Hidden Talents

Hidden Talents

ERICA
JAMES

LONDON NEW YORK SYDNEY TORONTO

This edition published 2002
by BCA
by arrangement with Orion
an imprint of the Orion Publishing Group

CN 109238

First published in Great Britain in 2002 by Orion,
an imprint of the Orion Publishing Group Ltd.

Copyright © Erica James 2002

Typeset by Deltatype Ltd, Birkenhead, Merseyside

Printed and bound in Germany by
GGP Media, Pössneck

All the characters in this book are fictitious, and any resemblance
to actual persons living or dead is purely coincidental.

To Edward and Samuel, my multi-talented sons.

Acknowledgements

*

As ever, countless thanks to everyone at Orion, in particular Helen, Jo, Ian, Linda, Erin, Maggy, Juliet, Jenny, Trevor, Malcolm, and Dallas. It wouldn't be the same without you all. (Even you Mr Taylor!)

Thanks too, to Anthony Keates for my precious paperweight and for the donkey story . . . And what would I do for days out were it not for Raymond, Jon, David, Dominic and Graham.

Thank you, Jane, for your continued support and keen editorial eye. And thank you, Susan, for telling me to stop whingeing.

Special hugs and thanks to Mr Lloyd.

Lastly, a whopping great thank you to Helena and Maureen for putting up with me.

Chapter One

*

Dulcie Ballantyne had made a lifelong habit of not making a drama of the unexpected: for sixty-three years silver linings had been her stock in trade. Moreover, she would be a rich woman if she had a pound for every time someone had remarked on her calmness of manner and her continually sunny and optimistic outlook. 'Overreaction serves no purpose other than to make a difficult situation a lot worse,' she would say, whenever anyone remarked on her unflappable nature. It wasn't a happy-go-lucky, trouble-free life that had given her the ability to cope no matter what, it was a wealth of experience. In short, life had taught her to deal with the severest catastrophe.

But as she sat at the kitchen table, waiting for the day to fully form itself, tearful exhaustion was doing away with the last remnants of her self-control and she was seconds away from making a terrible mistake. She had promised herself she wouldn't do it, but desperation was pushing her to ring the hospital to find out how Richard was. As his mistress, though – even a long-standing mistress of three years – she had no right to be at his bedside or have his condition explained to her. 'Are you family?' the nurse had asked her on the telephone late last night, when she had almost begged to know how he was. She should have claimed to be a sister or some other close relative, but shock had wrenched the truth from her and she was informed politely that Mr Richard Cavanagh was still in the coronary care unit in a stable condition.

Stable.

She hung on to this thought, closed her eyes, and willed the man she loved not to leave her.

How often had Richard said that to her? 'Don't leave me, Dulcie. Life would be intolerable without you.'

'I'm not going anywhere,' she had always told him. She had meant it too. Her affair with Richard had been infinitely better than any other relationship she had known since the death of her husband twenty-two years ago. Before she had met Richard, there had been a series of liaisons and one or two men had almost convinced her she was in love, but mostly they had proved to her that she enjoyed living alone too much to want anyone with her on a permanent basis. Commitment phobia was supposed to be the prerogative of men, but as far as she was concerned, commitment was an overrated phenomenon. Much better to let things take their natural course, to do without the restrictive boundary that was frequently the kiss of death to a relationship.

She swallowed hard, ran her fingers through her short, dishevelled hair, and only just kept herself from crying, 'No, no, *no*!' She had changed her mind. She wanted Richard to stay in her life for ever. She would give anything to deepen the commitment between them.

She heaved herself out of the chair where she had been sitting for the last two hours and set about making some breakfast. She hadn't eaten since yesterday afternoon when she and Richard had met at their usual restaurant for lunch – a hotel at a discreet distance from Maywood, where they'd hoped they wouldn't be recognised. It was while they were discussing the creative writers' group she was forming that he had grimaced, dropped his cutlery and clenched his fist against his chest. Horrorstruck, she had watched his strong, vigorous body crumple and fall to the floor.

It had been so quick. One minute they were chatting happily, wondering what kind of people would sign up for the group, Richard joking that he would join so that he could spend a legitimate evening with her, and the next they were in an ambulance hurtling to hospital, an oxygen mask clamped to his face. She had behaved immaculately: no hysterical tears; no distraught behaviour that would give rise to the suspicion that they were lovers. She had called Richard's home number on his mobile and left a message on the answerphone for his wife. She hadn't said who she was, just that Mr Cavanagh had been taken ill: a heart-attack. Half an hour later, though it was the hardest thing she had ever done, she had left the hospital before people started to ask awkward questions.

Now she wished she had stayed. Why should she care about the consequences of her presence at his bedside, or worry about anyone else's feelings but her own? Yet that would be so out of character. She *did* care about other people's feelings. Richard had once said to her, as they lay in bed together, 'You care too much sometimes, Dulcie. You're too understanding for your own good.'

'No I'm not,' she'd said, lifting her head from the pillow and gazing into his eyes. 'If I was that saintly I would think more of Angela and call a halt to this affair. It's very wrong what we're doing. It's selfish to be happy at someone else's expense.'

He'd held her tight. 'Don't say that. Don't even think it. Not ever.'

She had always thought that his need for her was greater than her need for him. Now, however, she wasn't so sure. She longed to see Richard. To tell him over and over how much she loved him.

Rousing herself, she cleared away her untouched breakfast and went upstairs to dress. Moping around in her old dressing-gown – not the beautiful silk one Richard had given her, which she wore when he was with her – wouldn't help anyone. It was time to pull herself together and become the cool, composed Dulcie Ballantyne everyone knew her to be.

From overpacked, higgledy-piggledy rails, she chose an outfit that would give her a superficial but necessary lift – a comfortable pair of wool trousers with a cream roll-necked sweater and a pink silk scarf, which she unearthed from the bottom of the wardrobe among her collection of shoes and handbags She thought of her daughter, and how much she disapproved of Dulcie's untidiness. Kate despaired of her, and had tried since the age of sixteen – she was now twenty-nine – to organise Dulcie's wardrobe. 'Colour co-ordination is the key, Mum,' she would say, riffling through the hangers and shunting them around. Curiously, and for no reason that Dulcie could fathom, it was the only area in the house, and her life for that matter, that she allowed to be muddled, where restful harmony didn't take precedence.

Once she was dressed, she looked down on to the walled garden from her bedroom window. Curved steps led down to the lawn, which was edged with well-stocked borders; some, despite the onset of autumn, were still bright with colour. Leaves had begun to drop from the trees, but the garden remained defiantly cheerful. In the middle of June, Richard had helped her spread several barrowloads of manure over the rose-beds. It had been a Monday afternoon and his family had thought he was away on business. But he had been with her. She'd had him to herself for a whole delicious two days. She smiled at the memory: a rare two days together and they had spent the afternoon shovelling horse droppings. They had laughed about that afterwards. He had claimed that that was what he liked about their relationship, its down-to-earth nature. 'You allow me to be myself,' he said. 'You expect nothing of me, which means I'm free when I'm with you.'

Their love was founded on a strong understanding of each other's needs and a companionship that was both passionate and close, something so many married couples lost sight of. She seldom wanted him to talk about his marriage, but often Richard felt the need to explain, or perhaps justify, why he, an ordinary man (as he called himself), was behaving in the way he was. From what Dulcie knew of his wife, she was an anxious woman who depended on him too much.

Turning from the window, she glanced at herself in the full-length mirror and tried to see beyond the stocky roundness of her body and the burst of lines around her blue eyes, beyond the short fair hair she had dyed every six weeks because she knew it took years off her, and beyond the skin that had lost its firmness. Beyond all this, she saw a woman who was a chameleon. She had played so many different roles in her life, and was destined, she was sure, to play a few more yet.

Downstairs in the kitchen, while she was trying to summon the energy to go out and rake up the leaves, the telephone rang. She snatched up the receiver, her heart pounding. Richard. Darling Richard. He was well enough to call her. Well enough to reassure her that he was all right.

But it wasn't Richard. It was a young girl enquiring about the creative writers' group. She had seen the card Dulcie had placed in the window of the bookshop in town, and wanted to know if there was an age restriction.

Chapter Two

*

Jaz Rafferty switched off her mobile and stared up at the sloping ceiling above her bed. It was covered with neat rows of Pre-Raphaelite prints she'd bought during last week's college history-of-art trip to Birmingham's City Art Gallery. Her favourite was *The Last of England* by Ford Madox Brown; the artist had been so dedicated to capturing the coldness of the day – the grey sea and sky, the couple huddled together in their thick winter coats – that he had forced himself to paint much of the picture outdoors, his hands stiff and blue. According to Miss Holmes, her teacher, the picture was all about the young couple and their child embarking on a new and brighter future, but within it there was also a sense of regret at leaving home.

To a large extent Jaz could empathise with the couple, she was all for leaving home as soon as she could, but she doubted she would feel a second's regret when that happy day dawned.

She put her mobile on her bedside table and relished a rare moment of blissful quiet. Added to this was the knowledge that she had a secret. Secrets were great, especially if she could keep them from her brothers and sisters, who were the nosiest, most interfering and irritating bunch on the planet. They were the pain of pains. The wonder was that she hadn't left home years ago. When she was thirteen she had gone through a phase of saying that she was adopted; anything to make people think she wasn't related to four of the most loathsome people alive.

Phin (short for Phineas) was the oldest at twenty-two, then Jimmy, who was twenty. Although they were both earning good money working for Dad's building firm – Rafferty & Sons – they still lived at home. 'And why would we want to live anywhere else?' they would say, whenever she called them mummy's boys for not finding a place of their own. 'Ah, it would break Mum's heart if we moved out.'

They were probably right. Mum loved and spoilt them to bits. Nothing was too much trouble when it came to Phin and Jimmy. 'Oh, go on,' she'd say, the minute Phin looked warily from the iron to the creased shirt he wanted to wear that night.

Pathetic.

And pity the poor girls who would be stupid enough to attach themselves to the Rafferty boys. They'd need to be certifiable to put up with them.

At seventeen, Jaz was next in line in the family pecking order. Every year on her birthday, 5 September, Dad always trotted out the same joke, that he'd had a word with the Almighty before she was conceived. 'Lord, I know how pushed you are, so I'll save you the bother of another boy. We'll make do with a girl this time round.'

Dad wasn't a religious man, not by a long chalk, but he used his Catholic upbringing in the same way he banged on about being so proud of his Irish heritage. 'Dad,' she said to him once, 'you're such a fraud. You wouldn't know a penny whistle if a leprechaun shoved one up your bum. You're as English as the Queen.'

'Yeah,' he'd grinned, 'and she's half German, isn't she?'

His hotline to God backfired on him, though: after a gap of several years, Tamzin (ten) and Lulu (eight) arrived. 'Sweet Moses,' he often complained, 'I'm overrun with women! What have I done to deserve this?'

More to the point, what had *she* ever done to deserve such a family?

From a very young age she'd had a feeling of being displaced. If it weren't for her colouring – so like her mother's – she would have believed that owing to some quirk of nature, or to a mistake made at the hospital where she was born, she had ended up in the wrong family. She could have been no more different from her brothers and sisters, who all took after their father: he described himself as being heartily robust of build and temperament. Jaz would have put money on Tamzin and Lulu having been born with fists clenched, ready to take on the world and destroy it. In contrast, she herself was small and pale with annoying childish freckles across

6

the bridge of her nose. Her hair was long, to her waist, and auburn ('*Not red!*' as she repeatedly informed her brothers, when they called her Gingernut), and she preferred to think rather than yack like the rest of her family. Family legend had it that she had been slow to talk as a toddler, and had been labelled 'a solemn little thing' by her father. Self-reliant from the word go, she had, at the age of six, briefly created her own make-believe friends to play with, but she soon had to lose them: they became as irritating as her brothers, crowding her with their insidious presence.

When the boys were old enough, they were allowed to help their father tinker with his collection of motorbikes. They also started to accompany him on trips to Manchester to watch boxing matches and to the horseracing in Chester and Liverpool. It meant that Jaz had her mother to herself, but not for long. When Tamzin was born, followed quickly by Lulu, Jaz accepted that she was destined to be the odd one out. Everyone but her was one of a pair: her parents, her brothers, and now her sisters. She withdrew and immersed herself in books, reading herself into other people's lives, happily escaping her own. With hindsight it seemed only natural that one day she would discover the joy of writing, that the simple process of putting words on paper – poems, short stories, rhymes, observations – would allow her to escape yet further.

She rolled off the bed, went over to her desk and switched on her computer. She checked that her bedroom door was shut, then opened the file marked 'Italian Renaissance'. She scrolled through the six-page essay she had written on Uccello's *The Hunt in the Forest*, for which she had been awarded an A, and stopped when a block of blank pages had flicked by and she came to the words 'Chapter One'. After months of messing around with poetry she was writing a novel. She had started it last week but, what with all the homework she'd had, there had been little time to devote to it. Being at sixth-form college was great, but the workload was crazy.

Vicki, her closest friend from school, had moved with her to Maywood College last month, and there was no shortage of new students to get to know. There was one in particular Jaz wanted to get to know better. He was a year older than her and was in the upper sixth. His name was Nathan King, and all she knew about him was that he lived near the park in Maywood. He was tall, wore his hair short, but not too short, and was never without his long black leather coat, which flapped and swished behind him as he strode purposefully to wherever he was heading. He looked as if he knew exactly what he was about, as if he had it all sorted. It was his confident manner that had singled him out to her on the first day of term.

Hearing the sound of feet thundering towards her room, she snapped forward in her seat and scrolled back to the start of the history-of-art essay.

The door flew open. 'Who were you talking to?'

Without bothering to turn round, she said, 'Tamzin Rafferty, get out! You, too Lulu. Can't you see I'm working?'

'You weren't a few minutes ago. We heard you talking to someone. Was it a boy? Have you got a boyfriend?'

She twisted her head, gave her sisters her most imperious stare. 'Were you listening in on a private conversation?'

They looked at each other and sniggered. Then they began to giggle in that high-pitched tone that grated on her nerves. She moved calmly across the room to the bookcase and her CD player. She picked up the remote control, switched it on at eardrum-bursting level and watched Tamzin and Lulu take flight. They hated her music, especially the Divine Comedy – they hadn't yet evolved beyond S Club 7.

'Sweet baby Moses on a bike! Turn that racket down.'

Her father, Pat (or Popeye, as her mother and their oldest friends called him), stood in the doorway, his massive body filling the gap. Jaz switched off the music and he came in. 'Jeez, girl, that was loud enough to shake the paint off the walls. How you can work with that rubbish playing, I'll never know.' He looked towards her computer. 'Much to get through this weekend?'

'A fair amount,' she said, sliding past him to sit down. She was worried he might decide to fiddle with the keyboard and acciden-tally find her novel. Her dad liked to give the impression he understood nothing about computers, but she knew that he had recently had the business kitted out with an expensive new system and had insisted on being shown how to work it. She kept her eyes lowered and waited for him to leave. But he didn't. He drew nearer, stooped slightly, and began to read aloud what was on the screen. '"Uccello was fascinated by perspective and this can be clearly seen in this painting, which is both richly coloured and ingeniously constructed . . ."' He straightened up, placed a hand on her shoulder. 'I've said it before, Jasmine, and I'll say it again, you owe it all to your mother. You get your brains from her. Never forget that, will you?'

She turned and smiled affectionately at him. He was always saying that, always making himself out to be the ignorant, silent partner in his marriage. 'Oh, I'm just the brawn in the Rafferty outfit, that's why they call me Popeye,' he'd say. 'It's Moll who knows what's what.' But let anyone make the mistake of taking him at his word and they'd soon regret it.

'You're not going to give me that old I'm-just-a-thick-Paddy spiel, are you?' she asked.

He returned the smile. 'But it's the truth. I couldn't read or write when I met your mother. She wouldn't marry me until I'd mastered *Janet and John*.'

'That's true love for you, Dad.'

He gave her a light cuff around the ear. 'Cheeky madam. Now, get on with your work. I'm expecting great things of you.'

'No pressure, then, Dad?'

He was almost out of the room when he stopped, turned back to her and said, 'So, has my little Jazzie got a boyfriend?'

She rolled her eyes. 'Chance would be a fine thing.'

'Hmm . . . best keep it that way until you've got college sorted.'

She watched him go. As dads went, he wasn't bad. Woefully sentimental at times, and scarily volatile but, beneath it all, she knew he was proud of her. He was always boasting to his friends about how clever she was. 'Mark my words,' he'd swagger, with a beer in his hands, 'this is the Rafferty who's going to put our family on the map. Jazzie's like her mother, book-smart.'

What he didn't realise was that his pride put unbearable pressure on her to perform. What if she let him down? How would he cope with the failure of a daughter on whom he'd pinned such high hopes? And did he have any idea how trapped she felt by the restrictions he placed on her in his desire to see her do well? He was happy for her to go out with Vicki, but heaven help any guy who showed the slightest interest in her. Dad would put him through untold tests before he would be satisfied that he was suitable. He never came right out and said it, but she knew her father wouldn't tolerate the distraction of a boyfriend at this stage in her life. But who'd be interested in her anyway?

She dismissed this line of thought and got back to the opening sentence of her novel. But the more she repeated it in her head, the

9

clumsier it sounded. It wasn't long before her thoughts strayed once more. To her wonderful secret.

Next week she would be going to the first meeting of Hidden Talents. Just think, a writers' group where she would be taken seriously. Where she could talk openly about her writing and not be laughed at. Because that's what her family would do if they ever found out what she was up to. She could hear her brothers now. 'Oo-er, little Miss Clever Clogs reckons she's an author, does she?'

She wondered what the other people in the group would be like. The woman she'd just spoken to, Dulcie Ballantyne, had sounded really nice. Hesitant, maybe, as though her mind was elsewhere, but quite friendly. Well, so long as the others were nothing like Phin and Jimmy, Tamzin and Lulu she would be sure to get on with them.

Chapter Three

*

Beth King was often told that she ought to invest in a dishwasher. 'You could easily whip out this cupboard here,' people would say, thinking they were the first to come up with the idea, 'and slip in a dishwasher, no trouble at all. Just think of the hours you'd save yourself. And the wear and tear on your hands.' This last consideration was a favourite of her mother's. 'Hands, more than anything, age a woman,' she would claim. 'You can have any amount of surgery done to your face, but your hands will always give you away.'

They were probably right, these well-meaning friends and family, but the truth was, Beth enjoyed washing-up – not for any strange, puritanical reason, but because the kitchen of the first-floor flat that she and Nathan had lived in for more than ten years overlooked Maywood Park. The view was a constant source of pleasure to her: there was always something different to watch – squirrels scampering across the grass, couples, young and old, strolling arm in arm along the winding paths that led down to the river and the tennis courts, mothers with prams, dogs and children playing on the swings and roundabout – which Nathan had enjoyed when he was little. And then there was the ever-changing look of the park. Now that it was autumn, the trees were losing their coppery leaves, and the fading leggy bedding plants that the council had planted in the summer would soon be replaced with pansies tough enough to survive the rigours of winter.

The last of the lunch dishes rinsed, Beth dried her hands and reached for the tub of luxury hand cream her mother insisted on sending her, along with the rubber gloves Beth always forgot to use. Her parents were wonderfully generous and still went out of their way to make her life easier.

As did her in-laws, Lois and Barnaby King.

But while she was grateful for her parents' generosity, which came from three hundred miles away – they had retired to warmer climes on the south coast – she found it difficult to feel the same enthusiasm for Lois's doorstep offers of help. Lois tried too hard and made Beth feel as if she were a charity case. 'Would you believe it?' Lois had said in April. 'I've stocked up at the supermarket and, without any warning, Barnaby's decided to take me away for the Easter weekend. You'd better have it, you know I hate to see good food go to waste.'

It would have been ungracious to refuse, especially as Beth knew Lois meant well. She always had. Ever since Adam's death, eleven years ago, she had committed herself to taking care of her son's widow and her only grandson. Occasionally Beth privately questioned Lois's motives, but she hated herself for thinking so cynically. What Lois did was kind and honourable and she should think herself lucky that she had such supportive in-laws. Nothing was ever too much trouble for them, and living just a few miles away in the village of Stapeley, they had always been there for her. Many a time Lois had despatched Barnaby to fix a leaking gutter or sort out a rotting window-ledge. 'Heavens! Don't even think of getting a man in to do it – you'll be charged the earth. Let Barnaby take a look for you. You know that's what Adam would have wanted.'

After all these years of living without Adam, it was difficult for Beth to know if Lois was right. Would he have wanted his parents to play such a central part in her life? Or would he have expected her to move on?

'Moving on' had become an irritating cliché to Beth. Everyone had served it up to her: her mother, her friends, the people she worked with – in fact, anyone who thought she should have remarried by now. Or at least found a serious boyfriend. 'You're not getting any younger, Beth,' her closest friend, Simone, had said only last month. 'You're forty-three, not twenty-three, in case it's slipped your notice.'

'Fat chance of that happening,' Beth had retorted, wishing that a sandstorm would engulf her friend's house in Dubai where she was currently living with her husband, Ben.

'Or are you working on the misplaced theory that the choice of eligible men increases with age?'

'No, I'm just being selective. I haven't met anyone who measures up to Adam.'

'Rubbish! You haven't allowed anyone near enough to see how they'd measure up. You're being a coward.'

Simone's words were uncomfortably near the truth. Fear and guilt had played a part in stopping Beth finding a new partner. She had hated the idea of being disloyal to Adam.

In the aftermath of his death, she had thrown herself into taking care of Nathan. He had been only six, too young to feel the pain of loss, but old enough to understand that his and his mother's lives had changed. Within six months of the funeral they had moved from their lovely house in the country, with its pretty garden, to this flat in Maywood. Money had been tight. Without her knowledge, Adam had taken out a second mortgage on their house and had invested what little savings they'd had in a business venture that had gone disastrously wrong. It had taken Beth some time to find work, but perseverance had paid off: she had landed a gem of a job at the recently expanded health centre in town. She had worked there ever since and had been happy; the hours were fairly flexible and the camaraderie had been good for her self-esteem. Her sanity too.

Her social life had not been so fulfilling: on a receptionist's salary she couldn't afford to do much. She was always totting up the pennies – a modest trip to the cinema plus a babysitter amounted almost to the cost of a pair of shoes for Nathan. Funnily enough, as supportive as Lois was, she never offered to babysit so that Beth could go out at night. Nothing was ever said, but Beth strongly suspected her mother-in-law didn't want her to meet anyone. To Lois, it was unthinkable that Beth could replace Adam.

But Beth's friends had had other ideas and before long they were dropping hints that it was time for her to start dating. Invitations materialised for her to meet unattached men at dinner parties. Simone had set her up with several unsuitable candidates – it was still a mystery to Beth where her friend's supply of single men came from. In those early years few got further than a second date. The first man she'd agreed to go out with had taken her for dinner in Chester. Just as she was beginning to think that he was almost 'promising', he had leaned across the table and asked about her favourite sexual fantasy. She hid her shock, and told him that an early night with a good book did it for her. Another man had bored her rigid with endless talk about his high-powered job and interdepartmental politics in the company. She had suppressed a jaw-breaking yawn, then nodded and politely said what she thought he wanted her to say.

When she grew tired of fending off men with whom she had no desire to form any attachment, she started to turn down Simone's invitations, using Nathan as an excuse – 'Sorry, Simone, I have to give Nathan a lift somewhere that night.' Or, 'Sorry, Nathan needs me to help him revise for an exam.'

Simone was no fool, and reminded Beth *ad infinitum* that time waits for no woman, especially a single one. Eventually she had said, 'How much longer are you going to use your son in this shameful manner? What excuse will you come up with when he leaves home? Or are you going to turn into an eccentric old woman who collects stray cats and makes marmalade that nobody will ever eat?'

'Anything would be preferable to the ear-bashing a so-called friend is subjecting me to. And if you really want to know, I'm putting things off until it's more convenient.'

'And as we all know, Beth, my poor deluded friend, procrastination is the thief of time.'

Beth knew that Simone was right, she *was* hiding behind Nathan. Plenty of parents struggle to come to terms with flying-the-nest syndrome, but she knew that because she and Nathan were so close she would undergo a painful period of adjustment next year when he left for university. She had never suffered from loneliness – mostly because she didn't have time for such an indulgence – but that might alter when Nathan went to college. Common sense told her that she had no choice but to fill the void his absence would create.

In preparation for this change, she had taken an important step this morning, which she hoped would expand her horizons. She was joining a creative writers' group. She had always enjoyed 'scribbling', as she called it. It had started after Adam died: when she couldn't sleep at night, she had written down the thoughts that were keeping her awake. It had been soothingly cathartic and before long she had grown confident enough to turn the random scribblings into short stories. She now had a collection that no one but herself had read. Or ever would. Those clumsily put-together vignettes were about the past. Now she wanted to write something to reflect the new life ahead of her.

This morning she had told Simone about Hidden Talents during their fortnightly phone chat.

'Good for you,' she'd said. 'Any men in the group?'

'I wouldn't know. We have our first meeting next week.'

'What else are you going to do to occupy yourself?'

'Isn't that enough to start with?'

'You tell me.'

'Goodness, you're giving me the choice? What's got into you? Has the sun fried your brain?'

'Crikey, it's time to come home to Cheshire if it has.'

For all Simone's bullying, she was a wonderful friend, and Beth missed her.

She screwed the lid back on to the tub of hand cream and put it on the window-ledge. Looking down into the park, she noticed a fair-haired man sitting on one of the benches; he had two young children with him. For a few moments she watched the smallest and blondest of the two little girls as she tried to catch a leaf that whirled in the wind. She wondered where their mother was, then chided herself for jumping to such a sloppy conclusion. It always annoyed her when people assumed she had a husband.

She was still staring at the man and his children when she remembered that Nathan was out for the rest of the afternoon and that she had promised to go downstairs to see her neighbour.

Adele – Miss Adele Waterman – had moved into the ground-floor flat a year after Beth and Nathan had arrived, which made them not just long-standing neighbours but good friends. To Beth's sadness, the old lady had decided, now that she was eighty-four, to call it a day: she was putting her flat on the market with the intention of moving into a retirement home. 'I'm under no illusion that my nephew wants the burden of me. He can never spare any time to visit so I'm spending his inheritance the fastest way I know how,' she had told Beth, with a chuckle.

Beth picked up a tin of home-made chocolate cake and went out, hoping that when the time came, Nathan would treat her more kindly than Adele's only relative had treated her.

Chapter Four

*

Jack Solomon switched off the car radio before Jimmy Ruffin's 'What Becomes Of The Brokenhearted?' could do its worst. The traffic-lights changed to green and he pressed his foot on the accelerator.

It was a typically tedious Monday afternoon. It was also his birthday. He was thirty-six, but felt more like sixty-six, and he certainly wasn't in the mood to celebrate. The girls in the office had surprised him with a card and a CD and he had been touched by their thoughtfulness, but less so by the choice of CD. He had nothing against Britney Spears, but it was too much of a cliché, men of his age listening to music aimed at a much younger generation. There was nothing worse than a middle-aged man trying to be hip. A wry smile twitched at his lips. He could have been describing that bastard Tony.

He felt the sudden tension in his shoulders and loosened his grip on the steering-wheel. He mustn't dwell on Tony, he told himself. But it was a futile instruction. Now that his brain had hooked on to the thought, he'd be stuck with it until he'd worked it out of his system.

Tony Gallagher . . . the best friend he'd ever had. Once they'd been inseparable. They'd grown up together, played and learned together. They'd smoked their first cigarette together, drunk their first pint together, and inevitably experienced their first hangover together. They'd shared practically every rite of passage. But Tony had taken 'togetherness' and 'what's yours is mine' too far and too literally.

Almost a year ago Jack had come home early from work one

afternoon with a high temperature and found Tony in bed with Maddie. Turned out they'd been having an affair for the last six months and dumb old Jack hadn't had a clue what was going on.

Dumb old Jack Solomon, that was him all right. Too blind to see what was going on under his own nose, in his own home. Too in awe of his old friend to think he'd ever betray him. Other men sank to those levels, but not Tony. Admittedly he'd been a bit of a lad, but he was one of the good guys. Imbued with an easy sense of entitlement and an air of confidence that drew people to him, he was a man you could trust.

But these things happen. Marriages fell apart all the time . . . apparently. Jack wished that every time some smug prat said this he could smack them in the face. 'These things happen' was supposed to make him feel better about losing his wife and only seeing his daughters on alternate weekends. Relegated to being a part-time father, he now had to trail his children round theme parks, cinema complexes, bowling alleys and fast-food restaurants. If he never had to order another burger and milkshake, he'd be a happy man. No, that wasn't true. It would take a hell of a lot more than that to make him truly happy.

Amber and Lucy had stayed with him at the weekend and, thankfully, the weather had been warm and sufficiently dry to make going out less of a chore. During the last year he had become a fanatical watcher of weather reports: if rain was forecast he had to plan indoor entertainment; if it was dry, he'd plan a trip outdoors.

On Saturday he'd taken the girls to the park in Maywood. Lucy had enjoyed it but, then, she was only seven and still young enough to feed the ducks and play on the swings. Amber, though, was eleven and fast becoming too grown-up for such childish entertainment. While Lucy had flung bread at the ducks, Amber had sat on the bench with him and watched her sister disdainfully. When Lucy's supply of bread had run out, she had skipped towards them, her face wreathed in smiles.

'Can we go now?' Amber had asked, getting to her feet and folding her arms across her chest. 'I'm cold.'

'But I want to play on the swings.' Lucy had pouted. 'Dad said I could.' She'd looked at him, eyes wide and pleading.

'Five minutes on the swings,' he'd said, 'and then it's Amber's choice what we do next.'

17

The peace had been kept and Amber's choice had been to walk back into the centre of town to have tea at McDonald's. During the weekend, he'd sensed friction between the girls, and when he was putting the tray loaded with burgers, chips, nuggets and milkshakes on to the table where they were waiting for him, he caught Amber telling Lucy off. 'Hey, what's the problem?' he'd said.

'It's nothing,' Amber said matter-of-factly and, assuming the role of dinner monitor, opened her sister's carton of nuggets and handed it to her.

'It doesn't look like nothing to me,' he persisted, putting his arm round Lucy. 'What's up, Luce?' He noticed Amber flash her a warning look and when Lucy began to cry, he said, 'Okay, that's it. What's going on?'

'I only said I was looking forward to our holiday.' Lucy sniffed.

'What holiday?' he asked, dabbing her eyes with a paper napkin.

She took it from him and blew her nose. 'Tony's taking us to Disney World for half-term. We're going to America.'

'That's nice,' he forced himself to say. He unwrapped his burger, knowing he wouldn't be able to eat it now.

'Well, I'm not going!' Amber announced. She looped a long chip and stuffed it into her mouth. 'I'm going to stay with Dad for half-term. I wouldn't go to America if you paid me.'

Atta girl! he wanted to cheer. But he didn't. Not when Lucy looked as if she was going to cry again. His heart went out to them both, caught as they were in an impossible situation. 'Is it definite?' he asked, playing for time. 'Has Tony booked it?'

Amber shrugged and reached for her milkshake.

Lucy nodded. 'He showed us a picture of the hotel we're going to be staying in. It's huge. And there's a pool with a slide and—'

'Shut up, Lucy.'

'Amber, don't speak to your sister like that.'

She looked at him, hurt.

Damn! He wasn't handling this at all well. Poor Amber, she was only trying to be loyal to him. 'Sorry, sweetheart,' he said, 'I didn't mean to snap at you. How's your meal? Burger up to standard?'

He drove them back to Prestbury the following day, to where Maddie had set up home with Tony. Home for her, these days, was a modern pile of impressive proportions and, with its over-the-top electric gates that positioned it on just the wrong side of good taste, Jack had nicknamed it Southfork. From what the girls had told

18

him, it had six bedrooms, three bathrooms, a sitting room the size of a football pitch and a sauna to sweat away the day's troubles. Well, yippity-do, hadn't Tony Gallagher done well for himself? Always ambitious and always on the lookout for a way to make a quick buck, Tony had come home after a holiday in Thailand and set up his own business importing Oriental rugs, furniture and knick-knacks. This had been in the early nineties, things had taken off for him, and he now had a string of shops throughout the North West. Oh, yes, Tony Gallagher had done very well for himself. Too damned well.

Tony opened the door to him and it took all of Jack's willpower not to shove the smug devil up against his expensive wallpaper and smear his brains right across it.

'I hear you're off to Disney,' he said, with false bonhomie as he passed the girls their weekend bags. Instead of rushing upstairs to their bedrooms as they usually did, they hovered anxiously in the hall.

'Yes,' said Tony. 'I thought it would do Maddie and the girls good. Some sun to cheer us all up.'

'You do surprise me. I thought you had everything you could ever want to make you happy.' His caustic tone rang out discordantly and Maddie materialised. As if sensing trouble, she placed herself between the girls, a hand on each of their shoulders. Even now, despite the bitterness that consumed him, he was reminded of the intense love he'd once felt for her. She was as slim as the day they'd met, and just as pretty. The girls had inherited her delicate bone structure, her clear complexion, and her pale blue eyes. Many a time when they'd holidayed in Greece, she'd been mistaken for a Scandinavian.

'Everything all right?' she asked, her chilly briskness telling him to back off.

'Oh, everything's hunky-dory, Maddie. Nothing for you to worry about. Although it might have been nice for you to inform me about your plans for half-term. But, hey, Amber and Lucy told me, so that's okay, isn't it?' Then, in a less acerbic voice, he said, 'Good night, girls. I'll see you when you get back.'

He moved forward to kiss them goodbye, but Amber wriggled free from her mother and said, 'You can't go yet, Dad. Lucy and I have something for you.' She shot upstairs and was back within seconds. She handed him a present that must have taken ages to wrap, judging by the amount of sellotape and the bulky edges of the paper around it. 'Happy birthday for tomorrow, Dad.' She gave him a fierce hug. When she stepped away, she narrowed her eyes and gave Maddie and Tony a pointed look.

He drove home, close to tears. All he could think of was the harm that had been inflicted on his children by his and Maddie's separation. Poor Lucy, so guilty and upset because she was excited about going to Orlando, and Amber defiantly refusing to go, but knowing she would have to. And how long had she been rehearsing the little scene when she had given him his present in front of Tony and Maddie?

Jack knew he had to come to terms with what had happened. He had to find a way to resolve his anger and bitterness.

He parked outside 10a Maywood Park House, where Miss Waterman lived. A shame it wasn't the whole house he'd been instructed to sell, but a flat in this area would be easy to shift, so long as Miss Waterman was realistic about the selling price. It never paid to go in too high. Fingers crossed that the old lady didn't have any greedy relatives manipulating her behind the scenes. Fingers crossed also that she wasn't too frail to make a cup of tea: he was parched.

He gathered up his clipboard and tape measure from the front passenger seat and locked the car. He examined the small front garden with a professional eye. It was well tended with laurel bushes and a lilac tree screening the ground-floor window from the road; established shrubs filled the narrow bed to the right of the path. So far so good. He wondered who was responsible for its upkeep. Surely not the elderly owner – a gardener, perhaps? Then he took the three steps up to the front door, which had its original lead-and-stained-glass fanlight. Again this was a good sign. There were two bells – one for 10a and one for 10b. He pressed the former, straightened his tie and tried to imagine Miss Waterman. From her voice on the telephone she had sounded the archetypal sweet old lady. He pictured her in a high-necked frilly blouse with a string of pearls and a pale mauve cardie, an embroidered hanky poking out from a pocket. There would probably be a ball of wool rolling about the flat, and the smell of cat litter, mothballs and throat lozenges.

The door opened. 'Er . . . Miss Waterman?' Either his client had undergone thousands of pounds' worth of plastic surgery and had

20

indulged in some super-strength HRT, or this was a relative who had been called in to check out the potentially scurrilous estate agent. She was an attractive woman with wavy fair hair, collar-length and tucked behind her ears: a tousled look that suited her bright, open face and went well with her figure-hugging knitted black suit. She looked vaguely familiar, but he couldn't think where he might have met her before. Perhaps she had been into the office at some time.

'No, I'm not Miss Waterman,' she said, 'I'm a neighbour. I live in the flat upstairs, which is where Miss Waterman is. I'm afraid her boiler's conked out and I insisted she stay in the warm with me. You must be Mr Solomon.'

'I am indeed. I didn't know neighbours like you still existed.'

'It helps that we're such good friends. Luckily I had the afternoon off. Come in.' She closed the door behind him and led the way along a communal hallway to 10a, her shoes clicking on the chequered tiled floor.

Inside the flat he was pleased to see that most of the original features were still intact. He stood for a moment to take in the proportions and features of the sitting room: the bay window, the fireplace, the high ceiling and the intricate cornice.

'I've been instructed to stay with you,' she said, observing him from where she stood next to a baby grand piano, which was home to a collection of framed black and white photographs and a vase of silk flowers.

'Quite right too,' he said. 'I could be anyone, after all.' He slipped a hand into the breast pocket of his suit and pulled out a business card. He gave it to her and noticed that she took it with her left hand and that she wore no rings – this was a skill he'd learned since he'd been on his own: he could spot a wedding ring at fifty paces.

She read the card and said, 'Well, Mr Jack Solomon of Norris and Rowan the Estate Agents' – her voice was playful – 'I've also been instructed to give you some tea when you've finished. Miss Waterman was most insistent on that. I should point out, though, that she'll drive a hard bargain with you over your commission. Be warned.'

And you'll see that she does, he thought, as he started making notes on his clipboard. But instead of feeling hostile towards Miss Waterman's helpful neighbour, he found himself warming to her.

Dodging the clutter of antique furniture, and being careful not to knock anything over, he pulled out a length of the tape measure and hooked the metal end into the edge of the carpet against the wall. It was going to be a tricky job, this one: no area of floor or wall space had been wasted. Corner cupboards and glass-fronted cabinets were stuffed with china and glassware. Tables, large and small, displayed silk-shaded lamps and yet more china.

'Do you need any help?' she asked.

'Only if you don't mind.'

'It'll keep me warm, having something to do.'

With the sitting room measured, they moved on to the dining room: it was also jam-packed with furniture, a veritable minefield of bits and bobs just waiting to be smashed. 'And what do you do when you're not looking after your neighbour?' he asked, reeling in the tape.

'I work at the medical centre in town. I'm what people refer to as an old dragon.'

He raised an eyebrow. 'Why's that?'

'I'm a receptionist, and most of the patients think I derive some kind of perverse pleasure in keeping them from seeing their doctor.'

Ah, so that's where he'd seen her.

The job didn't take as long as he'd feared, and he was soon being led upstairs to meet Miss Waterman. When he stood in the hall, inside 10b, he realised how cold he'd become downstairs. The warmth wrapped itself around him, as did his new surroundings. There was a homely smell and feel to this flat, which Miss Waterman's lacked: hers was too formal and prim for his taste. He thought of his own rented modern townhouse and acknowledged what he'd previously tried to ignore: that he didn't much like it. It wasn't a home, merely a stopgap, somewhere to lay his head until he found something better. When Maddie had left him, he'd sold their house almost straight away, finding it too painful to live there alone. She had refused her share of the money, and initially this had infuriated him. It was as if she was deliberately flaunting the wealth and status she had acquired as Tony's Gallagher's partner.

'Is that you, Beth?' called a voice.

'Yes, and I've brought Mr Solomon up.'

When he entered the main room of the flat, L-shaped and clearly used for sitting, dining and cooking, he came face to face with his client. She was sitting opposite a log-burning stove and he almost stopped in his tracks at the sight of her. Unbelievably, he'd pictured her perfectly, right down to the pearls and the colour of her cardigan. How extraordinary! One – nil to his vivid imagination.

'Goodness, Mr Solomon, you look like you've seen a ghost.'

Smiling, he stretched out his hand. 'Not at all, Miss Waterman. It's good to meet you at last.'

'I wanted to show you round myself, but Beth wouldn't hear of it. She's such a dear. I'm going to miss her dreadfully when I leave.'

While he and Miss Waterman discussed the marketing of the flat and the thorny issue of commission, he was conscious of his client's neighbour moving quietly at the other end of the room, where she was making a pot of tea and arranging some cake on a plate. As he warmed himself in front of the log-burning stove, he felt absurdly at ease. There was something calming about his surroundings, although there was nothing special about the way the flat was furnished and decorated – if anything it bordered on shabby: inexpensive pine units in the kitchen area had been painted cream and looked in need of a touch-up; the dresser beside the open brick hearth was chaotically filled with cookery books, photographs, CDs, and china that didn't match; the sofa was worn and lumpy; the rugs on the wooden floor were threadbare, and the blue and white cloth that covered the dining table was splattered with candle wax. For all that, it was one of the most charming homes he'd been in for a long while.

Out of the corner of his eye, he saw Beth pick up the tea-tray. He got to his feet. 'Here, let me do that.' He took it from her and noticed, for the first time, the view from the window. He wondered if she had seen him on Saturday in the park with the girls.

'That was delicious,' he said, after he'd eaten two slices of cake and drunk his tea, 'but I really ought to be going. I wish all my appointments were as convivial.' He meant it.

'Any chance of you knocking a chunk off the extortionate commission you'll be charging in return for our generous hospitality?'

'Beth, my dear, you shouldn't embarrass Mr Solomon like that.'

He smiled. 'Perhaps we'll do something creative with the marketing budget. Free advertising for the first month. What do you say?'

Miss Waterman tilted her head to one side. 'And a reduced rate for the subsequent month?'

The old lady was as sharp as her friend. 'Agreed, Miss Waterman. But I doubt that will be necessary, given the excellent location. We'll have sold your flat long before then.'

He shook hands with the two women, first with his client, then with her neighbour. 'Thank you for the tea and for your help downstairs. I hope you didn't get too cold.'

It was when he was driving back to the office, before going home, that he remembered it was his birthday and Clare, his girlfriend – *girlfriend*: even after five months he wasn't used to that expression – was cooking a special meal for him. He wished now that he hadn't eaten so much cake.

Chapter Five

*

From the garden, Dulcie heard the telephone ringing. She threw down the rake and, almost missing her footing on the steps, rushed to the house, hoping it was Richard.

It was Tuesday morning, four days since Richard's heart-attack, and for all she knew the unthinkable might have happened. So many times she had wanted to ring the hospital, but she knew how gossip could spread. Enquiries from an unknown woman about a male patient could mean only one thing and Dulcie could picture, all too easily, the scene of Angela overhearing a couple of nurses discussing her husband and the concerned caller.

Breathless, she snatched up the receiver. Before she could say anything, a man's voice she didn't recognise said, 'Hello? Who am I speaking to?'

'This is Mrs Ballantyne,' she answered, irritated by the pompous voice at the other end of the line. 'And who am *I* speaking to?'

'My name's Victor Blackmore and I'm calling about the writing group. I'd like to know some more details. Is it a serious group, or just an excuse for people to get together and chat over endless cups of coffee?'

'I'm sure there'll be coffee on offer for those who would like it,' she said coolly, instinct telling her that this man would not be an asset to Hidden Talents, 'and doubtless there'll be a lively exchange of views and opinions. After all, that's partly the function of a writers' circle. I would imagine it's safe to say that it will be as serious as its members want it to be.'

'Mm . . . So what can you tell me about the other people who have signed up for it? I don't want to get involved with time-wasting cranks.'

Bristling, Dulcie said, 'I'm not sure that's a fair question, Mr Blackmere. It rather depends on your definition of the word "crank".'

'Black*more*. Victor *Blackmore*. Perhaps I'd better explain. I'm working on a novel and I'm keen to find an expert appraisal. What are your qualifications for running a writing group?'

It was time to get rid of this ghastly man. Under no circumstances did Dulcie want him joining Hidden Talents. 'I have absolutely no qualifications whatsoever, Mr Blackmore. Now, it sounds to me as though our little group wouldn't suit you at all. We're very much on the bottom rung, just starting out, and you're obviously further on. Have you thought of submitting your novel to a publisher for a professional appraisal?'

'Publishers! What do they know?'

So he'd already been down that route and had his work rejected. She decided that her only course of action was to be firm. 'Oh dear, I must go, there's someone at my door. Goodbye, Mr Blackmore, I hope you find what you're looking for. Best of luck with the writing.' She replaced the receiver with a smile. It was the first time she had smiled in days and it felt good. She imagined telling Richard about the dreadful man and saw them laughing together. She loved it when Richard laughed: his face showed the lightness of his spirit.

Back out in the garden, she resumed her leaf-raking. There was rain in the air, but she carried on regardless, soon warm from the exertion. She was picking up the handles of the overflowing wheelbarrow to push it down to the compost heap when she heard the telephone once more.

She was getting too old for this, she thought, as she stood in the kitchen and caught her breath before answering it. She ought to have one of those cordless contraptions that Richard had suggested so many times.

'Mrs Ballantyne? Victor Blackmore again.'

Her heart sank.

'I wanted to go over a couple more points with you.'

'Does this mean you'll be joining us?'

'Let's just say I'll give you a try and see how it works out. Now, then, what will the format be?'

26

'Format?'

'I presume you've thought of that? If there's no order or structure to the classes, I can't see them working. Take my word for it, it will turn into an unmitigated shambles. I have years of managerial experience behind me so I know what I'm talking about. How much will you be charging?'

'Just a token amount to cover biscuits and coffee. I thought a pound wouldn't be unreasonable.'

Fifteen minutes later, her patience pushed to its limit, Dulcie managed to get rid of him. She wished now that she had never come up with the idea of forming a writers' circle. What had she been thinking of? And what if more people like Victor Blackmore wanted to join? So far he was the third person to make a definite commitment to Hidden Talents – there had been other enquiries, but they had come from people looking for something to do during the day. 'I'm afraid our meetings will be in the evening,' she had told them. 'Otherwise people who work will miss out.' Also, she hadn't wanted to end up with a group consisting only of retired people or young mothers who might have to rush off to collect a small child. Some of the enquirers had been surprised that the group wouldn't be meeting in a public room, and again this had been deliberate on Dulcie's part. The size of the group was important. If it was too large, people wouldn't get a chance to read out their work and would feel excluded. A small gathering would encourage members to relax, and once a bond of trust had been established, they would express themselves more openly – essential if the fragile buds of creativity were to blossom.

It was raining heavily now. Dulcie abandoned her intention to continue gardening, and decided to write instead. Which meant she would need a cup of tea to get her started. A biscuit or two as well.

She carried the tea-tray through to her study – like the kitchen, it overlooked the garden. The previous owners of 18 Bloom Street – a Georgian townhouse in the centre of Maywood – had used this room as their dining room, but Dulcie had known straight away that it would be her study. It was beautifully proportioned, and very elegant. She had painted the walls herself, a creamy buttermilk shade, and had chosen a carpet of royal blue to make a sharp but classic contrast – it was hopelessly impractical, showed every bit of fluff, but she loved it. It gave the room exactly the right feel. She set the tray on her desk, which was positioned in front of the sash window. Then, as the day had turned so gloomy she switched on the lamps and lit the fire. She had cleared away the ashes earlier that morning, so all she had to do was put a match to the kindling and the scrunched-up newspaper.

Within minutes she had picked up a pen and was reading through what she had written before Richard had suffered his heart-attack. When she had told the boorish Victor Blackmore that she had no qualifications to lead a writing group, she had been a little economical with the truth. For years now she had had modest success with writing short stories for magazines. She had also picked up the occasional prize for her literary endeavours. And a long time ago, before moving to Maywood, she had been a member of a writers' group, although she had never led one. But, of course, none of this would impress Victor Blackmore. Only Salman Rushdie as their tutor would have impressed a pompous twit like him.

She had always written, even as a child, yet had never seen it as anything more than a hobby. She had played with words – like others played squash or tennis to amuse themselves – bouncing them around on the paper until they formed just the right pattern. It was immensely satisfying. However, it had been a sporadic hobby. Marriage and children had been her priority, but once Kate and Andrew had left home, she had been able to devote more time to it. Before then, and while the children were young, she had nursed her husband for almost six years until his death. Parkinson's disease had turned him into a chronic invalid, but he had borne the debilitating illness with great dignity. Sadly for him, he had been a doctor and had known his future better than anyone. She would never forget how brave he had been, or how hard he had tried to lessen the effect his illness had on them as a family. Kate and Andrew had been wonderful and had taken it in their stride. For them he was still plain old Dad and they accepted his limitations. In their eyes, it didn't matter that he couldn't kick a ball around the garden with them: he could read to them instead, help them with their homework, or play chess. When the tremors in his hands became unmanageable, they watched his eyes to see which piece he wanted them to move on his behalf.

But his death was a shattering blow. She and the children had grown so used to the permanency of him being ill that they had somehow convinced themselves they would carry on like that for ever. His departure created a haunting emptiness in their lives, especially hers. Dulcie had known she must do something positive, so she and the children had moved from south Manchester to Maywood to make a fresh start and to be nearer her closest friends, Prue and Maureen. For a while she busied herself with decorating their lovely new home in Bloom Street, but she soon recognised the danger of having too much time on her hands, and decided to form her own business, a relocation company. She had wanted to do this for some time.

It had been many years later, when she had been on the verge of selling the business and retiring, that she had met Richard. A company move from Wiltshire to Cheshire put him and his wife in contact with Home from Home – the name had been Kate's idea. Initially Dulcie dealt with Angela, who made it very clear she was moving north reluctantly. 'My friends and family all live in Wiltshire,' Angela had lamented, over the telephone. 'I don't know what I'm going to do without them.' She flitted rapidly from one line of conversation to another, and Dulcie had to work at keeping her client on track. 'We don't want anything modern, or anything that needs a lot of work doing to it. Oh, and nothing with those awful replacement PVC windows. I saw a programme on television once where a family perished in a house fire because they couldn't smash a window to escape. It was awful. Three children. All dead. A paddock would be nice. We want to be out in the country – did I say that? I'm sure I must have because I can't cope with being confined. I've never lived anywhere but the country. We'll need five bedrooms with at least two *en suites*. We have two grown-up children living in London and they will be frequent visitors, and we have another two still at home, Christopher and Nicholas. I'll need your help in finding them a suitable school.'

'And your price range?' Dulcie had asked, making notes of all these requirements, at the same time forming a mental picture of her client: she foresaw a long haul. 'I ought to warn you that house prices around Maywood are almost comparable with those in the south of England,' she added tactfully.

'Is that so? Well, my husband will sort that out. In the meantime, perhaps you can send details of what you have available and we'll come up and take a look.'

Two weeks later, with a string of viewings arranged, Dulcie drove to the Maywood Grange Hotel on the outskirts of town to meet her clients. Richard Cavanagh was waiting for her in the hotel lounge. He was doing *The Times* crossword, one leg crossed over the other, fountain pen poised mid-air, his chin tilted upwards as he tussled with a clue. He didn't notice her approaching, and when she said, 'Mr Cavanagh?' he started. 'Sorry,' she apologised, 'I didn't mean to make you jump.' She held out her hand. 'Dulcie Ballantyne.'

He put down his pen and paper, rose to his feet, slipped his tortoiseshell glasses into the breast pocket of his beige linen jacket, and shook hands warmly. 'Please, call me Richard. But how did you know it was me?'

She looked at the coffee table on which an open wallet file revealed a collection of house details. 'They don't call me Miss Marple for nothing.'

He smiled. 'Would you like some coffee before we set off?'

She checked her watch. 'Yes, thank you, though it will have to be quick. Our first appointment's at eleven.'

'Plenty of time for you to sit down, then.' He indicated the sofa, where he'd been sitting, and took a hard upright chair for himself. She felt the warmth from his body in the cushions when she sat down, and watched him attract the attention of a young waitress. He was older than she had expected, but attractive with it. His eyes were blue and his hair silvery grey; it curled boyishly into the nape of his neck, and looked good against the dark blue of his shirt. He passed her a cup of coffee. 'My wife sends her apologies. Our youngest has chicken-pox and she didn't want to leave him with anyone else.'

As the day wore on – and with six houses viewed – Dulcie discovered quite a lot about Richard Cavanagh. He was charming and quick-witted, clear about what he did and did not want in a home, and appeared a thoroughly nice man. To say that he captivated her would have been an exaggeration, but she was certainly attracted to him.

But, and it was a colossal but, he was married, and therefore out of bounds. End of story. Married men were to be avoided at all costs.

Yet she allowed herself to be drawn in. He invited her to join him for dinner that evening. 'Don't let me suffer the ignominy of dining alone,' he said. 'I'll have everyone feeling sorry for me.'

'Nonsense! You'll have all the waitresses rushing to keep you amused.'

'I'd rather *you* kept me amused.'

They were sitting in her car in the hotel car park, and he'd turned to face her as he said this, his gaze as direct as his words.

She didn't answer him, but she didn't need to. He knew she would accept, just as she knew what the consequences would be.

That had been three years ago, and now she was in love with a man who . . . who, for all she knew, might be dead.

She put down the pen she had been holding – a fountain pen Richard had given her on the first anniversary of their meeting – and lowered her head into her hands. It was no good. She couldn't take the not knowing any longer. She removed her reading glasses and went to make the call from the kitchen where she had the number of the hospital pinned to the noticeboard beside the phone. She was almost across the room when the telephone on her desk rang. Probably that annoying Victor Blackmore again, wanting to know what type of coffee she would be serving.

But she was wrong. It was Richard. She sank into her chair and, at the wonderful sound of his voice, she burst into tears.

'Dulcie?'

'Oh, Richard, I've been so scared. I'd almost convinced myself you were dead.' Tears of relief were flowing.

'Ssh, my darling, I'm fine. Well, fine for a man who's recovering from his first heart-attack. They've let me use a phone today, which I'm taking as a positive sign. I'm no longer hooked up to the main grid so I must be over the worst. Oh, Dulcie, I'm so sorry to have put you through this. How are you bearing up?'

'Oh, you know, not bad for a mistress whose lover has suffered his first heart-attack.'

'Don't speak like that. You know I hate that word. You're not my mistress, you're the woman I love. Oh, hell, I can't talk any more, I have to undergo yet more tests in a few minutes and I can see a posse of nurses and junior doctors heading in my direction. I'll ring you again as soon as I can. I love you, Dulcie.'

'I love you too. Take care.'

'And you.'

After she had put down the phone, Dulcie went outside and stood in the rain, her face turned up towards the sky. It was the maddest thing she could think to do. She was so unbelievably happy that nothing but an act of sheer lunacy would satisfy her. Only when she was wet through did she go back into the house.

Chapter Six

*

By rights Jack should have been looking forward to the evening – he'd had some excellent news during the afternoon, and that, combined with seeing Clare, should have made him feel a whole lot happier.

But last night he and Clare had argued. It wasn't the first time, but the nature of the exchange had made him feel awkward about seeing her again. He would have preferred to get together with her later in the week, but that would only have upset her more: they'd already had to reschedule this evening's dinner, arranged for him to meet Clare's parents.

The cause of their row still rankled. Clare had accused him of being obsessed with Tony or, more specifically, with what Tony had done. 'Just get over it,' she'd said. 'What's done is done. My husband left me for someone else, but do you hear me banging on about it?'

'Banging on?' he'd said in disbelief. 'Is that what you think I'm doing?'

She screwed up her napkin and threw it on to her empty plate. 'Face it, Jack, you've done nothing but moan about him this evening. It's your birthday and I've gone to a lot of trouble to cook you this meal – which you've hardly touched. I'm bored of hearing you complain about your soon-to-be-ex-wife who, allegedly, is stopping you seeing your children. What's more—'

He put down his knife and fork. 'I think you've made your point.'

She got to her feet and started to clear the table, stacking the plates and dishes with noisy haste. 'Have I? And what point exactly do you think I'm making?'

He stood up too, and took the crockery from her. 'That I'm making a mountain out of a molehill.'

In the kitchen, they moved around each other warily and in stifling silence, putting things away, making coffee. 'Jack,' she said, at last, 'we have so much going between us, but I can't compete with Maddie and the girls.'

'I don't want you to.'

'That's how it feels.'

'Then that's your problem.'

She pressed the plunger down on the cafetière, looked at him sharply. 'Surely it's *our* problem?'

Exasperation made him say, 'I have enough problems of my own without taking yours on board. If you can't hack the idea that I have two daughters whom I love and need to see, then that's something you have to deal with. I can't do it for you.'

'Can't or won't?'

'Don't be pedantic.'

'That's right, Jack, run away from the question rather than answer it. Frightened of the truth, are you?'

'What truth would that be?'

'That you haven't moved on. It's time you accepted that Maddie and the girls are making a new life. Okay, it doesn't include you, and that doesn't seem fair, but it's all that's on offer. You have no choice but to make the best of it. Because if you don't, you'll end up lonely and miserable, an embittered man whom Lucy and Amber won't want to see. Is that what you want?'

He hadn't stayed the night, as they'd planned. Instead he drove home, wondering why the hell he was bothering to be in a relationship with Clare.

They had met through mutual friends – the usual scenario for recently separated people who had unexpectedly found themselves back in the singles market. 'Clare's great,' Des had told him, during one of their boys-only curry nights at the beginning of May. 'She's one of Julie's work colleagues, a friend too. She's recently divorced, but prepared to give the male species the benefit of the doubt. You'll hit it off, I'm sure.' Des ran the Holmes Chapel branch of Norris & Rowan, and Jack had accepted the offer of dinner with cautious interest. Much to Des's satisfaction, Jack and Clare had hit it off.

So tonight, five months on, Jack was meeting Clare's parents.

'It's no big deal, Jack,' she'd said, when she'd first put the suggestion to him. But he knew it was. And he didn't feel comfortable with it. It was too soon. It made him feel as if he were living on a fault-line: the ground might crack open beneath his feet at any moment.

He drove in through the gates of the Maywood Grange Hotel, and parked his car in the last remaining space, next to Clare's Audi TT. He switched off the engine, drummed his fingers on the steering-wheel, and wondered why he had allowed himself to be manoeuvred into this situation. 'Come and meet the folks' was tantamount to saying, 'Do you fancy a finger buffet or a sit-down meal at the reception?'

The thought sent a chill through him and he felt a sudden urge to start the car again and head home.

Clare had apologised for what she'd said – she'd phoned him at the office this morning. 'Oh, Jack, I shouldn't have said those things. Of course the break-up of your marriage is a lot harder to come to terms with than mine was for me. I don't have any children to complicate the issue. Are we still on for this evening? Mum and Dad are really looking forward to meeting you.'

'Clare, I'm not sure—'

'I've said I'm sorry, Jack.'

Aware that he was being unfair to her, he'd said, 'Okay, what time do you want me there?'

Clare saw him before he saw her. She came over and kissed him. 'I was getting worried,' she said, wiping lipstick off his cheek. 'Thought perhaps you might have . . . Well, it doesn't matter what I thought, you're here now.' She straightened his collar. 'Okay?'

'Fine,' he lied. He took her hand. 'Come on, then, introduce me to your parents.'

Mr and Mrs Gilbert – oh, please call us Terry and Corinne – were trying too hard to be nice, probably at Clare's instruction. Every now and then he caught a knowing wink, even the odd smile of collusion. The unease he had felt outside in the car was now magnified many times over. Their eagerness for their only daughter to remarry – and doubtless provide them with grandchildren – was shockingly obvious. But when they started asking after his own children, suggesting that he and Clare should bring them over for tea one day, he found their manner disturbingly intrusive. He changed the subject abruptly and said, 'Clare, I forgot to tell you, I had some good news today. I've been invited to—'

'Oh, yummy, look at that,' she said, eyeing the sweet trolley as it was pushed past their table and on to the next. 'The tiramisu looks to die for. Sorry, Jack, what were you saying?'

He fixed a smile to his face and said, 'It's okay. I'll tell you later.'

But later didn't come. After the goodbyes, Clare had squeezed his arm and said, 'There, that wasn't so bad, was it?' Then he had driven home alone. Except he didn't go home. He put the car into the garage then went for a walk. The row of townhouses he lived in overlooked the river and, following the path alongside it, he headed towards the centre of town. He was in the mood for a drink.

His timing was awful. The first pub he went into was packed; last orders had been called and a crowd of youngsters had descended on the bar. The next pub he tried was the same: music blared and eye-watering smoke filled the air. Feeling old and curmudgeonly, he gave up on the idea of a drink and decided instead to walk his bad mood out of his system. Anyway, turning up for work tomorrow with a hangover would not be a wise move. It would hardly give the right impression, not now that he had been invited to become a partner.

That was what he had tried to tell Clare during dinner. His reaction to her lack of interest – not to tell her – now seemed more akin to the behaviour of a petulant child than a grown man. Why was he behaving so badly?

If he was honest with himself, he hadn't wanted to share his good fortune with Clare. Which, he supposed, spoke volumes about his feelings for her. He had to end it, he knew. Deep down, he had known it for weeks. He had met her too soon after his split with Maddie, when he was still vulnerable, and had thought her to be the answer to his loneliness and hurt pride. And although she might never admit it, Clare had probably viewed him as the means to get herself back on-line with her plan to be happily married with children. He didn't begrudge her that – after all, a family had been what he and Maddie had most wanted. They had both experienced fragmented family life while growing up – Maddie's parents had divorced when she was twelve, and his had died in a car accident when he was in his late teens. It was important to them to create what

35

they felt they had missed out on. Children would give them security, stability and continuity. And they had, until Tony had intervened.

Tony had never married. 'I'm too busy to settle down,' he had claimed in the past, whenever Jack and Maddie teased him about becoming a disreputable *roué*: as he grew older, his girlfriends became younger. Not so long ago, and in a moment of drunken self-pity, he had confessed that he envied Jack. 'You have everything I've ever wanted. A beautiful wife who adores you and two children who think you're the best thing since sliced bread.'

'But you're the one with the Porsche and a different girlfriend for every night of the week.'

'It means nothing,' Tony had said, putting his arm round Jack, as he always did when he'd had too much to drink. 'Take it from me, it means absolutely nothing unless you feel you can't live without that woman.'

And, if Tony was to be believed, that was what he now felt about Maddie. 'I'm sorry, Jack,' he'd said, after Jack had found them in bed, 'but she means the world to me. I can't live without her.'

'Neither can I!' Jack had roared. And, landing a direct hit on Tony's jaw, he'd knocked him to the floor. 'She's *my* wife and you're not having her!'

If he had thought violence was going to put an end to the affair, he had misjudged Tony. And Maddie. That very night she had taken the girls and moved in with Tony. She instigated divorce proceedings immediately. One minute Jack had been a happily married man, the next he was alone in Dumpsville. Friends had rallied round to bolster his confidence by telling him he was a great catch and that his only problem would be fending off all the gorgeous women who would come his way.

All rubbish, of course, but they had meant well. One or two had even admitted they were jealous, that they wished they were single again and weren't tied down by the Three Ms – marriage, a mortgage and a monastic sex-life. It was all talk. None of them would want their marriage to end in the way his had. Or for their children to suffer as his did.

The streets were busier now: it was chucking-out time and the carefree youngsters who had monopolised the bars were now filling the cold night air with their boisterous laughter. Sidestepping a couple who had fallen into each other's arms for a passionate kiss, he crossed the road and turned into the main street of Maywood.

He passed Turner's, an old-fashioned department store that, against all the odds, had kept going, and went on towards Boots, Woolworths and W. H. Smith where the road had been pedestrianised. The shops were smaller here, and more individual. There was a bridal shop, a jeweller's, a florist (all three conveniently placed together), an Aga shop, an excellent delicatessen and, across the road, two shoe shops (side by side), a dry-cleaner's, a pine shop, a hair-dressing salon and Novel Ways, the town's only bookshop. Last year the owner had acquired the next-door premises – Jack had been in charge of the sale – so that he could knock through to provide his customers with a coffee shop.

Before Clare had appeared on the scene, Jack had often browsed the shelves before sitting down to a café latte and a quiet read. Clare wasn't a reader: she was a doer who preferred her time to be action-filled. Nostalgia for those pre-Clare days made him cross the road to look in the window of Novel Ways. He saw that the latest Harry Potter was out and made a mental note to pop back tomorrow and buy it for Amber and Lucy. He and his daughters had read all the previous ones together and the thought of sitting down with them to enjoy this one lifted his spirits. It would be something to look forward to when they returned from America.

But what if Tony bought it for them before Jack could?

He gritted his teeth and was about to walk away when something caught his eye. It was a piece of paper stuck to one of the panes of glass in the door.

Ever thought of writing a book, or penning a few lines of poetry? You have? Then why not join a writing group, where, among new friends, you can discover those hidden talents you never knew existed?

He read it through one more time and thought of all the song lyrics he had written as a teenager. He had given up when he'd met Maddie, dismissing his work as immature ramblings. But writing again might be cathartic. It might be an outlet for all the anger and bitterness he didn't know what to do with.

Without giving himself time to change his mind, he hunted through his pockets for a pen. He found one and wrote down the contact name and phone number on the back of his hand.

Chapter Seven

*

It was the last lesson of the day – double English with Mr Hunter – and Jaz was impatient for it to be over. It had been a long week for her, but at last it was Thursday and, the way things were going, she wouldn't have much homework to do tonight.

Her parents thought she was going round to Vicki's for the evening, and as long as all went to plan, they would think the same every Thursday night. She didn't like lying to Mum and Dad, and she rarely did, but she knew that the alternative, in this instance, was unthinkable. Better to keep quiet than put up with the teasing from her brothers and sisters.

At three forty-five the bell rang and, as he always did at the end of his lessons, Mr Hunter bowed and said, 'Thank you for your time, ladies and gentlemen. You may now take your leave of me. But remember, I want that Seamus Heaney essay in by Tuesday. That instruction extends to you also, Ross Peters.' Books and files were slapped into bags, and chairs scraped noisily on the tiled floor. Outside in the corridor, Jaz caught up with Vicki, who was getting something from her locker. They usually walked home together, unless one of them had an after-college activity. Vicki had just landed the role of Gwendolen in the drama department's production of *The Importance of Being Earnest*; from next week she would have rehearsals on Mondays and Wednesdays, leaving Jaz to walk home alone. More crucially, Vicki, with her enviably sleek long hair the colour of jet and her flawless skin, which tanned the second the sun shone, would be spending all that time with Nathan King, who was playing Algernon.

From the moment Vicki had told her about the play, Jaz had

debated with herself whether to let Vicki know that *she* had her eye on Nathan. Yesterday, after several days of torturing herself, she went against her instinct to keep quiet and confided in her friend.

'Nathan King,' Vicki had said, with a wide grin, 'I like your taste, girl. But you might need to take a ticket and get in line.'

'What? You mean you're interested in him?'

'I'm teasing. But there is something tempting about him. Oh, don't look like that! Billy the Kid is more my style.'

'Billy Kidswell?'

'Yeah. He's playing Ernest.'

If Vicki was considered to be the hottest date in the lower sixth, Billy the Kid was the fittest, most lusted-after guy in the upper sixth. It was rumoured that he kept the underwear of all his conquests. Though why on earth Vicki wanted her knickers to be added to his Lycra trophy collection was a mystery to Jaz. She could think of nothing more demeaning.

Her friend's declared interest in Billy should have put Jaz's mind at rest. But it didn't. Of course Nathan King would fancy Vicki so there was little point in Jaz getting worked up about him. Never in a million years would he look twice in her direction. And if he did, once he knew what kind of a family she came from he'd make himself scarce. She didn't like to think that she was ashamed of her family, but she was. Mum was okay, but her father was embarrassingly larger than life and always had to know what she was up to, and as for her brothers and sisters, well, they were just savages with as much sense between them as a peanut. She seldom invited Vicki home with her, and only when she knew Tamzin and Lulu wouldn't be there.

'So tell me again about this writers' group,' Vicki said, shutting her locker and swinging her bag over her shoulder. 'Won't it be a load of frustrated old women writing about men in bulging riding breeches?'

Jaz laughed. 'It might be, for all I know. I'll find out tonight.'

Vickie stared at her. 'You're a strange girl, Jaz. Way too secretive for your own good.'

'As the middle child of a big family, it's the only way to survive. It's okay for you, you're an only child. You don't have to keep things from pathologically annoying brothers and sisters.'

'And I've told you before, it's not that easy being the centre of your parents' universe. Whoa, hold up! Look who I see.'

Ahead of them, and standing within a group of other students, mostly girls, were Billy the Kid and Nathan King. Billy looked towards them and waved. His fair hair was highlighted with blond streaks and it was cut so that part of the fringe flopped artfully down on to his face, partially covering his trademark sunglasses. 'Yo, my precious Gwendolen, how's it going?'

'Ernest, my love, how sweet of you to enquire. Truth to tell, I'm feeling quite faint and in need of a handsome Adonis to carry my bag home for me.' She tossed her shiny black hair with an exaggerated sigh. 'If only such a man existed.'

Jaz marvelled at her friend. How did she always manage to do and say the right thing?

Billy grinned. 'Then, my sweet, allow me to oblige and give you a lift in my carriage.'

'I didn't know you'd passed your test,' Vicki said, assuming her normal voice and somehow becoming part of the group, leaving Jaz on the edge.

'I passed yesterday, so I'm quite legal.' He pushed a hand through his hair affectedly. 'Fancy a ride . . . home?' he drawled.

Vicki ignored the innuendo and said, 'Jaz too?'

Everyone turned and looked at Jaz. Including Nathan. Was it her imagination, or was he staring at her harder than the rest? She shrivelled inside and felt an excruciating flush creep up her neck. No! With her hair and skin tone, blushing was the kiss of death! She wished the ground would open up and swallow her. 'It's okay,' she said, 'I'd rather walk—'

'You haven't got room, Billy,' Nathan interrupted her rudely, 'not with all the other groupies you've offered to drive home.'

She felt the sting of his words. So, she was just another groupie, was she? A silly little groupie for whom Billy the Kid didn't have room. Well, she'd show him. In a gesture that Vicki would have been proud of, she tossed one of her long plaits over her shoulder. 'I'll see you, then, Vicki.' She walked away quickly, her head held high. She kept on walking, out of the college gate and right to the end of the road, where she turned left. Only then did she slow down to catch her breath. Bloody Nathan King! Whatever had she seen in him?

'Do you always walk this fast?'

She spun round. Oh, hell! It was him. 'Yes,' she snapped. 'I find it preferable to hanging round people who don't have any manners!'

He fell into step beside her, his long, languid strides outpacing her short, hurried ones. She waited for him to say something. But he didn't. They walked on in silence, past the supermarket and towards Mill Street. They stopped at the level-crossing, and he said, 'Carry your bag for you?'

She turned and saw there was a faint smile on his face. He was teasing her. 'I doubt you'd manage it,' she said and, seeing a gap in the traffic, she darted across the road.

He followed her. 'Would I be right in thinking I've done something to annoy you?'

'Yes. So leave me alone.'

'Oh,' he replied. 'Well, fair enough.'

With his hands deep in his pockets, the tails of his leather coat flapping rhythmically behind him, he sauntered beside her. She wished he'd get the message and push off.

But at the bottom of Chester Street, he said, 'And does everyone get this treatment, or have I been singled out specially?'

Enough! She stopped dead and gave him the kind of contemptuous look she practised in front of the mirror for Tamzin and Lulu's benefit. 'Don't flatter yourself that I'd single you out for anything.'

He tilted his head. 'Any reason why?'

She shifted the heavy bag on her shoulder and started walking again. 'Figure it out for yourself.'

'Give me a clue. Am I wearing the wrong aftershave, or am I just not your type?'

'My type? That's a joke! You'd never be my type. Not in a million years. Not even if you learned some manners. Not even if you were the last guy on the planet with a pedigree that stretched from here to Uranus.' She paused for breath, regretting her choice of planet. Why couldn't she have picked Pluto? He'd be bound to seize his opportunity for some more fun at her expense.

But he didn't. 'Aha,' he said, 'we're getting somewhere. So it's my behaviour that's rattled you. Something I said? How about we rewind the last fifteen minutes? My first words to you were when Billy offered your friend a lift home. What did I say?'

She shot him a furious look. 'Short-term memory not what it used to be?'

'Evidently not.'

'You told Billy not to give me a lift home with Vicki because he already had a carload of groupies to bolster his ego. Now, you can take this as a first official warning: I am nobody's groupie. Got that?'

'You think I snubbed you? Is that it?'

'Oh, please, give the boy a round of applause!

'Listen, if you hadn't gone stomping off, you would have heard what I was going to say next.'

'I didn't go stomping off . . .' She hesitated. 'What *were* you going to say next?'

'That rather than let you risk your life in Billy's death-trap of a car, I'd walk you home.'

She looked at him suspiciously, far from convinced. 'And why would you want to do that?'

He thought for a moment, then smiled. 'I guess I must get some sort of perverse pleasure out of girls giving me a hard time.'

Chapter Eight

*

Beth felt as if she were a child again getting ready for the first day of the school term. She had made so many last-minute checks – A4 writing pad, biros (two, in case she lost one on the way or one failed to work), pencil, and lastly . . . What else did she need to take with her to the first meeting of Hidden Talents?

Nothing, she told herself firmly.

'How about a ruler? Or maybe a dictionary? Better still, a thesaurus.'

She looked across the kitchen to where Nathan was helping himself to an apple from the fruit bowl. 'Don't tease me, Nathan,' she said. 'I'm nervous enough.'

He leaned back against the worktop, a picture of easygoing nonchalance. 'Keep it chilled, Mum, that's what you've got to tell yourself.' He bit into the apple and chomped noisily.

She smiled. 'I'm not sure I like all this role reversal.'

'It's the future. Which reminds me, I'll see to your computer for you tonight while you're out.'

'There's no hurry.'

'Yes, there is. I want you hooked up to the Net and best-friends with it before I leave home. How else will I be able to keep an eye on you?'

'By telephone?'

'Old ground, Mum. We've been there before. Email's much better, a piece of cake to get the hang of. Now I must learn my lines. Oscar's waiting for me in the bedroom.' He swept past her in a flourish of camp theatrical posturing.

It was a fifteen-minute walk to Bloom Street. She could have driven, but since it wasn't raining she decided to walk the nerves out of her system.

It was ridiculous that she was so keyed up. She was only going to a writers' group. Even if it was a departure from the norm, it was a necessary one, she reminded herself. She was on a mission: to convince all those doubters, herself included, that she would be able to cope when Nathan flew the nest. She was a capable woman – as Simone frequently reminded her – she had a comfortable home, a reasonable job and a brain that functioned relatively well. Now she had to learn how to enjoy exploring the unfamiliar.

She wished she could be more like Nathan, who took everything in his stride: exams were a challenge, as was standing up on a stage and performing for an audience. She could never do that. Just the thought of looking out at a sea of expectant faces made her stomach lurch. It was bad enough watching Nathan, because although he was extraordinarily good at learning his lines, she always sat in the audience rigid with worry that he might miss a cue.

His outward self-assurance came from his father. Nothing had seemed to faze Adam, which had made his untimely death all the more shocking. He had hidden his anxiety well. Too well. If only he had been more open she might have been able to help him.

She arrived at number eighteen exactly on time. Bloom Street was considered the prettiest street in Maywood, the most sought-after address in town. Having said that, her own address had become almost as highly prized – if the asking price that the estate agent had put on Adele's flat was anything to go by. There had already been two couples to view it and Beth knew that both were keen to go ahead with the purchase. She hoped for her elderly neighbour's sake that things would go smoothly.

She rang the bell, admiring the creamy white pansies and trailing ivy in the window-boxes at either side of the handsome wooden door. It was painted a deep blue and was finished off with a shiny brass knocker in the shape of a lion's head. Whoever Dulcie Ballantyne was, she had style, Beth decided.

To put everyone at ease, Dulcie had decided to offer a glass of wine before the meeting got under way. They made a small gathering, but an interesting one. That was the thing about writers' groups;

they brought together a diverse mix of people who, on the face of it, had little in common. She, for example, wouldn't ordinarily socialise with a man like Victor Blackmore. She doubted that any of the others present would either. He had been in the room for just a few minutes, but it was patently obvious that he was a spanner in the works. She put him in his late fifties; he had thinning, sandy grey hair, and was very pale with beady eyes tinged with pink. He was wearing a pair of seen-better-days trousers that were too short – an inch or two of shiny, hairless white shin was exposed as he nursed a bulky file on his lap – and a selection of pens was clipped to his breast pocket. He looked ill at ease as he sipped his red wine.

Nearest to Victor, and sitting on the sofa, was Beth King. She had been first to arrive and, when Dulcie had opened the door to her, had looked ready to turn tail. She was an attractive, fair-haired woman, somewhere in her early forties. In a navy blue polo-neck sweater with straight-legged jeans, she wore no wedding ring, so was possibly divorced. She had a son at the local college and his name had already been mentioned several times during the conversation. Dulcie wondered how dependent Beth was on him. When Philip had died she had seen how easy it would be to rely on her children, to live her life through them, and she had done everything in her power not to make that mistake.

It was good to see that Victor Blackmore wasn't to be the sole man of the group. With a bit of luck Jack Solomon's presence would keep the dreadful man from thinking he could lord it over the rest of them. He was good-looking, if a little sombre, and cut a striking figure in his dark blue suit and silk tie. But she detected a sag in his shoulders and a tiredness in his eyes. He had apologised when he'd arrived for being so formally dressed, but apparently work had run on. 'Don't worry,' she'd said, taking him through to the sitting room where everyone was gathered. 'You won't be marked down for it. Now, let me you introduce you.' It turned out that he had already met Beth King, and they seemed surprised to see each other. A little awkward, too.

The most interesting member of the group was Jaz Rafferty. Dulcie was delighted that someone so young wanted to be involved. If she could bear to be with a bunch of old fogies, which was probably how she viewed them all, she would add a fresh and exciting dimension to the group. She was a delicate sprite of a girl and probably had no idea how pretty she was, with her striking auburn hair and charmingly freckled complexion. There was a delicious defiance in her manner – heavily booted feet crossed at the ankles, arms clamped across her chest – and she bristled with that beneath-the-surface defensiveness of teenagers. Dulcie thought she was lovely and envied her her youth and tiny body, which looked so endearing in the minuscule black skirt and oversized baggy jumper. She had forgotten how fascinating and intense teenagers could be; how terribly serious life was for them.

It was time to get things started, and Dulcie had an opening exercise in mind; something lighthearted to set the right note and help everyone relax. She offered everyone a top-up of Shiraz, except Jaz, who was sticking to orange juice, and said, 'How would you all feel about playing a little game, just something daft to get us in the right mood?'

Victor was first to speak. 'I haven't come here to play games,' he muttered.

The rest of the group was galvanised.

Jack said good-humouredly, 'Squash or tennis? Either way, I'm afraid I haven't brought my trainers.'

'Sounds okay to me,' smiled Beth, 'so long as it doesn't involve a Trivial Pursuit board.'

'Is it role play?' asked Jaz doubtfully. 'We used to do a lot of that at school in Drama.'

'No, it's not role play,' Dulcie assured her. 'It's basic story-telling, and I'm sure you'll all have played the game before, as adults or as children. We each take it in turns to add a sentence to the story. We'll go clockwise, just to be conventional. Victor, perhaps you'd like to set the ball rolling.'

'Very well.' He leaned back in his seat, closed his eyes, steepled his fingers together and inhaled deeply. He let out his breath and they waited for him to speak.

Nothing.

Complete silence.

Beth looked at Dulcie, who winked at her.

Still nothing.

Someone – Jaz? – cleared their throat.

Victor's eyes remained shut. 'I'm thinking,' he said, in answer to the not-so-subtle prompt.

Another deep inhalation. And then it came. 'It was the best of times, it was the worst of times.' He opened his eyes and looked about him as though expecting a round of applause. Across the room, on the sofa next to Jack, Dulcie was aware of Jaz stifling a snigger. She swallowed to stop one escaping her as well and said, 'Good start, Victor. Beth, your turn now. And perhaps go for a slightly longer sentence, something for the rest of us to play with and get our teeth into.'

'It was the best of times, it was the worst of times,' Beth repeated slowly, her gaze focused on the clock on the mantelpiece, 'but no one could have been prepared for the awful calamity that struck, that wild, windy night, on exactly the stroke of midnight.'

With visible relief, she turned to Jack, who dived in straight away. 'Not even Gibbons, the one-armed gardener, who could never steer a straight course with a wheelbarrow, especially if he'd spent the morning in the potting-shed savouring his favourite tipple of potato gin and absinthe.'

'But despite his strange drinking habits,' said Jaz, 'and the loss of his arm during a fight over his prize-winning marrows, Gibbons was a crack shot, and was quite used to killing trespassers who came on to the master's land.'

It was Dulcie's turn next and she was glad to see that the game was working well and, with the exception of Victor, that the others were enjoying themselves. 'Now, the master was a curious man,' she took up the story, 'and it was generally rumoured within the village that he was not all he claimed to be. Some said he had never been the same since the incident with the pitchfork, while others claimed that his time in Africa had left him with a fever for which there was no known cure.'

After several more rounds, which had them all laughing – the master, Jack told them, was a cross-dressing lap-dancer and Gibbons a Mafia boss on the run from his domineering mother – Dulcie pronounced an end to the game. She had decided that Jack was a quick-witted good sport, an asset to the group.

'And the point of that exercise?' asked Victor, drumming his fingers on his file.

'To relax us,' Dulcie said. 'And to make us see how easy it is to slip into clichés and stereotypes,' she added, more seriously. 'Something we need to avoid, if we're going to write anything of worth and originality.'

'Quite so,' Victor agreed. 'First rule of writing, avoid clichés like the plague.'

Surprised at his ready wit, Dulcie laughed. Then, seeing the dead-pan expression on his face, she stopped short. Oh, Lord, the wretched man wouldn't know a cliché if it whacked him on the bottom. 'Right, then,' she said, careful to avoid Jack's eye – which she knew would betray his amusement at Victor's gaffe. 'Now that we know one another a little better, why don't we discuss what we each hope to gain from these sessions? Perhaps we could also be brave enough to share a few details about ourselves and say why we write.' Across the room, she saw Victor lean forward. 'Beth, would you like to leap in first?'

'Oh. Well, it's ... Oh, goodness. Well, I've been writing for some time, um ... since my husband died, eleven years ago. I suppose you could say it's been cathartic for me. Oh dear, that sounds terribly like a cliché, doesn't it?'

'Not at all,' Dulcie said encouragingly. 'When my husband died I wrote frantically. Any spare moment I had that might leave me dwelling on Philip, I filled with words. Have you had anything published?'

'Oh, no. I've only ever written for myself. I've never wanted other people to read my thoughts.'

'So what are you doing here?'

They all looked at Victor. Dulcie could have slapped him.

'Surely that's the whole point of writing,' he continued, 'to know that one has a talent and share it.'

'That's a fair enough theory,' said Jack, leaning back in his seat and looking directly at Victor, 'so long as one is sure one has such a gift.'

'Yes,' agreed Jaz, recrossing her legs and bouncing a booted foot in the air. 'No point in shoving a load of opinionated rubbish on people in the mistaken belief you can write. I can't think of anything worse.'

Good for you two, thought Dulcie. 'So, Beth,' she said, 'what would you like to get out of our meetings?'

'Oh, um, basic teaching, I suppose. Someone to show me where I'm going wrong. I know I'm not very good, and I'd like—'

'You can't teach people to write. You're either born a writer or you're not.'

'That's an interesting point that we'll discuss another time, Victor,' said Dulcie smoothly. He was such a textbook case of prejudice and arrogance, she was almost enjoying the verbal tussle

48

with him. It was like dealing with a truculent child; a child of whom she would get the better. Smiling, she said, 'I ought to say at this stage that every time one of us apologises for our writing, or says, "I'm not very good," a fifty-pence piece will have to be put into the Self-belief Box.'

Beth laughed. 'In that case, do you take credit cards?'

'How about having a Know-it-all Box?' muttered Jaz. She was examining a silver ring on her thumb, but no one could have doubted at whom her remark was aimed.

Dulcie was growing ever fonder of the youngest member of the group. 'Jack, how about you tell us a bit about yourself and why you're here?' she asked.

'Not much to tell, really. I'm at a point in my life when I need to have a rethink, try something new, and, well, it was a spur-of-the-moment thing when I saw your card in the bookshop window.'

'And hopefully you're not regretting having responded to it?'

'Not yet,' he said, with a smile.

'Any writing experience?'

'Nothing published, if that's what you mean. I wrote some rather poor song lyrics when I was very young and probably when I was very drunk. More recently I've been thinking of keeping a diary.' He turned to Beth. 'More catharsis for the soul, I guess.'

'And your expectations of the group?' asked Dulcie.

He ran a thumbnail the length of the crease in his trouser-leg. 'I'm not sure I have any. Like I said, I just wanted to try something new.'

Victor clicked his tongue. 'This was what I was afraid of. Unless we're all serious about writing and getting published, this group will be a waste of time.'

Dulcie saw Jack's hand clench. She reminded herself that patience was a virtue. 'I don't think that's a helpful thing to say, Victor. For all we know, Jack may turn out to be the next Tony Parsons.'

'Tony who?'

Jaz rolled her eyes. 'Tony Parsons. He wrote *Man and Boy* and *One For My Baby*.'

'Well, I've never heard of him or his books.'

'I think we may be missing the point,' Dulcie intervened. 'We're not here to judge one another. We're here to offer support and helpful criticism. Jaz, do you want to take a turn?'

49

'Okay. I've just started writing a novel, so you could say I'm very serious about writing.' She shot Victor a direct glance. 'That's it. Nothing else to say.'

'Was there a particular reason why you decided to write?'

Jaz paused. 'Hmmm . . . I like doing stuff on my own. I suppose I like the power it gives me.'

'Yes,' nodded Dulcie, 'writing does empower you. It's just you and that piece of paper, and when you've filled it, you know no one else had anything to do with it. A nice point, Jaz. And finally, Victor, you're obviously a seasoned writer. We'd love to know more about the book you're working on. Also, how and why did you start writing it?'

He squared his shoulders, ready to take the stage. He'd probably been wondering if he'd ever get a turn. 'It's a thriller set in a fictitious state, somewhere between Macedonia and Albania, and encompasses everything from drug trafficking and prostitution to political intrigue.'

'That's quite a canvas you're working with,' Dulcie said. 'What gave you the idea? A trip to that part of the world?'

'A programme on television, not that I watch much – rubbish, most of it, these days. And no, I haven't been there. But writers should learn to depend more on their imagination than on mere bricks and mortar.' He tapped his forehead. 'It's all in here.'

'How much have you written?' asked Jack.

'Two hundred thousand words,' Victor said proudly. 'And still going strong.' He opened the file on his knees.

Dulcie's heart sank. From what she could see it was an editor's nightmare. There were pages and pages of tightly packed old-fashioned type, smudged ink and Tipp-Ex. 'Don't you use a word-processor?' she asked.

He shook his head so vehemently that she might have asked him if he wrote in blood. 'I wouldn't feel the same creative flow using a computer. I feel more in tune with the spirit of being a real writer when I'm bashing away on my old Remington. Hammering on the anvil of true creativity, that's what I'm doing.'

'Goodness, how do you find time to write so much?' asked Beth, staring in awe at the manuscript.

'I'm very focused,' he replied, crossing his legs and revealing more white shin.

'You'd have to be,' said Jack. 'I couldn't begin to think of writing to that extent after a hard day's work. I take my hat off to you.'

Jack's praise caused Victor to blush with pride, and he gazed at his file lovingly. 'It's all in the focus,' he murmured.

Later, when Dulcie was showing them out, having set a simple exercise to be completed by next week, she knew that as much as Victor had initially harangued the group, he would continue to grace it with his awkward and at times antagonistic presence. Doubtless he was secretly delighted that he had written more than anyone else in the group: it put him above the rest of them. Which meant that deep down, just like everyone else, he was hopelessly insecure about himself.

Chapter Nine

*

'Mother, I'm shocked! *Who* was that man I saw you with?'

Despite knowing Nathan was teasing her, Beth felt her cheeks colour. She shut the door behind her, removed her jacket, and hung it up on the row of hooks. She decided to play along with him. 'And what man would that be?'

He wagged a finger at her. 'Don't come the innocent with me, my girl. I saw the two of you, bold as brass out there in the road for all the neighbours to see.' He shook his head. 'I don't know, I've tried my best to bring you up properly and this is all the thanks I get. What's a son to do?'

She squeezed past him and planted a kiss on his cheek. 'For starters you can put the kettle on and I'll tell you all about it. You wouldn't believe one man who was there. He was such a bigoted know-it-all. I don't know how we got through the evening without taking a swipe at him.'

They sat at the kitchen table with their mugs of tea. Nathan had kept the log-burning stove alight while she'd been out, and Beth felt herself relax for the first time that evening. She knew she had given a less than impressive performance in Bloom Street, and she didn't like to think too hard about what the rest of the group must have thought of her. Probably had her down as a simpering idiot. She hoped she scored higher in their estimation than Victor Blackmore.

'So, first off, who was the guy in the Beamer?' asked Nathan, his bare feet stretched out towards the stove. 'The bigoted know-it-all?'

Momentarily distracted by Nathan's long legs – she never failed to be surprised by the size of him – she said, 'No, that was Jack

Solomon. Coincidentally, he's Adele's estate agent and is really quite nice.'

Over the rim of his mug, Nathan raised an eyebrow. 'How nice?'

She swatted him with one of the cork tablemats. 'Not in that way. He's much too young for a decrepit thing like me.'

'Oh, Ma, give it up! I bet you were easily the best-looking woman there. And the youngest to boot.'

'Wrong again. There was an interesting girl about your age. Goodness knows what she thought of the rest of us. I expect she wrote us off as the local bunch of ageing crazies. You might know her, she goes to Maywood College.'

'Name, rank and number?' He pulled out an imaginary notebook from his pocket and pretended to flick through it, searching for a character match.

'Jaz Rafferty and she lives on—'

He looked up. 'Marbury Road,' he finished for her.

'You know her?'

'I walked home with her after college today. Did she know you were my mother?'

'Why? Are you worried I might have told her the truth about you and put her off?'

'Now, Mum, don't let this fiction business go to your head.'

Beth laughed. She told him about the game the group had played.

'Transvestite lap-dancers? I'm beginning to have reservations about this writing group. Perhaps I ought to come along as your chaperon and keep an eye on you.'

'Spoilsport.'

Later that night, soaking in a scented bath, Beth took stock of the evening. She concluded that it had gone well. She had enjoyed herself more than she'd expected to, and felt a sense of achievement. She put this down to Dulcie Ballantyne: with her quiet, reassuring manner, she had led the group firmly but not autocratically. She had given encouragement without resorting to patronage. It was just a pity they had had to put up with Victor. It was possible that by next week he would have pulled out – and also that new members might join. It was selfish of her, but Beth hoped this wouldn't happen. She wanted the group to stay as small as it was. Excluding Victor, she had liked everyone. Maybe it was because Victor was such a pain that the rest of them had gelled so nicely.

She soaped a leg with a banana-shaped sponge Nathan had given her for her last birthday and recognised she was being a wimp. *Courage, mon brave!* she told herself. It was odds on that no one else from the group was having these pathetic thoughts. Certainly not Jack Solomon. She wondered what he had meant when he had said that writing would be cathartic for him. What did he have to work through? He had seemed relaxed and confident to her. But no one knew better than she did that appearances could deceive.

If any of the patients from the health centre had seen or heard her mumblings this evening, they wouldn't believe she was the same person who had to stand firm when they claimed their sore throat was life-threatening and they just *had* to see the doctor. Often, in such cases, the only life under threat was hers – she was the one who had to deflect the tirade of abuse thrown at her down the telephone line.

Her mind still preoccupied with the group, she thought of Jaz Rafferty. Had she imagined it, or had Nathan shown a little too much restrained interest when she'd mentioned the girl's name? As popular as he was with girls – the phone was always ringing for him – there had never been anyone 'special' for him. He joked that he liked to keep his options open and play the field, but she knew it wasn't in his nature. That was more Billy's style. While Billy's *raison d'être* was clocking up as many broken hearts as he could, Nathan's was attracting girls as friends.

With an expert nudge of her foot, she turned on the hot tap and wondered why women were so often attracted to the wrong sort of men. Handsome, shallow men who would do them no good.

A knock at the door interrupted her thoughts.

It was Nathan. 'Will you test me on my lines?' He came in and settled himself in the creaking wicker chair beside the bath. It was a familiar routine between them. For years she had tested Nathan like this, whether it was lines for a play or vocabulary for a French test. When he'd hit adolescence she'd assumed he'd stop coming into the bathroom when she was in the bath, having decided he was too old for such openness, but he hadn't. It amused her that it didn't work the other way round: whenever he was in the bath the door was locked.

She turned off the tap. 'Go on, then. Pass me a towel.' After she'd dried her hands she took the script from him.

'If you start at the top of the page, I'll come in from there.'

Assuming her best Edith Evans accent, Beth began to read the part of Lady Bracknell, the high ceiling of the bathroom giving her voice an extra resonance: "'It really makes no matter, Algernon. I had some crumpets with Lady Harbury, who seems to me to be living entirely for pleasure now.'"

"'I hear her hair has turned quite—", Nathan broke off. 'What is it? What's wrong?'

She handed him the text. 'Quick, fetch me a pen and a piece of paper.'

He returned within seconds and watched her scribble in large block capitals the words, LIVING FOR PLEASURE.

'What do you think?' she said. 'Good title for a book?'

'Not bad. But why not give Oscar full credit and go for "Living Entirely for Pleasure"?'

She shook her head. 'No, it's snappier my way.'

Beth went to bed happy that night. The homework Dulcie had set the group had been to think of a suitable title for a novel, and to put together an opening page. 'Key features to get across,' Dulcie had said. 'You need a hook to grab the reader's attention, a sense of time and place, and the general tone of the story.'

Well, she'd stumbled across the title. Now all she had to do was write the necessary three hundred-odd words.

As Nathan might say, a piece of cake – surely?

Chapter Ten

*

On Sunday morning Jack woke with one of Clare's arms draped over his chest. He lay for a moment without moving, his eyes fixed on the narrow gap in the curtains: rain was pattering against the window. Another wet, miserable day, he thought. Thousands of miles away, Amber and Lucy would be enjoying blue skies and sun-drenched days in Florida.

He looked at the digital alarm clock on the bedside table and saw that it wasn't yet seven. There was no need for him to be up early – it wasn't a work day – but he knew he wouldn't get back to sleep. Not wanting to disturb Clare, he lifted her arm gently and slid out of bed.

He shut himself into the bathroom and stood beneath the shower, letting the powerful jets of water batter him into full consciousness. He wondered if this was such a good idea. In his present mood, it might be easier to get through the day in a state of hazy detachment.

Out of the shower, he wrapped himself in a large towel, wiped away the condensation from the mirror above the basin, and reached for his shaver. When he wasn't working he often liked to skip the tedious monotony of shaving, but Clare was a stickler for a stubble-free chin, especially if they were going out. Today they were meeting Des and Julie for lunch at the Italian in town. It had been Clare's idea to celebrate him becoming a partner, but Jack didn't feel comfortable at the prospect. He knew that Des had expected to be offered the same promotion, but nothing had materialised for him, and this would rub his nose in it. What was worse, a step up the career ladder would have been a welcome break for Des: six months ago his wife had given birth to Desmond Junior. But Clare had arranged it behind Jack's back, then delivered it to him as a *fait accompli* last night. 'I was going to keep it as a surprise,' she'd said, hooking her fingers round his neck and kissing him, 'but you know what I'm like with secrets. Completely hopeless.' She had manoeuvred him down on to the sofa, and before he'd known what he was doing he was undressing her, not slowly and tenderly as he normally did, but roughly, suddenly filled with the need to feel the effect of his own strength. To feel *something*. Afterwards he had fallen asleep with a chilling sense of desolation growing within him.

He had finally got round to telling Clare about his partnership on the day of the writers' group's first meeting. They were speaking on the phone, late afternoon, and she had immediately suggested they go out for dinner. 'Sorry,' he'd said, 'it'll have to be another night, I'm busy this evening.'

'Oh? Got something or some*one* better lined up?' Her words were playful, but beneath them he caught an edge of jealousy.

He hadn't wanted to tell her about Hidden Talents and had said, 'Now I'm a partner there'll be even more late nights I'm afraid, regular meetings I'll be expected to attend.' As soon as he'd said this, he'd realised he'd given himself a plausible alibi for every Thursday evening when he would be attending the group.

'Oh, well,' she'd replied, more happily, 'that's the price of success, I suppose.'

He slipped back into the bedroom, helped himself to some clothes from the wardrobe, and returned to the bathroom. Once he was dressed, he went downstairs. The kitchen was on the middle floor of the house and looked over the river. When he'd viewed the property this had been its one redeeming feature. He didn't like modern houses – an opinion, in his line of work, that he kept to himself. But necessity had quashed any aesthetic preferences: he had needed a place to live that was convenient for work and affordable. Maywood was an established pocket of affluence in Cheshire where, for many years, demand had outstripped supply. If beggars wanted to live in Maywood, they could not be choosy. He could have rented in a cheaper area, but he hadn't wanted to do that. One didn't have to be an estate agent to know that location, location, location was everything. What he wouldn't give to live in Bloom Street. Or Maywood Park Road.

Making himself some toast and a cafetière of coffee, he envied Beth King and Dulcie Ballantyne. He didn't know their circumstances, just that they were both widowed, but they seemed to have coped and got on with life. Perhaps if he got to know them better, he might learn something from them. He had given up looking for help and advice from his immediate circle of friends: all happily married, they had no comprehension of what he was going through. Besides, he sensed that they were tired of that particular conversation. He didn't blame them. What could be worse than another man's obsession? For that was what it seemed like, some days. How long, he wondered, had it been before Beth King had sorted herself out? Dulcie too.

It had been interesting seeing Beth last Thursday evening: she had seemed quite a different woman from the one he had met a few days earlier when she had been determined to make sure that old Miss Waterman wasn't duped. The other night she had been less sure of herself.

Maybe she had thought the same of him. He had told the group he was thinking of writing a diary, and after he'd driven home that night – having given both Beth and Jaz a lift – he had dug out an old notebook and made his first entry. After several lines, he had decided instead to write on his laptop. It was more private – less chance of Clare happening upon his innermost thoughts.

He stood looking at the river: it was as grey as the sky. The rain was coming down harder now. It wasn't the kind of day that induced one to go out. Much as he liked Des and Julie, reading the papers stretched out on the sofa with a bottle of wine would be more the mark for him today. He also wanted to spend some time writing. He had that exercise to do for next Thursday evening. He hadn't had time to make a start on it yet, but he was itching to do so. Trouble was, Clare had stayed over since Friday and he didn't want her to know what he was doing. He wanted to have something that was his, and his alone. He chewed his toast, and reflected that this was why he and Clare had no future together. She wanted too much of him: if they were to be together she would expect him to hand over his life to her lock, stock and barrel, and he wasn't prepared to do that. He couldn't share so much with another person: he wasn't ready, not so soon after Maddie.

Or was he oversimplifying matters, like that pretentious prat Victor Blackmore? He poured himself a second mug of coffee and, in spite of his morose mood, he smiled. Now there was a bloke who needed to be taken down a peg or two. Who in the group would be first to tell him to shove it?

His money was on Jaz. Sitting next to her that evening, he had felt her bristle whenever Victor had opened his mouth. She had reminded him of Amber or, more precisely, had made him think that this was how his elder daughter might be when she reached seventeen. Amber was only eleven but she was already showing signs of becoming a feisty teenager. He hoped she would never become so troubled or distant with him that they couldn't talk. The thought of anything spoiling his relationship with his precious daughters caused him to grip his mug so tightly that he almost snapped off the handle.

Then an even greater fear took hold of him: what if his inability to come to terms with what Tony and Maddie had done jeopardised his relationship with the girls, as Clare had warned him? He set down the mug on the worktop unsteadily. 'That must never happen,' he told himself. 'If you make just one promise for the rest of your days, Jack Solomon, it's to protect Amber and Lucy from the person who can hurt them most. You.'

During lunch, Jack drank too much and found himself drifting in and out of the conversation. Clare had never been interested in Des and Julie's baby son, but today she seemed inordinately keen to know everything about Desmond Junior: had his nappy rash cleared up, was he giving them many sleepless nights with teething problems? Once or twice Jack made eye-contact with her, and in return she rubbed her foot against his leg. He almost wished he could make it work between them. It would be so easy. So convenient. She was intelligent – her job as a solicitor was proof of that – attractive, and eminently capable of making someone a good wife. Any number of men in his shoes would leap at the chance to have her. Why couldn't he?

Because he didn't love her. And never would. It was as simple as that, and she deserved better. The sooner he ended it, the better off they'd all be. He decided that when and how he told her would be crucial. He wouldn't rush it; he would take his time to ensure an amicable split. He took another thirsty gulp of his wine, suddenly annoyed that he was treating his brief relationship with Clare as if it were a marriage. Five months, that was all it had been.

'Hey up, Jack? What's thee dreamin' of?'

He shook himself out of his reverie. 'Nowt you'd understand, Des, my lad.'

Julie groaned. 'Oh, they're off again, Clare, speaking int' northern tongues.'

It was a joke between the four of them: Clare and Julie had grown up in leafy Cheshire, as they called it, while Jack and Des both hailed from hardier climes – Lancashire and Greater Manchester respectively. When sufficient alcohol had been consumed, Jack and Des would slip into their Monty Python routine of *lookshree* living in a soggy paper bag.

'Oh, let's leave them to it and go to the loo,' Clare said, folding her napkin and rising from the table. 'We can talk about them behind their backs,' she added, with a smile.

When they were alone, Des topped up their glasses – the girls had offered to drive. Jack had drunk more than he would normally, and could feel that it was making him lightheaded and belligerent, but even so he allowed Des to fill his glass to the top.

'You okay, Jack? You're very quiet. Everything all right *chez* Solomon?'

As he looked at Des's concerned face, Jack was tempted to confide in him. Maybe that was all he needed to do. Perhaps it was nothing more than a case of cold feet that was making him back away from Clare. He hadn't known Des very long – just two years – but he was a good and loyal friend, someone he trusted, in and out of the office.

Someone he trusted.

The words played themselves over inside his head.

Someone he trusted.

Someone like Tony.

He raised the full glass to his lips and downed it in one. 'Nothing's wrong,' he said, holding out his glass for another refill. 'What the hell could be wrong with my life? Eh? I've got it made, haven't I? A fantastic girlfriend who I'd be nuts to lose, and a partnership thrown in for good measure. What the hell could be wrong with that?' His voice was sharp and much too loud. People at a nearby table looked in their direction.

Still holding the bottle of Valpolicella, Des stared at him. Then, 'You tell me, Jack.'

Chapter Eleven

＊

Marsh House was one of the coldest houses Nathan knew, and whenever he and his mother visited Grandma Lois and Grandpa Barnaby they always made sure they wore something warm. Today he was in jeans with his thickest sweater over a long-sleeved shirt and a T-shirt and Mum was wearing her Marsh Twinset, as she called it: a seriously uncool piece of expensive fluffy knitwear that Grandma had given her one Christmas. She only pulled it out of the wardrobe for a Marsh House visit. Usually, and at Mum's contrivance, his grandparents came to the flat, where Grandpa, unused to warmth, would doze by the fire. It wasn't that they were too mean to heat their large house properly, it was just that, according to Mum, they were of a generation that had been brought up to believe that the cold was good for you.

'Watch out for the cyclist, Nathan.'

'Relax, Mum, I saw it way back.' He indicated, overtook the cyclist and turned to smile at his mother.

'Eyes on the road!'

'Mum, I know the road. Pop another Prozac, then sit back and relax.'

He drove on in silence, ignoring his mother's right foot, which twitched on an invisible pedal. He knew it was difficult for a parent to be a passenger, everyone at college said they got grief from their parents, but at least Mum let him drive as often as she could. Whenever they went anywhere together, she always passed him the keys and said, 'You drive.' It would be great to have his own car, like Billy, but they couldn't afford it. He didn't mind: one day he would earn enough money not to worry about how expensive things were. When he'd got his law degree and was in London, things would be different. It would be a hard slog to get there, and he'd probably get a part-time job while he was at college, but he'd do it.

Unlike Billy and most of the others at Maywood College, who saw university as a means to extending their childhood, Nathan had the next five years of his life carefully worked out – as long as he got the right grades next summer he hoped to go to Nottingham – and he was determined that nothing would spoil his plans.

Billy was planning on a gap year in which he would travel at his parents' expense. Nathan wasn't envious. But, then, he'd never been envious of Billy. That was why their friendship worked. Billy, who couldn't be serious if his last pot of hair wax depended on it, had a simple outlook: he wanted nothing more than to enjoy himself with the least amount of effort. Nathan, however, knew that hard work paid off.

There was no rivalry between them, because Billy was Billy and Nathan was Nathan. They rarely argued, and while Nathan thought Billy was an idiot when it came to girls, and told him so, they never fell out. 'They know the score,' Billy once said, when Nathan had chastised him for the cruel way he had treated one particular girl. From what Nathan could see of the relationships that went on at college, the aftermath, when a couple split up, was invariably a minefield of who was no longer speaking to whom. He preferred to be friends with everyone; it kept things from getting messy or complicated. Anything else would blur the edges of the bigger picture he had drawn for himself.

Even so, he couldn't deny his interest in Jaz Rafferty. There was a spiky independence about her that appealed to him. He'd noticed her around college since the start of term and liked the distinctive way she dressed and spoke; she clearly wasn't a girl who would dumbly follow the crowd. But he suspected that her huffy manner, when he'd walked home with her on Thursday, had had nothing to do with his apparent snub, but everything to do with her fancying Billy. It was always the same: the girls who didn't receive a second glance from Billy always claimed they couldn't understand what anyone saw in him.

He drove through the gates of Marsh House and tried not to give in to the temptation that always seized him when they arrived: to increase his speed and spin the wheels recklessly before screeching to an abrupt stop at the front door, gravel flying.

Grandpa Barnaby opened the door to them. He was wearing an apron and a wide smile. 'Good-oh,' he said. 'Now that you're here Lois will let me have a drink. I was so worried you'd be late.' He shook hands with Nathan, which he had always done, even when Nathan had been knee high, and kissed Beth, who almost got lost in the enthusiasm of his embrace.

When she emerged, salvaging a crushed bunch of flowers, she said, 'You sound as if you're in dire need of one, Barnaby.'

He grinned and stroked his moustache, tilting his head towards the inside of the house. 'When am I not? Anyway, come on in. Lois is beavering away in the kitchen. Got all manner of delights in store for you. She's had me on spud duty for the last hour. You know there's no holding her back when she gets the bit between her teeth. I hope you brought healthy appetites with you.'

They followed him through the house, their shoes clattering noisily on the polished wood floor. As well as being cold, Marsh House was as silent as the grave. Rarely was there any music playing, or Radio 4 on in the background, like there was at home. As a young child the quiet stillness of Marsh House had unnerved Nathan and he had tiptoed round the place warily, half expecting someone, or something, to leap out at him. He could remember staying here when he was about five, when his parents had been away, and being terrified of going to bed alone. Grandpa Barnaby had sat with him for ages, reading book after book, until finally he had fallen asleep with his head wedged under the pillow.

Now, at a standstill in the kitchen doorway, Grandpa Barnaby said, 'Look who I've found, Lois! A charming couple bearing gifts of the horticultural variety.'

This was a variation on one of the many lines Grandpa came out with when they visited. It had started as a joke for Nathan's benefit when he'd been little but had become part of the ritual of their every arrival. *Look, Lois, two of the finest people in the county have come calling.* Or: *Lois, did you know we had royalty visiting today?*

But Grandma Lois never played along. She usually made a face at her husband and tutted. Now, with rubber-gloved hands held aloft, she turned from the sink where she was washing a large cauliflower. 'Ah, Beth dear, there you are. Oh, and how lovely you look. That really was such a good buy, that angora twinset I gave you, wasn't it? I can't believe you get so much wear out of it. And, Nathan, look at you in your smart leather coat. Very dashing. What a fine young man you've become. So tall.' She sighed and Nathan knew what was coming next. 'The spitting image of your father.' They'd been in the house less than two minutes and already the first comparison had been made.

Although he had promised himself he wouldn't react, Nathan clenched his jaw. Out of the corner of his eye, he saw his mother glance at him. She was trying to reassure him, but it didn't stop him wishing they weren't here. He hated having to keep quiet for his mother's sake, and for keeping up the pretence that had become an absurd reality for Grandma Lois. This whole day – his father's birthday – was a mockery, and he no longer wanted to be part of it.

Why were children punished for telling the most innocent lies, when adults could go to extraordinary lengths to conceal the truth and never once be accused of deceit?

'Nathan, you've been jolly quiet. What have you been up to recently? More apple sauce?'

'No thanks, Grandma.' His grandmother was a great cook, but she always overdid it: there was enough food on the table to get them through the entire winter. They were in the dining room, possibly the coldest room in the house with its north-facing windows. The walls were painted an acidic yellow which, rather than brightening the drab room, accentuated its chill.

At the head of the table, opposite Nathan, Grandpa Barnaby chuckled and gave him a conspiratorial wink. 'Careful, Lois, he's a good-looking young man, there's bound to be any number of things he'd rather keep private.'

She clicked her tongue. 'What nonsense! What could he possibly want to keep from his grandparents? Another roast potato, Nathan? Perhaps a parsnip?'

Knowing that there would be a choice of at least three puddings, he refused politely. This was one of those occasions when several brothers and sisters to share the burden of grandparental spoiling would have come in handy. To deflect his grandmother, whose eyes were roaming the table for something else to offer him, he said, 'Did Mum tell you I'm in the college play?'

'Ooh, are you? How exciting. Which one?'

'*The Importance of Being Earnest*. I'm Algernon.'

64

She turned to her husband, then to Beth. 'The best part, of course. Adam was the same. He could always land the lead in a school production.'

Irritated, Nathan said, 'It's essentially an ensemble piece. I think you'll find Lady Bracknell steals the show once or twice.'

But Lois seemed not to hear him. 'Barnaby, do you remember the time Adam played Puck in *A Midsummer Night's Dream*, and afterwards everyone kept coming up to us saying what a natural he was and that he ought to consider a career on the stage?'

Nathan stood up abruptly, knocking his plate askew. He caught his knife before it fell to the floor. 'Shall I clear away for you, Grandma?'

She turned from her husband and beamed at him. 'How kind of you, Nathan. But there's no need, I'll see to it.'

From the other side of the table, Beth also got to her feet. 'That's okay, Lois, you sit down and rest. Nathan and I will tidy up. It's the least we can do.'

'Sorry, Mum,' he whispered, when they were alone in the kitchen, 'but I can't stand it when she goes on and on about him.'

His mother put the pile of plates on the draining-board and rested a hand on his arm. 'I know, Nathan, but it's only for today. It's her way of coping with it.'

'But she's *not* coping with it. She's simply denying everything that really happened. Is that what Dad would have wanted?' He turned and stared out of the window, his resentment growing. 'And it's not as if it's just for today. She's doing it more and more. I can't tell her anything without her comparing me to him. Sometimes I just want to shout at her, "I'm *me*, *Nathan* King! Not Adam King, the deceased golden boy of Lois and Barnaby King."' He lowered his head, vaguely ashamed of his childish outburst.

His mother's hand moved from his arm to his shoulder. 'Look,' she said softly, 'this isn't the moment to talk about it. For now, let Lois remember her son the way she needs to. Okay?'

A brief silence passed between them. The rage inside him began to subside. He felt leaden. 'We're trapped . . . defined by what happened to Dad. You'll always be the widow and I'll always be the orphaned grandson.'

She frowned. 'Excuse me, but you're not an orphan. You have a mother who loves you very much. And if you weren't so keen to drive us home, she'd suggest you had a drink.'

He made an effort to smile. 'It's come to something when my own mother's encouraging me to hit the bottle.'

'How do you think Barnaby gets through the day?'

They went to investigate the pantry, where Lois had told them she had put the desserts. On the highest shelf, alongside jars of home-made jam, pickles and chutney, were two old-fashioned china basins. Tied with string, they each bore a lid of greaseproof paper and a flowery label that read, 'Christmas Pudding'. 'I see Grandma's ahead of the game as usual,' Nathan remarked. Neither of them commented on the assumption Lois made every year, that they would spend Christmas together at Marsh House.

On the lowest shelf they found what they'd been instructed to uncover, and removed the tea-towels, clingfilm and aluminium foil to reveal a pavlova, a chocolate mousse, and a large trifle, which, as he was repeatedly told by his grandmother, had been one of his father's favourite puddings. 'He couldn't get enough of it,' she would say. 'I made it for him every Sunday.' Nathan wondered, as he so often did when he was at Marsh House, how his father had survived, growing up with a mother like Lois.

His father's death seldom got to him, these days. It was only when he was forced into a position of recalling a time before it had been just him and his mum, like today, that he thought of what it meant to lose a parent. He had been six when his mother had told him his father was dead. She hadn't been as brutal as that, of course, she had softened the words – he couldn't remember how, exactly – and she had held on to him so tightly that he had said, 'Mummy, you're hurting me.' Funny, he could remember that part of the conversation, but not what had come before. There had been tears. Lots of them. Once he'd realised that she was crying, he'd been scared and started to cry with her.

And then Grandma Lois had appeared in his room. He hadn't known that she was in the house. She had one of her cardigans draped around her shoulders and seemed sort of hunched. Older suddenly. She had stepped on one of his Lego animals, but didn't seem to notice it sticking out from beneath her shoe. In a chilling voice he had never heard her use before, not even when he'd tripped over a light flex and broken one of her expensive Chinese lamps, she said, 'Beth, stop this at once! You're frightening Nathan. That isn't what Adam would have wanted.' What Lois didn't know was that, in that moment, she had scared him more than his mother's tears had. He could remember vividly how his mother had tensed, how she had looked as though she had just been slapped. But, then, that had been his grandmother's intention, to bring his mother to her senses. In Lois's world you didn't admit to sadness or loss. You gritted your worn-down teeth and got on with it. As a result, his father's death was never referred to directly at Marsh House. Instead, he was revered and held up as the perfect son.

The perfect husband.

The perfect father.

Just once, Nathan would have liked someone at Marsh House to tell the truth so that his remaining memories – the honest ones – of his father could be treasured, not tainted with Lois's deluded portrayal of a man who had only ever existed in her mind. No one could have been *that* perfect.

When Nathan and his mother went back into the dining room, and Grandpa Barnaby saw the quantity of desserts on offer, he groaned and clutched his stomach. 'Oh, Lois,' he said, 'you'll be the death of us all.'

Nathan winced. In any other household a remark like that would have meant nothing, but Lois shot her husband a look of total horror.

'It was a joke,' Barnaby back-pedalled. 'A slip of the tongue.'

But the damage was done. Lois's face was drawn, her lips a thin line, and when she spoke, her voice was tight and brittle. 'I really don't think it's appropriate, today of all days, for you to use me as the butt of your stupid schoolboy jokes.' She pushed back her chair, stood up and walked out of the room.

'Oh, Lord,' muttered Barnaby. 'Do you think I ought to go after her?'

Already on her feet, Beth said, 'How about I go and talk to her?'

'Would you? I'd be eternally grateful. You girls always manage to smooth ruffled feathers better than us chaps.'

Nathan watched his mother leave the room. 'Sorry about this,' his grandfather said to him. 'You'd think I'd know better at my age.'

Nathan nodded, then realised that for once he and his grandfather were alone. Normally Lois was with them, which meant she dominated the conversation. He didn't mean that unkindly: she just had a habit of taking over, leading people in the direction she wanted them to go. She did it particularly with his mother. It used to annoy him that his mother became a different person when Lois was around. The Beth King he knew was strong-willed, determined and fun to be with. When Lois was on the scene, she withdrew into herself. She lost some of her confidence, became diminished. Sometimes Lois went too far and trampled over his mother's feelings. On the few occasions when there had been a hint of a man in Beth's life, Lois had been quick to stamp on it. On one occasion he had overheard her say, 'Really, Beth, what are you thinking of? The man's clearly only after one thing. And what kind of a stepfather would he make for Nathan?'

Her voice hesitant, his mother had said, 'But, Lois, we've been out for dinner twice, that's all. Marriage is as far from my mind as it could possibly be.'

'You must be careful, Beth. Nathan's at an impressionable age. You don't want him getting the wrong idea about you. Mothers have to be above reproach. Surely I don't need to spell it out for you.'

Oh, yes, thought Nathan. Lois could be cruelly manipulative. But she could also be extremely generous – yet even that was not without its own agenda. While she was paying for things – driving lessons, school trips – she had a hold over them. His mother would never admit it, but he knew she didn't like the situation. That was why, when he had passed his GCSEs, he had insisted on leaving the private school Lois and Barnaby had paid for since he was seven. Instead, he'd opted to go to Maywood sixth-form college. 'I need to spread my wings,' he'd said, when his mother had asked him why. They both knew the truth of his decision, though: it was his way of releasing the vice-like grip Lois had on them.

It wasn't like this with his mother's parents. They never interfered. When they'd offered him the money to buy his leather coat for his birthday, he had accepted with grateful thanks. If Lois had made the same offer, he would have turned it down flat.

The ugly truth of this gave him a prickle of misgiving. He was being too hard on his grandmother. She meant well, he knew that. She and Grandpa had been very good to him and his mother. It was just that, like her Sunday lunches, she went too far and overdid it.

Beth found Lois upstairs in her bedroom. She was sitting on the bed, crying. When she saw Beth, she gave her eyes one last stoic dab then pushed the handkerchief inside her sleeve. 'Silly of me, I know,' she said, her voice frayed with edgy cheerfulness. 'Barnaby's such a fool, I shouldn't let him get to me.'

Beth stepped further into the room, the heels of her shoes sinking into the soft peach carpet that had only been fitted last week: it still had that slightly oily smell. 'He didn't mean anything by it,' she said, with a shiver, and noticed that one of the windows was open. 'He was just showing off for Nathan's benefit.'

Lois said nothing. She stood up, smoothed out the pleats in her skirt.

'He probably thought he was helping to make light of the day,' Beth added.

The pleats were now dealt with. As was Beth's attempt at offering sympathy. 'Well, he failed badly,' Lois said, and moved away from the bed. 'I don't suppose he's thought to put the coffee on, has he?'

She was past Beth now and standing at the door, a hand raised to it. The moment to talk, really talk, about Adam and how Lois still felt about him was gone. Perhaps a stronger woman would have taken her by the scruff of her neck and made her confess, but Beth would never be able to do that. When the two of them were together, she became a coward. She despised herself for it, but doubted she would find the courage to change. Her own mother said repeatedly that it was folly to play along with Lois. That if anyone should make a stand, it was Beth. But how, after all these years, could she make Lois understand that living the lie only made it worse for them all?

She followed her mother-in-law down the wide staircase, and once more the curtain went up on another Lois King performance. Like Norma Desmond, Lois was an expert on putting on the face she thought the world wanted to see.

They had their coffee in the sitting room, and just as she and Nathan had known would happen, Barnaby was assigned the task of setting up the old projector and screen. For the next hour they sat in semi-darkness watching jumpy images of a skinny, dark-haired boy grow into a handsome teenager. Last year Barnaby had suggested they should have their old cine films transferred on to modern videotape, but Lois had vetoed the idea. She had been terrified that the precious canisters of film might get lost or damaged – like her son, they were irreplaceable. From the scratched and faded reels of 8mm film, they progressed to turning the pages of Lois's photo albums. Beth knew that Nathan was finding this annual ritual more of an ordeal than ever, and her heart went out to him. Years ago he had taken a more active role in flicking through his father's past, asking his grandmother questions that helped her relive Adam's life, but today he was quiet and showed little interest. In response, she found herself compensating for him, drawing Lois on the names of other people in the photographs, or deliberately misremembering a crucial detail so that Lois could correct her.

It was dark and raining when they left Marsh House. Nathan was driving faster than Beth would have liked and she told him so.

'Worried I might put us out of our misery by killing us both?' he said savagely.

Horrified, she did not reply. How could he have said that? What terrible anger had fuelled such words?

'I'm sorry,' he said, some minutes later when he'd dropped his speed. 'That was a shitty thing for me to say.'

'Yes, it was.' Then, with false brightness, she said, 'And, anyway, an accident would result in a dreadful mess in the boot.'

He groaned. 'How much stuff did she offload on to you this time?'

'Oh, just the usual amount. Two puddings, the remains of the joint of pork and half a cauliflower.'

'What it is to be poor!'

'We're not poor,' she said crossly. 'Compared to some people, we live in the lap of luxury. Remember that, Nathan.'

'Doesn't it ever get to you, this constant supply of leftovers and hand-me-downs?'

She looked straight ahead of her. 'I think I'm beyond caring.'

He changed into fourth gear with a clumsy jerk. 'Doesn't pride make you want to say no occasionally?'

'Of course it does, but I also recall how grateful I was in the early years when keeping you in socks and shoes was a constant worry. You've no idea how fast you grew then, or what an expensive liability your feet were.'

The rain came down harder and Nathan flicked at the switch to make the wipers go faster. After a few minutes, he said, 'I know it hasn't been easy for you, Mum, but I do want you to know that – that my enormous feet and I are very grateful for all you've done.'

In the light cast by the street-lamps she could see that there was now a softness to his face. 'I'm glad to hear it. And maybe you'll think more of me when you know that I did refuse one of Lois's kind offers today. A carpet.'

'You're joking!'

'Her and Barnaby's old bedroom carpet. Apparently she thought it might replace the tatty one in your room, with a piece left over for the hall. You see what I saved you from? A flowery nightmare of the worst order.'

'You're a star, Ma!'

'I know. It's a knack I have. Watch your speed, there's a camera just up here.'

Nathan smiled. 'And there was me thinking I'd steal a Kodak moment to record the day.'

As if they'd ever need one, Beth thought miserably.

Back at the flat, in the warmth once more, their mood picked up. There was a pretty card from Adele Waterman inviting Beth to have a drink with her tomorrow evening, and a message on the answerphone from Simone in Dubai. 'Just thought I'd give you a ring and see how you got on today,' her friend's cheerful voice rang out. 'Was lunch as awful as it always is? I'll ring again tomorrow.'

In bed that night, Beth thought of Nathan's anger in the car. Never had he spoken with such bitterness before, and it scared her. She wished he didn't know the truth about his father's death. If he hadn't overheard her conversation with Simone all those years ago, he would have believed it was a tragic accident. A terrible twist of fate. But he knew the truth. That his father had gone out that night and deliberately killed himself. He had stopped off at the local off-licence, bought a bottle of cheap whisky, drunk half of it then driven into a tree. He had died instantly.

And that was what Lois had spent eleven years refusing to accept. She simply would not admit that Adam had been so depressed he had taken his own life as a way out of his problems. Despite all the evidence to the contrary, she wanted to believe it had been an accident.

Beth had always believed that the reason behind Lois's denial was her inability to forgive her son for being less of a man than she had thought him.

Poor Adam.

And poor Lois.

But there would be hell to pay if Lois ever discovered that Nathan knew the truth.

Chapter Twelve

*

Des couldn't sleep. And if Jack knew what he knew, he doubted his friend could either. From the look of Jack at lunch, it wasn't likely that he was getting much sleep anyway. Des had never seen him put away so much booze and he hoped it wasn't becoming a regular thing.

He turned over and gazed at his wife in the semi-darkness. A thick lock of hair lay across her cheek. He pushed it away carefully, his fingers light on her warm skin. She stirred, but not enough to wake. I'm a lucky man, he thought. If he hadn't felt so troubled, he might have kissed her and woken her so that he could make love to her. But he wasn't in the mood.

All he could think of, and be grateful for, was that he wasn't in Jack's shoes. What a mess Jack's life had become. He didn't know what he would do if he came home one day and found Julie in bed with Paul, his oldest and closest friend. For starters he'd beat the hell out of Paul, and then he'd do it again.

He ran a hand over his face, then slipped out of bed. He went into the room next door and stared at his tiny son as he slept in his cot. It was only now as a father that he knew he would do anything to protect and preserve what he had. Love made you vulnerable, but it also made you strong; tough enough to fight to the death, if it ever came to it.

Outside, rain lashed against the window and a gust of wind rumbled in the blocked-off fireplace behind him. He thought of what Jack had said at the restaurant while the girls had been in the ladies'. How he knew he had to break it off with Clare but that he was scared of hurting her.

'But I thought it was going so well between the two of you.'

'It was, but then . . . Oh, it's just getting too heavy. Too serious.'

'You'll hurt Clare even more if you carry on deceiving her,' Des had said, matter-of-factly. He had accepted that there was no point in trying to change his friend's mind: it was clear from his face that it was made up.

'I know, but it makes me feel such a bastard. She keeps dropping hints about getting married. We hardly know each other but I bet she's even drawn up a guest list in her head.'

'Jack, you have to talk to her. Tell her what you've told me. She'll understand. She'll be upset to begin with, but then see it just wasn't meant to be.' Then he'd tried to lighten the tone of the conversation: 'And she'll realise what a lucky escape she had.'

But Jack hadn't laughed. He didn't seem able to, these days.

In the car afterwards, when they were driving away from the restaurant, Julie had said, 'You must promise not to say anything, especially to Jack, but guess what Clare told me in the loo during lunch.' Without giving him a chance to open his mouth, she'd pressed on eagerly: 'She's not a hundred per cent sure, but she reckons she might be pregnant.'

'You're kidding!'

'Do I look like I'm doing a stand-up comic routine?'

'I wish you were,' he'd muttered.

Coming to a stop at the traffic-lights in the town square, she'd regarded him thoughtfully. 'Something you're not telling me, Des?'

'Only that I don't think Jack's ready to be a father again. Not after everything with Maddie and the girls. It's too soon and, besides, technically he's still married.' He didn't like lying to Julie, but if things were going to get sticky between their friends, it would be better all round if they stepped back from it, tried to remain impartial.

Julie had shrugged. 'Then perhaps he ought to have been more careful in bed with Clare.'

He kept the thought to himself that maybe Clare had deliberately 'allowed' the situation to develop. She wouldn't be the first woman to do that, and she certainly wouldn't be the last.

Des pulled up the covers over his son and wondered who would confess first – Jack, that he wanted to end things with Clare, or Clare, that she was pregnant.

Either way, they were both in for one heck of a shock.

Chapter Thirteen

*

It had rained all day on Monday and for most of Tuesday, but this morning the sun was shining and the sky was a brilliant blue, the kind of fresh, clear sky that Dulcie associated with autumn. She had gone to Scotland once at this time of year and had fallen in love with the clarity of the wide open skies and vastness of the beautiful landscape. Now, as she pedalled her bicycle along Bloom Street and turned into Jameson Street, she was filled with that same *joie de vivre*. The older she became, the more she believed that it was the simple things in life that provided the most pleasure: the sun on one's face and a happy heart. It wasn't much to ask for, was it? She pedalled faster, feeling that nothing could take the shine off her day.

Richard had been discharged from hospital yesterday and he had phoned her earlier this morning to give her the good news. 'I can't talk for long,' he'd whispered. 'Angela's in the shower, so five minutes is all I have.'

Five wonderful minutes of hearing his voice had been enough, and to know he had made such a good recovery that he was now at home. 'The bad news is that I'm still confined to bed,' he'd complained.

'And you must stay there until your doctor thinks you're well enough to be up and about.'

'Goodness knows when I'll be allowed to leave the house. Alone.'

She'd heard the wistful longing in his voice and knew he was saying he wouldn't be able to see her for some time. She said, 'Richard, I want you to promise me something.'

'Anything, my darling. You know I'd do anything for you.'

'You mustn't be silly and think you know better than the doctor. You mustn't convince yourself that you're well enough to sneak out of the house behind Angela's back to come and see me.'

There was a pause, during which Dulcie knew that that was exactly what had gone through his head.

He said, 'You're not very good with numbers, are you, Dulcie?'

'I beg your pardon?'

'That's two promises by my reckoning.'

'And you're too sharp for your own good.'

'I love it when you tell me off. Look, I can hear Angela coming out of the shower. I'll ring you when I can. Love you.'

Despite the brightness of the sun, the day was cold, but Dulcie glowed with an inner warmth. She pedalled across Bridge Street warily, staying as close to the kerb as she could, then turned into the relative quiet of Crown Street. She waved to Mr Colroyd, who was selecting flowers for a customer from his galvanised buckets at the front of his shop. She pedalled on further, towards the town square, and hopped off her bicycle at Churchgate; she was slightly out of breath. Gardening and cycling were her only forms of exercise, and the latter she only did when the weather tempted her to blow the dust off her daughter's old Raleigh. She locked it to the railings of St Cecilia's, unclipped her basket from the handlebars and went back to Crown Street where she had some shopping to do before meeting Prue and Maureen for lunch.

Every three weeks she and her friends got together for lunch and a gossip. Although they were close and had known each other for many years – they had children of roughly the same age – she was selective in what she shared with them about her personal life. She had never confided in them about Richard, believing that the fewer people who knew about her affair, the less chance there was of it becoming known to Angela. She liked to think that Prue and Maureen had their own secrets.

She called in at the delicatessen for some cheese for supper that evening and a couple of her favourite rolls, one baked with caraway, the other sprinkled with poppy seeds. She also bought a large tub of black olives, shiny with oil and flavoured with garlic. With these purchases carefully stowed in her shopping basket, and knowing she had a bottle of excellent red wine at home, she looked forward to the evening ahead.

76

It was one of the nicest things about living alone: she could eat what she wanted without having to consider anyone else. Just occasionally she wondered if she wasn't in danger of becoming self-absorbed, but whenever this thought surfaced, she reminded herself that she had devoted most of her life to others – Philip and the children. Now it was time to pamper herself a little. It was too easy to slip into the habit of justifying one's happiness. If she allowed that to happen too often, she might forget to relish the joyful simplicity of her life.

She never took her happiness for granted. She knew all too well how fortunate she was, that financially she was better placed than a lot of people she knew. She had used the money paid to her from Philip's life-insurance policy to buy the house in Bloom Street and knew it was the best investment she could have made. When the time came for her to sell up, it would provide her with the means to live out her old age in relative comfort.

She would never have dreamed that she would be so suited to living alone. She had turned into a most self-contained person. Not for her the frantic need to be constantly occupied or entertained: a good book, a glass of wine and she was content. And it was only now, at sixty-three, that she had discovered that if she demanded nothing of another person no demands were made of her.

It was this philosophy that was at the heart of her relationship with Richard; it was why it worked between them. Given the immovable parameters of their affair, neither could be possessive of the other. Few people would understand, and fewer condone, what she was doing, but she had come to know that there was no such thing as a one-size-fits-all dream. It suited her to have an affair with a married man: it meant that she could retain her singleness yet feel as if she were part of a couple.

Next she called in at Novel Ways to see if the book she'd ordered last week had arrived. It had and she handed a ten-pound note to the girl on the till. While she was waiting for her change, she heard a voice behind her: 'Come on, Nicholas, do hurry up and choose what you want.' There was something disturbingly familiar about the thin, careworn voice. She turned her head, cautiously, and her suspicions were confirmed: it was Angela. She looked just as she had the last time Dulcie had seen her – harassed, hair tied back in a childish, unflattering ponytail, tall, spare body swamped by a tatty waxed jacket. She was hovering over an angular boy with a sensitive face – currently buried in a rock-star biography – and in her hands was a pile of paperbacks; the latest Ian Rankin, a Robert Harris thriller, and two John Grishams. Books to occupy Richard while he was convalescing? Dulcie thought of the sweet little book of poetry he had given her – a collection of love poems from which he often read to her.

With a trembling hand, she took her change from the girl behind the counter, pocketed it and fled.

By the time she slowed her pace, she was standing outside St Cecilia's, her heart thudding painfully, her legs shaking. She felt sick, panicky and guilty. And weepy. She glanced over her shoulder; it was a long while since she and Angela had met but she was convinced Angela would have recognised her and come after her. It was nothing short of extraordinary that until today she had never bumped into the woman. This was partly because Richard and Angela lived in a village on the outskirts of Chester, rather than in or around Maywood. Richard had often said that Chester satisfied all of Angela's shopping needs: why, then, had she chosen to come into Maywood all of a sudden?

It was an irrational thought and one with which Dulcie quickly dispensed: Angela had the right to shop wherever she chose.

Relieved that there was no sign of her now, Dulcie walked slowly to the side of the church. It was still too early to meet Prue and Maureen for lunch in the café opposite, so she pushed open the door of St Cecilia's, and went inside. She had what she called a 'religious temperament' but rarely attended a Church of England service: she found the atmosphere too chaotic – modern vicars were inclined to allow unruly youngsters to run up and down the aisles. In a secular sense, she was a frequent visitor to St Cecilia's because of the many concerts it hosted – Maywood boasted a fine choir, of which both Prue and Maureen were members.

The gift shop was on her right and two elderly ladies were browsing though the racks of books and postcards and other assorted Christian paraphernalia of tea-towels and monogrammed teaspoons. No one else was about, and after walking the length of the nave, Dulcie turned to her left to sit in the small side chapel where an exquisite stained-glass window caught the bright autumnal sunshine. St Cecilia – famous since the sixteenth century as the patron of musicians – looked down benignly at her from the colourful window: in one hand she held a lute, and with the other she indicated an intricately decorated organ.

Dulcie closed her eyes. She didn't feel she deserved such a look of kindness. Sitting on the hard pew she felt horribly unworthy, and strangely isolated, as though she were being punished for loving Richard. The happiness that had filled her only a short time ago had gone. Now her heart was heavy.

Still with her eyes shut, she considered how an affair was generally acknowledged to be a roller-coaster ride of out-of-control emotions: at one minute its participants would be wallowing in insecurity and doubt; at the next, they'd be euphorically high on the exhilaration of sexual fulfilment. But it hadn't been like that between her and Richard; she had never put herself through the he-loves-me-he-loves-me-not game. Nor, until recently, had she spent hours waiting for the phone to ring, or wasted time wondering where he was, or what he was doing. Grounded in her own sense of who she was, and the fulfilling life she led, she had been perfectly content with what they had. 'I will not be a demanding and possessive lover,' she had promised him at the outset. 'I will never disgrace myself by doing that.'

'Not even a little bit?' he'd teased. 'It might flatter me if you were.'

'Then you've picked the wrong woman to have an affair with.'

They were having lunch in the hotel that would soon become the scene of many such occasions. He had reached across the table, taken her hands and said, 'I've picked the *only* woman I would have an affair with. Betraying my wife and my marriage vows is not something I make a habit of.'

She had never harboured the hope that he would leave Angela: he had made it very clear that he wouldn't. 'I couldn't leave her,' he confessed. 'It would destroy her.' Also, there were the two younger children to consider – they had been eleven and nine at the start of the affair, and Dulcie knew that Richard was a devoted father and loved them dearly. To leave his wife would be to leave his sons, and it was out of the question. He simply wasn't that kind of man.

There were four children in all, the older two – Henry and Victoria – were grown-up and living in London, but Christopher and Nicholas had come along late in the marriage. Angela had just turned forty-one when she discovered she was pregnant with

79

Christopher: Richard had been forty-seven. As with so many parents who find themselves with an unexpected addition to what they had imagined was a complete family, they decided to have another so that Christopher would have company.

Dulcie respected Richard for his devotion to his family, but questioned his belief that Angela would be destroyed if he left. From the dealings she had had with Angela when she'd helped them to find a house, she had formed the impression that Angela was an inefficient woman, who, like a clockwork toy, rushed around in ever-decreasing circles before winding down having achieved nothing. But she also had a streak of stubbornness. From what Richard had told her, Dulcie concluded that what Angela wanted, Angela invariably got. This didn't mean that Richard was weak. It was just that finding the middle ground through compromise came more naturally to him than all-out confrontation.

When he'd told Dulcie that he had never been unfaithful to Angela before, she believed him. In the early stages of their affair, he had been overwhelmed by guilt. One evening, she had told him that perhaps it would be better if they called a halt to it: she couldn't bear to see him so miserable. He had looked at her, sadly. 'Is that what you want?'

'No,' she'd said truthfully. 'But I don't want to be the cause of your unhappiness.'

They hadn't stopped seeing each other, but after that their relationship slipped into another gear and they became more at ease with the situation.

Right from the day they had met, in the lounge of the Maywood Grange Hotel, there had been a spark between them, and the first time they had kissed, Dulcie had known it was only a matter of time before they slept together.

After she had had dinner with him, he had walked her to her car. Several awkward moments had passed before he had asked if he could kiss her goodnight. Mute with longing, she had nodded, and he'd raised a hand to her hair and stroked it gently, then her cheek and her neck. Lost in the intensity of his gaze, all she could think was that it had been years since she'd felt like this. When their lips had touched, they had held each other with quiet, loving relief. It was as if they had both waited a very long time for the moment.

*

80

Prue and Maureen were on fine form, which was just what Dulcie needed to lift her spirits. Where would we be without our friends? she thought, as they ordered their lunch and got down to discussing Maureen's impending holiday in the Algarve and how she was going to avoid playing golf morning, noon and night with her husband, Geoff.

'Just tell him you can't see the point in hitting small white balls for hours at a time,' Dulcie said.

'Oh, that's easy for you to say,' Maureen remonstrated. 'You've lived alone for so long you've forgotten what husbands are like. They sulk if they don't get their own way.'

'Yes,' agreed Prue. 'Count yourself lucky that you can go on holiday without the impediment of a husband. You have no idea how envious we are of you. I can't think of anything better than a week all to myself.'

It was a measure of their close friendship that Prue and Maureen were able to refer to Dulcie's single status so offhandedly. Others tiptoed around it, either in fear that it might be contagious or that it was still a sore subject. It had taken years for them to reach their current level of candour and Dulcie loved them for it.

'Then why not do exactly that?' Dulcie said to Prue. 'If you want some time alone, tell Robert.'

Prue shook her head. 'Don't be silly, Dulcie, you know it doesn't work like that. Robert would immediately put on the spoilt-little-boy act – pouting lip and silences. Husbands hate the idea of their wives enjoying themselves without them.'

'Then you have to box clever. Choose to do something Robert would think was a hardship. Go on an activity holiday like I have in the past. I had a wonderful week in Provence learning to paint.'

Frowning, Prue said, 'I'm not sure that's really my scene.'

Dulcie laughed. 'Then stop whingeing and make do with what you've got.'

They ordered their meal, and while the waitress organised their cramped table to accommodate the basket of bread and carafe of house wine, Dulcie thought of the last trip she'd made: a touring holiday to Florence and Rome. She had had a wonderful time, and had met so many interesting people. Next summer she was hoping to go to the Italian lakes and she already had a couple of brochures to browse through. She loved Italy and always felt at home there. Richard said it suited her carefree temperament and that he could easily picture her sitting on a balcony sipping a dry Martini and watching the world go by from beneath the brim of a large hat. 'And, of course, you'll be inundated with advances from countless unsuitable men,' he'd elaborated, 'but you'll handle them in a demure and politely English manner.'

'Goodness, you make me sound like a character out of an Anita Brookner novel.' She'd laughed.

He had kissed her, and said, 'No, you're much too passionate for that.'

At her age it was nice to be described as passionate. She glanced at her two friends and wondered if Geoff or Robert ever thought of them in that way.

Just as the waitress appeared with their plates of quiche and salad, Dulcie caught sight of someone else approaching their table. For the second time that day, she felt wrongfooted and panicky.

It was Angela. From the expression on her face, it was clear that she had just recognised Dulcie and was coming over to say hello.

Chapter Fourteen

*

It was at mealtimes that Jaz most envied Vicki. Her friend had no idea how lucky she was to be an only child. If she were here now to witness the racket, she'd soon count her blessings.

It was a typical night around the Rafferty supper table and, with a book resting on her lap, Jaz was speculating as to what a visiting alien would make of it. His report home would make interesting reading:

> It would appear that the sole purpose of these sessions is to shout louder than the earthling sitting next to you. Nor does it seem to matter that the yelling goes unheeded. There would also appear to be some kind of ritual contest taking place: the more food these primitive life forms can grab and shovel inside themselves, the more unpopular they become with each other, which in turn provokes yet more yelling and shouting, particularly among the smaller and uglier female members. It is a spectacle that requires much rational thought to discern any point in the proceedings.

'Hello, Jazzie's got that faraway look in her eyes again. Either that or she's stopped taking the medication.'

Jaz looked up from her book and pulled a face at her brother. 'I was imagining myself a million miles away from you, Phin, if you must know.'

'Oo-er! How about I make your dreams come true and help you pack?'

'You wouldn't know how. When was the last time you managed

to fold your own arms, never mind cope with something as tricky as a bag of clothes?'

'Snappy, snappy,' mocked Jimmy. He helped himself to the last of the mashed potato, then elbowed his brother in the ribs. 'Probably that time of the month again. I'd go careful if I were you. You know what a Rottweiler she turns into.'

'Oh, that's *so* original. A girl outsmarts a man and she's accused of being hormonally unbalanced. Well, for your information I'm not pre-menstrual.'

Lulu and Tamzin leaned into each other and sniggered. They were still of an age to laugh at the mention of bodily parts or functions.

'Hey, hey, *hey*! Less of the dirty talk, if you don't mind.'

'Dad, menstruation isn't a dirty word.'

Popeye Rafferty dropped his knife and fork and reached for his beer. 'It is when I'm trying to eat. Cut it out. And how many times have I told you it's rude to read at the table?'

Jaz turned to her mother for support, but Molly Rafferty seemed preoccupied and oblivious to the commotion going on around her. She was absently spooning an extra portion of peas on to Phin's dinner plate.

'Helpless baby,' Jaz muttered under her breath, scowling at her brother. Ignoring her father's reprimand, she returned her attention to the book on her lap and reminded herself that she would have the last word. And in a way her brothers and sisters could never imagine. The novel she was writing was based on them, and the more she wrote, the more empowered she felt. She didn't think she was a vindictive person, but every jibe they made about her, every put-down they laughed over, was a point they scored against themselves. Oh, revenge would be sweet!

Later upstairs in her room, Jaz switched on the computer. She wanted to read through what she would be taking to the writers' group tomorrow evening. When she'd finished checking it, had changed a couple of lines, then put them back to how she'd written them originally, she decided to leave it well alone. All Dulcie had asked them to do was produce the opening page of a novel (with title), which, of course, she'd already written, so she hadn't had much to do. She clicked on SAVE and PRINT, and wondered how the others had got on with the assignment.

Being with a group of adults had been more fun than she had

84

thought it would be. Maybe it was because they had treated her as one of them, not as a child. They'd all been really nice to her and, apart from Victor, hadn't patronised her. Victor was a right pain, though. Nobody had said anything during the meeting but she'd reckoned, from looking at their faces, that they'd all thought as she had about him. She was proved right in the car on the way home, when Jack had remarked, 'I shouldn't say this, and don't either of you quote me on it, but where on earth was Victor dug up?'

Beth had laughed and said, 'I don't know, but he should be put back straight away.'

'Oh, please! Let's start digging a hole for him right now.'

'First-rate idea, Jaz,' Jack had said. 'And we'll give you the honour of pushing him into it.'

Jack and Beth were a laugh, and it had been kind of Jack to drive her home. Both she and Beth had said they'd walk when he'd asked if anyone needed a lift. Then Dulcie had opened the front door, they'd seen the rain coming down and changed their minds. Victor, she'd noticed, hadn't offered to take anyone home. He hadn't even bothered to say goodbye, just dashed rudely to his car further up the road and driven off.

So that she didn't give the game away with her family, about where she'd spent the evening, she'd asked Jack to drop her on the corner of Marbury Road. 'It's a dead end,' she'd said, already undoing her seatbelt, 'so it'll be easier for you if you let me get out here. Save you having to turn round.'

'It's no trouble,' he'd said.

But she'd insisted, said goodnight to them both and got out. Hurrying home, she hoped he hadn't thought her ungrateful. She also thought how weird it was that she had spent the evening with Nathan King's mother when she'd talked to him for the first time that afternoon. How spooky was that?

She had thought a lot about Nathan since that day, but couldn't decide what to make of him. Why had he walked home with her? To report back to Billy and tell him what a klutz she was, so they could laugh at her behind her back? Or had he been genuine? But why would he want to spend time with her? And, more importantly, why was she wasting her valuable time and energy thinking about him? He was a whole load of trouble she could do without. She had decided that, close up, he was even better-looking and would be no more interested in a girl like her than Billy would.

She would have to be careful when half-term was over and she was back at college. Not for a minute must she let him think she had ever been interested in him. He had hinted, but he might have been joking, that maybe he would walk home with her again some time. Whichever way she looked at it, worse things could happen to her than being seen in the company of a good-looking bloke from the upper sixth. Perhaps he'd tag along again when Vicki was busy. Immediately she saw the flaw in this: she'd be walking home alone on the days when Vicki, Billy and Nathan would be rehearsing the college play.

A knock at the door had her clicking on CLOSE.

'Okay if we come in?' said a voice.

Her mother was the only person who respected the sign on her bedroom door that read, 'Private – Please Knock Before Entering.' Everyone else ignored it and burst in, but Mum was different. She was eight years younger than Dad, and Jaz had always thought her beautiful. Dad joked that when he'd first set eyes on her his legs had turned to overcooked spaghetti. 'That was because you were so drunk,' Molly would say, a soft smile brightening her face.

'A touch mellow,' he'd acknowledge, 'but the truth of the matter is that it was love at first sight.' Dad was such a screaming sentimentalist.

Nothing was too much trouble for Mum. She could always be relied upon. But not so much, these last few weeks. Most of the time she seemed lost in a world of her own. Jaz had been talking to her last night, telling her something about a parents' evening at college, only to realise that her mother hadn't heard a word she'd said. She was practically nodding off.

'What's wrong?' she asked, when both of her parents came in. They only ever put in a double appearance if they had something important to say. Like that time they'd sat either side of her on the bed and told her Granddad had died.

'Nothing's wrong, Jazzie,' her father said. 'Now, why would you think that?'

She shrugged. 'Dunno. Something to do with your serious faces? Hey, you're not getting divorced, are you? Because if you are, I want it understood that I'll go with whoever doesn't want custody of Tamzin and Lulu.'

Her mother, who looked exhausted, tutted and cleared a space on the bed to sit down. 'You know you don't mean that.'

'Don't you believe it.' Oh, hell, if her mother was sitting down, this *was* a serious newsflash. Had they found out that she'd lied about being at Vicki's last week?

She pushed away the thought. 'So what's up, then?' she asked. Her money was on some nosy neighbour having filed a report to her parents claiming she'd been seen with Nathan.

Suddenly a huge grin appeared on her father's face and, after exchanging a look with her mother, he said, 'Jaz, we've got brilliant news, and your mother wanted you to be first to know. She's pregnant.'

Nothing could have surprised Jaz more. She fumbled for a response. 'You're . . . you're joking, right?'

They were both grinning at her now. Oh, this was terrible. 'You're kidding,' she repeated. *Oh, please, say you're having me on. I couldn't stand another brother or sister.*

'And what's more,' her father said, putting a hand on her mother's shoulder, 'we've hit the jackpot. It's twins.'

Chapter Fifteen

✳

It was Thursday evening and once again the group was assembled in Dulcie's sitting room. They were listening to Victor, who had just summed up his *magnum opus* – *Star City* – and was now giving an over-the-top reading of his opening page. Predictably he'd elected to go first and was intent on getting across the dramatic content of his writing. Dulcie would have liked to ask him to start again and read it with a little less theatrical conviction, but she didn't think it would be fair on the group to have to hear it twice.

'Thank you, Victor,' she said, when at last he paused. 'What a lot you squeezed into one page.' She wanted to add, 'Are you sure it was only three hundred words?' but she knew there was no point. They all knew he'd read out at least twice the specified amount.

He nodded and leaned back into his seat. 'That, of course, is my objective,' he said. 'I want to hit the reader right between the eyes with as much action as possible. Grab them by the throat.'

A shame if it all ends up sticking there, thought Dulcie. She said, 'An ambitious opening such as that requires skilful handling to pull it off. Anyone else want to make a comment? Jack? What was your reaction?'

Dressed in jeans and an open-necked shirt, Jack was looking less formal than he had last week, but he didn't appear to be any more relaxed. He looked tired and drawn, like a man with the weight of the world on his shoulders.

'Ah,' he said carefully. 'To be honest, I got confused. There seemed to be a great number of characters thrown at us. It was difficult to keep up with what was happening.'

'I thought that too,' agreed Jaz. 'And they all had foreign names ending in *avinski*.'

'That's because they *are* foreign,' Victor said waspishly.

'I think the point they're making,' Dulcie said, picking her way cautiously, 'is that you gave a tad too much information. Remember what we discussed last week? To create the all-important hook to draw the reader in, you need to offer some tantalising details, but you must treat them as magic ingredients and use them sparingly. Perhaps you could cut back on some of the characters. Ideally, just have one or two. And was that second explosion really necessary?'

Victor cleared his throat. 'Essential.'

'You don't think it weakened the effect of the first?' suggested Beth.

Before Victor exploded, Dulcie said quickly, 'Good point, Beth, and one we should all bear in mind. Less is frequently more when it comes to writing. But well done, Victor, for sharing that with us.' Trying to encourage him, she said, 'Victor's given us a hard act to follow, but who's going to be brave enough to go next? Any takers? Jaz, how about you?'

'Okay. So long as I'm not queue-jumping.' She glanced at Jack and Beth, who shook their heads.

'No, you go ahead,' Jack said.

'It's called *Having the Last Laugh*,' she said, then launched into reading her work in a clear, confident voice. When she'd finished, she looked at Dulcie for her verdict. 'What do you think?' she asked. 'Was it okay?'

Dulcie smiled. 'Jaz, that was more than okay. It was brilliant. My only quibble is that you stopped when you did. I wanted more.'

'Me too.'

'And me.'

Blushing, Jaz smiled at Jack and Beth. 'Really? You're not just saying that?'

The only person not supporting Jaz was Victor. Dulcie had noticed that while she had been reading, he'd been making notes on his A4 pad. 'I have a couple of quibbles,' he said, clicking his biro. 'What's a head-mash? And don't you think it's risky using modern-day parlance? I was under the impression that it limits your audience and dates the book before it's even published.'

A protective motherly instinct made Dulcie want to come to Jaz's aid, but she needn't have worried.

'A head-mash is when you've scrambled your brains trying to work something out,' Jaz said levelly. 'I expect you get that a lot, Victor, don't you?' He looked at her uncertainly and she smiled sweetly at him. 'I know I do after a long day at college and then three hours of homework. As for worrying about writing a book that's unpublishable, I don't give a monkey's. I'm writing for my own satisfaction. No one else's.'

A case of putting that in one's pipe and smoking it, thought Dulcie happily. Goodness, youngsters today could easily hold their own. At the same age, she wouldn't have said boo to a day-old gosling, never mind a grumpy old gander like Victor.

Dulcie went next, and then Beth took her turn, a little nervously, but with an amusing central character called Libby, an insecure self-confessed self-help junkie. It was titled *Living For Pleasure* and, like Jaz, Beth had written the piece in the first person. Unlike Jaz, she made the mistake of apologising for what she'd written. Dulcie waved the Self-belief Box under her nose. 'I warned you.'

Beth laughed and reached for her bag to pay her fine.

And then it was Jack's turn.

'I'm afraid it's still a bit rough,' he confessed. Dulcie rattled the box at him, and he smiled and added a coin to Beth's. 'But here goes anyway. It's called *Friends and Family*.' He cleared his throat and fiddled with the neck of his shirt. '"By their friends shall ye know them. That's what I'd been brought up to believe, and believe it I did. Until now. Now I know differently. Friends are rarely what they seem. Friends come and go. Like chameleons they change their colours to suit the moment. I once had such a friend. But, there again, I once had a wife."' He swallowed, straightened the papers on his lap, then continued, his voice low.

Dulcie listened intently. She saw the profound sadness in Jack's face as his eyes moved across the page. Poor man, she thought. But how brave to put it down on paper and share it with the group. When he'd finished, the room fell quiet. Nobody rushed to speak. Not even Victor.

'Sorry,' Jack murmured, 'was that a bit too much of the Misery Joe's?'

Both Jaz and Beth reached for the Self-belief Box at the same time and rattled it in front of him. It broke the tension in the room and Dulcie, feeling faintly troubled, suggested they discussed his opening page over a cup of coffee.

'Would you like some help?' asked Beth.

'No need, I've got everything ready. All I need to do is put the kettle on.'

Out in the kitchen, while she waited for it to boil, Dulcie listened to Victor telling Jack that what he needed to do with his opening page was lose some of the introspection and liven it up with a bit more action. Dulcie sighed. What with? A couple of car crashes? The man didn't know the words 'subtlety' and 'sensitivity'. With him it was wham, bang, wallop. Horribly patronising too.

Not dissimilar from how Angela had treated Dulcie yesterday lunchtime.

'I thought it was you,' Angela had said, her voice so loud that everyone in the café had turned to look. 'I said to Nicholas, "Isn't that the woman who helped us move house?" But, of course, he couldn't remember. How are you? Still running your little business?'

Dulcie had bristled to hear her livelihood dismissed as no more than a hobby. 'No,' she'd said. 'These days I'm a fully fledged lady of leisure.'

'Oh, good for you. I wish I could say the same, but with Christopher and Nicholas to chase after, my leisure time is non-existent. And now I have Richard at home.'

'Oh?' Dulcie had tried to make her voice neutral, as though she didn't know what Angela was referring to. 'Is he working from home, these days?'

'Dear me, no, he won't be working for some time yet. He's just recovering from a heart-attack. He gave us all a dreadful scare. I've been on at him for years to slow down, but you know what men are like, they never listen and always think they know best, and the next thing you know, you're a widow passing round the sherry at a funeral.'

Dulcie had cringed at Angela's overly jolly manner. Or was she simply trying to hide her concern for a husband who had nearly died? And might well have done so, if he had been alone.

'You must give him my best wishes,' Dulcie had said.

'Thank you, I will. But I doubt he'll remember you. He has the most shocking memory. Anyway, I must press on. I've left Christopher to keep an eye on Richard and I promised we wouldn't be long. What a coincidence meeting you like this, after all this time. I seldom bother coming into Maywood, such a funny old-fashioned little town. I usually go to Chester, but I thought this would be quicker.' She rolled her eyes. 'But it's proving otherwise. I can't find half the things I need.'

And then she was gone, hurrying back to her son who was sitting at a corner table, absorbed in one of the novels they'd bought for Richard.

As perceptive as ever, Maureen had said, 'Whoever that woman was, you didn't much care for her, did you, Dulcie?'

'Oh,' she'd said airily, hoping her face wouldn't give her away, 'she was one of those clients who tend to be a thorn in one's side. Nothing was ever right for her. She had very high expectations.'

'Doesn't look like anything's changed,' observed Prue. Both Dulcie and Maureen had followed her gaze to where Angela was ticking off her son for having his elbows on the table. He frowned with a trace of petulance and retreated further behind his book.

It was a frown Dulcie recognised: she had seen Richard look just the same. He didn't often frown, or behave petulantly, but when he did, it made her laugh. She wondered how long it would be before she saw him again, how many weeks or months before he was well enough to drive. It was tempting to speak to her son, a doctor, about Richard, but even to discuss him in vague terms – 'Andrew, I know someone who's recently suffered a heart-attack, how long do you think it will be before he makes a full recovery?' – broke the rules of being a mistress. She must never allude to Richard. Not even as a friend or one-time client. There was always the chance that a casual reference could give them away.

After talking to Angela, she might have expected to feel guiltier about her affair with Richard but, perversely, the reverse had happened: Angela's offhand manner – as if his heart-attack had resulted from his own carelessness – had irritated her, and she strongly believed that Richard deserved the love and happiness she could offer him. Any pangs she had experienced while sitting in St Cecilia's had vanished.

Now, pouring boiling water into the mugs, she thought of Jack. There was no doubt in her mind that what he had written and read out to the group was autobiographical. How would she feel if she was in his position?

Or, more to the point, in Angela's shoes?

Stop it, she told herself. Life can't be so neatly pigeonholed. People make mistakes. They fall in love with the wrong people. They don't mean to, but it goes on all the time.

Yet as resolute as she tried to be, when she took the coffee into the sitting room and passed round the mugs, she found herself unable to meet Jack's eye.

It was raining again, and after dropping off Jaz at the end of her road, then Beth, Jack drove home. It was just after ten thirty when he let himself in. He helped himself to a beer from the fridge, then checked his answerphone. There were two messages: one from Des suggesting a boys' night out, and another from Clare.

'Jack, if it's not too late when you get in, give me a ring. There's something I need to talk to you about.'

He took a long swig of his beer and erased the message, as though it had never existed.

Chapter Sixteen

*

After a relatively wet but mild October – the warmest on record – the back end of November was making up for the earlier discrepancy. Winter had arrived, with icy mornings and bitter winds that shook the last remaining leaves off the trees.

Maywood Health Centre was always busier when the weather turned cold and, on this particular Monday morning, it was teeming with what Beth called winter-sickies. She had a theory that the first note of a piped Christmas carol was the harbinger of medical doom and gloom. She also believed that if sufficient people banged on about the threat of a flu epidemic there would be one. And now that they were only a week away from December, and a short step from the onslaught of Christmas, everyone was convinced they were suffering from the most virulent strain ever endured.

The waiting room was packed this morning, and as she listened to the endless coughs and sniffles, Beth knew, without any medical training, that most of the patients weren't as critically ill as they claimed. Beth felt sorry for the elderly, those who suffered in silence, who would not dream of troubling their overworked doctor.

Only a couple of days ago, she had called on Adele Waterman and found her in a terrible state. She had immediately called out the old lady's doctor – Rose Millward from the health centre – who diagnosed pneumonia. 'Lucky we caught it when we did,' Dr Millward told her patient. 'Otherwise we'd probably have had to whisk you into hospital.'

Beth and Nathan were taking it in turns to keep an eye on her, ferrying down food and drink at regular intervals. Before leaving for work this morning, Beth had given Adele a flask of hot vegetable soup for her lunch and hoped she would eat it. Nathan had promised to call in as soon as he was home from school, and Beth knew Adele would benefit from his company. The old lady had said that if she was feeling up to it she would help Nathan with his lines for the play: it was curtain up in two weeks' time.

Beth would miss Adele when she moved. According to Jack, if all went well with the sale, she would be leaving in the New Year. Just as he'd predicted, there had been no shortage of people interested in the flat and the full asking price had been offered. 'You see,' he'd joked with her over coffee one night at Dulcie's, 'I'm not the shark you thought I was.'

'I never said you were,' she'd responded.

'You didn't need to. It was in your eyes.'

'Oh, surely not?'

'That and a look that said, "Mess with my neighbour and you're a dead duck."'

'Sharks and ducks – goodness! What a mix of metaphors. Are we allowed to be so careless?'

Thursday nights had become part of her routine, and Beth looked forward to seeing the group each week. Apart from Victor, who never spoke of his life outside Hidden Talents, they were learning about each other. It had occurred to Beth that, without exception, they all had a raw spot, or an area that was strictly out of bounds. As open as Jaz was, she refused to speak about her family, even the fact that her mother was pregnant – Beth only knew this from seeing Mrs Rafferty at the health centre for an antenatal check-up – but she wrote amusingly, perhaps tellingly, about a fictional family from hell. Jack, clearly going through a painful divorce, wrote in poignant detail about the break-up of a marriage, and only last week had hinted to her in the car on the way home that he'd got himself into a mess with a subsequent relationship. Surprisingly, Dulcie was the most reserved of them all, but unlike Victor, who was breathtakingly rude when any of them enquired how his week had gone, she always answered questions but somehow managed never to tell them what she'd really been up to. Perhaps she didn't get up to anything. Maybe that was why she had started Hidden Talents. As plausible as this sounded, Beth didn't think it was the whole truth.

But the really good thing, as far as Beth was concerned, was that she was gaining in confidence with regard to her writing. *Living For Pleasure* was growing fast, and almost had the feel of a novel. Well, all five chapters of it. She didn't think she would ever be as good as the others – Jaz and Jack undoubtedly had a natural flair for it, Dulcie too (the less said about Victor, the better), but she got a lot out of their evenings together and that was what counted. Dulcie had encouraged them to have a go at entering a short-story competition, which none of them had considered before. It had been advertised in *Writing News* – a magazine to which Dulcie subscribed – and it was the group's latest piece of homework: they had two weeks to complete the task.

'Thank heaven for that,' said Wendy, when the last of the patients had been seen and the waiting room was clear.

Magazines and healthy-eating leaflets lay strewn about, toys, books and puzzles were scattered everywhere, and a wastepaper bin had been upturned. It was twelve thirty. Lunchtime. 'You put the kettle on,' Beth said, 'and I'll put this little lot straight.'

There were three receptionists: Wendy and Beth worked full-time, while Karen came in for the afternoons and early-evening surgeries; she also covered when Beth and Wendy were on holiday. They made a good team, so going to work was a pleasure rather than a chore. As they relaxed in the staff kitchen over their lunch, Wendy said, 'You know, we ought to start thinking about where we're going to have our Christmas beano this year. If we leave it too late we'll miss out.'

'What's wrong with Bellagio's? I thought everyone enjoyed that last year.'

Wendy groaned. 'Same place, same faces, same everything. I fancy somewhere new. We don't have to stay in Maywood, we could go further afield. We could live dangerously and go into Chester. Any chance of you bringing a *friend* along this year?'

Beth smiled. 'No.'

'Isn't there anyone from your writing group you could ask?'

'No again.'

Wendy dipped a spoon into her blueberry yoghurt. 'You know, I reckon I could write a book. It'd be a raunchy bestseller. I'd give it so much of the sizzle factor I'd become the Jackie Collins of Maywood.'

'Well, they say there's a book in all of us,' Beth told her.

'At the last count, I've got three or four. But before I put pen to paper and make myself a million, how about I find you someone for our Christmas bash?'

'I'm repeating myself, I know, but no. And I certainly don't want one of your cast-offs.'

A big jolly divorcee, Wendy was a thirty-eight-year-old party girl. She had been single for three years now and always had a smile on her face, even when she was dealing with a particularly irritating patient. A horrid man had once called her a power-crazed fat bitch because she told him he would have to wait more than an hour to see a doctor. 'Save your breath, Mr Austin. You'll not get to see the doctor any faster by flattering me,' she had replied. She had no children, but she did have a hectic social life and never seemed short of men to go out with. Beth teased her that she must be suffering from RSI – repetitive strain injury – from all the first dates she went on. 'Can I help it that I get bored easily?' was Wendy's favourite retaliation. She probably wanted to hold their Christmas dinner out of town because she'd exhausted Maywood's supply of eligible men.

Stirring her yoghurt, Wendy gave her a hard stare. 'How long before Nathan goes off to college?'

In exchange for all the times Adele had babysat Nathan, Beth did the heavier work in her neighbour's garden and took her to the local supermarket each week. It was a delicate balance, which Beth was careful to respect. She would never dream of interfering with the old lady's independence. Didn't she suffer enough of that herself? And not just from Lois.

But today Beth had carried out an extra errand for Adele – a trip to the library to stock up on her reading matter. With her coat buttoned, her head bent into the biting wind as she carried the heavy load of books, she walked home in the dark, disconsolate. All that afternoon she had thought of what Wendy had said, and been thoroughly annoyed by it. Why did people think they had a right to try to organise her life for her? Why did they keep implying that she lived it through Nathan?

She didn't.

She absolutely did not!

As his mother, she had simply put Nathan's needs before her own. And what was wrong with that?

She let herself in to the flat and called, 'Hi, it's me, I'm back.' No answer.

She hung up her coat, put the pile of historical romances on the hall table, and was struck by the emptiness of the flat. Before long, this was how it would feel every day when she came home from work. She shrugged off the disagreeable thought and went through to the kitchen to put the kettle on and think about supper. It was then that she remembered where Nathan was.

'He's been such delightful company,' Adele said to Beth, when she went into the flat below.

'He hasn't been wearing you out, has he?' she asked, placing the library books on the ottoman at the foot of the bed. She noticed the play script on Adele's bedside table and a chair pulled up close: Nathan was making tea.

'Of course he hasn't. He's cheered me up wonderfully. And he's word perfect with his lines. He's going to make an excellent Algernon. I do hope I'll be well enough to come along and watch. How was your day?'

'Oh, the usual, Wendy and I playing good cop, bad cop with the more tiresome patients.'

Nathan came in with a tray. 'Okay if I leave you to it? I have an essay I need to make a start on.'

When he'd gone, Adele said, 'He's a real credit to you, Beth, but how on earth will you manage without him?'

She sighed inwardly. 'Oh, I expect I'll find a way.'

Late that night, and long after Nathan had gone to bed, Beth poured herself a glass of wine and switched on the computer. It had belonged to Nathan, but when her parents had offered to buy him a more up-to-date model, it had been passed on to her. Although she had used the computer at work for some time, and readily enough, she had never been a fan until Nathan had bullied her out of her technophobia. He had given her several evenings of instruction, and now she was hooked and did all her writing on it. The best part was that she was in daily contact with Simone by email, just as Nathan had said she would be once she'd got the hang of it.

By shifting the furniture around, she had created her own little bit of 'personal space' where she could write in the kitchen, beneath one of the windows with a perfect view of the park. Now, she checked to see if there was an email from Simone. There was. She spent more than twenty minutes replying, then hesitated before she switched off the machine. Last night, she had done the craziest thing: she had visited a chat room. She blamed Simone: it had been her suggestion. At first Beth had been dubious about doing it. 'What if I get chatting to some pervy anorak type?'

'Not everyone using the Internet is a raging weirdo,' Simone had emailed back. 'Of course, if you're not sure how to go about it, you could always ask Nathan to help you . . .'

There had been something in Simone's tone that had made Beth want to explore a chat room on her own. Just to prove to her friend, and herself, that she could do it. It was all about motivation, and scoring a point off her old friend was motivation enough. To her surprise, not only had it been straightforward but there were several chat rooms specifically for writers. She had picked one at random and was soon reading a selection of messages in the 'meetings' room. It all seemed innocent enough: critiques wanted, word-processor services offered, listings of poetry workshops and crime-writing events advertised. Someone wanted to know how to go about writing for children, and another was seeking advice, tongue-in-cheek, on how to get even with a publisher who had just rejected his novel.

She hadn't plucked up the nerve to respond to any of the messages, but tonight she thought she might give it a go. She accessed the chat room she'd been in last night. One message in particular caught her eye:

I'm new to this, and as someone once wrote, 'One should always be a little improbable,' so I'm giving it a whirl. I've had one of those days, and to quote again from the same source, 'I am sick to death of cleverness.' Anyone on the same wavelength? Mr Outta Laffs.

After a brief tussle with the warning voice in her head, Beth typed:

I know just what you mean, Mr Outta Laffs. 'Everybody is clever nowadays. You can't go anywhere without meeting clever people.'

She signed herself BK.

A few seconds passed. Then another message appeared.

'The thing has become an absolute public nuisance.'

Her brain working overtime, her fingers flicking at the keys, she wrote,

'I wish to goodness we had a few fools left.'

'We have.' And how refreshing to find someone who knows their Oscar Wilde so well. Bravo! Are you a fan?

My son is currently rehearsing The Imp of Earnest. He's playing Algernon.

'Professionally?'

No, it's for his sixth-form college.

As soon as she clicked on SEND, she regretted it. Even in a chat room she had resorted to mentioning Nathan.

I'm a parent too [came the reply]. My daughter once played Gwendolen and after spending weeks helping her learn her lines, I became hooked on Oscar Wilde. By the way, if I may be so bold, you sound like you're a woman. Am I right?

She hesitated before answering, suddenly picturing the pervy in the anorak hunched up over his keyboard. Too much information, perhaps? Quoting Oscar Wilde again, but this time, from *An Ideal Husband* – she and Nathan had only recently hired the video – she typed:

'Questions are never indiscreet. Answers sometimes are.'

Point taken. But let me assure you, I'm no cyber Peeping Tom!! I'm a very respectable man, whose only vice, thus far, is to have come on-line (for the first time) to chat, instead of getting on with my novel. I seem to be stuck. Any advice?

I find a glass of wine helps.

Way ahead of you. On to my second. What's your preferred drug of choice? In terms of writing, that is! Which genre?

I'm very much a novice. A history of unpublished (and unpublishable) short stories behind me, but now I'm trying my hand at a novel. And you?

Oh, this and that. Novels primarily. Occasionally the odd short story. And I mean odd. But odd as in quirky!

How long have you been writing?

Years. What's your book about?

A self-help junkie.

Autobiographical?

NO!

I'll take that as a yes. Title?

Living For Pleasure.

Aha, do I detect more overtones of Mr W?

Guilty as charged. Time for me to go now. Goodnight, Mr Outta Laffs. It's been . . . interesting.'

Well, thought Beth, as she stood in the bathroom brushing her teeth, whoever Mr Laffs was, he had taught her that chatting on-line was as easy as pie. That was one in the eye for Simone.

She went to bed wondering what he was like. For all she knew she had just spent fifteen minutes in the presence of a nerdy type who believed in crop circles and aliens.

Or, worse, a dead ringer for Victor.

As was her habit before giving in to sleep, she read for a quarter of an hour. Beside her bed was her inspiration for writing *Living for Pleasure*: a stack of self-help books Simone had given her over the years. There was *The Road Less Travelled*, a selection of *Chicken Soup* paperbacks and her current favourite, *Feel the Fear and Do It Anyway*.

She'd certainly done that tonight. She awarded herself a gold star and a wide, smug smile.

Chapter Seventeen

*

For obvious reasons, people preferred not to move house during the winter and estate agents often had to resign themselves to a period of quiet tedium. It was now, during the predicted lull, and despite feeling terminally exhausted, that Jack chose to overhaul the office filing system. It wasn't going as well as he would have liked. The back of the office, the part the public didn't see, was a scene of paper carnage. He was a tidy man by nature and found himself growing steadily more irritated each day when he came into work and found the mess no better. If anything, it appeared to be getting worse.

Just like his life.

When Clare had told him she was pregnant, he had been poleaxed, as though the world had crashed in on him. 'Are you sure?' he'd asked, once he could think straight enough to string a sentence together. They were having a drink at her place – he'd wondered why she was drinking bitter lemon, not her usual vodka and tonic.

'Yes,' she'd said, 'I've done a test.' And then she'd smiled, a smile that told him just how she felt about the situation. He thought he would never forget that look on her face. Or the sense of being trapped by it.

'But I thought you were on the pill, that that was all taken care of.'

'All taken care of?' she'd repeated. 'What a funny way to describe something so important.' She suddenly sounded every inch the legal adversary she was.

He put his glass down on the coffee-table and turned to face her, moving slightly away. He needed space. 'I notice you haven't answered me,' he said, barely able to keep his voice level.

Her gaze didn't quite meet his. 'I'd been having trouble with the pill,' she murmured, 'so I was using something else.'

'What? Ignorance? Hope? Faith?' He was getting angry now, could feel his head throbbing. She'd done this deliberately, he knew it. This was her way of making sure that she got what she wanted.

She stood up. 'What's got into you, Jack? I don't understand why you're taking this line. I thought you'd be pleased. You love children, you told me that.'

He went and stood as far away from her as he could. He stared out of the window, on to the small fenced garden of her modern estate house. He had never felt so confined before. He pushed a hand through his hair. 'I was talking specifically about my own children, Amber and Lucy. Not every Tom, Dick and Harry's children.'

Now it was she who sounded angry. 'This child is yours, Jack, not Tom's, not Dick's or anyone else's. It's yours. *Ours*.'

He made no response, and they were quiet for a long, threatening moment. Until Clare said, 'Thank you for making your feelings so clear. At least I know exactly where I stand. I think you'd better leave.'

He turned from the window, suddenly ashamed. 'Look, Clare, it's the shock. I never expected this to happen. I had—'

She raised a hand to stop him. 'No, Jack. You can't unsay what you've said.' He could see that she was trying to tough it out, but there were tears in her eyes.

'We need to talk about this,' he said, more gently, his anger and resolve faltering.

'I don't think I want to hear anything you've got to say right now. Please, just go.'

He didn't move. 'Clare, don't try to twist the situation. It's bad enough without you doing that.'

'Bad enough?' Her voice was low. 'Bad enough? Oh, that's good. You should try viewing it from where I'm standing.' She started to cry. He went to her and put his arms around her, then led her back to the sofa, where she clung to him. 'Oh, Jack,' she cried, her tears warm, then cold, against his neck. 'I know what you're thinking. That I was deliberately careless. I wasn't. Please believe me. And please don't go. Don't leave me. I love you.'

He held her tightly, moved by the strength of her need for him. But as he tried to comfort her, he knew he was caught. It was too late now to walk away from her. From her and the baby.

No matter how much he wanted to.

The phone rang on his desk, making him start. He picked it up and was told that Mr Mitchell was on the line for him. The news wasn't good. The sale of the man's property in Altrincham had fallen through and consequently he was withdrawing his offer on Miss Waterman's flat. They were back to square one again. Damn. He was more than usually upset that a vital link in the chain had been broken. Miss Waterman was one of their nicer clients and he had wanted everything to go through smoothly for her. She was also Beth's friend, which made it more personal. He went over to the chaos of the filing cabinets, riffled through a drawer, found Miss Waterman's file and was about to sit down again to telephone her when he changed his mind. He decided to deliver the bad news in person. Just once, he'd leave early.

He slipped on his jacket, then his coat and scarf, and went through to the front office where Janine and Nicky were sitting at their desks discussing when to put up the Christmas decorations. 'I'm off for the day,' he said. 'Can you put 10a Maywood Park House back in the window, please? Mr Mitchell's sale has bitten the dust. Oh, and not a single decoration up for at least a fortnight,' he added, with a smile.

He drove out of the small car park at the rear of the office, and joined the stream of early-evening traffic. It was almost dark and the shop fronts along Bridge Street were brightly lit. By next week he wouldn't be able to move for twinkling lights and sprayed-on snow.

The thought of Christmas depressed him. Maddie still hadn't got round to letting him know when he would see the girls – apparently Tony had some grand notion about taking them skiing during the festive season. Jack had only just got over hearing about their half-term holiday. Lucy had raved about it and shown him all the clothes and cuddly toys Tony had bought her while they'd been away. Amber had been less enthusiastic to talk about the trip, but he'd done his best to be ambivalent and tried to coax out of her what she'd enjoyed most. Gradually, she'd lowered her guard and shown off an expensive pair of trainers Tony had given her. Judging from her expression, they were the latest word in high-tech footwear and he'd made all the right noises about how cool they made her look and how well they went with the cropped jeans – another Uncle Sam export, of course.

Good old generous Tony.

He parked outside Maywood Park House and saw there were lights on in both flats. Perhaps he'd call on Beth when he'd talked to Miss Waterman.

But when he rang the bell for 10a, it was Beth who answered the door. 'Hello,' she said, stepping back to let him in from the cold. 'Is Adele expecting you? She hasn't mentioned your visit.'

'No. I've called on the off-chance, with bad news, I'm afraid, which I thought I'd impart face to face.'

'Oh dear, that's the last thing she needs right now. She's in bed with pneumonia.'

'I'm sorry to hear that. And I certainly don't want to add to her troubles. I could always ring tomorrow. Or leave a message with you to pass on.'

She hesitated, as if weighing up the options. 'Hang on. I'll go and have a quick word with her. Why don't you go through to the sitting room?' She reached past him and switched on the light.

While he waited, he prowled round Miss Waterman's antique furniture. The flat was a lot warmer than it had been on his last visit and he found himself liking it more. He felt awkward for intruding, though. A phone call would have sufficed. He was standing with his back to the room and looking at his haggard reflection in the blank window when Beth returned.

'Adele says you're welcome to see her, as long as you behave like the perfect gentleman and don't look too closely at her. Cup of tea?'

'That would be great.'

Miss Waterman was propped up with several pillows behind her, the bedclothes decorously drawn up to her chin. He could see straight away that she wasn't at all well and he apologised for barging in. 'I should have telephoned,' he said. 'Please forgive me.'

She waved aside his words and indicated a chair. 'Nothing to forgive. Now, then, why don't you give me your news. It's bad, I presume.'

He took off his coat and laid it across his lap as he sat down. He told her about Mr Mitchell withdrawing his offer. 'Of course, as soon as you're feeling better,' he continued, 'we'll get people viewing again. It's a pain, I know, especially with Christmas just round the corner, but I'm sure we'll find another buyer in no time.'

'What about the others who viewed and who were so keen?' asked Beth, coming in with a tray of delicate cups and saucers.

'I'll chase them first thing in the morning, but they've probably found somewhere else by now.' He took the cup offered to him and watched her sit on the bed with Miss Waterman.

'You look tired, Mr Solomon,' Miss Waterman said. 'Are you working too hard?'

He smiled. 'Please, it's Jack. And, no, I can't admit to working too hard.'

Beth laughed. 'That's not what your client wants to hear.'

He saw the funny side. 'Oops, bit of a slip-up, that.'

'You two may be joking,' Miss Waterman remarked, and eased herself into a more comfortable position, 'but I'm being serious. You look nearly as bad as I feel, Mr Solomon – Jack.'

If anyone else had been as frank, he might have felt insulted, but coming from this sweet old lady, he took the words in the spirit in which they had been voiced. 'A few personal problems at the moment,' he said lightly. 'Nothing that will get in the way of me selling your flat, I assure you.'

'The flat be damned,' she said, with surprising feeling. 'You look as if you need a good hearty meal to build you up. Beth, as Nathan's out this evening, why don't you invite Jack for supper?'

It was difficult to know who looked more astonished, Beth or Jack.

'I think Adele might have been trying her hand at a little matchmaking,' Beth said to Jack, later that evening when he was helping her to lay the table. 'I hope you weren't embarrassed.'

'Not in the least.'

She gave him a handful of cutlery. 'Well, just so long as you don't think I put her up to it. If I didn't know better, I'd say she's been overdosing on romantic novels. It's time for me to change her prescription for library books.' She went back to the cooker and stirred a pan of ratatouille. 'But she's dead right, Jack, about you looking tired.'

'Do I really look that awful?'

Still stirring, she turned her head to look at him. 'To be brutally honest, and speaking as a friend, yes.'

'Then I must do something about changing my friends. I'm not sure I can handle such honesty.'

While Beth took a small plate of supper downstairs to Adele, leaving him to open a bottle of wine and put on a CD, Jack was struck again by how comfortable he felt in Beth's flat. It had an almost magical ability to make the rest of the world and its troubles disappear. He wished his own home had the same effect on him.

He had nearly turned down Beth's offer of supper – knowing that the idea hadn't entered her head until Miss Waterman had put it there – but he was glad now that he had said yes. He liked the idea of spending an evening with someone who was straightforward and easy to talk to. He didn't even feel guilty that he was in the company of a woman Clare had no knowledge of. And, anyway, there was nothing going on between him and Beth. It was a platonic friendship, nothing more. But he had the feeling that Clare would need convincing on that score. Since she had told him about the baby, she had become increasingly possessive. She had wanted to move in with him, but he had held off. 'Let's just take it slowly,' he'd said, 'one step at a time.' He had used Amber and Lucy as an excuse to preserve what little privacy he still had, claiming that he didn't want to unsettle or alarm them. He had also asked her not to tell anyone just yet that she was pregnant. She had been disappointed by this. 'What about Mum and Dad?' she'd asked. Especially not them, he'd wanted to say. He was being a coward, he knew. As if keeping it a secret would somehow make it seem less real. Less of a mess. She had later confessed that she had confided in Julie. Which meant Des knew. Funny he hadn't said anything.

Clare's possessiveness also stretched to her badgering him about his regular absences on Thursday evenings. He still hadn't let on about the writers' group, determined more than ever to keep that secret from her. Sometimes he thought it was only his new-found passion for writing that kept him sane. Whenever he sat down in front of his laptop to write his diary or his novel, the words tumbled out of him, an unstoppable outpouring from the heart.

He was just switching on the CD player when Beth came back. 'I'm under orders to feed you till you burst,' she said brightly, 'and to get to the bottom of what's troubling you.'

'I could always fob you off.'

'You could. But how productive would that be?'

They sat down to eat, and before long he found he was telling her everything. About Maddie and the girls, Tony and Clare, and now the baby.

'Oh, Jack, what a load you've been carrying. I'd sort of guessed about Maddie and Tony from what you've read to us at the group, but I had no idea that you were so unhappy with Clare.'

He sighed heavily. 'I've only myself to blame. I shouldn't have rushed into things with her as I did. At the time I thought she was the answer. Now I know differently. I've been bloody stupid.'

'Don't be too hard on yourself. You haven't said, but presumably Clare wants the baby?'

'Very much so. And I wouldn't want her to do anything . . . well, you know, anything drastic like get rid of it.'

'I'm probably letting the sisterhood down, but you don't have to marry her.'

He looked grim. 'I feel as if it's inevitable. But that's a long way off. For now I'm still married to Maddie.'

'But you mustn't marry Clare if it means the pair of you will end up hating each other. You have to be sensible. Look long-term, Jack. You have a duty to the child, but also to be true to yourself. And there's Amber and Lucy to consider. If you're unhappy, think what that will do to them.'

He was no nearer to solving his problems, but the evening spent with Beth had cheered him, and the first thing he did when he got home was not to pour himself a large drink, as he'd got into the habit of doing, but go to bed. It had been good sharing so much with Beth, even the painful stuff. He knew now that he'd deliberately not confided in Des because of Julie. He'd wager the last coin in his pocket that those two kept few secrets from each other, and therefore whatever Jack shared with Des about his current situation would go to Julie, then straight to Clare. It was a risk he couldn't take.

But thank goodness for Beth.

He slept well that night. The best sleep he'd had for what seemed like for ever.

Chapter Eighteen

*

Richard Cavanagh knew he was taking a risk – to himself and others. Driving a car so soon after a heart-attack wasn't advisable. The medical view was that he should wait for at least another month, but he simply had to see Dulcie. He missed her so much it hurt. This evening, while Angela was out with the boys at a school function, he was seizing his opportunity.

He reversed his beloved old Aston Martin out of the garage: he hadn't driven it for nearly six weeks and the controls felt unfamiliar. At one time his beautiful classic car had meant the world to him. He had lavished untold care and devotion on it, had polished it lovingly, restored it, even tinkered with the engine, convinced that no one understood it better than he did. Now he knew it was nothing but a stylish and extravagant piece of machinery. With nothing to do while he'd been recovering from his heart-attack, he'd thought a lot about his life: what was important to him, and what wasn't. And before it was too late, he had to make the most of what was left to him. His near-death experience had taught him a lot. It was a wake-up call he could not ignore.

It was dark and he flicked on the lights, then closed the garage door with the remote control, turned the car on the gravel and drove away slowly. He didn't have much time, but he knew better than to hurry. If he only got to be with Dulcie for half an hour, it would be better than nothing. The possibility that she might be out had crossed his mind, but there had been no question of telephoning, not when he knew she would be furious at the risk he was taking and try to stop him.

Gaining confidence, he squeezed the accelerator, enjoying his moment of freedom. With Angela taking his convalescence so seriously, fending off calls from work and insisting he mustn't be exposed to stressful situations, he had been kept a virtual prisoner in his own home. He lowered the window, just to feel the cold evening air on his face. It made him feel truly alive. And so very glad to be so. When he'd been lying in that hospital bed, he'd had plenty of time to count his blessings and grasp just how fragile life was. How easy it was to take it for granted, to imagine that one was immortal. He had thought of his children often – Christopher and Nicholas in particular – and had hated the idea that he might not see them grow to adulthood.

The doctors had put down his heart-attack to an unaccountable change in his blood pressure. It was all they could come up with, because in all other areas he had a clean bill of health: he'd never smoked, had never had a problem with cholesterol, and hadn't worked himself into the ground as so many of his colleagues did. He had been unlucky, was their conclusion. At least at the time Dulcie had been with him. Her prompt action had ensured that within the hour he was in the coronary-care unit. It meant that the severity of the attack had been reduced and any permanent damage limited. That morning he had told Angela before leaving for work that he would be taking an extended lunch break to drive down to the classic-car garage on the Whitchurch road – something he often did when he needed a replacement part for the Aston Martin; it was only half a mile from the Belfry Hotel where he and Dulcie met occasionally. When Angela had asked who had come to his aid, he had lied. He had told her that because he'd been feeling unwell he'd stopped off at a hotel for a drink, and had got talking to a woman in the bar. 'What a pity we don't know her name or where she lives,' Angela had said. 'It would have been a nice gesture to write and thank her for what she did. She probably saved your life.'

He could have told a partial truth, he thought later. Would there have been anything so odd about a chance encounter with the woman who'd helped them move house?

Angela's innocent reference to the supposed stranger who had saved his life might have caused him to flinch a short while before, but now it didn't. Ever since she had told him how she and Nicholas had bumped into Dulcie, his heart had hardened towards her. 'I expect you can't remember what she looks like, but I don't recall her looking so old,' Angela had gloated. 'And I'd bet a pound to a penny she's put on weight.' Angela had never had to worry about her weight. She had been in her coat, fresh from her shopping trip in Maywood, and was bustling absentmindedly around the bedroom, a carrier-bag in her hand. 'It would explain why she's still a widow,' she'd added, further annoying him.

With his hands forming fists under the duvet, he'd said, 'How do you know she hasn't married again?'

'Oh, Richard, you men are so hopelessly unobservant. She wasn't wearing a ring, of course.'

He rushed to defend the woman he loved – and also decided to buy Dulcie a ring at the earliest opportunity. 'That doesn't mean a thing in this day and age. She might live with a loving partner who cares passionately about the woman within, not the superficial exterior of size and looks.'

She had stared at him as if he were mad, then switched her glance to the plastic bag in her hand. 'Oh, I bought you some books.' She held the bag out to him and he took it without a word of thanks.

He couldn't say with any certainty when or why he had stopped loving Angela but, like middle age or a change in season, it had crept up on him, a gradual dawning that they had run their course as husband and wife and had become more like brother and sister – older brother and little sister. At times he felt choked by her neediness, stifled by her inability to stand on her own two feet. Ironically, it was this very trait that had attracted him when they first met. In those days she had been painfully shy and he had got a kick out of being able to make her smile, to make her happy, to give her the strength and confidence she so badly lacked. Being needed – *wanted* – was powerfully seductive.

How arrogant that made him sound. Years later it had been an independent spirit and a quiet sense of self-containment that had attracted him.

Often it was the silly things that got to him about Angela, like her haphazard approach to housework, the way she could never keep on top of the ironing and left the kitchen to tidy itself. He tried hard not to show his disapproval but, being obsessively tidy himself, he frequently stepped in and did the job for her.

Angela had her good points. She was a wonderful mother: she gave her all to the children, ensuring that she was always there for every play, every parents' evening, every concert. It was him who was at fault. He had forced too much upon her. He had chased a good promotion at work to satisfy his own needs – more money, greater status, bigger challenges. He had justified uprooting Angela and the younger children by saying it would get them out of a rut, that it would give them an exciting new start. It hadn't worked. Angela had never settled: she missed her friends and family, particularly her old schoolfriend, Rowena. She felt isolated, cut off from all that she knew, became more dependent on him.

Looking back on that time, when he had realised he no longer loved his wife – long before they'd moved to Cheshire – he often wondered if she ever sensed he was drifting away from her: as he'd retreated, she had advanced on him, becoming more affectionate and loving. Then she had told him she was pregnant and the future he had begun to imagine was snatched from him. He had no way of knowing, but he had always suspected that Angela had deliberately become pregnant with Christopher. Oh, she'd done an excellent job of pretending she was as shocked as he was, but something in her manner – her readiness later to provide Christopher with a younger brother or sister – told him that this was all part of the plan to bond them together for a long time yet. She had probably told herself she had given their marriage a new lease of life.

And in much the same way, his heart-attack had done the same for him.

He didn't mind admitting that being in hospital had terrified him. Even now, when the expert opinion was that he was well on the road to recovery, he often went to bed at night frightened that he might not wake up. Every time he had the slightest twinge of pain, or a change in the rhythm of his heartbeat, he worried that he might be dying.

It took him almost thirty minutes to reach Maywood. As he turned into Bloom Street his heart pounded at the thought of seeing Dulcie. He forced himself to breathe slowly and deeply, and stopped the car a short distance from her house: there were lights on and it was all he could do to resist the urge to quicken his step towards the door.

Dulcie heard the front-door bell and stopped mid-sentence. She had been absorbed in what she was writing. Annoyed at the interruption, she took off her reading glasses and reluctantly went to see who it was. If it was another of those young men with holdalls of dusters and ironing-board covers, she would give him short shrift.

'Richard!'

'Hello, Dulcie. It's not a bad time to call, is it?'

They held each other tightly, kissed, and cried with the sheer joy of being together again. It was a while before either of them could speak.

'You've no idea how much I've missed you,' Richard said, when they'd calmed down and were in the sitting room.

'Oh, I do. It's been the same for me.' Then, more seriously, she said, 'But you broke the promise you made. You risked too much by doing this. What if—'

He took her hand and pressed it to his lips. 'I'm sorry but I had to see you. I thought I'd go crazy if I didn't. Don't be cross.' He put his arm round her and drew her close. 'I can't stay long, though.'

'I know. I understand.'

'But one day I will. If you'll agree, I'd like to stay for ever.'

She looked deep into his eyes and saw the conviction in them, and the love. But still she doubted what he'd said. He was speaking from his heart, not his head, and when the emotional trauma of what he'd been through had settled, he would know that his place was with his family. They both knew it. For now, though, none of that mattered. They were together for a few precious moments and she didn't want anything to spoil it, least of all let the dull thud of reality impinge on their happiness.

He took her face in his hands and kissed her. 'I don't suppose you'd take pity on a sick man and make love to me, would you?' he whispered.

Smiling, but gently chiding him, she said, 'I'd like nothing better, but I'd rather not have your demise on my conscience or have it take place in my bed. I'm squeamish like that.'

He hushed her with another kiss. 'But what a way to go.'

Chapter Nineteen

*

'William Kidswell, you're such a tart!'

Billy slid into the passenger seat of the car, lowered his sunglasses and gave Nathan one of his classic lazy-eyed looks, the kind that he knew was such a turn-on for girls. He smoothed down his suit and flicked at the absurdly floppy points of his enormous collar. 'Takes one to know one, darling.'

Nathan laughed. 'I can't make up my mind if you're playing the camp dandy or the seventies game-show host.'

'Either way, it's Friday night and I'm in the mood for *lurve*.' He reached inside his jacket pocket and pulled out a small bottle of tequila. 'Something to help the party along.'

Nathan wound down his window. 'But did you have to smother yourself in so much CK? I'm dying of passive aftershave poisoning here.'

'Do you mind? It's Paul Smith. But drink it in, boy, it might just do the trick and give you the necessary to pull tonight.'

'Yeah, right, like I need your help in that department. The king of dump 'em and run.'

Billy grinned. 'So what's the score between you and that cute little redhead, *Jasmina* Rafferty? And give me the real score – I don't want you holding back on me.'

Keeping his expression inscrutable and concentrating on the road, all Nathan said was, 'Her name's Jasmine. Jaz.'

It turned out that Nathan had got it wrong about Jaz being interested in Billy. She'd been horrified when he'd suggested as much. Scornful, too. 'Oh, please,' she'd said, 'credit me with more sense. Billy's so into himself he's in danger of vanishing up his own bum.'

'Vicki seems to think differently,' Nathan had ventured.

She'd laughed. 'I think you'll find Billy may have met his match there.'

He was glad that she was smart enough to see through Billy. He and Jaz only saw each other at college; occasionally they walked home together. They talked about the kind of books and films they enjoyed and her writing. She was different from most other girls he knew, more serious and intense. Occasionally she gave him a contemplative smile, but more often than not her manner was defensive and prickly. It made for some great exchanges between them. Once or twice he had wondered if it wasn't an act she put on for his benefit. If so, why?

And why did he feel he was surrounded by people putting on an act?

Jaz.

Billy.

And, of course, the greatest of them all, his grandmother.

Lois had phoned last night. 'Sorry, Gran,' he'd said, 'Mum's not in. Can I pass on a message? Or get her to ring you when she comes back?'

'Oh, is she working late?'

'No, she's at her writers' group.'

'Her what?'

He'd seen his mistake immediately, but had known there was no way to wriggle out of the situation. Lois was a determined inquisitor when she wanted to be. He tried to play dumb, but everything he said seemed to rouse his grandmother's curiosity further. 'It's just an evening out for her,' he said.

'And what goes on at this group?'

'Writing, I suppose.'

'But why?'

'Why what?'

'Why does your mother want to do something so peculiar? Is this another of Simone's harebrained schemes? I've never known anyone so faddish. It was her who passed on all those absurd self-help books to your mother. As if she needed that kind of thing when she had us.'

Nathan had always known that his grandmother disapproved of

Simone, but it was only recently that he had realised the extent of it. Hack away the veneer of Lois's attempts at humour and it was patently clear that she saw Simone as a threat.

When his mother arrived home, humming to herself in the hall as she removed her coat and hung it up, he told her that he'd dumped her in it with Lois.

'Oh, Lord,' she'd said, after he'd explained and apologised. 'Now I'll be cross-examined on the dubious company I'm keeping. Not to worry, it was bound to happen sooner or later. Lois has a nose for sniffing out a secret.'

Humming again, she went through to the kitchen and put her writing file on the small desk where her computer was. He was surprised that she didn't seem bothered by what he'd told her. Only a short time ago, she would have tried to justify her right to have a life that Lois knew nothing about. Things were changing for the better, he decided.

Was it possible that her mood had been influenced by a certain man from the writers' group – Adele's estate agent, Jack Solomon? Hadn't they had supper together the other night?

Nathan and Billy arrived at the party to find the usual suspects present from the upper sixth, as well as several cast members from the play who were in the lower-sixth. It was Kirsten Dempsey's eighteenth birthday – she was playing Cecily Cardew – and because she was friendly with Vicki, Nathan had hoped secretly that Jaz would be there.

He left Billy to his admiring fans, including Vicki, and went in search of a soft drink – he'd drawn the short straw and was the designated driver that night, which meant he'd stay stone-cold sober. Billy would probably need to be put into the recovery position on the back seat of the car.

There was no sign of Jaz. Disappointed, he stared round the sitting room, which the Dempseys had wisely stripped of most of its contents, and wondered where she was and what she was doing.

He hoped she was enjoying herself more than he was.

Jaz was furious. How could her parents do this to her? It was so unfair. And why was it always she who had to babysit Tamzin and Lulu? Why did they never ask Phin or Jimmy? And it wasn't just for tonight: they were away for a long weekend staying at the apartment in Tenerife. 'My Molly-doll deserves a bit of pampering,' Dad had announced at breakfast, 'and a blast of sun too. So long as we can get on a flight, we'll be off this afternoon.'

Jaz hated it when Dad used his pet-name for her mother: it was so childish. And what did they think they were doing at their age by having more children? Why couldn't they just accept that they were past their sex-by date?

Every time she thought of her mother being pregnant, she felt sick. She had been eight when Lulu was born and had never forgotten that dreadful night. Tamzin had been two (for a change she had been fast asleep in her cot and not trying to climb out of it), and apart from Jaz and her mother, no one else was at home. It was St Patrick's Day and her father had taken the boys to Dublin to expose them to their Rafferty roots. To be fair to her father, he had dithered about going – the baby was due in three weeks – but mum had insisted she'd be okay and he'd headed out of town. That night she had gone into labour. The first Jaz knew of this was when her mother woke her and said, 'Jaz, I need your help. The baby's decided to come early.'

Instantly bolt upright, Jaz had said, 'What do you want me to do?' Her mother's face was covered with a sheen of perspiration. She looked awful.

'Don't look so worried. I've phoned for an ambulance and until Mrs Dalton can get here, I want you to take care of Tamzin while I'm at the hospital.'

'Why can't Mrs Dalton come sooner? She's only next door.'

'I can't get hold of her – she must be out for the evening.' Her mother's face twisted and she gasped. Frightened, Jaz threw her arms round her. She wanted to cry, but somehow knew it wasn't the time. 'It's okay, Jaz,' her mother said, moments later, 'everything will be fine.'

But it wasn't fine. Mrs Dalton didn't come back from wherever she was and the ambulance took for ever to arrive. Within minutes of it showing up, Lulu was born, but not before Jaz had heard her poor mother cry out with a pain she swore she would never experience.

'I thought it was supposed to get easier the more you had,' her mother said to Dad, after he and the boys had got home – they had caught the night ferry.

'Maybe after the tenth it does.' He'd laughed. 'We'll have to carry on and find out.'

From the foot of the bed, Jaz had watched her father cradle the scrawny baby, which was squirming like a horrible worm in his large hands. She had prayed for all she was worth that he had been joking.

And now her mother was going to go through all that again. With twins. Jaz had a sneaky feeling that her father viewed babies as a badge of honour: the more who bore the name of Rafferty the better.

With her head in her hands as she sat at her desk, Jaz shuddered. She had long since grown out of believing in the Catechism and the Catholic God of her upbringing, but she offered up a new prayer: 'Please, God, don't ever let me be stupid enough to get pregnant.' She couldn't think of anything worse: all that screaming and disgusting mess. She tried to block the nightmarish thought from her mind, but was distracted by an almighty racket from downstairs. She gritted her teeth, ready to read the Riot Act to Tamzin and Lulu. She took the stairs slowly, planning a suitably satisfying punishment for her sisters.

She found them in the sitting room, the television blaring and a sweating Robbie Williams strutting his half-naked, tattooed body across the screen. There were crisps, Cheerios, peanuts, and feathers all over the carpet. A small table lay on its back and one of Mum's china ornaments lay broken among the chaos. From where they were standing on the sofa – feather-leaking cushions in hand – Tamzin and Lulu stared at her. Both were out of breath with hysterical laughter and both had covered their faces in what Jaz could only hope, from the empty pot on the floor, was chocolate mousse.

It was the most surreal moment, and when her scream came, she gave it full vent. Once she had started, it was difficult to stop, especially when she saw the effect it was having on her sisters. They jumped off the sofa and managed to look almost contrite. She was still yelling at them when she heard the doorbell ring.

'That'll be the police,' she said, blurting out the first thought that came into her head. 'I called them from upstairs and they said they'd get here as soon as they could to take you away. I hope you enjoy spending the night in a cell.'

Lulu was young enough to be taken in and she looked horrorstruck. But Tamzin wasn't so convinced. 'I don't believe you,' she said, sticking out her chocolaty chin. She had probably watched sufficient police dramas to know that they never arrived quite so quickly.

Jaz went to answer the door. She did a double-take when she saw who it was.

Nathan stood hesitantly on the doorstep. He'd heard the commotion and was now confronted with an expression so hostile he wished he'd remained at the party. When Vicki had told him Jaz had had to babysit her sisters, he'd come up with what he'd thought was a brilliant idea to surprise her and see if she fancied some company. But from the drawn brows and the arms pinned across her chest, she plainly didn't want him here. He was all set to leave when she seemed to change her mind: 'Look, you can come in, if you like, but you'll have to put up with my awful sisters. They're a right pair of savages, evil personified. Riff-raff. Trash. You name it. Collectively, they're Public Enemy Number One.'

He smiled. 'Every family should have one.'

'So why did mine end up with two?' She stepped back to let him in. 'Hey, I don't suppose you'd do me a favour, would you?'

'What? Adopt them?'

'What a spectacularly wonderful idea, but no. Could you pretend you're a policeman and that you've come to arrest them? You'll understand why when you see what they've done.'

He laughed. He was already having more fun than he'd had at the party. 'Anything to oblige, miss.'

With the collar of his leather coat pulled up and an authoritative swagger, Nathan walked into the middle of the sitting room and tried to look every inch the plain-clothes detective inspector as he surveyed the damage. It was awesome.

He shook his head.

He tutted.

He inhaled deeply.

He exhaled deeply.

He shook his head again.

Most of all, he tried not to laugh. He'd never seen anything like it. Even the Dempseys wouldn't be confronted with a sight on this scale after Kirsten's party. How could two kids create such a scene of devastation? And what the hell was that muck they'd smeared over their faces?

'I told you it was bad, Officer,' Jaz said, switching off the television. She put down the remote control, folded her arms again and looked fierce.

'Strikes me that I came in the nick of time.' He stepped towards the pair. 'What do you have to say for yourselves, then? And I must caution you, anything you say will be taken down and used as evidence.'

The smaller of the two girls took a step behind her sister, but the bigger one held her ground. 'How do we know you're a real policeman? Where's your badge? You could be a piddyfile for all we know.'

Nathan was taken aback. When he was their age, he'd never heard the word 'paedophile'. He ignored her request to see his badge and said, 'You must be the ringleader, eh? Would I be right? Name, please.'

Her eyes darted nervously from him to Jaz, then back to him. 'I know my rights,' she said, rebelliously. 'I'm allowed to make a phone call. I'm going to ring Mum and Dad.'

'Yes,' said Jaz. 'You do that and I'll tell them what you've done here, broken ornament and all.'

Nathan was beginning to feel that they'd carried the joke as far as they could. 'Seeing as it's a first offence,' he said, 'how about you tidy up the place and we'll say no more about it? But I'm warning you, you've committed several serious offences here tonight.' He held up his hands and counted off their crimes on his fingers. 'Breach of the peace, aiding and abetting, unlawful conduct, and violation of section 16a and 22b of the Law and Order Act.' Gratified to see their jaws drop, he added sternly, 'Now, don't do it again. Do you hear?'

They nodded and began to clear up. Except they made it worse. Their hands were covered in the same stuff as their faces and everything they touched stuck to their fingers. They tried to shake off the feathers and Cheerios, but began to giggle when a feather landed on the end of Lulu's nose. 'Oh, for heaven's sake,' Jaz shouted, 'go upstairs, have a bath and then go straight to bed. I'll sort this out. Go on, *scram*!'

When she and Nathan were alone, she closed the door, leaned against it and groaned. 'You see what I have to put up with? It's like that twenty-four hours a day. Please don't judge me by their awfulness.'

He had taken off his coat and was crouched on the floor picking up the broken china. 'Hey, it's okay, I'm on board with the gruesome-sister act. No comparison made.'

'I can't wait to leave home. University can't come quick enough.' Then, registering what he was doing, she went over to him. 'There's no need for you to do that. I'll see to it.'

'It's okay, I don't mind helping. I think we're going to need a cloth, a bin-liner and a vacuum-cleaner. I doubt that this china can be glued back together.'

They worked together, binning, scrubbing and hoovering, until at last the place looked as it should. After she'd been upstairs and checked on her sisters – making sure they were in bed, not flooding the bathroom – she said, 'The least I can do is offer you a drink. Or would you like something to eat?'

Out in the kitchen, she made some hot chocolate and two fried-egg sandwiches. They kept their voices low, so as not to bring her nosy-parker sisters down again. She was glad now that she'd invited him in. Her initial reaction at seeing him had been of acute embarrassment. But this was great, sitting here in the kitchen: it was as if they were proper friends. Since that first time, they'd walked home together quite often, and occasionally they chatted during their lunch breaks in the college cafeteria. Usually there were others at the table with them, but once or twice they'd had a moment to themselves. Those were the times she'd liked best. She was relieved that he didn't fancy her: it meant they stood a chance of developing a friendship that might last – he was good company. And now that Vicki and Billy were hitting the smooch button, Jaz spent less time with Vicki, and more with Nathan. She was still wary of him, though, reluctant to show too much of her real self in case he didn't like it.

'So, how was the party?' she asked.

'You didn't miss anything, believe me.'

'I guarantee it would have been better than my evening here. What made you leave?'

'Oh, you know, I'd heard that there was a better gig going on in this upwardly mobile neighbourhood.' He looked about him, assessing the large and expensively kitted-out kitchen. Jaz knew where Nathan lived and that he and his mum had just a small flat.

She was suddenly aware of how others might perceive her – spoiled little rich kid. 'What does your dad do for a living?' he asked, confirming her thoughts.

'Don't be so sexist. My mum might have been the one to fund all this.'

He raised his hands in mock surrender. 'Okay, okay, I'll keep my big mouth shut.'

'Actually, you were right.' She relented. 'Dad runs a building firm. My brothers work for him now.' She gave a short laugh. 'That's because no one else would be stupid enough to take them on.' She took a bite of her sandwich, then ran her tongue over her lips to catch a dribble of melted butter and egg yolk. She noticed he was staring at her. Self-conscious, she said, 'What? Have I missed a bit?'

He shook his head slowly, his gaze still on her lips.

She didn't believe him, so got up and went over to the cupboard where her mother kept the kitchen roll. She ripped off a piece, wiped her mouth, then went back to the table, taking another square with her in case she made any more mess. He was still staring at her. 'You're beginning to spook me. What is it?'

He brushed some breadcrumbs off his fingers and cleared his throat. 'I was just thinking how much I'd like to kiss you.'

Stunned, she wiped her mouth again. But instead of thinking how much she might enjoy him kissing her, she was suspicious of his motives. Suppose he was trying it on? Suppose Vicki had told him at the party that her parents were away and he had come here with the express intention of taking advantage of her being alone . . . of trying to get her into bed? She had a horrible vision of Billy, and everyone else at the party, urging him to do exactly that. Then a far worse picture came into her head: what if she succumbed and got pregnant? Vivid flashes of her mother in labour swam before her. She drew back from the table sharply. 'I think you should know there's absolutely no chance of you getting me into bed. Got that?'

He frowned, looked genuinely perplexed. 'Well, I'm glad we've got that sorted out.'

She was saved from having to respond by the sound of a door slamming upstairs. Grateful for the distraction, she excused herself. She took the stairs two at a time, wishing, as the distance grew between her and Nathan, that she could turn back the clock on the last five minutes.

What had just happened?

How could she have made such a fool of herself?

Of course he hadn't been trying to jump her. All he'd asked her for was a kiss. It was no big deal.

When she'd taken out her embarrassment on Tamzin and Lulu, she went back to the kitchen and found Nathan waiting for her. He was in his coat, ready to go.

She watched him drive away, knowing she'd blown it.

Now they wouldn't even be friends.

Chapter Twenty

*

There was a very different atmosphere among the group that evening: they were relaxed and enjoying themselves – and they had Victor to thank for that. He hadn't turned up.

Until now, no one had missed a meeting and Beth was surprised that Victor had the first black mark against his name. She almost wished that his absence would not be a one-off and that he had decided Hidden Talents wasn't for him.

At Dulcie's suggestion last week, they were trying something new. From now on they were taking it in turns to lead the group. The reason behind this, according to Dulcie, was to induce a greater level of participation. Beth had dreaded being picked first, but all credit to Jack: he had risen to the challenge and volunteered. He was now explaining what they had to do.

'I'll come clean,' he said, 'I pinched the idea from a how-to-write book, so it's not original. It's an exercise to teach us the importance of fair-minded characterisation. To kick off with we have to create a character in no more than fifty words that no one in their right mind would like. Don't hold back, make him or her as nasty as you want. Okay?' He pointed to the clock on the mantelpiece. 'We have precisely ten minutes to do that.'

After a few moments of rustling paper and cranking up their brains, they fell quiet and concentrated on the task in hand. Minutes passed before Beth wrote anything. Then, with the pressure on, she panicked and scribbled the first thing that came into her head. To her shame, she found herself caricaturing Lois – the archetypal interfering mother-in-law.

She had nearly lost her temper with Lois at the weekend and the memory still hurt of what the other woman had said. Lois had shown up unexpectedly at the flat – usually she phoned in advance to check that they would be in – and had gone round the houses before she got to the real purpose of her visit. She wanted to know all about the writers' group. 'What kind of people would go to something so extraordinary?' she'd asked. 'I could scarcely believe it when Nathan told me what you'd been up to. You're turning into quite a dark horse, Beth. How many more little secrets are you keeping from us?' Her light, tinkling tone barely disguised the brittle hardness of her words and Beth regretted that she hadn't got this over and done with sooner. She should have returned Lois's call, as Nathan had said she would. She looked across the kitchen table to where Lois was unashamedly reading an electricity bill and said, 'Hardly a dark horse, Lois. I've joined a creative-writing group, not the Ku Klux Klan.'

'But what on earth for? I wouldn't have thought you'd have time, what with Nathan so busy in his final year at Maywood College.'

A flutter of anger released itself inside Beth. She knew she had to take a stand, had to put an end to Lois's insidious need to control her. It was outrageous that Lois should use Nathan to manipulate her like this.

'Lois, Nathan is quite capable of taking care of himself while I treat myself to the odd night out.'

'But it's such an important time for him. And it's not the odd night, is it? It's every week, so I understand from Nathan. You know, if he fails to get the grades he needs, you'll never forgive yourself. I was always there for Adam. I always put him first.'

Beth stared at Lois and wondered if she had any idea how cruel and absurd she sounded. 'I think you're exaggerating,' she said, more calmly than she felt. She got up from the table, suddenly confronted with the shocking discovery that she was on the verge of hating Lois. She didn't want to hate anyone, least of all Adam's mother. She went and stood at the window, stared down on to the park. A strong wind was scattering the clouds and a father was teaching his young son to ride a bicycle without stabilisers. For a moment she was disoriented as she recalled Adam doing the same with Nathan. Finally she spoke. 'Lois, I don't think you have any idea how offensive or hurtful you've just been to me. I've always put Nathan first.' She turned slowly from the window. 'But that's not what's really behind this, is it?' They were dangerously close to a point of no return and, more than anything, Beth wanted to clear the air. It was time to confront the lies and pretence. They couldn't go on as they were.

Lois's normally composed face twitched. A hand went to her throat and fiddled with a beaded necklace. 'I'm not sure what you mean. I'm . . . I'm sorry if I've offended you in some way, but I was merely showing concern. Taking too much on is never a good idea. I should know, I've done it myself countless times.' She gave a shrill laugh, fanned her reddening face and looked at the fire reproachfully. 'Goodness, it's warm in here. Oh, did I tell you about Barnaby cutting his hand on a broken pane in the greenhouse? I don't know how often I've warned him to get it fixed. What he thought he was doing out there at this time of year is anybody's guess.'

And that was it. In one of her classic manoeuvres, Lois had made her point then moved the conversation on so that it would appear churlish to retaliate or pursue the argument further. She went on to discuss Christmas and what they would all be doing. 'I thought I'd do us a nice goose this year. What do you think?'

As if Lois cared what Beth thought.

Beth was about to put a line through what she had written when Jack called time.

'Right,' he said, 'now fold up your pieces of paper and hand them to the person on your left. Don't read them until I say so.'

Beth handed hers to Dulcie, hoping that Dulcie wouldn't guess at the extent of her unkindness.

'We now have twenty minutes to create a believable scenario in which we can turn round our neighbour's character,' Jack said. 'We have to make him or her not just likeable but redeemable.'

Dulcie nodded approvingly, but Jaz said, 'Flipping heck, Jack, you're not asking much, are you?'

Jack smiled. 'For a smart girl like you, Jaz, it'll be a breeze. Oh, and I forgot to say, we have to write this in the third person.' He looked at the clock again, and said, 'Okay, you may now turn over your exam papers.'

A collective groan went round the room. Beth read through the paragraph Jack had given her, and her heart sank. From what she knew of his circumstances, she could see that he had described the man who had once been his closest friend and was now living with his wife, Maddie.

It was interesting, but with the exception of Victor and Dulcie, who was the most experienced member of the group, everything they wrote was in the first person, which was probably why Jack had specified the third person now. No one had mentioned it before, but it was glaringly obvious to Beth that she, Jack and Jaz were writing about themselves. Apparently most writers did this when they embarked on their first novel. Other than Victor, they seldom spoke about getting published: they were all writing for the fun and challenge.

And, more importantly perhaps, for the escapism it offered.

Over coffee last week, Dulcie had said that while she was absorbed in writing, she didn't brood over things she couldn't control. It was a rare confidence that took Beth unawares, as Dulcie, so self-assured and congenial, didn't seem the anxious type. After this, and curling one of her long plaits around her finger, Jaz had said that she loved writing because it took her away from her brothers and sisters, who never gave her a minute's peace. 'I guess it's a power thing,' she said. She'd then admitted that her fictitious family, the Clacketts, was based on her own (not that they had needed to be told that) and Beth wondered if they were as riotous as Jaz painted them. But, then, wasn't it always the case that truth was stranger than fiction? Neither Victor nor Jack had contributed to this part of the conversation, but Jack had already told her, the night she'd cooked for him, that there were times when he thought he was writing his way out of the black hole he'd been sucked into.

She still cringed when she remembered Adele's attempt at matchmaking. 'You're not to do that again,' she had told the old lady the next day, when she'd popped in to see her before going to work, 'or I shan't fetch any more books from the library for you. It was mortifying for the poor man.'

'Nonsense,' Adele had said. 'He was charmed by the idea.'

'You mean he was struck dumb with shock.'

'But you had a good evening, didn't you? It was hours before he left.'

'Adele Waterman, you're the sneakiest neighbour I've ever had the misfortune to know. If you weren't so ill, I'd give you a proper ticking off. Now, behave yourself and take your medicine. And don't forget to have some of the soup I've made for you.'

Adele had looked at the Thermos beside the bed and smiled. 'It's not poisoned, is it?'

'Not on this occasion, but if you try to set me up again with Jack, I might just consider it. Anyway, he's seriously involved with someone else so you were wasting your time.'

Settling back into the pillows, which Beth had rearranged for her, Adele had said, 'Then he should look happier.'

Beth didn't tell Adele what was bothering Jack. What he had shared with her had been extremely personal, and she knew that he wouldn't want one of his clients to be privy to such information. To gossip about him behind his back would also be disloyal.

That was another aspect of the group that had surprised her. They hadn't known each other for long, yet a bond was forming between them. At the outset, Dulcie had said that the aim of the group was for them to support and encourage each other, not to criticise and demoralise. Maybe it was because they were writing about such personal things, and being brave enough to share them, that trust was developing. It was as if, without meaning to, they'd formed their own self-help group. She made a mental note to explore this thought more deeply: it might come in hand for Libby, her self-help junkie in *Living For Pleasure*.

She dragged her thoughts back to the here and now and wondered why Victor hadn't come. Perhaps he'd gone down with one of the many pre-Christmas bugs doing the rounds. For the first time it struck her how little they knew about him. Was he married? Or did he live alone? If so, and he was ill, did he have anyone he could call on for help?

Later that night, when she had tidied the kitchen, taken a load of washing out of the machine and put it to dry in front of the fire, Beth settled at the computer and tried to get on with Chapter Eight. It had been annoyingly obstinate in its unwillingness to play ball with her, but now she was determined to get the better of it. She had set herself a goal of a thousand words a day, and the more she wrote, the more convinced she became that an author often had little say over a character's input to a story. At first she had thought that this was because she was inept, but apparently the most experienced writers suffered from this phenomenon.

Mr Outta Laffs had told her this. Since their introductory chat on-line, they had slipped into a nightly habit of emailing each other. She wasn't a secretive person, but she had decided to keep quiet about Mr Outta Laffs. She knew what people would say if they were aware of what she was doing: that he could be anyone – at best a saddo with a dandruffy centre parting who wore white socks and grey shoes and still lived at home with Mother, or at worst, a serial murderer who would track her down and add her to the scores of bodies he had buried under his patio.

But instinct – or was it misplaced hope of delusional proportions? – told her that Mr Outta Laffs fitted into neither category. He seemed as sane as she was, which, admittedly, didn't say much about him, and was just as concerned for his own safety as she was for hers.

How do I know you're the full shilling? [he'd asked in one of their early chats, after she'd admitted she was a woman.]

What made you think I was?

Clever reply, a bona fide madwoman would have gone to great lengths to convince me she was firing on all cylinders.

I could be double-bluffing you.

Shucks, I hadn't thought of that. So where does that leave us?

Watching our backs, I guess.

Would that be before or after one of us has revealed themselves to be the psycho? No, don't answer that, I like a bit of suspense in my life. Tell me about your book. How's it going?

She liked the way he showed an interest in what she was doing, and that he understood how frustrating it could be. So far they had discussed little of a personal nature and had only broached the subject of their real names last night. Mr Outta Laffs had said,

In the spirit of you show me yours and I'll show you mine, my real name is Ewan. Yours?

Beth.

Short for Elizabeth?

No. Bethany.

Nice. Does anyone ever call you Bethany?

Not since I was a child.

Then I shall distance myself from the crowd and from time to time address you by your proper name. That's if you don't object.

She hadn't minded. Quite the reverse, in fact. It added an element of intimacy to their correspondence – not even Adam had called her by her full name. As Simone would say, the whole thing was straight out of the Tom Hanks and Meg Ryan movie, *You've Got Mail*.

At midnight, and after Nathan had announced he was going to bed, Beth logged on to the Internet. She was looking forward to chatting with Mr Outta Laffs – or, rather, Ewan.

But there was no message waiting for her as there usually was. She left one for him, rearranged the washing in front of the fire, wrote a few Christmas cards, then checked to see if there was a reply.

Nothing.

Disappointed, she switched off the computer. She felt almost as though she'd been stood up.

Ewan Jones gave the keyboard one last thump of frustration. But it was no use: no amount of coaxing was going to get the machine working again. The damn thing had crashed. For good. To his disgust, he knew he was looking at a complete overhaul. He'd had his faithful Hewlett Packard for almost six years, and he viewed the prospect of change with annoyance. He would have to summon help first thing in the morning. While he was about it, he ought to do the sensible thing and buy a laptop too. If nothing else, it would provide him with some decent back-up. For a borderline techno-phobe, this was pioneering stuff.

He turned out the light in his office and made his way to the kitchen, where he filled the kettle and plugged it in. While he waited for it to boil, he read the letter he'd left on the table earlier that evening after he'd got in from a hectic day in London. It was from a publisher who had read the first three chapters of his novel, *Emily and Albert*. It was a love story set in the fifties and based, loosely, on the illicit relationship between his parents, a young schoolteacher who taught at the local village school and a GP who was married to a well-heeled woman ten years his senior. They had never married but, after causing much scandal in their strait-laced Welsh mining community, they had fled across the border to take up residence in Shropshire where they produced a child: Ewan. For all sorts of reasons, his book was a secret project – only his daughter knew about it – and to his delight the publishers were interested and wanted to see the rest of the manuscript. All he had to do was finish it, along with everything else that needed doing yesterday. Which was why it was so irritating that his computer had chosen to give up the ghost. Still, as Alice would be the first to say, 'Stop moaning, Dad. Just bite the bullet and replace it.'

How easy life was for a twenty-year-old girl who possessed sufficient self-confidence to reduce Anne Robinson to a quivering jelly. Everything was achievable for Alice. She was resourceful and resilient, and since she'd left home for university, he'd missed her. The frequency and length of her visits were shrinking, and he was looking forward to her coming home for Christmas

They had always been close, but when Alice had turned nine her mother had left him for a man in deepest Devon – a tofu-eating Buddhist – father and daughter had become inseparable. Now and again Alice received a letter from her mother, but she had never gone to see her, although Ewan often suggested that she should. Over the years, he'd discovered when not to push things with a headstrong daughter.

He looked at the clock on the kitchen wall and thought about ringing her to share his good news, but as it was just after midnight, he decided it was too early. Alice had an active social life in Leeds, and she wouldn't be available to chat until the clubs had closed. Lord, how did she do it? He was no slouch when it came to late nights – invariably he burned the midnight oil to write – but that was different: the only energy he was exerting was brain-power. At the age of forty-six, that seemed to be all the heavy-duty excitement on offer to him.

He was continually told by friends and Alice – especially Alice – that he didn't have enough going on in his life. That he had to do something about his long-term single status. He sipped his tea thoughtfully, and wondered if an on-line friendship counted.

Chapter Twenty-One

*

It was a freezing Saturday afternoon. A misty blanket of fog shrouded the whitened banks of the river and elegant willow branches drooped with brittle stiffness; here and there, gossamer cobwebs hung petrified with a dusting of sparkling frost.

In the warm, and to the sound of 'Walking In the Air' playing on the radio, Amber and Lucy were decorating the Christmas tree. Jack was regretting his choice – an artificial one from Taiwan that smelt of the polystyrene chips in which it had been packed, which now lay scattered over the living-room floor. He should have chosen a richly scented pine tree from the outdoor display at the garden centre, but it had been so cold that it had seemed a better idea to rush inside for a boxed one. He had given the girls free rein on choosing the ornaments and they had shown scant restraint for taste or expense. Consequently he was going to spend Christmas with the most kitsch tree this side of *It's A Wonderful Life*. There were strings of twinkling multicoloured fairy lights, gaudy baubles of every shape, size and colour, swathes of tinsel and beads. These were now being draped over already heavily laden branches, and there was a strong possibility that the tree might collapse under the strain.

But Jack was happy to let the girls go wild: to watch their eager faces as they worked together so industriously was reward enough. Amber had complained earlier that they hadn't been allowed to touch the tree Tony had put up last night: he'd told them that he and Maddie would be decorating it when the girls had gone to bed. According to Lucy, the Norwegian blue spruce was so tall it had had to stay in the high-ceilinged hall. Doubtless Tony had gone into the forest, hacked it down with his bare hands, then carried it home over his heroic shoulder.

Down, boy! Jack told himself. Remember, this is the season of goodwill to all men.

And that includes Tony.

When he'd shown up first thing that morning to fetch the girls, Maddie had been at the hairdresser's getting ready for the party they were giving that evening – that was why he had been allowed to have the girls for two weekends on the trot. Tony had offered him a drink, but he'd refused, just as he always did, and had stationed himself in the hall, his hands shoved deep in his trouser pockets. He was there for one purpose only, to collect his daughters. Polite chit-chat wasn't on the agenda. Never would be.

'What do you think, Daddy?' Lucy was looking at him expectantly. 'Do you like it?'

He studied their handiwork, then scooped up his younger daughter so that she was eye to eye with the angel on top. 'It's the best I've ever seen. We'll be the envy of everyone in Maywood. Once word gets round, they'll be queuing up for a look.'

Giggling, Lucy pushed her face into his neck and kissed him. He lowered her to the floor, smiled at Amber and gave her a high five. 'Great work, partner! How about a drink and a mince pie?'

Lucy, always hungry and pin-thin, set off towards the kitchen. 'Are they home-made like Mummy's?' she called over her shoulder.

'But of course.'

Amber looked at him doubtfully.

'Okay,' he admitted. 'A hardworking chef at Marks and Spencer made them for me.'

The kitchen was too small to eat in, so they took their drinks and plates into the living room to admire the tree. It had a worryingly drunken tilt to it, but neither Amber nor Lucy noticed this defect. 'We'll need to put some presents around it,' Lucy said, sitting on the floor and surrounding herself with squeaking polystyrene chips. 'It looks too bare at the bottom. Have you got any?'

'Only yours.'

Lucy's eyes lit up.

Amber came and sat on the sofa next to Jack. 'Don't be stupid, Lucy, you can't have them yet. It's too soon. Christmas isn't for another two weeks.'

Lucy's face dropped and her chin disappeared into the neck of her sweater.

'Well,' said Jack slowly, 'you could have them this weekend if you want, seeing as I shan't be with you over Christmas.'

Lucy perked up again, but Amber, who was becoming more grown-up each time he saw her, shook her head decisively. 'No. I want to keep mine until the day. I want Dad's present to be special.' She snuggled close to him.

'So do I,' added Lucy, but her voice lacked conviction.

'And don't forget,' he said, 'you'll have lots of presents from Father Christmas too.' He knew Amber was too old to go along with such things, but he hoped Lucy was still a happy believer. She had been forced to cope so young with so much harsh reality and he wanted her to enjoy what innocence was left in her childhood.

With her legs stretched out in front of her, knees and ankles together, she looked at him thoughtfully. 'Do you think he'll be able to find us in France?'

'Of course he will. And, what's more, he'll deliver the presents to you before all the children here in England.'

'Why?'

'Because France is an hour ahead of us,' said Amber. 'Honestly, don't you know anything?'

'I know lots of things.' Lucy rallied. 'Like I know it's about to snow.' She picked up a handful of polystyrene chips and threw them at Amber. Laughing, Amber got down on the floor and started to tickle her sister. They rolled around together like a couple of puppies and Jack thought how good it was to see Amber relax: these days, she hardly ever let herself go.

Maddie had finally informed him last week of the arrangements for Christmas and New Year, and it was just as he'd feared: the girls were going to France for a two-week skiing holiday. 'Good of you to keep me up to date,' he'd said drily.

'Please don't be like that, Jack,' she'd said, impatiently. 'We've only just decided what we're doing.'

'And I don't suppose it crossed your mind that I might like to make plans for Christmas?'

'Look,' she sighed, 'I'm sorry. It's not as easy as you think.'

'What's so damned difficult? Tony looks at his calendar, reaches for his chequebook and that's it, you're off skiing. I should be so lucky to have that much choice.'

'If you can't be civil, Jack, I'd rather not speak to you.'

'Oh, believe me, the feeling's mutual.'

'I would have thought, if only for the sake of the children, you would make more of an effort.'

That had hurt and he'd lost his temper. 'And if you'd cared more for the children in the first place, you wouldn't have been carrying on with Tony behind my back!'

It had been another disastrous conversation, and once again he had told himself that it would be their last angry exchange. He would keep a lid on his anger. He would swallow his pride. And his bitterness. Except he didn't seem able to.

'Who's for another mince pie?' he asked, when the squeals of laughter died down.

'Me, please!' panted Lucy.

Jack smiled at her. 'Go on, Luce, help yourself. Amber?'

'No, thanks.'

'You sure?'

She pulled her ponytail back into shape. 'I'm on a diet.'

Convinced he'd misheard, Jack said. 'Come again?'

'It's no big deal, Dad, I just don't want to get fat.'

'There's about as much chance of that happening as there is of me becoming prime minister. What's brought this on?'

She shrugged.

'Does your mother know?'

Another shrug.

Appalled, he reached out to her and pulled her on to his lap. 'Listen to me carefully, Amber. You're perfect as you are. Girls of your age don't need to diet.'

She leaned away from him so that she could look him in the eye. 'But, Dad, all the girls at school are doing it.'

He stroked her cheek lovingly. 'Maybe that's because they're not as beautiful as you.'

She didn't say anything, but she leaned back into his embrace and he was reminded of all the times he'd held her as a baby and a toddler. She had been such a tactile little girl. Nowadays the hugs were rarer, but no less precious. He suddenly thought of the baby Clare was carrying and, to his sickening shame and dismay, he couldn't imagine feeling the same strength of love for this new child as he'd always felt for Amber and Lucy.

The next day, Jack drove the girls to have Sunday lunch with Clare. They were meeting her for the first time. He was on edge, as were they. He'd told them about Clare last night while they were eating a Chinese takeaway supper. He had tried to describe Clare as a friend, someone he'd got to know since he'd been on his own. It was the truth, but a little economical. He hadn't wanted to give Amber and Lucy any reason to think they weren't his number-one priority. 'If she's just a friend, why are *we* meeting her?' Amber had asked, her eyes weighing him up shrewdly. Lucy had stopped chewing on a spare-rib and was staring at him too.

'Well, I suppose she's a special friend and I'd like you to meet her.'

There was a pause.

'Are you going to marry her?' asked Lucy. The spare-rib was on her plate now and she was looking at him intently. He leaned across and wiped her chin with his paper napkin. 'There's a chance I might one day. But that's a long way off.'

'But you can't marry her! You're – you're still married to Mum.'

He switched his gaze to Amber. She looked as surprised by her outburst as he was. 'I know that,' he said soothingly, 'but one day I won't be.'

'But why?'

'Why what, Luce?'

'Why do you want get married again? Don't you love us?'

'Love you? I'm mad about you. You mean the world to me. And nothing's ever going to change that. You'll always come first with me.'

He could tell they weren't buying it. They spent the rest of the evening bickering between themselves and went to bed tired and fractious. At breakfast Amber had refused to eat anything and Lucy had cried when her sister had knocked over her favourite mug, breaking the handle off and spilling juice over the floor.

It was not the start to the day he might have wished for, and as Jack parked in front of Clare's house, he had a feeling that things were about to get worse.

Straight away Jack could see Clare was tired. It was also clear that she had put a lot of effort into creating the perfect lunch for Amber and Lucy, food that she was sure would appeal to them – spaghetti Bolognese, then apple crumble and Häagen Dazs ice-cream. More than that, he sensed she was uptight, probably because she knew she was facing the two most critical judges she would ever encounter.

As the four of them sat at the table – decorated with Santa-shaped candles and red and gold crackers – the conversation grew ever more limited. Slumped in their seats, Amber and Lucy were picking uninterestedly at their food.

'Come on, you two, eat up before it gets cold,' he told them.

'But there are bits in the sauce,' Lucy complained, prodding her meal with her fork.

'Bits?' Clare repeated. She looked at the offending item on the plate and laughed. 'That's a mushroom.'

Lucy pulled a face. '*Ugh!* I don't like mushrooms. Mummy never gives them to us. They're slimy – and they might be toadstools. Toadstools are poisonous, aren't they? I saw it on television.'

'I promise you they're harmless, from the fruit and veg counter in Tesco's. Why don't you cover them up with some Parmesan and see if they taste any better?' Clare passed her the dish.

But Lucy didn't take it. 'Can I have some proper cheese, please?'

'Lucy, I don't think—'

'It's okay, Jack,' Clare interrupted. 'There's plenty of Cheddar in the fridge. It won't take me two seconds to grate some.'

He watched her leave the dining room, then turned to his daughters. 'Eat as much as you can, girls,' he said quietly. 'Clare's gone to a lot of trouble for you.'

Neither of them said anything, and when Clare came back into the room, he noticed she was frowning. 'You okay?' he asked, taking the dish of cheese from her. 'You look tired.'

She smiled unconvincingly. 'Knowing my luck I've got that bug that's doing the rounds at work.' She sat down heavily and drank some orange juice.

Ten minutes later, when it was apparent that Amber and Lucy weren't going to eat any more, Clare said, 'You can leave that if you want. I'm sorry I made something you don't like. Next time I'll check with you first, shall I? Perhaps the two of you could put a list together of your favourite meals. We'll call it your Yummy List. What do you think?'

An indifferent shrug was all she got in answer. Embarrassed by his daughters' behaviour, Jack was about to reprimand them when

Clare stepped in before him. 'Hasn't anyone told you it's bad manners not to answer a question?'

Amber looked up sharply. 'And hasn't anyone ever told you to shut up?'

In the silence that followed, Clare stared at her across the table, then at Jack, who was as shocked by Amber's rudeness as Clare had been. 'Amber, what on earth's got into you?' he said. 'Apologise this instant.'

'No!'

'Amber, I'm warning you. Say you're sorry.'

'Why should I when I'm not? I didn't want to come here and I certainly didn't want to eat this!' She raised her hand to point at her unfinished lunch, misjudged the distance and the plate, plus its contents, flipped over. Amber began to cry. 'I hate you,' she cried, looking straight at Clare, 'and I wish you'd drop down dead and leave my daddy alone.'

Jack got up abruptly and knocked his glass: red wine bled into the tablecloth. 'Amber, please, that's no way to speak to Clare, not when she's tried so hard to – Clare, are you all right? *Clare?*'

He watched her try to stand, but she swayed towards him. He grabbed hold of her and held her firmly. 'What is it, Clare? What's wrong?'

'Bathroom,' she whispered. 'You'll have to help me.'

Before they'd got as far as the stairs she was out cold. Keeping as calm as he could, Jack carried her through to the sitting room and laid her on the sofa. Lucy and Amber hovered behind him anxiously. 'Is she all right?' Lucy asked.

'She'll be fine,' Jack said, willing Clare to open her eyes. 'Don't worry. She'll be fine in a minute.'

'Is she going to die?' asked Amber.

His daughter's voice was so faint that Jack had to strain to catch it. He held her hand and squeezed it. 'Of course not,' he replied, keeping to himself that for most of the hair-raising journey to the hospital he had been terrified by the same thought. This is all my fault, he'd thought, driving as fast as he dared. What if she dies? How will I live with the guilt? And why didn't I call an ambulance? All the while, Clare had been dipping in and out of consciousness, alternating between gasps of pain, and frightening silences. Everything told him that she was losing the baby, but that this was no ordinary miscarriage. Des and Julie had lived through that nightmare twice, and he knew from them that what was happening to Clare was different.

'I didn't mean it when I said I wished she'd die,' Amber murmured. 'I'm sorry, Daddy. And I'm sorry about the spaghetti too.' Tears filled her eyes.

Jack hugged his daughter. 'None of that matters, sweetheart. Everything's going to be all right. Clare knew you didn't mean it.'

On his other side, Lucy was swinging her legs and flicking through a tattered comic. She said, 'But what's wrong with Clare, Daddy? What made her suddenly be so ill? Do you think it was those mushrooms? Maybe they *were* toadstools.'

'I don't know,' he lied, unable to meet her gaze. 'Let's wait and see what the doctor says, shall we?'

Chapter Twenty-Two

*

It was the day before Christmas Eve and Dulcie stared in disgust at the amount of food she had just lugged in from the car. It hadn't seemed such a mountain of greed when it had been in the supermarket trolley, but here, in her kitchen, it looked obscene. She began the tedious task of putting everything away in the cupboards, the fridge and the freezer.

If it weren't for her children's nostalgic fondness for a traditional Christmas with all the trimmings, Dulcie would have been happy to kiss goodbye to the whole wretched business and stay in a cottage somewhere remote and beautiful. Even being at home on her own had its appeal: she would be perfectly content with some simple but tasty food in the larder and a few bottles of wine. She never felt the need to live life at a hundred miles an hour, like Prue and Maureen who, if they didn't have a full diary of events, became bored and miserable and longed for the phone to ring. Or invented some reason to ring someone else. Prue had done exactly that yesterday morning, interrupting Dulcie's train of thought when she was trying to finish the short story she was submitting for a competition. She had admitted to the group only last Thursday that writing competitions were her weakness: 'They're addictive,' she had told them, 'so be warned.' With all the festive commitments, they had decided to take a couple of weeks off for Christmas and wouldn't be meeting now until the New Year. She would miss the group over the holiday period.

The last of the food put away, Dulcie stuffed the bundle of plastic carrier-bags into the bin and made a pot of tea. She rewarded her efforts with a glance at the newspaper, ignoring the beds she still had to make up and the towels that needed putting into the guest bathroom. There was plenty of time yet. Kate and Andrew – plus an unknown friend – wouldn't be arriving for another three hours. She had offered to drive across to Crewe to meet them off the London train, but they'd insisted they would catch the connecting train to Maywood – it would only add another forty-five minutes to their journey.

Andrew had been curiously secretive about his friend, saying only that he was bringing someone he was keen for her to meet. Which, naturally, added to Dulcie's speculation that she might soon be on the verge of a new role, that of mother-in-law. She liked the idea. She had asked Kate on the telephone what she knew, but Kate had replied, in what Dulcie recognised as evasive tones, 'Hardly anything, Mum, only that the pair of them seem ideally suited to each other. I don't think I've ever seen Andrew so happy.'

'So it's serious, then?'

'Depends what you call serious,' Kate said. 'Now, stop interrogating me, Mum, it's not fair. Have you put the tree up yet?'

'Yes.'

'The lights working?'

'You want lights?'

'Oh, Mum, don't say you haven't . . . Oh, you're kidding, aren't you?'

'I might be. And before you ask, yes, I've bought chocolate money for you and several kilos of Brazil nuts, which will still be here for Easter.'

'But you can't have Christmas without Brazil nuts. It wouldn't be the same.'

'I know, darling – but just once, I'd like someone to eat them.'

At half past four, just as he'd promised he would, Richard telephoned. He was back at work now, part-time and under strict orders to take it easy – only two and a half days a week. That meant he was able to call Dulcie more regularly. They had even met for lunch. He was looking much better, and Dulcie grew more confident that he would soon be his old self.

But his opening remark had her clutching the receiver in panic. 'Dulcie,' he said, 'you don't have to agree to this, but we're throwing one of our usual Christmas drinks parties and Angela wants to invite you.'

141

'*Me?* Why? Oh, my goodness, does she know? Perhaps she wants to test us, observe us at close quarters as we try to avoid each other. Is that it, do you think?'

'Darling, calm down. It's nothing of the sort. Ever since you met that day in Maywood she's wanted to show off the house to you.'

'I don't care if she's turned it into a version of Graceland with Elvis singing "Love Me Tender" at the door, I don't want to see it.'

He laughed. 'But if it means we can be together for a few hours, wouldn't it be worth it?'

Dulcie couldn't believe what she was hearing. 'Are you saying *you* want me to come?'

'Yes, I do.'

'You're crazy!'

He laughed again. 'Only for you.'

'Richard Cavanagh, these dreadful clichés are going to have to stop.'

'There speaks the writer. So, you'll come?'

'I haven't decided. And you haven't told me when the party is being held?'

'Boxing Day.'

'But Kate and Andrew will be here.'

'Then bring them. The more the merrier. Besides, I'd like to meet them.'

She hesitated. 'I don't know, Richard. What if we give ourselves away?'

'Then so be it, I'm tired of the—'

'Richard,' she interrupted, 'you can't be serious.'

'I've never been more serious. I want to be with you, you know that. Oh, hell, my other phone's ringing, I'm going to have to go. Listen, Angela will probably call you later this evening, so do your best to sound surprised.'

'That won't be difficult.'

It was dark and raining hard when Dulcie drove to the station, but her spirits were high. On reflection, and despite the risk she was taking, she was pleased that she would see Richard over the Christmas period, which she never had before. A mistress was invariably denied such a pleasure.

When she drew up outside the station she saw that the London train must have arrived: the entrance was crowded with people sheltering under umbrellas waiting to be met. She spotted Kate and Andrew before they saw her, and she pipped the horn to attract their attention. Kate saw her first and Dulcie was just wondering where Andrew's girlfriend was when she caught sight of a dark-haired young man. He stood out from the crowd, tall and elegantly dressed in a thick overcoat with the collar turned up. He was strikingly handsome.

I don't think I've ever seen Andrew so happy.

Dulcie drew in her breath and hated herself for feeling shocked. Why had Andrew never told her? Had he thought her so narrow-minded?

These thoughts hurtled through her head in the time it took Kate to lead the way to where Dulcie was parked. Ordinarily she wouldn't get out of the car, would leave the children to throw their luggage into the boot, but on this occasion she felt she should act differently. She had to make it clear from the outset that she was delighted to meet her son's friend. Her son's *boyfriend*? Or was *partner* the more politically correct term? She went round to the other side of the car to hug and reassure Andrew: he looked strung out.

Miles proved the perfect houseguest and Dulcie liked him enormously – not just because he had presented her with a large box of her favourite *pâtes de fruits*. Throughout supper he had been amusing and helpful, and had further endeared himself to her by insisting that he and Kate would tidy the kitchen so that she and Andrew could have a quiet chat. 'Here you are,' he said, pulling a bottle of port out of a bag Dulcie hadn't noticed before. 'Take it with you to the sitting room. Oh, and perhaps you might enjoy this.' A Fortnum and Mason's ceramic pot of Stilton magically appeared.

She watched her son move nervously about the room, picking up a card from the mantelpiece, straightening a candle on the bookcase, even rearranging a bauble on the Christmas tree. She poured two glasses of port and waited for him to speak. She knew Andrew didn't like to be hurried: as a small boy he had always taken his time, whether it was in tying his shoelaces or spooning up the last drops of milk from his cereal. It had been a habit that had driven his sister mad. 'Hurry up!' she would yell at him, as she stamped her feet on the kitchen floor, terrified that she would be late for school. He never had made Kate late, but his placidity inflamed his hot-headed, volatile sister. Mothers instinctively know their children's strengths and weaknesses, and Dulcie had never doubted Kate's ability to cope with whatever life threw at her, but she had worried that Andrew, who had always been a gentle, thoughtful boy, would be taken advantage of. So far, her fears had been unfounded and Andrew had shown himself to be as tough as his sister. If not tougher. He worked ridiculously long hours in a London teaching hospital in a busy ear, nose and throat department. He'd always wanted to be a doctor, and his father would have been so proud that he had achieved his dream.

'I'm sorry, Mum,' he said at last, with his back to her as he examined another Christmas card. 'I should have told you, but the time never seemed right.' He put the card back into its place, turned slowly and met her eye. 'Are you okay about this, or are you putting on one of your famously brave faces?'

'Oh, Andrew, how well you know me, but how little too. Of course I'm all right about it. I'm just disappointed you thought you had to pick your moment to tell me. Surely you never doubted my reaction?'

He smiled. 'Telling your mother that you're gay – even as a supposedly intelligent grown man – isn't easy.'

'How long have you known?'

'Most people say they've known, deep down, for ever, but I wasn't sure until I left home. And before you ask and start to lose sleep over it, I haven't been promiscuous.'

She tried not to look too relieved. But he swooped in on her expression. 'I've always been selective, Mum. And careful.'

'And Miles?'

'Him too.'

'Good.' She kicked off her shoes and tucked her feet under her. Would Philip have handled this so well, she wondered. She liked to think so, but men could be funny about these things. After taking a sip of port, she said, 'How long has Kate known?'

'I told her – or, rather, she guessed – last year. Until then I'd done an excellent job of covering my tracks. Which was stupid and pointless.'

Disappointed that Kate, not normally known for her observational skills, had been more perceptive than she had, Dulcie said, 'I

144

like Miles a lot. Kate told me she'd never seen you so happy. Is that true?'

He nodded and sank into the soft cushions on the sofa opposite her. 'It feels right with Miles.'

Thinking of Richard, she gazed into the flickering flames of the fire. 'I know exactly what you mean.'

'Is that what it was like between you and Dad?'

Dulcie was about to agree, when she changed her mind and decided to share her own secret life with her son. 'This might come as a surprise, Andrew, but I've been having an affair with a married man for the last three years. We're very much in love and I can't ever see the relationship coming to an end.' It was remarkably satisfying to see the shock on his handsome young face.

Especially when he smiled.

Chapter Twenty-Three

*

Lois sighed for the second time. 'Barnaby, do we have to have the television on?' she asked irritably. 'It's so antisocial. We ought to be playing a game. Anyone for Scrabble? Nathan you'd like that, wouldn't you? Beth?'

It was Christmas Eve and they were in the sitting room at Marsh House. Seconds after setting foot over the threshold earlier that afternoon they had been under attack from a steady bombardment of food – ham and mustard sandwiches, mince pies, dates, a chocolate Yule log. Supper had followed, salmon *en croûte* with boiled or mashed potatoes, and a medley of vegetables. They'd got off lightly with dessert – there was only one: pear and almond tart with custard. The waistband of Beth's trousers already felt tight and she dreaded tomorrow when Lois would be up at the crack of dawn to prepare a mammoth lunch that would have brought a team of Sumo wrestlers to their knees. Beth had tried to limit their stay to one night, but Lois had insisted, 'Oh, Beth, you must stay a minimum of three. We see so little of you.'

Once Lois had decided on something, it was futile to resist. Over the years, Beth had tried several times to wriggle out of this annual duty, saying her parents wanted her and Nathan to spend Christmas with them. But Lois had no hesitation about playing her trump card: 'Since we lost Adam,' she'd say, in a small, wavering voice, 'you're all we have. If it weren't for you and Nathan we wouldn't bother with Christmas. There'd be no point.'

Other than wilfully upsetting her, Beth could see no way to change the situation. She supposed that the time would soon come when Nathan would make up his own mind how he would celebrate Christmas. Before long he would be armed with a variety of excuses: newly made friends to visit, work commitments to honour. Oh, how she envied him. Meanwhile, she would still be undergoing this ordeal.

Barnaby had switched off the television, bringing an abrupt end to a Christmas special of *Jonathan Creek*, which Beth had been enjoying, and was now back from his foray in the cupboard under the stairs where Lois kept their collection of ancient board games. 'Scrabble it is,' he announced, with a flourish. He began to set out the board on the coffee table and shook the bag of plastic tiles vigorously.

'There's no need to be quite so rough,' Lois reprimanded him. 'You'll rub off the letters. Nathan, you can go first. Now, then, where are the pencils and the pad of paper I always keep in the box? Barnaby?'

'Clueless on that score, I'm afraid. Drink, anyone?'

As usual they let Lois win – the trick was to give her access to a triple-word score – and as usual they went to bed with strict instructions not to mind Lois getting up early on Christmas morning. 'No, no, Beth, there's no need for you to help. You make the most of a well-deserved lie-in.' Beth had taken her at her word one year and poor Barnaby had spent most of Christmas Day being subjected to mutterings that no one had offered to help.

After a whispered conversation with Nathan, who was in the room next to hers, Beth got ready for bed, slipping quickly into her thickest fleecy pyjamas. She had put a hot-water bottle into the bed earlier: now she shifted it down to her icy toes and pulled up the duvet around her neck.

An hour later she was still wide awake. If she'd been at home she would have got up and made herself a drink, but nothing would entice her to do the same at Marsh House. Instead, she switched on the bedside lamp and reached for the book she was reading. Ewan had recommended it and she was enjoying it immensely. Every time she opened it she felt as if she were connected to him in some way. Their correspondence, which was always a lively and entertaining exchange of views and opinions, had moved on considerably. Their favourite topic was the pros and cons of being a single forty-something.

Would you agree that people in their forties are at their most

reflective and have become more aware of their age and
appearance? [she had asked Ewan].

Only those who are single. The married ones are too busy for
such navel gazing. They have their hands full pretending to their
divorced friends that couples have a much better time.

So that's why my married friends are obsessed with trying to fix
me up. They want me to be in the same boat as them.

Got it in one!

   She knew now that Ewan was forty-six, that he was divorced
and had a daughter called Alice, who was two years older than
Nathan. In his own words he had 'reluctantly' let his only child fly
the nest to go to university:

It was the worst day of my life driving her to Leeds and leaving
her there. I was tempted many times during the journey home to
turn around and go back for her. I'm afraid that makes me
sound a hopeless case.

But I shall be far worse when the same thing happens to me
next year. I shall behave very badly, I know. I'll worry all the
time about the state of his diet and underpants.

But that's the prerogative of being a mother: you're allowed to
behave badly. It's we fathers who are supposed to wear the stiff
upper lip.

   She had also discovered where Ewan lived: in Suffolk, on the
coast. It sounded idyllic: a writer's paradise with views out to sea.
She had told him a little about where she lived and that her view
when she wrote was of the park. She was itching to know what he
looked like, but couldn't pluck up the courage to ask for fear of . . .
well, appearing shallow. Or, worse, pushy, as if she was angling to
turn their correspondence into something it clearly wasn't. All the
same, it would be nice to have an image of him rather than the
mugshot she had created in her mind. She'd decided that he had
short dark hair with just a hint of grey and that he was tall,
perhaps a little overweight – he'd mentioned he was allergic to
strenuous exercise, but that he liked to take a daily constitutional

along the beach, either first thing in the morning before work, or in the evening. When she'd asked what he did for a living, he'd told her he ran his own public-relations business:

My job is to make people suspend their disbelief and accept what they wouldn't ordinarily go along with. It's all in the spin, as they say.

She still hadn't told anyone about the mystery man in her life, as she now thought of Ewan, and she knew that it was dangerous to become fond of someone she had never met. It would be so easy, in view of how little she knew about Ewan, to turn him into something he wasn't, to attach feelings to him that, in reality, were misplaced. It was all very well having a few things in common, such as single parenthood and writing, but what did they *really* know of each other? For all she knew he was a foaming-at-the-mouth racist. And, of course, there was still a chance that he was a serial killer.

But why should any of this matter? she asked herself, as she turned over, still waiting for sleep. Because, as naïve as it sounded, she liked her mystery man, and was convinced that if they met they would get on. She had missed him when he hadn't emailed her for some days – it turned out that his computer had gone wrong and he'd had to replace it. When he'd reappeared on her screen, she'd been so pleased that she'd had to acknowledge how disappointed she'd be if their e-correspondence ended.

She had also forced herself to accept that part of the attraction for her was that Ewan was safe. He was a man with whom she could chat quite openly and not feel threatened. Or, more importantly, because he wasn't 'real' – he was a virtual man floating around in cyberspace – she could allow herself to like him and not feel disloyal to Adam. No one needed to tell her that this was absurd, that after all these years of widowhood she was at liberty to have a relationship with another man, but with Lois's determination to keep Adam's memory alive it was often an uphill struggle to believe it.

At least it was progress. She was now thinking in terms of climbing the hill. And, if she was honest with herself, she got a thrill out of having a secret man in her life. She could let her imagination run wild and conjure up any number of lovely scenarios. It was easy to be in love with someone you hardly knew – you could fill in the rest to your own liking and have the best of all worlds. At the end of the day, romantic love was only a projection of one's thoughts, and why shouldn't she indulge in a little of that?

Nathan woke to the sound of his grandmother singing along to 'Once in Royal David's City', which was playing on the radio downstairs. It was still dark but the noise in the kitchen beneath his room told him that Lois had been up for a while. He buried his head under the pillow. 'Happy Christmas, one and all,' he muttered.

He thought of Billy – lucky Billy – who was spending Christmas in Barbados with his family. His friend had invited him to join him, but even if his mum had been able to afford the air fare he wouldn't have left her to cope alone at Marsh House. To torture himself, he pictured Billy sitting in the shade of a palm tree downing a beer. He held the picture in his mind's eye for some time, telling himself that, one day, that would be him.

But at least he was having a break from college. It had been a busy term, what with *The Importance of Being Earnest* and applying for a place at university. Exeter had made him an offer, as had Sheffield and Hull; he was still waiting to hear from his first choice, Nottingham. He would have to be patient.

The play had gone well and he'd been the only one in the cast not to dry. Even Billy had messed up on the opening night and had had to rely on Nathan to carry him until he'd recovered and got back on track. Lois and Barnaby had had front-row seats on the last night; afterwards, Lois had said how like his father he was on stage. 'Nathan has such a very real presence when he performs,' she'd said to his mother, 'and we all know from whom he gets that.' Nathan had wanted to ask why his mother could never be allowed to take her share of the credit.

That night Jaz had been in the audience, too. He'd hoped she might come to the end-of-show party, but she hadn't.

They hadn't spoken since the night he'd gone round to her place and he'd stupidly asked if he could kiss her. She couldn't have made it any more obvious that she didn't fancy him – not that he'd had any intention of getting her into bed. The memory still made him flinch.

Christmas Day wore on slowly and tediously. Vast quantities of food were pressed upon them, paper hats were worn, terrible jokes were read out. After the Queen's speech, they were given the go-ahead to exchange presents.

As a child it had always been Nathan's job to gather up the parcels from beneath the tree and hand them round. Now, at eighteen, it was still his job: Grandma never saw the point in doing away with a tradition of her own devising. She'd probably get him to act the part of Marsh House Santa when he was a father. In her eyes, he would always be a small boy, the image of her own small boy. Just as his mother would never be anything but Lois's daughter-in-law. Her possession, in other words. He gave his mother a present from Lois. Neither of them needed to unwrap it to know that it was a tea-towel. They had a kitchen drawer stuffed full of them. Next he handed Barnaby a small book-shaped gift with a tag on it bearing Lois's handwriting. Again, no surprises here. It would be a pocket-sized Lett's diary.

'Nathan, dear, before you give me anything, I want you to find a present for yourself. There's a special one for you.'

He did as his grandmother said and reached for a large, flat object, which he knew would be yet another wildlife calendar. He'd been mad about animals when he was six, but now he couldn't give a toss if every panda or red-arsed monkey disappeared off the face of the earth. 'No, not that one,' Lois said. 'The small one to the left of it.'

He held up a long, thin package. 'This one?'

She smiled. 'Take care how you open it – you'll see why.'

He was suddenly the focus of the room. Dreading what he'd find, and preparing himself to look pleased, he sat next to his mother. The wrapping paper dispensed with, he held an old velvet jewellery box. He sensed his mother stiffen beside him, but Lois was leaning forward in her seat. He opened the case and saw a watch inside. It was a Rolex, old and scratched, but he knew its significance. He took it out of the box and looked at it closely. He had no recollection of it.

'It belonged to your father,' Lois said unnecessarily. 'I was keeping it for when you were twenty-one, but I thought that since you've grown into such a sensible young man, you'd be careful enough to have it now. Go on, put it on. Let me see how it looks on you.'

But he couldn't do as she asked. Burning from within, he felt an uncontrollable desire to throw the watch on to the carpet and grind it under the heel of his shoe.

'Nathan?'

He looked up, saw the expectation on his grandmother's face. He was confronted with a choice: he could either do as she said and allow her to bully and manipulate him and his mother for ever, or he could take a stand. He swallowed and made his choice. Very carefully, he put the watch back into its box and snapped the lid shut. He stood up and gave it to his grandmother. 'Thank you,' he said, 'but I don't want it.'

She stared at him, as if not understanding what he'd said. 'But, Nathan, it was your father's. We bought it for him for his twenty-first birthday. He wore it every day. He—'

'Didn't you hear me? I said I don't want it. And if you make me take it, I'll throw it away. I want nothing from my father. Absolutely nothing. I'm sick to death of hearing his bloody name.' He was almost shouting, and out of the corner of his eye he could see that his mother was pale and shocked. Across the room Barnaby's jaw had gone slack. Nathan could see that he was hurting everyone, but he didn't care. This had been waiting to happen for a long time. Wanting to hurt Lois some more, he said, 'And if Adam King was such a fine man, as you keep saying, why the hell didn't he sort out the mess he'd created? Why did he have to dump us in it by killing himself? He was nothing but a pathetic coward and I hate him for what he did to Mum.'

He heard his grandmother start to cry, but he didn't hang around. He grabbed his coat from the hook in the hall, the keys in the pocket, and slammed the door after him. He threw himself into his mother's car, started it and hit the accelerator. Gravel flew into the air as he took off down the drive. He didn't know where he was going, or what he would do when he got there, but he had to get as far away from his grandmother as he could.

Beth stood on the doorstep and watched her son narrowly miss colliding with one of the gateposts. Near to tears, her arms locked around herself, fear flooded her.

What if history repeated itself?

Consumed by a frightening anger she had never known before, Beth went back into Marsh House. Lois was going to pay for this.

Because of her selfish, blind stupidity she had made Nathan act dangerously out of character. If anything happened to him – God forbid that it did – she would see to it that Lois carried the guilt of this day to her grave.

Chapter Twenty-Four

*

After checking that the oven was at the right temperature, Richard slid a tray of vol au vents on to the top shelf. Behind him, Henry and Victoria, home for Christmas, were slicing oranges to go into the mulled wine. The three of them were chatting and laughing together. They didn't notice Angela come into the kitchen. 'You all seem very cheerful,' she said. Her brisk voice instantly quietened them.

Closing the oven door, Richard said, 'How about a drink, Angela? A quick gin and tonic before everyone descends on us?'

'Thanks,' she said. 'I think I will.' She reached for her apron to protect the new blouse and skirt she was wearing and tied it round her waist. Her decisive movements suggested she was making the effort to take charge. She picked the wooden spoon out of the pan of mulled wine, put it on the draining-board and found a ladle. 'Don't you think you ought to go and change, Henry?' she said.

'Plenty of time yet.' He shambled across the kitchen towards his father and added a splash more gin to his own glass. It was nearly twelve o'clock, and Henry was still in his pyjamas and dressing-gown; his hair was sticking up in clumps on top of his head. As a small boy he'd hated getting dressed and had gone to extraordinary lengths to avoid it – he still did. But it was a trait at odds with the ambitious and hard-working thirty-four-year-old man he had become. He worked in the City as a broker for an American bank, drove a Porsche, and had recently bought a flat in Canary Wharf. By his own admission, he was filthy stinking rotten rich. Richard always found it difficult to equate the confident Henry of today with the bungling little boy he and Angela had frequently taken to hospital because, yet again, he had tripped and bumped his head.

He handed Angela her drink and joined his daughter, who was clearing up the mess around the chopping-board, fastidiously wiping and tidying: a habit she had picked up from him. Out of the four children Victoria was the quietest and, perhaps, the most intuitive. She kept her opinions to herself, and only expressed them if pushed. When she did, they were always worth listening to. She rarely judged others and could always be relied upon to defuse an inflammatory situation. In many ways, she reminded Richard of Dulcie: they were both easy to be around.

Nervously drumming her fingers on the steering-wheel while she waited for the traffic-lights on Bridge Street to change, Dulcie wondered if it wasn't too late to back out. She must have been mad to accept Angela's invitation. She had even tried to use her children as an excuse to stay away.

'Oh, bring them too,' Angela had said.

'But Andrew's got a friend with him. We couldn't possibly impose—'

'Nonsense. She's perfectly welcome too.' Like Dulcie, Angela had assumed that Andrew's friend was a girl.

'I'm not sure.'

'Henry and Victoria will be here so there'll be other young people for them. They won't have to stick with us old codgers.'

Dulcie had taken umbrage at that: Angela might see herself as past it, but Dulcie certainly didn't.

'Wakey, wakey, Mum, the lights have changed.'

She looked at her daughter. 'What? Oh, silly me.' She drove on. 'I hope you won't be too bored at this party,' she said. 'You could have stayed at home and amused yourselves.'

'It's always good to broaden one's horizons,' Kate said. 'And, anyway, didn't you say an eligible man's going to be there? I need to cast my net wherever I can – I'm not getting any younger.'

In the back of the car, Miles laughed. 'Oh, Kate, don't sell yourself too cheap.'

'It's all right for you two soul-mates,' she retaliated, with good humour. 'You've joined the ranks of the happily hitched. I'm almost thirty – only five months to go – and if I'm not careful I'm going to turn into a bitter old spinster. So, Mum, tell me again about the eligible bachelor.'

'I never said he was eligible, or that he was a bachelor,' Dulcie said, disconcerted. 'He'll probably turn out to be thoroughly obnoxious with bulging eyes and buck teeth.'

Kate tutted and Dulcie exchanged a look of concern with Andrew in the rear-view mirror. Having shared her secret with him, she had made him promise not to tell anyone about her affair with Richard, and she knew from his expression that he was thinking as she was – that it would be disastrous for Kate to form an attachment with Richard's son, Henry. She considered telling Kate now about her and Richard, to warn her off, but she decided against it. Andrew could be relied upon to be discreet – hadn't he proved that with his relationship with Miles? – but Kate could not. As a child, Kate's face had always given her away. Philip used to say that she was as honest and open as a book. With Fiery Kate, as he called her, you always knew where you stood. But despite her apparent toughness, she was easily hurt and capable of holding a grudge for as long as it took the guilty party to make amends. She had tremendous staying power, which Dulcie presumed was an asset in the dog-eat-dog world of advertising where Kate worked.

But perhaps she was being unfair to her daughter, pigeonholing her too rigidly. Hadn't she kept quiet about Andrew's relationship with Miles? For a split second Dulcie was seriously tempted to tell her daughter about Richard, but the moment was lost when Kate leaned forward and switched on the radio, then tutted at her mother's choice of music station. 'How can you listen to that bland trivia?' she said, fiddling with the buttons until the authoritative tones of Radio 4 filled the car.

Richard had almost given up hope of Dulcie coming. All the other guests had long since arrived, even those who made a habit of being late. With several drinks inside them, they were happily swapping Christmas Day gripes: of turkeys that hadn't tasted of anything, pullovers that would have to be returned to M & S, of livers and waistlines that would never be the same again. As well as friends and neighbours from the village, and the odd parent from school, they had invited some of his colleagues from the office, and if he hadn't been on such tenterhooks waiting for Dulcie to appear, he would have considered the party a success.

He was on his way to the kitchen to make sure that plenty of wine and soft drinks were available when he heard the doorbell ring. His heart leaped. Dulcie? 'I'll get it,' he called to Angela, who was in the sitting room instructing Christopher and Nicholas to pass round the canapés.

He opened the door and saw, to his delight, that he'd been right. He smiled the smile of a congenial host and shook hands with Dulcie. 'Mrs Ballantyne, how lovely to see you again, and after all this time. How are you? Come on in.' Her reply was lost in the moment of closing the door behind them, and he switched his attention to her family. He introduced himself, recognised Kate and Andrew at once from the numerous photographs Dulcie had of them around her house. Her son, he noted, took after her: he had the same wide cheekbones and the broad forehead that Dulcie covered with a wispy fringe. The daughter was pretty, with dark eyes and an expression that was alert and friendly. She had her mother's wide smile. Lastly, he shook hands with a good-looking man whom he suspected might be of interest to Victoria. 'Hi,' he said. 'You must be Andrew's friend up from London.'

'That's right. Miles. That's the name, not the distance. Sorry, it's a shocking joke and I really ought to know better by now.'

Richard smiled, grateful that someone was helping the conversation along. 'Let me take your coats and get you a drink.' He ushered them in the direction of the kitchen, weaving a path through the crush of guests. He hoped he appeared to anyone observing him as good old Richard getting drinks for a group of new arrivals, not a man who was cheating on his wife and had had the audacity to bring 'the other woman' into the family home. Some would be appalled by what he was doing. 'Who'd have thought Richard Cavanagh capable of such duplicity?' he could hear his critics say. 'And we thought he was such a decent man. But you know what they say, it's always the quiet ones. The ones you'd least suspect.'

Yet as contemptible as his behaviour might seem to others, it didn't feel so awful to him. What's more, he wanted to put an arm round Dulcie's shoulders and declare to everyone that this was the woman he loved, that he had never felt so strongly for anyone as he did for her. He wanted to share his good fortune, to say, 'Look, happiness is a choice. Leave it too late, and you'll regret it.'

Much as he was tempted to devote his time to Dulcie and her

family, he couldn't: there were other guests to see to, drinks and food to organise. Moreover, he ought to find Angela and tell her that Dulcie had arrived. But before he did that, he stood back to observe Dulcie as she chatted with Juliette, a young legal executive who'd recently joined his department at work. Seeing how relaxed and fully composed Dulcie was, and loving her for it, he knew with certainty that this was the woman with whom he wanted to spend the rest of his days.

He was so sure of what he wanted that he knew the time had come to tell Angela. He would go quietly. He would do everything in his power to make their parting bearable. He would give her the house, most of their savings, and whatever percentage of his pension she was entitled to. More, if necessary. And the boys, Christopher and Nicholas, they mustn't suffer. He would do whatever it took to keep the pain, the confusion and upheaval to a minimum.

From across the room, Dulcie caught him looking at her. She gave him one of her half-smiles and his heart swelled. He raised his glass to her and wandered off to the conservatory to find Angela. She was nowhere to be seen, but he discovered that this was where the 'young people', as Angela called them, were hiding. They seemed to be getting along well enough. 'Sorry to barge in,' he said. 'You all okay for drinks?'

'Fine, thanks, Dad, though some food wouldn't go amiss.'

He smiled at Henry. 'Give me a hand, then, and we'll get you sorted with some supplies.'

Back in the kitchen, loading up a tray of dips, crudités, canapés and anything else that was going, Richard said, 'How's your sister getting on with Miles?'

Henry shook his head. 'Definitely not her type.'

'You surprise me. I would have thought he was exactly her type. Smartly dressed and very good-looking.'

Henry lowered his voice. 'And very gay, Dad.'

'Oh. Oh, I see.'

'He's Andrew's partner.'

'Really? Dulcie never . . . I mean Mrs Ballantyne never said anything.'

'Don't sound so middle-class and shocked. Why should she say anything? It's no one else's business. But, between you and me, I'm rather taken with the lovely Kate.'

'Kate?'

'Your memory going, Dad? Mrs Ballantyne's daughter. I think if I play my cards right, we'll be seeing each other in London. Often, if I have anything to do with it.'

Richard slowly absorbed what his son was saying. He pushed the tray of food at Henry. 'I've just remembered something I was supposed to do.' He hurried back to the sitting room to find Dulcie. He had to tell her that under no circumstances could *his* son and *her* daughter become involved with each other.

Chapter Twenty-Five

*

Intolerable: insufferable, impossible, from hell, insupportable, unendurable, unbearable.

Jaz closed the thesaurus with a weighty slap. None of those words came close to what she had to put up with. If Dr Roget and his pals had had first hand experience of a Christmas with the Raffertys, they'd have thought of something far more explicit and appropriate. But, try as she might, she couldn't think of any one word that expressed the horror of living with her family. Finally, she admitted defeat and picked an adjective at random: *insufferable*. It would do for now, until she could think of something better.

The more she wrote, the more she found that sometimes words were inadequate: they just didn't supply the right meaning. It was as if they turned into a strait-jacket that wrapped itself round her brain. She knew how she felt, right enough, but couldn't convey it on paper. The thought depressed her: now even the secret world in which she lost herself was mocking her. Maybe she wasn't cut out to be a writer: she had been fooling herself all along.

She switched off the computer, and went to lie on the bed and stare up at the sloping ceiling. It was proving the longest, most boring Christmas known to mankind. They'd trailed round all the relatives, or had had them here, and if Tamzin and Lulu asked her one more time to play Twister with them she'd have to hit the booze cupboard big-time. To make it worse, there was no one to hang out with or chat to on the phone – Vicki was away, visiting her grandparents. Never before had Jaz longed so much for a holiday to be over. She'd done all her homework and was all revised-out in readiness for her mock exams the first week of the new term. There was nothing else to do.

She'd hoped that her mother might take her clothes-shopping when the sales started, but it looked like it wouldn't happen now. Not with Mum being pregnant. Dad was worse than a hen these days, fussing over his Molly-doll as if she was a piece of china. And Mum had gone all airy-fairy. She hadn't been the slightest bit cross when she came home from Tenerife with Dad and found her favourite ornament broken and a stain on the carpet. The only good thing to come out of that incident was that her sisters had kept quiet about the policeman who had reprimanded them. To this day, they still thought Nathan had been a real plain-clothes officer, and every now and then, when they really got on her nerves, she would remind them quietly that if they didn't leave her alone she would tell Mum and Dad they'd behaved so badly that she'd had to call the police.

She thought again of what a good job Nathan had done in putting the wind up her sisters, and smiled. Anyone who could do that was a true hero. But the smile soon disappeared when she thought of what an idiot she'd been. She had overreacted and now she had lost Nathan as a friend. And she would give anything, right now, to have his company.

She flipped over on the bed and buried her face in the pillow. Oh, she'd made such a mess of it. Hundreds of times she had wanted to pluck up the courage and apologise to him, put things back to how they'd been, but she hadn't been able to face him. She had watched him in the play and thought him brilliant – far better than Billy, who everyone always raved about. She hadn't gone with Vicki to the party after the last-night performance: her pride wouldn't let her. She couldn't bear the thought that he might throw her apology back in her face, in front of everyone.

Once, at the writers' group before Christmas, when Jack was talking to Dulcie, she had almost asked Beth how Nathan was, just to see if he had mentioned her to his mother. But, again, her nerves and pride had got the better of her.

If she thought of Nathan too much, and how he must despise her for her immaturity, she felt sick with shame, so it was better to push him out of her mind.

It was a pity the writers' group wasn't meeting during the

holiday – at least that would have given her something worthwhile to focus on. She missed her secret Thursday nights out.

Bored, and restless with frustration, she decided to go for a walk. She hunted for her favourite baggy jumper among the pile of clothes on the end of her bed. On her way downstairs she met Phin coming up. From the look of him he was just back from a night out. There was a massive love bite on his neck and he stank of booze and fags. He yawned hugely and messed up her hair. 'Hey there, little sis, how's it going?'

'Fine until you appeared stinking like a brewery. I see you've had some old bat chewing at your neck again.' She tried to slip past him, but he didn't move, just stood there grinning at her. 'Phin, can you figure on your own how to shift yourself, or do you want me to help?' She dodged round him and made her escape. Her mother was in the kitchen, listening to the radio while she stripped the turkey carcass – it would be turkey curry that evening, it always was the day after Boxing Day. She noticed how tired she looked, and felt sorry for her. 'Need a hand, Mum?' she asked.

Molly looked up. 'That's okay, Jaz, I'm just pottering. Where are you off to?'

'I need to fill my lungs with some of that stuff they call fresh air. Are you sure you don't need any help?'

'No. Off you go and enjoy yourself.'

Disappointed, Jaz shut the back door behind her. She hadn't wanted to do anything as gross as pick over turkey bones, but part of her would have liked her mother to want to include her in something. They never did anything together, these days. She frowned. When had she become an outsider in her own home, so out of step with everyone else?

The day was cold, almost freezing, and the sky was grey and heavy with the promise of snow. There was that lovely quiet muffled feeling in the air that she'd loved as a young child. She had always known when it was going to snow. She pulled down the long sleeves of her jumper, covered her hands to keep them warm and headed towards the park.

At a loose end, Nathan was standing at the kitchen window. The park was busy with young families: small children wearing helmets were trying out new bikes, and others were showing off their skills on shiny new scooters. But there was no mistaking the solitary figure in black jeans and knee-length baggy sweater that came into his field of vision from the right of the park. It was Jaz.

He watched her play with one of her long plaits as she settled on a wooden bench, and thought how much he missed her company. Missed her as a good friend, someone with whom he could talk. It still annoyed him that he had botched things so spectacularly. Perhaps he should apologise. He decided that there was no time like the present, slipped on his coat, locked the door after him, and went downstairs to tell his mother – who was knocking back mince pies and dry sherry with Miss Waterman – that he was going out.

He took the short-cut route to the park, through the gate at the end of Miss Waterman's garden. He made his way over to where Jaz was still sitting on the bench. 'Hi,' he said casually, when he was almost upon her.

She looked up, startled. She must have been deep in thought. 'Oh. Hi.'

'Okay if I join you?'

She slid along the wooden seat to make room for him. 'Good Christmas?' she asked.

'You don't want to know.'

'It must have been better than mine. You've met Tamzin and Lulu. Need I say more?'

'Yeah, well, while you were having a picnic with them, I stirred up World War Three.'

'Who with? Not your mum, surely?'

He shook his head. There were many things in his life that he would always remember, but the look on his mother's face when he'd arrived home late on Christmas night – he'd known she would be at the flat, just as she'd known he wouldn't go back to Marsh House – was one that would stay with him for ever. She had been crying, and he'd known why: he had put her through seven hours of hell. She had been convinced that he was lying dead in the wreckage of their car. But she hadn't lost her temper, as he'd expected her to. 'I was too relieved that you were alive to be cross with you,' she'd admitted later. 'Besides, I took out my anger on Lois.'

'Really?'

'I'm afraid that, between us, we've blotted our copybook at Marsh House. We won't be welcome there for a long time.'

'I didn't mean that to happen.'

'I know. But until your grandmother sees sense and understands

163

why you lost it with her, I think we have to accept that she will not be 'at home' to either of us in the foreseeable future.'

'You're making light of this, aren't you?'

'I'm not sure I can do it any other way.'

He didn't ask for the details of what had been said in his absence, but before going to bed, she said, 'Nathan, promise me that you'll never drive again when you're not fully in control of your emotions. Driving while out of your mind with anger is as dangerous as being drunk behind the wheel.'

It was only in the morning, in the cold light of day, that he realised how selfish he had been. He hadn't thought about anyone's feelings but his own. He had never known such rage, and it had been directed solely at his grandmother. He had hated her with all his being. Hated her for pretending she could make his father live through him.

Aware that a silence had settled on them, and that he hadn't given Jaz a proper answer to her question, Nathan turned and saw that she was looking at him intently, but when his gaze met hers, she lowered her eyes. He couldn't work her out, couldn't decide whether she liked him or not. 'You look cold,' he said. 'Do you want to walk?'

She was on her feet almost before he'd got the words out. 'It looks like it's going to snow,' she said.

They wandered down towards the pond where a family with two young children were feeding the ducks. They continued along the path, and when a boy riding a bike much too big for him, came careering in their direction, Nathan instinctively pulled Jaz out of harm's way. When the boy had passed, he let go of her, embarrassed. 'Sorry,' he said. 'That's an even blacker mark against my name, isn't it? Rough-handling in the name of safety probably goes down as well as asking for a kiss.'

She stared at him, her brows drawn together. For a nasty moment she looked so furious that he thought she was about to thump him. But then, just as he noticed a snowflake land on top of her head, her face broke into a tentative smile. Once again, just as he had on the night of Kirsten's party, he had the urge to kiss her. This time, though, he didn't ask permission, simply leaned in close and pressed his mouth gently to hers. Her lips were icy cold, the same as his, but he sensed no coolness in her. He wrapped his coat around her shivering body and looked down into her pale, lightly freckled face. 'Just for the record,' he murmured, 'I have no immediate plans to drag you off into the bushes for a mindless shag.'

She stiffened within his arms. 'Please don't tease me.'

He held her firmly, understanding, now, the real reason why she had brushed him off before: she had thought he would treat her like Billy would. 'I'm not,' he said. 'I'm trying to put your mind at rest.' He felt her relax and kissed her again. And, as the snow fell slowly around them, he felt strangely at peace. Being with Jaz made him happy. Holding her made the rest of the world disappear.

No more Lois.

And no more Adam King.

Chapter Twenty-Six

*

For five consecutive years Des and Julie had thrown a New Year's Eve party, but this year, now that they had Desmond Junior, they had agreed to give tradition a miss and settle for a low-key evening with a bottle of bubbly and Angus Deayton on the telly.

But, to Des's disappointment, even those simple plans had been thwarted.

After he had given in to Julie's last-minute insistence that her friend couldn't possibly spend New Year's Eve alone – 'Not after all she's gone through' – Clare had arrived yesterday afternoon to stay the night. When she wasn't berating Jack for being such a bastard, she was begging them, as the wine flowed, to make him see sense. 'I'm sure he's terrified of being hurt again,' she'd said weepily, clutching at the finest of straws. 'That's why he's done this. He cares for me, really. I know he does.'

It didn't matter what he or Julie said, Clare wouldn't listen: it wasn't advice she wanted but the opportunity to vent her feelings. She was wretchedly unhappy and, in Des's opinion, given her weakened state after what had happened, she shouldn't have been drinking so much. If at all. In the end, so that they could go to bed and get some much-needed sleep – it was nearly four in the morning – Des had promised to talk to Jack.

Now, at five past seven, while he was giving a perky little Desmond his breakfast, Des knew it wouldn't do any good. Jack had made his decision and, for what it was worth, Des was right behind him. Okay, maybe his timing might have been better – telling Clare it was over while she was still recovering from an ectopic pregnancy hadn't been the smartest or most sensitive way to handle it – but the upshot was that Clare had to accept she and Jack were finished.

Spooning mushy Weetabix into his son's open mouth, then scraping off the excess goo, Des hoped that his friendship with Jack hadn't been damaged. Friends were often expected to take sides in these situations and currently Julie had little sympathy for Jack. What she refused to acknowledge was that while Clare had been carrying his child Jack had been prepared to do the decent thing and stick by her, even though he had admitted to Des that he didn't love her and didn't think he ever would.

Lost in his thoughts, he didn't hear footsteps coming into the kitchen. Clare was standing right next to Desmond Junior's high chair before he noticed her. 'Hi,' he said. 'How're you feeling?' He didn't need to ask: still in her nightclothes with traces of yesterday's makeup – what had survived the tears of last night – smudged around her eyes, she looked hollowed out.

'In need of a cup of coffee,' she murmured.

Desmond Junior whipped his head round at the sound of her words and the spoonful of Weetabix that Des had been about to slip into his mouth smeared across his cheek. He put up a small chubby hand, grinned, then rubbed it into his hair. Des put the bowl of cereal prudently out of reach and fetched a cloth from the sink. 'Sit down and I'll put the kettle on for you,' he said. 'Breakfast will be a while yet. If you and Julie are good, I might do us one of my famous fry-ups. Gotta start the year as we mean to go on.'

She dropped into the chair opposite the one he'd vacated. 'Sorry, Des, I'll have to pass.'

'Nonsense,' he said cheerily. 'You need building up, and there's nothing like a plate of eggs, bacon and devilled kidneys to put the colour back into your cheeks—'

He didn't get any further. Clare's complexion had turned green – not quite the colour he'd had in mind – and she rushed from the kitchen to the downstairs loo. Poor girl. A hangover as well as a broken heart. Hardly the best way to start the New Year. He wondered how Jack was feeling this morning.

Jack had been up since six thirty and was on his fourth cup of coffee. He was in the spare room doing the one thing that kept him from dwelling on Clare. So long as he focused on the troubles and dilemmas of his characters, he could block out the events of the last few weeks.

But not entirely. He would always feel responsible for putting Clare through such a painful ordeal. The guilt he'd felt while she had been undergoing the emergency operation to remove the tiny foetus that had caused one of her Fallopian tubes to rupture had been unlike any he had ever known. And while it was far from ideal that Amber and Lucy had witnessed the frightening scene of Clare's collapse, he had been glad they were with him at the hospital: they gave him something to think of other than his own culpability. When he had been told that the operation had been a success and that Clare was going to be all right, he had almost wept with relief.

Shortly afterwards, and he knew it had been unthinkably selfish, he remembered that he'd had a lucky escape, and that he had to act on it . . . as soon as Clare was over the worst. But decisive action came sooner than he'd intended.

With her parents staying while she convalesced at home, Clare started talking in earnest about how much she wanted Jack to move in with her. He couldn't lie to her or give her false hope and, as her mother loaded the washing-machine downstairs and her father fixed a wonky cupboard in the kitchen, he'd found himself telling her it was over between them, that if she were honest, she would admit that she had known this for some weeks too. He'd held her hands and looked her straight in the eye as he'd spoken, knowing he would never have been able to forgive himself if he'd done it any other way.

'You bastard!' she'd murmured, withdrawing her hands from his. 'Couldn't you at least have waited until after Christmas?'

The irrationality of her question hadn't struck him till he was driving home. Of all the things she could have accused him of, it was his poor timing that had mattered most. It struck him then that it more or less summed up how superficially Clare viewed him. She expressed her love for him readily enough, but the reality, he was sure, was that she had been in love with the fantasy of a happy ending.

He hoped that there would come a day, soon, when she would accept that they were never meant to be more than friends. But when he'd voiced this thought, she hadn't been ready to hear it. 'Don't you dare suggest that that's what we should now become. I never want to set eyes on you again. Because of you, I'll probably never be able to have children.'

He hadn't argued with her, although the surgeon who had operated on her had said it was still possible for her to have a normal pregnancy in the future. 'I'd advise against rushing things,' he had said, 'but essentially you're still in with a good chance of producing a healthy baby.'

For Clare's sake, Jack had to believe this was true.

At half past nine he finished the chapter he'd been working on since yesterday morning. He set the printer running and took his empty coffee cup to the kitchen. He was ravenous. He opened the fridge and helped himself to a packet of sausages, some bacon, two eggs and a tomato. Within half an hour he was back in the spare bedroom eating his breakfast and reading through the printed pages. Anything he wasn't quite happy with, he marked with a pencilled comment in the margin. On the whole, he was pleasantly surprised by how well the chapter had come together. He didn't kid himself that what he had written would put him on the shortlist for the Booker Prize, but it struck him as eminently readable. According to Dulcie, *Friends and Family* could be categorised as 'bloke lit', which sounded disparaging, but as this was the term used to describe the books of Tony Parsons, Nick Hornby and Mike Gayle, he considered himself in excellent company. In the last month he'd read all the books by these authors and had quickly noticed that he was writing from the same perspective – guess what, guys have feelings too!

His breakfast eaten, he leaned back in his chair, his hands clasped behind his head. It wasn't just having written another chapter that pleased him, it was knowing that he was starting the year on a positive note. He had made an important decision on the stroke of midnight last night, a New Year's resolution, you could say, which seemed to have been staring him in the face for some weeks. He intended to make an offer on Miss Waterman's flat.

The idea had come to him out of the blue, but perhaps it had been there subconsciously for a while. A new start in a new home was just what he needed. Admittedly he hadn't been all that taken with the flat when he'd first seen it, but it had grown on him. Probably because he'd seen what Beth had done with hers. She had made it into a real home – and that, more than anything, was what he wanted. If he closed his eyes he could picture himself living there, could even visualise knocking through from the kitchen to the sitting room to make one large comfortable room – again, as Beth had done upstairs. The flat also had the added advantage of the park being right on the doorstep: the girls would be able to let off steam there. Okay, Amber was getting too old for swings and slides, but the tennis courts might appeal to her. If she fancied it, he could find a coach and she could have lessons.

Now that he had resolved matters with Clare, he could plan for the future.

At what he considered an appropriate time to call, bearing in mind that it was New Year's Day, Jack phoned Beth to enquire after Miss Waterman. 'She's well on the mend,' Beth said, 'much more her old self. Why? Have you got good news for her about the flat?'

'I might have,' he said carefully. He didn't want to say anything to Beth before he spoke to his client. 'So, you think she won't mind if I give her a quick call?'

'I have a much better idea. Why don't you come here for lunch? Adele's joining us. As is a friend of Nathan's. Someone you might know.' There was a hint of a laughter in her voice.

'Are you sure? I don't want to intrude.'

'If that were the case I wouldn't have invited you. It'll be very informal. No need to get dressed up.'

He spent the next hour showering, shaving and dressing, not because he wanted to impress Beth but because he was in dire need of smartening himself up. While he'd been off work – four days at home alone – he'd adopted some distinctly slovenly habits: he wrote all day in his scruffiest clothes and didn't bother to shave. If it hadn't been for his writing, he didn't know how he would have survived Christmas and New Year. By absorbing himself in the world of *Friends and Family*, he had escaped the mess of the one in which he lived. It wasn't only the guilt of what he'd done to Clare that had weighed so heavily on him: it was also being apart from the girls. This was the first Christmas when he hadn't been with Amber and Lucy and he missed them like hell. On Christmas morning he had unwrapped their present and had spent the next hour deciding which photograph to put in the frame they'd given him. He finally settled on a photo he'd snapped of the two of them in the summer when they'd gone on holiday to Devon – hair bleached by the sun, faces freckled, and smiles widened by the good time they were having.

The streets were empty as he walked to Maywood Park Road, his footsteps echoing along the deserted pavements. A hard frost had left gardens and grass verges cloaked in a whiteness that sparkled in the sunlight. But there was no warmth in the sun and his breath hung in the cold, sharp air. At bang on one o'clock, he rang Beth's doorbell. Minutes passed before she appeared. 'Happy New Year,' he said, and passed her the bottle of champagne he'd had in the fridge but hadn't felt inclined to open last night.

She took it from him with a smile. 'How very kind of you. *Brr* . . . come on in! It's freezing out there.'

He followed her upstairs and through to the sitting room, where Miss Waterman was resplendent in what had to be a 'special occasion frock'. She looked regal and a lot better than when he'd last seen her. He told her as much when they shook hands. 'It's the sherry Beth keeps giving me,' she said, pointing to a small glass on the table beside her chair. 'That and the delicious food she's spoiling me with. I've decided. I should be ill more often.'

'I'm not sure that's such a good idea, Miss Waterman' Jack said.

'Please, don't be so formal. Call me Adele.'

From behind him, he heard a familiar laugh. He turned to see Jaz coming through the front door – so this was the someone he might know whom Beth had mentioned on the phone. Following hot on Jaz's heels was a tall lad whom Jack took to be Beth's son.

It was during lunch that Jack brought up the reason for his visit. 'I've found you a buyer, Adele,' he said, 'and one I have every reason to believe will be a dead cert. There's no chain involved at his end so it would be a straightforward sale.'

'Really?' she said. 'How wonderful. This *is* good news.'

'Hang on a moment,' Beth said, pausing with a dish of roast potatoes she was passing to Jaz. 'No one's been round to view Adele's flat for ages. Who's made an offer?'

'Ah,' he said, amused by her sharpness, and her continued protectiveness of the old lady. 'Time to come clean. It's me. I'm making an offer.'

'Is that ethical?' asked Adele.

'It is if he's divvying up the full asking price,' said Beth.

'Everything will be done above board and correctly,' said Jack. 'Have no fear on that score. And, yes, I'm offering the full asking price. What's more, so that you can be sure there's no funny business going on, I'll pay for you to have the property independently valued. That way you'll know I've priced it correctly.'

'Well,' Adele beamed, 'I'm delighted with the news. I can't think of anyone I'd rather have moving into my flat.' She raised her glass. 'To you, Jack. I hope you'll be very happy living here in Maywood Park Road.'

'Thank you. I'll be instructing my solicitor first thing tomorrow morning. So long as no one has any objections.' He looked directly at Beth.

'And what possible objections could I have?'

'I'm just making certain that I meet with the approval of the chief custodian of my client's business affairs.'

'It goes without saying that there'll be a detailed questionnaire for you to complete before your offer is accepted. One can never be too careful.' Then, looking round the table, she said, 'If everyone's finished, I'll clear away.'

'That's okay, Beth,' said Jaz. 'Nathan and I'll see to this. Won't we, Nathan?'

'Will we?'

'Yes, so on your feet and be quick about it.'

Adele winked at Jack, and when Jaz and Nathan were stacking dishes over by the sink and making a noisy job of it, she said, 'Don't they make a lovely couple?'

'Stop it, Adele, or I shall have to send you home. Without your party bag. More wine, Jack?'

'Please.'

Beth topped up Jack's glass, then her own – Adele was sticking with sherry – and while Nathan and Jaz larked around at the other end of the room, she let Jack talk business with his client. Surprised though she was by his announcement, she welcomed the prospect of having him as her new neighbour. She had dreaded neighbours from hell moving in. The only downside to the arrangement would be that she would now have her work cut out convincing the mischievous Adele, and the sceptical Nathan, that there was nothing going on between her and Jack. She had seen the look on Adele's face earlier and knew all too well what the old lady was thinking.

But her neighbour's misplaced determination to bring about a romantic union for Beth was the least of her worries. She hadn't

172

seen or spoken to Lois since Christmas Day, and not for lack of trying. Each time she had telephoned Lois had cut her dead. 'I have no wish to talk to you, Beth,' she had said. 'You've treated me abominably. And after all I've done for you and Nathan. What really hurts is that I believe you've deliberately turned my only grandson against me by filling his head with lies about my poor Adam. I shall never forgive you for that.' Her voice had been shrill and she was evidently on the verge of tears.

'But, Lois, you know as well as I do that Adam committed suicide. Every report that was made on his death reached the same conclusion. The coroner's verdict was—' She got no further. Lois slammed down the phone.

There had been many moments when Beth had regretted her outburst at Marsh House after Nathan's dramatic departure on Christmas Day. She had turned on Lois with a viciousness she hadn't known she was capable of. 'You stupid bitch!' she had yelled at her mother-in-law. 'You stupid, unthinking bitch! Have you any *idea* what you've done to my son? And do you even care?' Backed against the bookcase, Lois had stared at her, her mouth open, her eyes wide. But she didn't answer Beth.

Barnaby had tried to intervene and cool things down. 'Come on, Beth,' he said, patting her arm. 'Shouting won't help anyone. Let me get you a drink and we'll discuss this—'

She shrugged him off. 'You're wrong, Barnaby. On this occasion, shouting is exactly what's needed. I just wish I'd done it years ago.' Her gaze was back on Lois. 'The truth is, you don't give a damn, do you? You're so obsessed with keeping a pathetic myth going, a myth nobody else believes, that you've lost sight of what's going on around you. Nathan despises you because you've refused to accept that his father was anything but perfect. He was a normal human being, Lois. A man who, when the chips were down, couldn't go on.'

It was then that Lois spoke, and she attacked Beth the only way she knew how. 'If you had been a better wife Adam would never have been so depressed!'

'You don't think his upbringing was responsible? It was you who brought him up to believe that no member of the King family was allowed to fail. Poor Adam, you taught him that there was only one rule by which he had to live, and that was to win. But when it came down to it, he wasn't the tough fighter you wanted him to be. And when he realised that it was too late. He was set on a course from which there was no escape other than to end his life.' She pointed her finger at Lois. 'You made him do it, Lois. You made Adam so ashamed of failing that you might just as well have handed him the bottle of whisky and car keys yourself.'

Lois swallowed hard, and held her head high. 'I want you to leave, Beth. I want you out of my house. Now.'

Barnaby had offered to drive Beth home and she had accepted. 'I'm sorry, Barnaby,' she said, once Marsh House was behind them. 'I've put you in a bloody awful situation. But right now, this very minute, I'm not sorry for what I said. That will probably come tomorrow and I'll feel terrible.'

Barnaby didn't say anything. He just nodded, his face sad and tired. He helped her into the flat with her bags, Nathan's too, and stood awkwardly in the hall. 'I'd better not stop,' he said, staring miserably at his shoes. 'Lois will be needing me.' He reached out to open the door, then hesitated. 'He was my son as well, you know. I think people forget that sometimes.' His eyes misted over, but before Beth could say anything, he had pulled the door shut and was gone.

Beth had kept all this from Nathan, not wanting to burden him any more than he already was. She blamed herself for not having seen the signs, for not having realised just how deeply affected Nathan was by Lois's constant comparisons between him and his father. Both Simone and her mother had been right: they had warned her to put a stop to Lois's make-believe version of Adam's death. And life. Her only hope now was that time would heal the rift. An outside hope was that Barnaby might find the courage to talk to his wife. But that was unlikely. Barnaby might tease Lois, but he would never go behind her back. He was the most loyal of husbands.

She had waited hours for Nathan to come home that night, despairing of ever seeing him alive again. It was the longest wait of her life, and when she'd heard his key in the lock, she had rushed to meet him. They were both too wrung out to talk properly about what had happened, but in the morning they went for a long walk to clear their heads, and the awkwardness between them. 'How did you know I'd come home?' he asked.

'I didn't think you'd show your face at Marsh House so soon and, anyway, I was asked to leave. I'll tell you about that later. For now, talk to me about your father. You don't really hate him, do you?'

'Sometimes.'

'He doesn't deserve that.'

Nathan kicked at a stone on the path and frowned. 'You speak as if he's still alive.'

'I meant his memory. What's left behind of him doesn't deserve to be treated that way.'

'But I have so little memory of him. And what I do have has been spoiled by Lois.'

'Then we have to work on that. I don't know how, but we'll do it. I promise.'

Meanwhile, Beth was left with myriad feelings of guilt, anger and confusion. Not so long ago, if faced with a crisis, she would have looked automatically to Simone for advice and support, but she hadn't this time. Instead she had turned to Ewan, telling him everything that had happened, recounting all the ghastly details as if she was writing it out of her system.

By sharing the problem with an outsider, she felt less disloyal to Lois. When she had mentioned this to Ewan, he'd said,

It's loyalty to Lois that's helped to create this mess. How about a bit of loyalty to your own self-respect? Sounds to me as if Lois has tried systematically to diminish you, Bethany.

That sounds harsh.

It was meant to be. No point in dressing up what you already know to be true.

Ouch. And double ouch. Are you always this blunt?

Only with . . . those who I care about.

Flummoxed by his comment, she hadn't known how to respond. A further message appeared on her screen.

Strike that disclosure from the record if you'd prefer. My fingers are getting above themselves.

No [she'd typed, after another brief hesitation]. It was nice. It took me by surprise, that's all.

An okay-ish surprise?

Yes.

In that case, I have a favour to ask. But first, do you have a scanner?

Nathan has one. I could use that. Why?

How do you feel about exchanging pictures of ourselves?

Smiling, she'd replied,

Only if you promise not to cheat.

What? Like do some sneaky cutting and pasting to enhance my naturally cute features?

Something like that, yes.

Hand on heart, I'll play it as straight as you do.

This had taken place last night and they'd agreed to do the exchange this evening. The photograph Beth was going to use was one that Nathan had taken of her at Ben and Simone's farewell party last year before they'd left for Dubai. She hoped it showed her at her best.

She was shaken out of her thoughts by Jaz and Nathan clattering dessert plates and cutlery on to the table. She glanced up and noted how relaxed her son was as Jaz flapped a napkin at him. Before yesterday, when Nathan had asked if it was all right for him to invite Jaz to lunch, she'd had no idea that they were such good friends. Or, rather, such *close* friends.

With the horror of Christmas Day still hanging over them, it was good to see him so happy.

Chapter Twenty-Seven

*

Whenever Ewan was anxious, frustrated or under pressure, he had a fail-safe method for taking his mind off what was bothering him: he opened a bottle of wine and made bread. At the time of his divorce, when he had been struggling to hold down a job and look after Alice, he had stumbled by accident upon this little-known form of therapy.

One afternoon, when Alice hadn't been feeling well, he'd offered to cheer her up by making one of her favourite treats: gingerbread. The tray of gingerbread men – stumpy fellows with misshapen legs and arms – had been such a success (they were edible!) that he had felt compelled to flick through the cookery book to see what else he could turn his hand to. Bread looked easy enough and, working on the theory that the end result of throwing grains of yeast into warm water and sugar was no more mysterious than basic chemistry, he had taken on a white loaf and found the task immensely absorbing. And relaxing.

His début baking days were long behind him, and now his repertoire included pizza bases, wholemeal plaited loaves, potato bread, garlic and herb bread cooked in terracotta pots, and cheese and chilli flatbread. Tonight he was making a poppy-seed loaf and as he sank his fingers deep into the soft dough he felt the soothing effect almost instantly.

It was usually when his brain went into overload that he turned to the flour bin for solace, but on this occasion the reason was that he was having second thoughts about exchanging photographs with Beth. They had agreed to do the deed at midnight, and as the time grew nearer – it was eleven thirty-six – he couldn't shake off his rising doubts.

Would it be a mistake?

And wasn't this just what he'd wanted to avoid?

What annoyed him most was that he had no one to blame but himself. He had sent himself down this particular route, so if anything bad happened as a consequence it would serve him right.

The stupid thing was that he was genuinely bothered by what Beth might think of him. He'd never considered himself a looker: in his opinion, he was just an ordinary middle-aged man with lines fast developing around his eyes, grey hairs aplenty and the kind of filling-out face that was as average as it was unmemorable. Even he sometimes had trouble in the morning recognising himself. Who the hell are you? he'd think, when he looked in the mirror to shave. Where's that energetic young man I used to be? Alice said he was getting too hung up on his age, that he should stop being such a vain old slapper.

While his daughter had been at home for Christmas, he'd confided in her about Beth. 'Are you out of your mind, Dad?' she'd cried. 'What was it you used to lecture me about? Oh, yeah, I remember. I wasn't to talk to strangers.'

'This is different,' he'd said defensively, all too aware of the truth of what she was saying. If the boot had been on the other foot and Alice had struck up an on-line relationship with a man she didn't know he'd be waving the parental big stick at her.

'Different?' she'd said. 'Like hell it is! For all you know this "Beth" could be a man getting off on some weird sexually perverted game he's playing with you.'

'Credit me with a modicum of savvy,' he'd replied.

With her hands on her hips – a typical Alice stance – she'd argued, 'Show me an ounce of evidence that you know who or what she really is.'

It wasn't the first time their roles had been reversed – and certainly wouldn't be the last. As he stared into her stormy face, all he could say was 'Sometimes one has to take a chance in life. Some risks are worth taking.'

'I'll remember that when I'm hitching a lift home at two in the morning, shall I?'

'Oh, Alice, it's not the same.'

'Seems to me that it's a case of don't do as I do, do as I say.'

There was no arguing with his headstrong daughter so he'd agreed to disagree. 'Whatever does it for you, Dad,' she'd said, helping herself to a slice of cold turkey from the fridge, 'I would have thought there were easier ways for an eligible man like you to pull.'

'I'm not on the pull!'

'Then perhaps you should be. You have a lot to offer, Dad. You're a better catch than you think you are. You're intelligent, funny, and not bad-looking. The only downer is that you're as rich as Midas. But, hey, nobody's perfect.' She opened the fridge again and helped herself to more turkey.

'Why don't you get the whole thing out and make a sandwich?' he suggested.

'Too much effort.' She shrugged. 'Mm . . . these chipolatas are great. Any cranberry sauce left?'

'Second shelf down.'

After another rummage in the fridge, she turned to him and said, 'Oh, and something I have to ask, as the only responsible adult round here. Are you indulging in regular cyber-sex? Because if you are, I hope you're taking precautions.'

'What? Like wearing a spellchecker at all times?'

She smiled. 'Just be careful, Dad. I know you think you're a great sage with all the answers, but really you're just an innocent. You haven't had enough experience with women.'

'Oh, go right ahead and build a man's confidence up, why don't you?'

She pointed at him with the stubby remains of a sausage. 'Okay, then. How many women have there been since Mum?'

He scowled. 'A few.'

'Too few. And it's not as if you don't get plenty of offers.'

'Yes, but they're not from anyone I'd be interested in.'

'But this Beth character does interest you?'

He hesitated. 'As a friend, yes. And . . . and if it so pleases the prosecution, may I be excused any further interrogation? I have some mail to see to. Of the snail variety, I might add.'

A glance at the kitchen clock told Ewan that it was now eleven forty-five. He kneaded the dough some more and pondered over his feelings for Beth. Despite all of Alice's warnings, innuendoes and jokes, he really did view Beth as a friend – and a friend he wanted to get to know better. It was obvious that their correspondence meant a lot to both of them; certainly Beth had shared some pretty personal stuff with him. But by taking this step of seeing what the other person looked like, were they running the risk of spoiling what they had? Odds on, and he reckoned he was a fair judge of human nature, if Beth didn't like the look of him, she would 'run out of things to write about' and the correspondence would grind to a halt. And, of course, it worked the other way too. If Beth had a smile on her like a snarling pit-bull terrier, he'd think twice about continuing.

It was inexcusably shallow, but it was the way the world worked. Always had. Always would.

He thought of the photograph he'd already scanned into his computer. It was slightly out of focus and lopsided, but he'd chosen it because, for once, he appeared as he actually saw himself. He had any number of better photographs to choose from, but they all tended to distort who he really was.

At eleven fifty-two he covered the dough with a damp tea-towel, put the bowl on the shelf above the radiator, washed his hands, poured himself another glass of wine, and approached his office.

'Okay,' he said aloud. 'It's Checkpoint Charlie time.'

Beth clicked on OPEN, closed her eyes, held her breath and waited for Ewan's picture to materialise, knowing that he would be doing the same in Suffolk.

It was the most excruciating moment. Would Ewan turn out to be the greasy-haired, bespectacled, nerdy anorak she'd always hoped he wasn't?

She opened a cautious eye and saw that the electronic wizardry had done its stuff. More bravely now, she stared at the screen and saw a face that . . . that she liked the look of. Reflected in his relaxed expression was the humorous warmth she had come to know through her exchanges with him. His smiling mouth was framed by two deep lines at either side, which gave the impression that he was holding back a laugh. She couldn't be sure what colour his eyes were, the picture quality wasn't that good, but she had a feeling they were blue. His hair, short and grey – no hint of a centre parting! – was receding. She hoped that her photograph was being equally well received in Suffolk.

Ewan's first thought was that Beth was just the kind of woman he would look twice at. It wasn't only the fair hair or the slim body that appealed to him, but the brightness of her smile.

His second thought was that he wanted very much to meet her. It was in his head for no more than a nanosecond before he squashed it flat. It was the dumbest thing he'd ever come up with.

Or was it?

Chapter Twenty-Eight

*

It was the first Thursday of the year and the first time the group would be together since half-way through December. There had been no word from Victor – not even a Christmas card in return for the one she'd sent him – and Dulcie decided to give him a call, to see if he was going to join them.

Using the phone in the kitchen, she tapped in Victor's number from her address book and waited for him to answer. She supposed that if he had left the group for good she should re-advertise Hidden Talents, although she would have to check with the others first. Dulcie sensed that Beth, for one, would prefer to keep things as they were. The doorbell interrupted her thoughts and she replaced the receiver with a feeling of relief, more than happy to put off the task of encouraging Victor back into the fold.

Richard was standing on the doorstep. 'What a lovely surprise,' she said. But straight away she could see that something was wrong. His arms didn't linger around her as they usually did when they embraced, and the kiss was on her cheek, not her mouth. 'Come through,' she said, keeping her voice light to disguise her concern. While she filled the kettle to make some coffee, she watched him prowl uneasily round the kitchen.

'What is it, Richard?' she asked, his behaviour making her anxious. 'Is it Angela? Does she know? I knew it was a mistake to accept her invitation to your party.'

He came over to her, put his arms round her shoulders and held her to him. 'You're jumping to conclusions, and that's so unlike you.'

She slipped out of his grasp, looked into his face. 'Then what is it? Have you been overdoing it and made yourself unwell again?'

He shook his head. 'No, I'm fine. But it's what we dreaded. Henry and Kate are seeing each other.'

'No!'

'I'm afraid it's true. Henry phoned last night. They've met up regularly since they got back to London. Oh, Dulcie, there was something so . . . so upbeat in his voice. And I know it's only a couple of weeks, but my guess is that this is more than a passing fancy. Henry has fallen hook, line and sinker for Kate. He's mad about her.'

Dulcie tried to think straight. This couldn't be happening. She and Richard had been scrupulously determined to keep their affair secret so as not to hurt his family, and now this. When Richard had first warned her at the party that Henry had hinted he was taken with Kate, she had been as shocked as he was. But what could they do? She had driven home reminding herself that Kate might joke about casting her net to catch a boyfriend, but the reality was – as Kate had often said – she was too engrossed in establishing herself at work to want to be sidetracked by a serious relationship. Thus Dulcie had reassured herself that there was no need for them to warn Kate off Henry. She had always agreed with Mark Twain when he wrote, 'I have spent most of my life worrying about things that have never happened.'

'Maybe it's one-sided,' she said finally. 'Kate hasn't mentioned anything to me.'

'When did you last speak to her?'

Dulcie tried to think straight. 'When she rang to thank me for Christmas. More than a week ago.'

Richard frowned. 'A lot could have happened in that time.'

'Well, it certainly seems to have,' Dulcie said stiffly. She made the coffee and they went into the sitting room. 'So what's to be done?' she asked, when they were settled on the sofa.

He stared across the room, through the french windows and out on to the terrace where a robin was pecking at the frozen water in the stone bird bath. 'I'm damned if I know,' he said.

She reached for his hand, and as her fingers touched his skin, she saw how things stood. 'You want me to warn Kate off, don't you? I have to tell her about *us* and the inappropriateness of there ever being a Kate-and-Henry?'

Slowly he faced her. 'You do see that it's the only way, don't you? I can't possibly tell Henry. I'd have to tell him why.'

An unexpected niggle of resentment rose in Dulcie. That, and the motherly need to fight for her daughter's freedom to go out with whom she chose. What right did she or Richard have to interfere with her life? 'I thought you no longer cared what others thought,' she said, her voice flat. 'I thought you were on the verge of telling Angela about us.'

If he caught the pointed bluntness in her words, he chose to ignore it. He passed a hand over his face. Suddenly he looked very tired. 'But not like this. This . . . this would be too brutal. I couldn't do it to her. Surely you understand that?'

Dulcie understood only too well. The world was full of women who had to carry out other people's dirty work.

The college library was packed with students doing what they weren't allowed to do: eating, drinking and chucking things about. A rubber landed on the A4 pad on which Jaz was making revision notes. Without looking up – she knew that the culprit was a greasy-haired, cretinous oik from the upper sixth – she placed it on the desk in front of her, wishing that Mrs Barr, the librarian, would come back. With so much noise going on, she gave up on her Seamus Heaney notes and allowed herself to think of something more interesting: Nathan.

It was official. Jaz Rafferty and Nathan King were an item. It was also official that they would not be one of those awful couples who slobbered over each other in the lunch queue or held hands in the corridor – like Billy and Vicki. One reason behind this was that Jaz didn't want to attract attention to herself or have people discussing how soon it would be before Nathan tired of her. Since Billy and Vicki had got it together, supposed friends were openly betting on who would dump whom first. It was all so sordid and shallow. Also, she didn't want anyone in her family to find out about Nathan. The thought of her sisters pestering her, her brothers teasing her and, worse, her father interrogating her had made her extract a promise from Nathan that he wouldn't call for her at home. 'And only ring me on my mobile,' she'd insisted.

'Are you embarrassed about me?' he'd asked.

'No. I just like to keep certain areas of my life private,' she'd said, not admitting that it was the rest of Raffertys who embarrassed her. 'I don't want everyone knowing what I do. Least of all my family.' To her shame, she was lying even more to her parents, telling them she was at Vicki's whenever she was with Nathan.

They saw each other most days. Usually they went back to his place after college. She liked where he lived: it was so quiet. When Beth was out at work, and it was just the two of them in the flat, they would lie on the sofa in silence. The first time they'd done this he had wanted to put on a CD for them to listen to, but she'd said, 'Please don't.'

'Why? Don't you like my choice of music?'

'It's not that.'

'What, then?'

She'd tried to explain how good it was to hear nothing but the beat of your own heart. That all she got at home was constant mayhem: doors banging, voices shouting, music blaring. 'If you had to put up with that you'd understand.'

He'd wound a lock of her hair around his finger and smiled. 'You're not like other girls, are you?'

She wasn't offended by his comment. She knew she was different and was destined never to fit in. People would always refer to her as strange, a loner. Often, as if peeping through the crack in a doorway, she caught glimpses of herself when she was older: she was always alone.

At the far end of the room, the door flew open and an instant hush fell on the library. It was Mrs Barr. Thank goodness for that, thought Jaz. Now she'd be able to get some work done.

When college was over Jaz walked home with Nathan. He wanted to call in at Novel Ways, and when he'd found the book he needed for some background reading on Virginia Woolf they decided to have a drink in the coffee shop. 'We'd better not stay too long,' she said, after they'd paid for their café latte and had found themselves a table. 'It's my writers' group tonight and I've still got some revision to do for my exam tomorrow.'

'No sweat, I know the score. Mum was on at me this morning not to be too late either.'

She smiled. 'How awful for you – two women nagging you.'

'Could be worse. I could make the mistake of listening to them. Hey, who's so interesting you can't tear your eyes off him?'

'Sorry. I've just noticed someone from the writers' group.' She lowered her voice. 'His name's Victor. Your mum must have told you about him. He's the biggest pain going.'

He followed her gaze across the coffee shop to where Victor, trousers half-way up his legs, pens stuffed into his jacket pocket, was tussling with a small sachet. When he managed to rip it open, sugar scattered over the table and several sheets of handwritten notes. Jaz could see exactly what was going to happen next and, sure enough, Victor waved a hand impatiently at the mess and promptly knocked over his cup. A puddle of brown liquid flooded the papers and dripped on to his trousers. There was something so pathetically hopeless about the silly man that Jaz felt sorry for him. She scooped up a handful of napkins and went over to help. 'Hi,' she said. 'I thought these might come in handy.'

He seemed not to recognise her. 'A cloth might be of more use,' he said ungraciously, on his feet now, shaking the papers so that the coffee dripped on to the wooden floor. Amused that he appeared to be holding her responsible for his own ineptitude, Jaz went to the woman behind the counter and asked if she had something with which to clear up the mess. The woman gave her a handful of paper towels. 'He's one we could do without. Every day he sits there scribbling away, and he's as tight as they come. He makes a cup of coffee last more than an hour. I hate skinflints.'

On her way back to Victor, Jaz raised her eyebrows at Nathan, who was smiling at her. 'There you go, Victor,' she said. 'Are your papers okay? Are they from *Star City*?'

He narrowed his eyes at her, and finally she saw recognition dawn. 'Oh, it's *you*,' he said.

'Well, it certainly was the last time I looked in the mirror. Are you coming to the group tonight? It's our first meeting since the Christmas break.'

Making a poor job of mopping up the puddle of coffee, he muttered something unintelligible. Jaz left him to it.

'Was that your good deed for the day?' asked Nathan, when she was sitting down again.

'For the entire month, more like. Honestly, he's such an ungrateful weirdo. I bet the words "thank you" don't appear in his vocabulary.'

She was still thinking this when, later that evening, she rang Dulcie's doorbell and recalled what the women who worked in the coffee shop had said about Victor always being there. If that was true, why wasn't he at work? The obvious answer, she decided, was that he was on holiday.

Chapter Twenty-Nine

*

From as early as Victor could remember, life had dealt him a rotten hand. As a child his hard work was never rewarded as it should have been. It didn't matter how hard he tried at school, his reports rarely reflected the true worth of his endeavours. He'd been surrounded by idiots, show-offs and bullies who boasted of never doing a stroke of work but somehow always got straight As for the end-of-term exams. He, who had diligently applied himself week in week out, was denied the grades he deserved. He knew it was because the teachers didn't like him. He'd once corrected the English teacher on a point of grammar – 'Sir, I think you meant to say, if I *were*, not if I *was*' – and was ridiculed for the rest of the term. Thereafter, and because of the flak to which he was continually subjected, he was known as Victor Flakmore.

It was no better when he left school at sixteen and started work as a junior clerk in the local council offices. From day one he was expected to be the general dogsbody and the butt of everyone's jokes. 'Oh, Victor, be a love and open a window for us,' the girls in the typing pool said to him on his first day, causing him to blush and fumble with the stack of papers he'd been sent to deliver. Fanning themselves with their long-nailed hands and undoing the buttons on their tight-fitting blouses, they'd sighed and swivelled on their typist's chairs, showing off their legs. The windows had been similar to the ones at school, high and narrow, the kind that required a long pole with a hook at the end to open them. A tall, busty girl from the front row of desks had risen from her seat and approached him with it. 'Just shout if you need any help, Victor,' she'd said, towering over him and thrusting her massive bosom into his face. Nearly suffocating from the smell of her cheap scent, he'd started to shake, stammered that he had to be somewhere else, dropped the pole and bolted. Their laughter had followed him the length of the corridor and up the stairs to the third floor, where he shared an office with half a dozen other men, all of whom were coarse and of below-average intelligence. They had sniggered at him when he burst in, and he'd realised that he'd been set up.

Just as he had at work before Christmas. He'd worked for J. B. Reeves and Company for almost twenty years. He'd started as a rep, driving round the North West of England with a bootload of office-supply equipment, but selling had never been his strong suit and after six months he was offered a job in the accounts department. Initially it meant a drop in salary and no car, but he didn't mind because at last he'd found his niche. He was a great believer in dotting Is and crossing Ts. There was also something satisfying about keeping an eye on the firm's money. He had a keen nose for sniffing out irregularities on expense claims and he had no qualms in summoning a miscreant to his office to explain himself. He knew that behind his back he was called Penny-pinching Blackmore, but he didn't care: his word was final. Ultimately they had to toe the line or not get paid. It made him unpopular, but his duty was to the company. It was his job to stamp out the cheats who thought they could steal from their employers, whether it was claiming for petrol that hadn't been used for business purposes or sneaking toilet rolls home in shopping-bags.

He had always done exactly what he was paid to do and a lot more besides. He had been a loyal, trustworthy employee who had given his all. He'd been punctual, consistently hard-working, seldom took his full holiday entitlement and had only once missed a day – and that had been to attend his mother's funeral. Which was why he felt so aggrieved by what had happened, just before Christmas, when he was called into the senior manager's office. He had been expecting news of the bonuses that came at that time of year, but instead he was informed that he had been made redundant. 'You're not alone,' Steve Cartwright had said, as if it would help. 'Cuts are being made across the board. People younger than you are being given their terms. It's them I feel sorry for, guys with families and mortgages to keep afloat. From your point of view, at least you only had six years to go before retirement. If I were you, I'd treat this as a lucky break, an excuse to go off and enjoy yourself with Mrs Blackmore.'

'There is no Mrs Blackmore.'

'Oh, I'm sorry to hear that. When did – when did she pass away?'

'She didn't. I've never been married.'

He'd returned to his desk, furious. Steve Cartwright had worked at J. B. Reeves for five years and hadn't known the first thing about one of the firm's longest-serving employees.

'Streamlining' was what head office was calling the loss of jobs. Indiscriminate bullying was what it amounted to, picking on those unable to fight back. Oh, it had been ever thus. But he'd show them. By God, he'd show them. Now that he had time on his hands, he'd finish his novel, get it published and revel in its success. He'd prove to the whole damn lot of them that while they thought of him as no more than Penny-pinching Blackmore – an expendable employee – he was a true winner.

Yes. Victor Blackmore was a winner.

He had programmed himself to say this, aloud (if he were alone), every half-hour, and as his digital wristwatch pipped the hour – eight o'clock – he put down his pen, closed his eyes and said, clearly, 'Victor Blackmore, you are a winner.' He repeated the words several times, visualising the glory of *Star City* displayed in the window of Novel Ways. He also pictured a long line of people queuing patiently to buy a signed copy.

Several years ago the company had brought in a supposed expert on team-leadership skills and one of the pieces of advice the woman had given was that self-affirmation was the key to fostering a strong belief in oneself. She had suggested they start their day with a mantra that would help them to feel more positive about themselves. Until he was made redundant he had ignored such preposterous psychobabble, but now he was writing in earnest, he was prepared to do anything to secure his future success as one of Britain's leading authors. It was this belief that got him out of bed every morning, stopped him losing faith. He reminded himself regularly that redundancy was the best thing that could have happened to him: hadn't it given him the chance to concentrate all his energy on his book?

What he disliked most about losing his job was the look on people's faces when they asked him why he wasn't at work. Only the other morning, as he put the rubbish out, his neighbour – a young man with a Vauxhall Astra that he washed and polished every weekend and parked in front of Victor's house – had asked him about his job. 'Working flexi-hours, are you now, Mr Blackmore? You're a lucky bloke, wish I could. What wouldn't I give for a lie-in?'

And what wouldn't he give for people to mind their own business? Like that girl this afternoon in the coffee shop. Poking her nose in where it wasn't wanted. Why couldn't people just leave him alone? Of course he wasn't going to bother with that absurd excuse for a writers' group. He had more talent in his big toe than the rest of those amateurs between them. He'd known it would be a mistake to join them and, once again, he'd been proved right. He really ought to trust his instinct. Hadn't his mother always said that the only person one could trust was oneself?

His love of books had come from his mother. She had read to him from as early as he could remember, and every Saturday morning they had gone to the library together. While she searched the shelves for a crime novel she hadn't yet read, he knelt on the dusty wooden floor to make his choice from the limited selection of children's books. Before long he was writing his own stories, tales of escape and heroic adventure, of good guys who would save the world from notoriously evil villains. He wrote and wrote, always in private, and always to blank out the daily grind of school and the bullying he had to endure.

He swallowed at the painful memory of there being no one to whom he could turn and, recalling that it was Thursday, he pictured the writers' group sitting in that smug woman's front room doing nothing more constructive than playing silly word games. What was the point in that?

Writing. That's what it was all about. Solid writing. Head down, words on the page, nothing to distract the focus.

He used to write downstairs in the dining room, but he'd found there were too many distractions – the noise of the children playing next door, the fussy pattern of the wallpaper, the creak of the table, the tick of the clock, the smell of burning dust from the electric fire. Now he worked upstairs in the smallest bedroom at the back of his terraced house. He'd emptied it of all clutter, removed the bed, the chest of drawers, the pictures on the walls, the carpet, the curtains, even the lightbulb from the overhead fitting. In place of these extraneous objects, he now had nothing but a desk and a chair, which he'd placed in front of the window. During the day, when he wasn't writing in the coffee shop, he worked there, and at night he lit the room with candles. He allowed himself no form of heating, other than a small Calor Gas burner on which he boiled water for mugs of tea and heated cans of baked beans or tomato soup. If he felt the cold while he was typing, he wrapped a blanket around his shoulders. And there was no danger of being interrupted by the telephone: he'd had it disconnected.

He had made a proper artist's garret to work in, and by depriving himself of any comforts he hoped to dig deep into his creative soul and produce his best work.

The thought that he might be taking things too far never crossed his mind.

Chapter Thirty

*

Dulcie woke with what was now a familiar sense of foreboding.

It had been the same every morning since Richard had told her about Kate and Henry. That had been more than two weeks ago and, as she'd promised Richard, she had called her daughter some nights later, prepared to explain the situation. But on hearing the happiness in Kate's voice as she had talked so enthusiastically about Henry – she couldn't believe how well they got on, how ideally suited they were, and how much they had in common – Dulcie had lost her nerve: she couldn't bring herself to burst the bubble of her daughter's euphoria. All she could hope for was that whatever was going on between Kate and Henry would fizzle out within a month or two. Kate bored easily and boyfriends never lasted long.

She had told Richard this over lunch the day before yesterday. Sitting in the kitchen, with the low January sun streaming brightly through the french windows giving the illusion of a warm spring day, there had been a tension between them that she had never known before. 'I disagree,' he'd said, when she'd explained how she felt. 'I'm convinced that Henry wants something to come of this relationship with Kate. He'll pursue her until he gets what he wants. He was like that as a child. He might not look the determined go-getter but, believe me, beneath the affable exterior is a will of iron.'

'Have you spoken to him again?' she'd asked.

He shook his head. 'No, but Angela has. He phoned last night while I was out. When I got home she was full of what he'd had to say. She seems to find it enormously amusing that life should be taking this particular turn. "We could end up being related to Dulcie Ballantyne."'

'What did you say?'

'I said I thought it highly unlikely, and that she was jumping the gun somewhat.'

'But you don't believe that, do you?'

'No. There just seems something horribly inevitable about the situation.'

She'd reached across the table and touched his hand lightly. 'This isn't like you, Richard. I've never known you so fatalistic.'

'I can't help it.' He sighed wearily. 'It's how I've felt right from the start when Henry first mentioned Kate at the party. It's as if we're destined not to be together.'

'Nonsense,' she'd said robustly. But she couldn't think what else to say to reassure him.

Out of bed now, she poured a few drops of the aromatherapy oil Andrew and Miles had given her for Christmas into her bath water, and went downstairs to see what the postman had brought that Saturday morning. Her heart gave a tiny jolt when she saw a large, buff-coloured envelope with her own handwriting on the front. She left the rest of the mail on the hall table but took this upstairs to read in the bath.

Once she was settled in the warm scented water, she dried her hands on the towel beside the bath and opened the letter. She let her eyes skim over the first few words. This time there was no rejection. No 'Sorry, better luck next time.'

Dear Dulcie Ballantyne,

I am delighted to inform you that your short story 'Young At Heart' has won first prize in our annual creative-writing competition. We had a record number of entries this year, of an extremely high standard, but the judges were particularly impressed with your clear use of narrative and full understanding of your central character.

You might like to know that all winning entries are to be published in our quarterly magazine, which we will, of course, be forwarding to you when it is to hand.

Please find enclosed your prize money. May it encourage

you to go on to bigger and better things.
   Yours sincerely,
   M. Cadogan
   (Competition Secretary)

Paper-clipped to the back of the letter was a cheque for fifteen hundred pounds.

Her earlier mood was immediately replaced with a burst of pure happiness. Elated, she sank back into the water and allowed herself to gloat with satisfaction. At her age she had experienced the full gamut of highs and lows that life could offer, but nothing matched the thrill of having one's writing accepted. She had won prizes before, admittedly not as large as this one, and she'd had nearly a dozen short stories published, but the thrill never diminished.

Her happy mood stayed with her for the rest of the day. Until the phone rang early that evening.

'Hello, Kate. How are you?'

'I'm fine, Mum. Well, better than fine. Lots better, in fact.' Girlish laughter – which Dulcie rarely heard from her daughter – echoed down the line. 'The thing is, I'm ringing to let you know that I'm moving in with Henry. We only decided this afternoon, but as of tomorrow I'll be living in—'

'Kate, slow down! When did you decide to take such an important step?' Even to Dulcie's ears, her question sounded heavy-handed.

'Oh, come on, Mum. You must have guessed this would happen sooner or later.'

'You don't think you're hurrying things a little?' Dulcie struggled to keep her voice level.

Kate was quick to go on the attack. 'Did you say that to Andrew and Miles?'

'No, but that was different. They'd known each other a lot longer before they—'

'Don't you like Henry? Is that it?'

'How can I answer that when I hardly know him?' She was stalling. Hopelessly so.

'Then you'll just have to take my word for it. I wouldn't be moving in with him if I didn't love him. He's everything I want in a partner. Oh, Mum, I really think he's The One.' There was more girlish laughter and Kate went on to list Henry's finest qualities.

Only half listening, Dulcie closed her eyes. It was just as Richard had feared.

'Mum, are you listening to me? Honestly, here I am, baring my soul, and you're not even—'

Rallying herself, Dulcie said, 'I heard every word. And I'm very pleased for you.'

'Good. So tell me what you've been up to since we last spoke. No chance of there being a man in your life, I suppose?'

Dulcie forced a laugh. 'Heavens, what made you ask such a question?'

'I don't know. Maybe it has something to do with being so happy myself. I sort of feel I'd like the same for you.'

The irony was not lost on Dulcie. 'I'm touched,' she murmured.

'You shouldn't leave it too late, Mum. I know you won't believe me but you're still a good catch. There's bound to be a man out there who'd be interested in you.'

'Thank you, darling. I'll try to remember that when I'm at a low ebb.'

'Rubbish! You've never been at a low ebb in your entire life. You're the most positive and upbeat woman I know.'

It was dark by the time she got off the phone and, sitting in the study in a pool of soft light cast from the lamp on her desk, Dulcie lowered her head. As a mother, she could not deny her daughter the chance to be happy, which meant she had to sacrifice her own happiness.

If there was to be a Kate-and-Henry, there could not be a Richard-and-Dulcie. The mix was too volatile. The pressure on Kate and Henry would be intolerable. The natural way of things was that sons gravitated towards their mothers, but if Henry wanted to be with Kate – whose mother had broken up his parents' marriage – how would he ever be able to look Angela in the eye? And how would Angela view Kate?

No. She had no choice but to end her affair with Richard.

Chapter Thirty-One

*

It had snowed heavily during the night, just as the weather forecasters had said it would. As Jack pulled back the bedroom curtains, he squinted at the brightness that met his eyes. Everything was covered in a blanket of sculpted whiteness. Along the riverbank, branches drooped under the weight of the snow and, from a crystal blue sky, the sun shone down on the intense beauty of the day. Lou Reed's 'Perfect Day' came into Jack's mind. He had the whole weekend off, the girls were with him until Sunday evening, and this afternoon he was taking them to see what would soon be his new home. Theirs too, albeit it on a part-time basis.

Almost a month had passed since he'd made his offer on Adele Waterman's flat and so far the purchase was going through without any delay. Owing to the efficiency of both solicitors involved, contracts had been exchanged and, if his luck held, he'd move in during the second week of February. As an estate agent, he had seen it all when it came to the best-made plans going awry, but he had every confidence that his own move would be accomplished without any hitches. He was looking forward to it: the purchase of a home was a step in the right direction. He knew how important it was for his daughters to believe that he was happy, and he had talked a lot about the new flat last night when he'd collected them from Prestbury. As they tucked into the takeaway pizzas they'd picked up on the way home, he'd stressed how great it would be once he'd made it his own. To do that, he told them, he needed their help. 'I want you to choose the wallpaper for your bedroom and all that kind of thing,' he'd said. 'You'll be much better at it than me.' Lucy had jumped at the opportunity, but Amber had been less enthusiastic. Unnervingly, she had looked at him as though she suspected him of manipulating her. Which, of course, he was.

'What's wrong, Amber?' he'd asked.

She'd shrugged her shoulders and poked a fork at her pizza.

He wasn't taking that from her. 'Come on, Amber, you can do better than that for an answer. Don't you want to decide how your bedroom will look? Leave it to me and you could end up with something totally naff, like ... like Walt Disney.'

She scowled and put down her fork. 'Will you really let us choose?'

'Sure. That's what I've just said.'

She didn't seem convinced. And then he understood why: she said, 'Mum and Tony said we could choose how to decorate our rooms, but every time I told them what I wanted Mum said I couldn't have it. She kept saying it wouldn't go with the rest of the house.'

'Well, never mind what goes on in Prestbury. So long as you and Lucy can agree on what you'd both like, you can have whatever you want. And that's a promise. A gold-plated one.'

They arrived at 10a Maywood Park Road slightly late and out of breath. They had left the car beneath its duvet of snow and walked across town. Except that it was a case of two steps forward and one back. In common with most children, Amber and Lucy treated the snow as something they'd never seen before, although they'd played out in it for most of the morning. If they weren't throwing snowballs at each other, or at him, they were shrieking at the top of their voices. Their enjoyment was infectious: he couldn't remember the last time he'd felt so happy and relaxed.

He rang the doorbell and in the following minutes, while he waited for Adele to appear, he checked out the girls: they were standing on either side of him gazing up at the house. He tried to see the property through their eyes so that he could gauge their reaction. It was important to him that they liked it. As if she was reading his mind, Lucy said, 'It looks old, Daddy.'

He interpreted this as a negative comment, and said, 'Oh, not very. Only about a hundred years.'

'It's quite dark,' she added, standing back from the covered porch and staring up at the brick walls, which contrasted sharply with the whiteness all around them. 'Do you think it might be haunted?'

He laughed. 'Not a hope.'

'I think it's nice.'

This was from Amber.

'Really?'

She nodded. 'Yes. It looks . . . sort of cosy. And friendly.'

Before he could respond, the door opened and there was Adele, dressed in a pleated skirt and lace-frilled blouse with a pale lilac cardigan. Suddenly he realised that he and the girls – boisterously red-faced and damp from snowball-throwing – weren't fit to cross this elegant lady's threshold. If she thought so, she didn't let on, but welcomed them in and asked if they would like to take off their wet shoes and boots. Then she offered to take the girls' coats and wet gloves and put them on the radiator in the kitchen. 'Let's see if we can have them dry by the time you leave,' she said.

Always more forward than her sister, Lucy said, 'My socks are wet too.'

'Are they? In that case we'd better dry them as well. What about yours, Amber?'

'Sorry to impose on you like this,' Jack said, when they were standing in the high-ceilinged kitchen, divested of anything wet. It was then that he noticed the tea-things set out on the small table in the corner of the room. There were dainty cups and saucers, plates of biscuits and crustless sandwiches covered with clingfilm. There was also a tiered cake-stand bearing an assortment of jam tarts and fairy-cakes, which had caught Lucy's eager eye. Exchanging a look with the old lady, he said, 'We won't keep you long, Adele, I can see you're expecting company.'

She looked at him, puzzled. 'Oh, I see.' She laughed. 'How silly of me. Of course, I should have said. I thought that when you'd shown your daughters round the flat you'd like to join me for some tea. Unless you have something else to do.' She switched her gaze from Jack to Amber and Lucy.

'I'd like to stay, Miss Waterman. And my sister would too.'

To Jack's surprise it was Amber who had spoken. How grown-up and polite she sounded.

'Excellent,' Adele said. 'Now, off you go with your father while I put the kettle on. Would you prefer juice? Or milk, perhaps? I'm afraid I don't have any fizzy drinks.'

'Tea's fine, thank you' replied Amber, not giving Lucy a chance to speak and already moving towards the door.

It didn't take them long to explore the flat, and Jack brought their tour to an end in what was to be their bedroom. Like all the other rooms, it was crammed with treasured possessions: a large wardrobe that took up an entire wall, a high chest of drawers, shelves of china figures, a full-length mirror on a mahogany stand, a double bed with an ornate wooden headboard, a waist-high bookcase packed with rows of faded hardbacks and a pair of bedside tables.

'So what do you think, girls? Will it do?'

'Will all this furniture be here when you move in?' asked Lucy, her tone unsure as she lifted the lid on a large sewing basket and peered inside.

'No. It belongs to Miss Waterman and she'll be taking it with her.'

Lucy moved her attention from the sewing basket to the chest of drawers and a selection of framed photographs. 'Where's she going to live? Will it be as nice as this?'

'She's moving into a retirement home, where she'll have lots of people to keep her company.'

Amber turned from the window where she had been looking down on to the garden and the park. 'I think she'd be happier staying here. This is her home. It doesn't seem right that you're pushing her out.'

'Your father is doing no such thing,' said a firm but kindly voice at the door. Adele came into the room and stood next to Amber by the window. In a gesture that Jack expected Amber to shrink away from, the old lady rested a hand on his daughter's shoulder. 'But you're right. This has been my home and I've been very happy here. Now it's time to let someone else enjoy it. And that's where you come in. I need to know that the three of you will like being here and that you'll take good care of it for me.'

They had their tea in the sitting room, in front of the old-fashioned gas fire that hissed and fascinated the girls. It was when he was watching Amber and Lucy warm to Adele that Jack realised how sad it was that they had no grandparents. Given the tension between himself and Maddie, some neutral adult company was probably just what they needed.

When Lucy started to fidget, Adele asked if they would like to go outside and play. 'You could build a snowman for me,' she said, making it sound as if they would be doing her an enormous favour. 'I haven't had one of those in my garden for many years. I think the birds would like it too. Something new for them to look at. I might have a carrot I could spare for a nose, but you'll have to think of something outside to use for his eyes.'

After the girls had bundled themselves up in their warmed coats and gloves and had slipped on their boots, Adele let them out and made a fresh pot of tea. When she and Jack were back in the sitting room, watching Amber and Lucy through the window, Adele said, 'They're lovely girls, Jack, you must be so proud of them.'

'I am,' he said simply. 'They mean the world to me.'

'I can see that. And you're a very special man to understand how important they are. It isn't every father who makes that connection with his children.'

'I've always felt this way about them, but . . . but nearly losing them when Maddie took off, well, let's just say the experience has sharpened my focus.'

She handed him his cup. 'You sound bitter, Jack.'

He swallowed. 'I am. Sorry if that sounds petty.'

'Certainly not petty. Just a great shame. Sugar?'

He raised his hand to the proffered bowl and silver sugar tongs.

'And Maddie, your wife, she's now with your oldest and closest friend – Tony, if my memory serves me correctly from one of our earlier conversations.'

Bristling slightly, he said, 'Your memory serves you very well.' But what she said next had him even more on edge.

'I fully understand your sense of betrayal and hurt, Jack, especially towards Tony, and please forgive an old lady's impertinence, but may I offer you a piece of advice? Or, rather, ask you something extremely personal?'

He shifted uncomfortably in his seat. 'I probably don't have much choice in the matter, do I?'

She smiled and took a sip of her tea. 'Think back to before Maddie left you when, for all those years, Tony was your best friend. If anything had happened to you, who would you have wanted to help Maddie take care of Amber and Lucy?'

Unable to meet her piercing stare, he looked beyond her, to the garden where his two precious daughters were playing in the snow. He didn't know if the old lady was psychic, but years ago he and Maddie had had it written into their wills that if anything happened to both of them, Tony would not only be the executor of their wills but would become Amber and Lucy's legal guardian.

Minutes passed before he spoke. 'I don't think that's a fair question. The circumstances have changed.'

'Indeed they have . . . and for all concerned. But I would imagine that Tony would want only the best for those two delightful girls. Give him the credit for that much, at least. You might be surprised by how much peace of mind that thought could give you. Now, then, tell me about your writing. Beth says you're quite the rising star of the group.'

Chapter Thirty-Two

*

It was rare for Beth to have an entire day to herself, but on this particular Sunday, early in February, she was entirely alone.

With January behind them, which meant Nathan's mock A levels were over – no more study leave and late-night revision sessions – an air of calm routine had returned to their lives. To reward himself, Nathan had borrowed the car and driven Jaz to Nottingham University for the day to show her where he hoped to be studying, come the autumn. He had been delighted when the letter from Nottingham had arrived last week and he'd been offered a place. Beth had wanted to caution him on the perils of counting chickens before they'd hatched – he had yet to sit the all-important summer exams and acquire the necessary grades – but she'd held her tongue and told him instead to drive carefully.

She sighed. Would he ever take her concern seriously? And would she ever learn to trust his judgement? How did a parent make that enormous leap of faith?

The only person she knew who had made and coped with this transition was Ewan – most of her friends either had much younger children or none at all, like Wendy, and Simone and Ben. But she and Ewan had had frequent conversations on the subject.

Ah, the eternal question [he'd said once], how to locate the on/ off button for being a parent. Let me know if you find it, won't you?

The only on/off button she could locate with any certainty was the one on her computer. Having spent the morning blitzing the flat after a chaotic week of late nights at the surgery – she had been covering for Wendy, who was basking in some winter sun in the Canary Islands – it was time to treat herself to an afternoon of uninterrupted writing. Armed with a mug of tea and a ham and tomato sandwich, she settled herself at her small desk and switched on the computer. Before losing herself in her novel – she was in the middle of a chapter that was proving particularly enjoyable to write – she would check her emails. There was nothing from Simone, which was disappointing, but understandable – her friend's parents were staying with her – but there was one from Ewan. She smiled and clicked on OPEN.

Hello Beth,

How about this? I'm all wired up with the latest in mobile phone and laptop technology. Yes, I know I've always been proud of my technophobe status, but this baby's a real cutie to play with. More importantly it means I can keep in touch while I'm away from home.

I'm currently down in deepest Cornwall, showing my face at a conference. Supposedly I'm here to work, but in reality I'm doing nothing more vital than shoring up the local economy by sampling the excellent seafood on offer. The local beverage isn't bad either. I'm here until Tuesday, and while I'm hanging out at an undisclosed address I feel brave enough to ask you something important.

I'm only too aware that I've taken enough liberties with you already, that I've pushed the envelope as far as is decent, that I've thrown my undeserving self upon your gentle nature once too often, that I've squandered your precious time in forcing reply upon reply to my inadequate electronic meanderings. And, oh, that an ill-favoured wretch such as I should even . . . 'Stop!' I hear you plead. So with a hey, and a ho, and a hey nonino, I shall cry, 'Havoc!' and let slip the dogs and get to the point.

Bethany, p-p-please . . . (huge intake of breath here, maybe even a drum roll) . . . p-p-please, if it so pleases your ladyship . . . (clears throat in attempt to cover up excruciating nervousness) . . . c-c-can we meet?

Your stuttering with nerves, humblest of lowly humble servants,

Ewan Barefaced-Cheek Jones

Beth laughed, and was all set to reply when the doorbell rang. What timing! She clicked on SAVE, hurriedly shut down the machine and rushed downstairs. Out of breath, she opened the front door to find Barnaby on the step.

'Am I welcome?' he asked.

It was almost six weeks since she had last seen Barnaby and the sight of him standing hesitantly at her door moved her to tears. They embraced each other tightly, and when he released her, she wiped her eyes with the backs of her hands. 'I'm sorry,' she said, 'it's just so good to see you.'

His eyes were moist too. 'I would have come sooner, only I didn't know how I'd be received. Didn't want to walk into hostile territory. You know what a shocking coward I am.'

It was on the tip of Beth's tongue, as she led the way upstairs, to say that anyone who lived with Lois was anything but a coward, but she refrained from making such an inappropriate remark. She took his scarf and overcoat and offered to make him his favourite drink.

They sat at the table with mugs of hot chocolate and the biscuit tin between them. Beth got up to put a couple of logs on the fire. 'How are things at Marsh House?' she asked. 'How's Lois?'

'Oh, don't you go worrying about Lois. She's keeping her spirits up by rapping me over the knuckles when the mood takes her.'

'That doesn't make me feel any better. Worse, if anything. It's hardly your fault she and I have had a falling out.'

'I'm more than used to a daily dose of admonishment. My day wouldn't be complete without a good scolding.'

She admired Barnaby for his apparent indifference, but Beth knew that he wouldn't be there unless he was upset about the situation in which they found themselves. 'Barnaby,' she said, adopting a firmer tone, 'we can't let this go on. There has to be a way. Lois has to understand that while I'm genuinely sorry for what happened there was a lot of truth in what I said. Does she know you're here?'

He dunked a chocolate digestive in his mug. 'Er . . . no. Thought it best to keep my visit under wraps. She thinks I'm at B&Q pricing Black and Decker Workmates.'

If the situation weren't so serious, Beth would have laughed at his subversive behaviour. 'Oh, Barnaby, if I didn't know better I'd say you were enjoying yourself. But what's to be done? Between us we have to make Lois see sense.'

He finished his biscuit and leaned forward in his seat. 'I have a plan. It's risky, but it might just work. I'll need your help. Nathan's too.'

Nottingham was busy with rush-hour traffic and it wasn't until they were heading towards the A50 that the congestion on the roads eased. Even so, Nathan wasn't taking any chances. It was dark, and with sleety rain obscuring his vision, he was keeping a healthy distance between himself and the car in front. He had no intention of arriving home with a crumpled bonnet. His mother had enough to cope with already without him adding to her worries.

Lately, though, he had noticed that his mother's confidence was growing. He'd put it down to the writers' group she had joined. Since she'd taken up with Hidden Talents she had changed. For the better. She was smiling more these days. Several times he had caught her staring out of the window, looking as if she was on the verge of laughter. 'Something amusing you, Mum?' he'd asked yesterday at breakfast.

'Oh, not especially,' she'd replied, her face inscrutable, as she waited for their toast to pop up. If he didn't know better, he'd suspect she was keeping something from him.

He stopped for a bus to pull out in front of them, and turned this thought over in his head: he was surprised by how much it bothered him. He supposed that, because he and his mother had always been so close, they had seldom kept things from each other. It made him wonder how he would react if that was to change. He explored this thought further, and a troubling feeling crept up on him. It was the disturbing realisation that he understood the root cause of his grandmother's problem. Perhaps her overbearing and sometimes bizarre behaviour stemmed from a basic need to be close to him and his mother. By trying to stop things changing, by denying the truth, she had hoped to preserve the safe little world she had invented for them all to live in.

A world that he had nuked ruthlessly on Christmas Day.

For the first time, he felt a wave of shame and regret. He had gone too far, he saw that now.

'You're looking very serious.'

He turned his head towards Jaz. 'Just thinking.'

A wry smile flickered across her face. 'Whoa, check out the man trying to do two things at once.'

He brightened instantly. 'Hey, I'm the one driving, so watch the attempts at biting wit.'

'Any chance of Michael Schumacher finding the brake pedal? I need the loo.'

A short time later they stopped at a Little Chef and leaving Nathan to join the queue for a table so that they could have a drink and something to eat, Jaz went in search of the toilets. In the cubicle next to her she could hear a woman talking: 'Stop it, darling, Mummy doesn't like it when you do that. That's better. Now, stand straight and Mummy will see to your buttons.'

She stood at the row of basins, washing her hands, listening to the stream of gibberish still coming from the cubicle. Before long, when the latest batch of Raffertys arrived, her mother would be speaking the same nonsense. She switched off the hot tap, grabbed a couple of paper towels and dried her hands. And who would be called upon to babysit? Good old Jaz. After all, she was the only sensible one who could be trusted with such a job. That's what her father had said last night when he'd come up to her room to tell her it was time she turned out her light. 'It's gone midnight, Jaz,' he'd said. 'Do you think I'm made of money and can afford to keep this many lightbulbs going?'

'Jimmy and Phin's lights are still on,' she'd countered, while surreptitiously closing down her computer.

'Yeah, but theirs aren't as bright as yours.'

'Like their brains, then.'

He came further into the room, laughing. 'Don't I always feed you the best lines? We could become a double act, you and me.'

'Let's not be hasty, Dad. I don't fancy being anyone's stooge. Was there something you wanted? Other than to keep me informed of your fiscal policies.'

He laughed again. 'You're a true Rafferty, Jaz, make no mistake. An answer for everything.' He sat on the end of her bed. 'Actually, I wanted to have a quiet word with you. I'm worried about your mother.'

Jaz gave her father her full attention. 'What is it? She's not ill, is she? The pregnancy isn't—'

He raised his hands, palms facing her. 'Calm down. It's nothing serious. But you must have noticed how tired she is.'

Jaz had. Most days now her mother looked washed out. She was sick a lot in the mornings too, usually after Jaz's father and brothers had left for work. While her mother was suffering in the bathroom, Jaz saw to her sisters' breakfast and got them ready for school – no mean feat, given the inherently cussed nature of Tamzin and Lulu. By the time Jaz arrived at college she was frazzled and in no mood to concentrate on her work. Several times she had found herself nodding off.

'So what I'm saying, Jaz,' her father had continued, 'is that I want you to help your mother as much as you can. I want to know that I can rely on you.'

'But what about the others?'

He chuckled. 'You mean your sisters? I think we can safely say they're as useful as a pair of chocolate candlesticks. Unlike you, they're not blessed with an ounce of common sense or reliability.'

She knew she was clutching at straws, but said anyway, 'There's Phin and Jimmy. They could do something.'

His expression turned stern. 'Are you saying you don't want to help?'

'No. It's not that, it's just—'

'Then stop making such a fuss.' He got up. 'Anyone would think I'd asked you to repaint the Vatican. Which reminds me, I want us all to go to Mass tomorrow. We've let it slip.'

'But I can't go. Not this Sunday.'

'Oh? Can't or *won't?*'

'I told you I was spending the day with Vicki.' The lie had tripped off her tongue, as they did so easily, these days. Her family still didn't know about Nathan and she intended to keep it that way for as long as she could.

Chapter Thirty-Three

*

'Dulcie, please, I beg you to reconsider. Don't do this to me . . . to us.'

'I don't have any choice.'

'But you do. Of course you do.'

'My mind's made up, Richard. Please don't make this any more difficult than it already is for me.'

Hearing the terrible finality in Dulcie's voice, Richard passed a shaking hand across his face. He had never felt more shocked. When he had arrived to have lunch with Dulcie there had been nothing in her manner to hint at the devastation she was about to wreak. He had just opened the sandwiches he'd bought from the sandwich bar near his office and put them on to their plates, when from nowhere she was telling him it was over between them.

He hauled himself to his feet, ready to try again. He had to make Dulcie see that she couldn't expect him to walk away from her. That he was never to see her again. His life would be over if that happened. He moved silently across the kitchen, went and joined her at the french windows where she had her back to him, arms folded across her chest, gazing at the rain that lashed against the glass. He placed a hand on her shoulder and turned her gently towards him. Tears filled her eyes and he saw his own pain mirrored in them. 'Dulcie, this is madness. We can't inflict so much pain on ourselves.' He took her in his arms and held her close. He feared she might resist, but she didn't, and burying his face in her neck, he kissed her soft, warm skin. He felt her quiver in his embrace, worked his mouth along the line of her jaw and kissed her deeply, wanting desperately to forget the pain of the last few minutes. He held her tightly against him, his body tense with the need to be reassured that everything would be all right. 'Let's go upstairs,' he whispered, his hand pressing on the nape of her neck.

But that was when he knew he couldn't change her mind. Tears were streaming down her cheeks. She pulled away from him. 'Please, Richard, I love you, and probably always will, but it's over between us. It has to be.'

He let go of her, bewildered. Angry too. Angry with Kate and Henry.

And Angela. It had been Angela's idea to invite Dulcie and her family to their wretched Boxing Day drinks party. If she hadn't come up with such a stupid suggestion Kate and Henry wouldn't have met and he wouldn't be facing the worst moment of his life.

The irrationality of this thought slammed into him. His head pounding, despair welled up inside him. He took hold of Dulcie's arm. 'Explain to me one more time why and how you can justify what you're doing.'

She looked at him sadly, her face still wet with tears. 'I'm not thinking of us. I'm thinking of your son. If you ever leave Angela for me, you put Henry in an impossible situation with his mother.'

'He'll get over it. So will she.'

She shook her head. 'No. Angela would feel doubly betrayed. By her husband *and* her son. What could be worse for her?'

'Then I won't leave Angela. We'll carry on as before.'

'You might be capable of doing that, but I'm not. I wouldn't be able to face Kate. The deceit would build and build. I just know I couldn't live with it.'

Her cool reasoning was too much for Richard. 'But, Dulcie, what they feel for each other is nothing compared to what we have. Our love is worth infinitely more than theirs.'

'How can you say that?'

'They're young. They're—'

'They're not that young, Richard. And if you loved your son as much as I love Kate, you'd want to give him the benefit of the doubt. After all, it was you who said you believed their attraction was more than a passing fancy.'

He drew in his breath sharply, felt as if she'd dealt him a physical blow. 'That's unfair, Dulcie. I wouldn't have thought you capable of such a cheap shot. You know how I feel about my children.

How important they are to me.' His voice shook. 'And who, I'd like to know, gave you the monopoly on familial love?'

In response, Dulcie's shoulders sagged and she wrapped her arms around herself as if she were cold. 'This isn't doing either of us any good,' she said. 'Please, let's finish it by being civil. We owe each other that, if nothing else.'

She was asking too much of him. 'No!' he argued wildly. 'I can't. I can't be civil. I won't give you up. I love you, Dulcie, and stupidly I thought you loved me. Perhaps . . .' he went on, more slowly, knowing he was being cruel, but wanting her to understand what she was doing to him '. . . perhaps I've been wrong all this time. You were never really committed to me, were you? Maybe that's why you didn't warn Kate off before it was too late.' She turned on him, eyes blazing.

'I don't think you're in any position to speak of commitment. You're a married man who's been sneaking around having an adulterous affair behind his wife's back. How's that for commitment?'

He knew when he was beaten and he slumped into the nearest chair. Resting his elbows on the table, he covered his face with his hands and wept. For a while he was aware of nothing but the sound of his own choking sobs. Then gradually he sensed Dulcie moving towards him and felt the slight pressure of her hand on his shoulder. 'I'm so sorry,' he mumbled. 'I shouldn't have accused you like that. Forgive me, please.'

She stroked his hair, a gesture that was so evocative of their being in bed together. He shuddered, knowing, and now accepting, that he would never experience that pleasure again.

Dulcie marched through the park gates. The moment Richard had gone, she had left the house, grabbing her filthy old waxed jacket from the back of the kitchen door, the one she only ever wore for gardening. But she didn't care how awful she looked: she needed to be outside, away from any physical reminders of Richard – her house contained too many memories of him.

The rain had eased off, but the biting February wind was gusting, sending leaves and a rogue crisps packet skittering as she strode past the swings and slides. She followed the path towards the duck pond. Already breathless, she increased her speed, as if to convince herself that her heart wasn't breaking.

But it was futile.

She had just made the ultimate sacrifice, had given up the man she loved for her daughter's happiness. She felt no virtuous gain for what she had done, only the deep ache of loss.

She wished that there had been a better way to end it with Richard, a way that wouldn't have hurt him so much. Would she ever forget the anguish in his face when they had held each other and kissed for the last time?

The park was almost deserted – just a couple walking their floppy-eared springer spaniel – and with the pick of the park benches overlooking the pond, she chose one directly beneath a large oak tree, so that, should it start to rain again, she would have a degree of shelter.

She recalled Kate's words – *You've never been at a low ebb in your entire life. You're the most positive and upbeat woman I know.*

Oh, Kate, if only you could see me now, thought Dulcie, as she stared through swollen, tear-filled eyes at the ripples caused by the wind on the surface of the pond. How had she found the strength to walk away from the man who had meant the world to her? Only a short while ago, when Richard had suffered his heart-attack and she had thought she'd lost him for ever, she had woken up to the extent of her love for him. And now, when she had never been surer of his love for her, she had thrown it away. What was the sense in that?

She lowered her head, and let the tears flow. What did it matter if anyone saw her?

But she changed her mind when, coming towards her in the distance, she recognised Victor Blackmore. Strangely, though, he wasn't walking in a straight line along the path. He was zigzagging between the trees in a bizarre fashion, glancing over his shoulder every now and then or stopping to tie a shoelace.

How very odd.

Chapter Thirty-Four

*

Victor was in character. With his hood up, his anorak zipped to his chin, his hands thrust deep into his pockets and dark glasses covering his eyes, he was Irving Hunter, special-ops agent, the protagonist of his novel *Star City*. Peering furtively over his shoulder, he was checking the trees, bushes and litter-bins for CIA agents secretly drafted in by NATO to take out Macedonian subversives.

He had started work on Chapter Ninety-six at five o'clock that morning, but the hours had slipped by and the words failed to flow. Something jarred. And then he'd got it. The situation hadn't felt real to him, and without further delay he'd left the house and thrown himself into acting the part of Irving Hunter. Prowling the streets, dodging in and out of shop doorways, following suspects, he was finally getting the feel of Irving's day-to-day routine. He'd found the experience both exhilarating and exhausting. His feet ached and were wet from the rain, but a little discomfort was a small price to pay. All the great writers had suffered for their art, and he was to be no exception. It was what put him above all the wannabe writers out there. What those fools didn't understand was that the noble craft of novel-writing was like scaling Everest – the harder and higher the climb, and the more one struggled, the more worthwhile the task and the finished result. If only he could find a publisher who had half a brain and the wit to take on his book, he knew *Star City* would be a huge success. In his opinion, it was written to a far higher standard than most of the rubbish on the shelves. It had pace, tension, and plenty of action. What more could a publisher want? It had blockbuster stamped all over it! And there was always the chance that it would be turned into a film. He was out of touch with actors these days, but a young Michael Caine would have done justice to the role of Irving Hunter.

He caught a blast of icy wind in his face, and was suddenly annoyed with himself. He'd got sidetracked, had slipped out of character and forgotten that he was Irving Hunter scouring the deserted streets of Skopje for Albanian rebels and ruthless terrorists.

He took in his surroundings, not sure how he'd got there. This was happening to him more and more: he would go out for a carton of milk and come back two hours later with a loaf of bread. He put it down to his absorption in his writing. Since his redundancy, *Star City* had become his *raison d'être*: nothing else mattered to him.

A swivel of his head informed him that he was in Maywood Park. And there, a few yards in front of him, sitting on a bench, was someone he recognised. It was Dulcie Ballantyne from the writers' group. He debated what to do. Should he walk past her and risk being recognised then be forced to make polite conversation, or turn and retrace his steps?

He hesitated. How would Irving Hunter react in this situation?

He would brazen it out. That's what he'd do. He'd stroll by and nonchalantly wish the woman a good day, while all the time never slowing his step.

The decision made, he picked up his pace and pushed on, acknowledging why he didn't like Dulcie Ballantyne. As self-elected leader of the writers' group, she had assumed she was better than the rest of them. With her posh house and fancy furniture, she had looked down on them. Him in particular.

He was almost level with the woman when a voice inside his head said, 'Why not stop and show her what you're really made of? Isn't that what Irving Hunter would do? Remember, you're a winner. *A winner*.'

Dulcie braced herself. 'Hello, Victor,' she said, rising quickly to her feet to give the impression she didn't have time to hang around. 'How's the writing going? We've missed seeing you on a Thursday evening.'

He lifted his sunglasses. 'I'm very well, Mrs Ballantyne. Thank you for enquiring. And, yes, the writing is going well. Never better. And yours?'

'Oh, you know, muddling along.' She thought it better not to mention anything about the short-story competition she'd won recently: with his rampant insecurity he would only think she was boasting. A gust of wind rattled a swirl of leaves around their ankles and for a moment she forgot her own problems and took in the shock of Victor's appearance. He'd lost weight and his bloodshot eyes had a strained, slightly manic look. Perhaps he was working too hard and wasn't getting enough sleep. But who was she to talk? With her tatty old jacket, hair all over the place, and face blotchy with crying, he was probably thinking what a mess she looked. The silence continued between them, until Dulcie's compassionate nature got the better of her and she said, 'Victor, I've been sitting here for some time and now I'm chilled to the bone. I don't suppose you'd like to join me in a cup of coffee at Novel Ways, would you?'

A downpour of sleety rain hastened their departure from the park. Dulcie didn't know what surprised her more – that she had made such an invitation, or that Victor had accepted it.

Chapter Thirty-Five

*

Jack was running late. After work he'd met up with Des for a drink. It was ages since they'd done that and he suspected it had something to do with Julie. She was still cross over the way he'd left Clare although, according to Des, she was coming round slowly. 'Best not to rush things,' Des had advised. 'You know what women are like. Once they get something into their heads, it's there carved in stone until time weathers it.' He'd asked after Clare and Des had told him she was much more her old self. 'Getting over you by swearing allegiance to the school of thought that denounces all men as Neanderthal numbskulls.'

'I still feel guilty about what happened,' Jack admitted.

'Good. That means there's hope for you.'

'Do you think it would be okay for me to get in touch to try to make my peace with her?'

Des had shaken his head vehemently. 'Take my advice and leave well alone for a few more months.'

It was raining hard when Jack drew up outside Dulcie's house. He checked his watch. Ten to eight. He should have been there twenty minutes ago. He reached for his file from the passenger seat, locked the car and hurried up the steps to number eighteen, the rain hammering on the road and pavement.

Beth answered the door to him. 'We'd almost given up on you, Jack.' Then, as he shrugged off his coat and draped it over the newel post at the foot of the stairs, she said softly, 'You'll never guess who's here – Victor.'

'Really?'

'Apparently Dulcie ran into him this afternoon and persuaded him to join us again.'

He rolled his eyes. 'Is she feeling okay?'

Still with her voice scarcely more than a whisper, she said, 'Between you and me, I don't think she is.'

'Any idea what's wrong?'

'No. But I'll try to get her alone in the kitchen at coffee time and see if there's anything we can do.'

Following Beth, Jack realised that he knew practically nothing about Dulcie. She had shared little with them about her family or friends. He couldn't even say for sure how many children she had. Or had he been so wrapped up in his own problems that he hadn't listened properly?

In the sitting room, Jack saw that Victor was occupying the chair he'd always sat in. 'Hi, Victor,' he said cheerily. 'Long time no see. How's it going?' Not good, he thought. The man looked wrecked. Dishevelled and ready to drop. And flakier than Jack remembered. He was dressed in his usual jacket, but the shirt beneath it was rumpled and his tie was marked with a greasy stain.

'I'm very well,' replied Victor, eyes darting. He crossed his legs and fidgeted with the A4 pad on his lap.

In response to the man's curt reply, Jack decided to be equally blunt. 'So, what brings you back to the group?'

Victor picked at one of his fingernails. 'It was Mrs Ballantyne. She insisted I came. She seems to think I have something unique to offer to you all.'

Jack was saved from making a reply to this extraordinary comment when from the kitchen, he heard Jaz talking to Dulcie. He turned to greet them. Instantly he saw what Beth had meant: there was an agitated air about Dulcie that was at odds with the calm woman he knew – and, if he wasn't mistaken, she'd cried recently.

Everyone was getting on with the exercise she had set them and, in the silence of their intense concentration, Dulcie was regretting her decision to go ahead with tonight's meeting. She should have been sensible and cancelled it. But she hadn't been thinking straight today. Why else would she have encouraged Victor to join the group again? Had it only been pity that had driven her to take him to Novel Ways for a coffee then sit with him for more than an hour while he regaled her with an in-depth, blow-by-blow account of where he was up to with *Star City*? If she was to believe half of what he said, his manuscript was on the verge of becoming the hottest property the publishing world had ever got its hands on.

It was all too easy to laugh at people like Victor, but her own vulnerability that day had given her an empathy towards him and she had fell an inexplicable urge to offer her protection. It was clear to her, even in her dazed state, that he was sick. Depressed, probably. She hadn't been able to turn her back on someone so obviously in need, who very likely didn't have many friends he could approach for help. As irritating as he was, she hoped the rest of the group would forgive her for foisting Victor on them again. Perhaps tomorrow she should ring them individually and explain the situation.

Across the room she could hear a distracting clicking sound. Victor was fiddling with his biro. He was breathing heavily too. My, how he filled a small space. It was pure madness what she was taking on, but rescuing Victor from himself would stop her agonising over Richard.

With fifteen minutes left in which to complete the writing exercise, Dulcie focused her thoughts. The group was writing a thousand words about a box. 'It can be any kind of box,' she'd informed them, 'and you can do anything with it.' At first Victor had declined to take part, but after gentle persuasion, he had relented, and she'd set the stopwatch. Her own piece of writing wasn't going well. It was chock full of clichés and embarrassingly sentimental. But how could she even think of writing when all she wanted to do was crawl upstairs and hide under the duvet for the rest of her life?

'Time's up!' declared Victor, so loudly that Dulcie jumped.

'How did we all get on?' she asked.

Jaz let out her breath. 'I think I may have gone on longer than a thousand words.'

'Show-off,' teased Jack.

'Beth, how about you?'

'It's not quite what I thought it would turn out to be, but I did finish it.'

'Good for you. And, Victor, how did you get on?'

'It was straightforward enough. I can rattle off a thousand words in my sleep.'

218

'That's excellent,' she said. 'Jack, would you care to be first off the blocks to read to us?'

The evening progressed with everyone taking a turn to read out their work. All except Dulcie. 'Sorry, everyone,' she apologised. 'I wouldn't inflict my attempt on my worst enemy. A very poor effort, I'm afraid.' And before anyone could argue with her, or shake the Self-belief Box, she put down her pen and suggested it was time for coffee.

'I'll give you a hand,' offered Beth, quick to get to her feet.

No sooner were they in the kitchen, Dulcie filling the kettle and Beth putting milk into a jug, than the telephone rang. Dulcie picked up the receiver, gesturing to Beth where the sugar was kept. The kettle almost slipped out of her hands when she heard who it was.

'Dulcie, please don't put the phone down on me. Just listen to what I have to say.'

'I'm . . . I'm afraid I'm rather busy at present.' Her voice sounded cold and stilted. She saw Beth shoot her a curious glance.

'Dulcie, I can't do this. I can't accept that I'll never see you again.'

'Perhaps we could discuss it later.' Again, the same toneless voice.

'You've got someone there?'

'My writing group.'

'*Dammit!* What time do they leave?'

She was about to answer his question when she realised that she wasn't brave enough to speak to Richard later, when she would be alone. Instead, she said, 'Goodbye, then.' Hating herself, she dropped the receiver on to its cradle with a clumsy clatter.

Then she burst into tears.

Beth was instantly at her side, a hand on her shoulder. 'Dulcie, whatever is the matter? What can I do to help? Shall I get rid of the group?'

Unable to speak, Dulcie leaned into her and sobbed. But there was no relief, the physical contact of another person made her cry all the more. Minutes passed, and to make things worse, Jack appeared in the doorway. 'Don't suppose I can hide out here with you two—' He stopped short. 'Anything I can do to help?'

'Yes,' said Beth, taking command of the situation. 'Tell the others Dulcie isn't feeling well.'

'There's no need for that,' Dulcie muttered fumbling for a tissue but not finding one. She felt such a fool for breaking down.

'Yes, there is,' asserted Beth, briefly leaving her side to fetch a box of Kleenex from a shelf above the fridge. Dulcie took a handful and blew her nose hard. 'Maybe Beth's right,' she said. 'Would you mind, Jack? Please say how sorry I am.'

'Of course. Leave it to me. I'll run Jaz home. Do you have anything stronger than coffee in the house? You look like you could do with a stiff drink.'

'There's nothing seriously wrong with her, is there?' asked Jaz, as Jack pulled away from Dulcie's house.

'I hope not.' And, making light of the situation, 'Maybe it was the shock of having Victor back in the group.'

Jaz smiled. 'That would be it, then. Did you know he was going to be there?'

'No. All Beth had time to tell me when I arrived was that Dulcie had bumped into him this afternoon.'

She cringed. 'I can think of any number of people I'd sooner bump into. He looked like a walking freak-show, didn't he?'

'He certainly wasn't at his best.'

'You don't think it's catching, do you? I mean, perhaps he and Dulcie have got some awful bug.'

'Here's a promise. If you start looking anywhere near as bad as Victor, I'll cart you off to Maywood Health Centre.'

'Cheers.'

He turned into Jaz's road and stopped the car on the corner. 'See you next week. And fingers crossed everyone's feeling better.'

She was just unbuckling her seatbelt, when a P registered Rav-4 came towards them, its headlamps shining straight into their faces. It stopped at the junction, just yards from where they were parked, music booming. Two men in their twenties sat in the front. At the same moment, they turned and looked down at Jack, then at his passenger.

'Oh, hell!' Jaz cursed.

'What? What's wrong?'

'Everything.' To his astonishment, she flung open the door and marched away down the road in the pouring rain. Puzzled, he watched her go. Then, realising that the car was still alongside him, he turned his head. The driver scowled at him with such menace that Jack had to look away. And then they were gone, tyres squealing.

The evening was getting weirder by the minute.

He decided he'd better stay to check that Jaz got in safely and watched her disappear up the drive of a large modern house. Then he sat for a moment to consider what he'd just witnessed. Perhaps the two men in the car were loony neighbours. He was certain Jaz knew them, and even more certain that she wasn't fond of them. Once more that evening he was shamed into admitting that he knew hardly anything about a member of the writers' group.

He turned the car and drove back the way he'd just come to Bloom Street. Again, Beth opened the door to him.

'Did you forget something?' she asked.

'No. I just thought I'd see if there was anything I could do to help. I also thought you'd need a lift home at some point.'

'Oh, that was thoughtful of you.'

'How's Dulcie?'

'Come and see for yourself.' Dropping her voice, she added, 'She hasn't let on what's troubling her.'

Dulcie was where he'd left her half an hour ago in the kitchen. He was pleased to see that she looked less agitated. On the table in front of her stood a bottle of whisky, a pot of tea, some mugs and a large plate of toast and honey. 'Comfort food,' she said, with an attempt at a smile. 'Beth's idea.'

'And an excellent one at that. Okay if I join you?'

'Of course. And I can't apologise enough for my loss of control. Very melodramatic of me. You can always trust a writer to go to pieces. It's the drama, I suppose.'

He pulled out a chair and sat down. 'If you apologise any more I'll have to fetch the Self-belief Box.' This elicited a proper smile from her. 'You would say if there was anything I,' he glanced at Beth, 'or we, could do, wouldn't you? I'm sure I read somewhere that it's *de rigueur* for writers to show a brothers-in-arms solidarity to each other.'

She patted his hand. 'That's very sweet of you, Jack, but I shall be fine. A long soak in a hot bath followed by an early night should do the trick. Now, then, who's going to help me polish off all this tea and toast?'

Her tone was brisk and hearty, and Jack had to accept that he had done as much as he could for her. 'Honey and toast, how could a man resist? Count me in.'

The three of them sat round the table talking about anything that was safely neutral: his imminent house move and how Amber and Lucy had taken such a shine to Adele Waterman, then Beth's son, Nathan, and how he and Jaz were such a cosy item. It prompted Jack to describe the incident when he had dropped Jaz at home.

'Goodness, how peculiar,' said Beth.

'Did Jaz give any clue that she knew these men?' asked Dulcie.

'She didn't say anything, but I'd put money on her knowing exactly who they were. She was off like a rocket when she saw them.'

Beth looked thoughtful. 'They must have been her brothers.'

'I didn't know she had any,' Jack said. 'She's never mentioned them.'

'Oh, yes, she has,' Beth corrected him. 'The novel she's writing is about the family from hell, the Clacketts. It's probably based on her own family. What's more, I'm sure Nathan once said something about a couple of brothers and how she can't stand them. She also has two younger sisters.'

'Well, that's that mystery cleared up,' Dulcie said.

But Jack wasn't satisfied. If the two men had been Jaz's brothers, why had they looked at him so threateningly?

They had moved on to Victor, when the shrill ring of the phone made them all start. Jack saw the frozen expression on Dulcie's face and registered also that she made no move to answer it. It rang three more times. He slid a glance in Beth's direction.

Another excruciating ring.

Still Dulcie stayed where she was.

'Erm . . . shall I answer that for you?' he offered.

She opened her mouth to speak, but nothing came out.

He sat through two more rings, his nerves jarring. 'Whoever it is, shall I tell them you're busy?'

'No,' she murmured, tight-lipped, 'let it ring. He'll give up.'

So that was it. The poor woman was being plagued by a nuisance-caller. No wonder she was so upset. When at last the kitchen was quiet again, Jack said, 'Dulcie, how long has this been going on?'

Her eyebrows came together in an uncharacteristic frown. 'I'm not sure that's any of your business,' she said primly.

'If someone I know is receiving obscene phone calls,' he said, 'I think it is my business. How long?'

'He's right, Dulcie,' said Beth. 'There's no need for you to put up with it. BT can do all sorts of things nowadays to track down these people.'

To their combined amazement, Dulcie smiled. 'Oh, you two wonderfully concerned people. If all I had to worry about was a heavy breather I'd consider myself most fortunate.' She drained her glass of whisky and seemed to come to a decision. 'I suppose it won't do any harm to tell you. Today I told the man I love that I couldn't see him any more.' She pursed her lips until they were almost white. 'That was him, probably. As it was earlier this evening.'

'But if you still love him, why stop seeing him?'

Jack and Beth spoke at the same time.

'Because—' Her voice cracked and she blinked hard. 'Because we've been living a secret life. He's married, and now my daughter's fallen head over heels in love with his son. A tangled web, wouldn't you say? Sounds like a novel.'

Jack could only nod in stunned agreement.

Chapter Thirty-Six

*

The second Jaz walked into the kitchen, she knew she was in trouble.

The radio wasn't on, as it was normally during breakfast, and the silence – so rare – was awesome. It told her that her sleepless night worrying about whether her brothers would say anything to their father had not been in vain.

Thanks to Jimmy and Phin, who were sitting on either side of their father, it was obvious they all knew. There was no sign of her mother – she must be feeling unwell again.

Jaz took a long, deep breath and sat down next to Tamzin. She poured milk over her muesli and stirred it, willing herself to eat at least one mouthful. But she knew she couldn't. Her stomach was draining away from her. It was currently on a level with the tops of her knees. In the silence that continued, she thought, miserably, Oh, just get on with it. Do your worst. 'How's Mum?' she asked.

'And what would you care?'

She lifted her chin, gave her brother a sharp, challenging look. 'A darn sight more than you, Phin. When was the last time you did anything round the house to help Mum?'

'Watch your tongue, young lady.'

She squared her shoulders, indignation overruling her earlier decision to toe the line. 'Why, Dad? Why shouldn't I speak the truth?' No! Not the right thing to say. Her father seized the opportunity she'd handed to him.

'Well, I'd like to hear you speaking the truth some time. Wouldn't that be a great thing?'

'Please get to the point, Dad. If you're going to accuse me of something, spit the words out and have done with it.' So much for meekness.

Her father seemed to grow in his seat; taller, broader. 'Let's get this clear, Jasmine Rafferty, I'll spit my words out when I'm good and ready. Not when you tell me to.'

A dangerous bubble of mirth rose in Jaz as the image of a gobbing camel popped into her mind. She gritted her teeth and swallowed hard. This was no time to laugh: she was about to be grounded for the rest of eternity. She'd be in solitary confinement for ever, all privileges withheld. She'd be lucky to go to college, never mind attend her writers' group. A worse thought came to her. What if she had to show her father what she'd been writing? Suddenly the Clacketts didn't seem such a great move on her part. 'Sorry, Dad,' she said, trying hard to sound as if she meant it, but failing hopelessly: it came out too loud, as if she was being sarcastic.

Her father asked Lulu to pass him the marmalade, and leaned back in his chair. 'Now, the problem I have, Jaz, is that on the one hand I'm led to believe you were at Vicki's for the evening, and the next I'm hearing from your brothers that last night they saw you getting out of some man's car. Either Phin and Jimmy need to get down to Vision Express pretty damn quick, or you've got a *doppelgänger* wandering about town. Or maybe, there's a third option. Any theories of your own?'

Everyone looked at her.

'It's no big deal—' she began.

'You're on dangerous ground, girl, so don't go giving me any of that old malarkey! You can't make an eejit out of me, your brothers saw you good and proper. I don't know how long you've been sneaking off behind our backs seeing this – this man, but let me tell you, when I get a hold of him, he'll wish he'd never set eyes on you. If he's so much as laid a finger on you, I'll – I'll bloody kill him!'

Jaz gasped. When she'd been lying in bed last night unable to sleep, she'd been so concerned about her father finding out about the writers' group that she hadn't considered he'd make such a mind-blowing assumption. Jack was old! Okay, he made her laugh and could write like a dream, but he was *old*! 'Dad, you've got it all wrong. It's not what you think.'

'Yeah, well, you would say that.'

'Phin, just butt out, will you? Dad, you've got to listen to me. Jack's a friend. He gave me a lift home.'

Her father banged his fist on the table; her sisters jumped. 'Oh,' he mimicked, in a mocking falsetto, 'Jack's a friend, is he? So maybe it's time he started hanging out with *friends* of his own age, instead of preying on a girl young enough to be his daughter! What is he? Some kind of pervert? Have I got be careful with these two as well?'

Tamzin and Lulu giggled.

'Look, Dad—'

'Don't give me any of that "look, Dad" stuff, you lied to your mother and me. You told us you were seeing Vicki when all along you've been seeing this man. And if you weren't seeing him, why the lies?'

Jaz stared at her father, knew it was pointless to argue with him. She knew also that if she told him about her writing and how important it was to her he'd want proof. Only trouble was, that proof would send him into orbit. The contents of her novel, *Having the Last Laugh*, would make everything worse. If he read a word about the Clacketts and sussed that she had been making fun of her family behind their backs, he would go ballistic. He would bring an end to the world as she currently knew it.

Beneath the table her knees shook. She was in serious trouble. Weighing up the odds – which all seemed unfairly stacked against her – she decided she'd be better off keeping quiet. If she said nothing, her precious writing would be safe. So what if they thought she'd been having secret assignations with a bloke as old as Jack? They didn't know who he was, or where he lived. It was bite-her-tongue time.

Chapter Thirty-Seven

*

At first Jack thought he was imagining it, but after several miles of driving along country lanes to and from meeting a new client and measuring up her charming thatched cottage in Bunbury, he had to admit that his imagination wasn't playing tricks on him. A car was following him.

He couldn't be sure but he thought the black Golf had been with him since he'd stopped for petrol a short distance out of Maywood. It was currently positioned one car behind his, and he couldn't see the face of either the driver or the passenger. He decided to flush them out. He lowered his speed to twenty-five miles an hour, which he knew would infuriate the driver of the Fiesta immediately behind, and sure enough, when they came to an appropriate stretch of road, the Fiesta accelerated past, leaving Jack with a clear view in his mirror of his pursuers.

To his amazement, it was the two men he'd encountered in the Rav-4 last night when he'd dropped Jaz off – the two men who might or might not be her brothers. But what in hell's name were they up to?

The Golf shot in front of him, then slammed on its brakes. His heart in his mouth, Jack jammed his foot on the brake pedal and skidded to a halt, inches short of the ditch at the side of the road. He made a grab for his mobile phone.

It was the wrong thing to do. He should have locked the door. The next thing he knew he was being hauled from his car and bundled into the Golf. They pushed him into the rear seat, sandwiching him between them. He was more shocked than scared. 'What's this all about?' he asked.

The young man on his right, the bigger of the two who was chewing gum, spoke first. 'We're gonna make this as simple as we can, mate. So listen up. You so much as set eyes on our Jaz one more time and we'll tear you apart. Got that?' He sounded like he'd watched one too many gangland movies.

Jack stared, open-mouthed. 'Does this mean you *are* Jaz's brothers?'

Now it was the turn of the man on his left. 'Don't play dumb, Jack. We saw you last night so we know exactly what you've been up to. And just so you know, we don't like it.'

'But I'm not up to anything.'

'Oh, yes, you are.' Jack turned back to the first man. 'We know all about you. It's amazing what you can find out about a person once you've got their car registration. The Internet's a wonderful thing. I expect you use it a lot, don't you? Men like you do. Perverts who can't keep their hands off girls half their age. Can't get yourself a real woman so you make do with jail-bait. But we're here to let you know that nobody messes with our little sister.'

Men like you ... Perverts ... Nobody messes with our little sister. What they were accusing him of was preposterous. Disgusting. 'Look,' he said, trying hard to sound reasonable, like an upright citizen – anything but a child molester! 'You've got this all wrong. There's nothing going on between Jaz and me. Honestly. You have to believe me. I was giving her a lift home from our writers' group. As I do every week.'

There was a pause.

'Writers' group?'

It was the brother on his left. 'Yes,' said Jack.

'What d'you mean, as you do *every* week?'

'There's five of us in the group and we meet on Thursday nights. But surely you must have known that. We've been meeting since October last year.'

At this, the two men exchanged looks. He saw doubt on their faces and, keen to seize the advantage, he said, 'If you don't believe me, ring the woman who runs the group. She'll back me up on everything I've told you.'

'Outside,' the first man instructed his brother. 'You stay where you are,' he said to Jack. Both doors were slammed shut so he wasn't able to hear what was being said, but the gist was plain. They had realised they'd cocked up and were now reviewing matters. Jack knew he was within his rights to threaten them with police action but, bizarrely, he respected them. Who was he to hold a grudge when they'd only been looking out for their sister? As a father, he knew all too well how far he would go to protect Amber and Lucy.

The door was yanked open. 'Seems like we . . . Well, how about a drink, mate?'

'Is that your way of apologising?' Jack asked, when a hand was thrust towards him and he was helped out of the car.

'We could throw in some lunch, if you want.'

Jack laughed. 'I wouldn't want to put you to all that trouble.'

'So, a drink to put matters straight?'

He smoothed down his suit jacket, amused at their front. 'I'd love to, gentlemen, but I have lunch planned already. Something a little less physical.'

'No hard feelings, then? Oh, and we'd appreciate it if you kept schtum. Don't tell Jaz, she wouldn't understand.'

He put a hand in the air, started to walk away, straightening his collar and tie.

'Hang on a minute. Before you go, tell us about this writers' group. What exactly do you do?'

'We write,' Jack said, over his shoulder.

'What about?'

'Life, fellas. You ought to try it some time.'

Perhaps he should have been more shocked by what had happened to him, but the more Jack thought about it, the more absurd and bungled the whole thing appeared. Why hadn't Jaz told her brothers about the group? But there again *he* hadn't let on about it to Clare, or even to Des and Julie, and for the simple reason he hadn't wanted to face a barrage of questions or be mocked for considering himself a writer.

Gradually, the more he thought about it, the less surprised he was that Jaz had kept Hidden Talents from her brothers. He might be doing them a disservice, but they didn't strike him as being on the same wavelength as their sister. However, what they lacked in sensitivity they made up for in their eagerness to keep her safe. He had a feeling, though, that Jaz wouldn't see it in quite the same way.

When he had told her brothers that he already had a lunch appointment, he hadn't been lying: he'd arranged to meet Maddie.

He had arrived at the office early that morning, and had called her on her mobile knowing that she'd be driving the girls to school. 'What a coincidence,' she'd said. 'I was going to give you a ring today.'

'Oh?'

'You first.'

'What?'

'I said . . . Oh, never mind. What do you want?'

'I wondered if you'd meet me for lunch. There's something I want to discuss with you.'

They'd agreed to meet in Maywood at Casa Bellagio and now, as Jack ordered himself a glass of orange juice, he thought how uncomfortable he felt about meeting Maddie like this, just the two of them. Which, after the experience he'd just gone through, was laughable. Having lunch with his soon-to-be-ex-wife should be a cinch in comparison with abduction.

Ex-wife. It still didn't seem possible. He and Maddie had been so convinced of their love for each other, but at some point it had gone wrong. When did she stop loving him? Had it been a Road-to-Damascus revelation when she had seen that their lives didn't fit together any more? Or had it been a gradual process, each day building on the disappointment of the one that had gone before? She had never given him a straight answer as to why she had felt the need to have an affair, and he'd been left to scrutinise his own input to their marriage. Certainly he'd often spent more time at the office than he had at home, but they'd known that that would happen. If they were to have the lifestyle they both craved – holidays abroad, his-and-hers BMWs on the drive – then he'd had to prove himself partnership material. It had seemed justification enough, but now he knew better. The choice had been there, he just hadn't picked the right one.

It had been talking to Adele Waterman that had set him on this line of thought, and it was why he was here today to meet Maddie. For the sake of the children, he wanted to put things right between them.

Maddie was coming across the restaurant towards him, hips swaying in that unconscious way he'd always loved, hair immaculately cut and perfectly framing a face that was still faintly tanned from the Christmas skiing holiday. He noted the cream leather trousers, the pale pink cashmere sweater, and the pashmina slung stylishly around her shoulders. Designer from head to toe, he reckoned, while he was in his Next suit and Principles shirt and tie.

'I'm glad you came,' he said, pushing back his chair and rising to his feet. For an awkward moment, neither knew how to greet the other.

A kiss on the cheek?

Out of the question.

A handshake?

Too formal.

They settled for a wary smile and a bob of the head.

They ordered just one course because Maddie said she couldn't stay long.

'So what was it you were going to call me about?' he asked, when their plates of pasta and salad had been delivered by a diminutive girl who didn't look much older than Amber.

'Oh, it'll keep,' she said airily, and pointed out to the young waitress that she'd forgotten the mineral water.

Jack smiled at the girl when she reappeared with it. Maddie took the glass without a word of thanks and said, 'In America you never get such sloppy service.'

'I wouldn't know. I've never been to the land of plenty where fries and doughnuts rain down from a sky of maple syrup.'

She looked at him sharply. 'Don't goad me, Jack.'

'I'm not.' He sprinkled extra Parmesan over his pasta and tried to relate to the irritable woman sitting opposite him. Where had the happy-go-lucky girl gone? In fairness they had all changed: Jack, Maddie and Tony. He forked up some pasta and thought of Adele's words, that Tony would have the girls' best interests at heart. It focused his mind on what he needed to say. He put down his fork. 'Maddie,' he said, 'I want to talk seriously. About you and Tony. But mostly about the children and their future.'

Her expression changed. Gone was the sharp defensiveness, and in its place a softening. A softening he knew so well. His heart ached that she could still have that effect on him. He watched her dab the corners of her mouth with her napkin. She said, 'And that's what I wanted to discuss with you.'

The waitress materialised beside their table. 'Everything all right?' she asked, a little breathlessly.

Jack smiled and said everything was perfect.

'Another drink?'

He shook his head. 'Maddie?'

'No.'

'I think we're fine,' he said, and she left them alone.

'Jack, I've got something important to tell you,' Maddie said.

His emotions went from nought to sixty in two seconds and all at once he was on full alert. Well, she wasn't about to tell him she and Tony were getting married – that couldn't happen until the divorce had gone through. Perhaps she was pregnant. But what did that have to do with him? 'Go on,' he said.

She looked him dead in the eye. 'Tony's got a new business venture that's really taking off in the States.' She paused. 'Nothing's definite, but we're considering going to live in California. It would be great for the girls. They'd have the time of their lives. It would be a fantastic opportunity for them.'

Her words knocked the breath right out of him. Along with all his good intentions. He sat back in his chair. 'Over my dead body. That bastard is not taking my children anywhere.'

Chapter Thirty-Eight

*

More than once during the day Jaz had considered the coward's way out, running away. Her father's parting words that morning had been 'I'm too angry right now to decide how to punish you, but by tonight I'll have cooled off enough to think straight. And make no mistake, Jasmine Rafferty, you'll not get off lightly this time.'

This time. He'd spoken as if she was always in trouble. As if he'd lumped her in with Tamzin or Lulu. If only Mum hadn't been upstairs feeling so rotten Jaz might have had an ally but, as it was, she had no idea what was going on. And, worse, Dad had warned her not to involve Mum. 'Do that, young lady, and you'll regret it. Your mother's suffering enough as it is without having this lot to worry about as well.'

Several times during the morning Vicki had asked her what was wrong and at first she'd pretended everything was fine. By lunchtime she'd relented and confided in her friend. Vicki lapped up every word. 'So your family reckons you're seeing some old guy on the quiet? How awesome is that? You're not, are you?'

'No!'

She looked almost disappointed. 'What does Nathan say?'

'He doesn't know. And . . . and I don't want him to know. You mustn't say anything. And not to Billy either, he'd go straight to Nathan with it.'

'Suit yourself. But this might not be a bad time to tell your parents about Nathan. I mean, your dad'll be so relieved you're going out with someone your own age, he'll think Nathan's an answer to a prayer. Which, let's face it, he is.'

Now, during last break, as Jaz waited by her locker for Nathan to tell him he'd have to walk home alone, she thought over what Vicki had said. Would it be such a bad idea to do as she suggested?

Yes, it would. She could picture the scene perfectly: her father demanding to meet Nathan so that he could interrogate him and her gloating brothers preparing to embarrass him. And what would Nathan think of them and, as a consequence, of her? Oh, it was so unfair!

'Hi, Jaz. You look serious, what's wrong?'

It was Nathan.

'Nothing's wrong,' she said. The sight of him made her want to fall into his arms, to be hugged and reassured that maybe the day wasn't going to end as badly as she knew it would.

'You sure?'

'Hey, what is this?' she joked, in an effort to convince him she was okay. 'Dr King making school visits, these days? Now listen up, I can't walk home with you as I'm staying on for a bit.'

'I'll stay as well, if you like. What are you doing?'

'There's no need. Anyway, I don't know how long I'll be.' And before he could ask any more questions, the bell rang for the end of break, she grabbed her rucksack and scooted off.

She found that her instinct to walk home on her own had been good. No sooner had she set foot out of the college gates than Jimmy's black Golf appeared: it crawled along the kerb beside her, its tweaked engine rumbling and making her feel like a gazelle being stalked by a hungry panther. This was the reason she hadn't wanted to walk home with Nathan. She'd known her brothers would come for her, checking that she wasn't slipping off for another assignation with her middle-aged lover.

Jimmy lowered the driver's window. 'Get in, little sis.'

'Push off. I'd rather walk.'

'Looks like rain to me,' said Phin.

'I don't care if a typhoon's heading this way, I'm not going anywhere with you two.' She walked faster, but Jimmy kept the car level with her, its engine growling.

'We met a friend of yours this morning,' he said. 'What was his name, Phin? It's slipped my memory. Was it John?'

'Nah. It was Jack.'

'Ah, that's right. Jack. Jack Solomon.'

Jaz froze. She stared after the car as Jimmy drove slowly down the road, her stomach churned and her mouth went dry. Her brothers had spoken to *Jack*? But how had they found out who he was? And what had they said? She chewed her lip. As teenagers Phin and Jimmy had both learned to box and once, as adults, much to Mum's horror, they'd been involved in a late-night brawl in Manchester. Someone like Jack – a man to whom they were determined to teach a lesson – wouldn't stand a chance. 'Wait!' She yelled after the car. 'Wait for me!' She sprinted after them, her heavy rucksack banging against her back. Phin got out of the front passenger seat and let her in.

'What have you done to Jack?' she asked, when she'd caught her breath. 'If you've hurt him, I swear I'll make sure he goes to the police and has you put away.'

Jimmy grinned at her in the rear-view mirror. 'Cool it. Jack's fine. We left him in more or less one piece, but why don't you tell us what you've really been up to? We know you haven't been putting it about with some dodgy old bloke.'

She hesitated. Did this mean what she thought it did? Were they on to her writing? Or did they know about Nathan? Perhaps they were only bluffing. 'I don't know what you're on about,' she muttered. Then, trying to deflect them, she said, 'How did you find Jack?'

'Easy as pie,' crowed Jimmy.

'Yeah, even for a pair of oiks like us,' added Phin. 'Which is how we know you view us, you being such an intellectual and all. But it looks like we might have outsmarted you for once.'

She leaned forward. 'So tell me how, then.'

'One word,' said Jimmy. 'Numberplate.'

Jaz's heart sank. 'You're nothing but a pair of loathsome yobs,' she said.

But what had Jack told them?

Her father was home early, his Jaguar parked on the drive alongside Phin's Rav-4. Jimmy snatched on the handbrake. Jaz told herself to keep calm, to say nothing until she knew exactly what she was accused of. Against all hope, she wanted to believe that she wouldn't have to own up to everything she had been doing since October. The thought of being ridiculed for her writing was bad enough, but the fallout, if her father got wind of the Clacketts, didn't bear thinking about – she'd decided during the day that she would have to delete *Having the Last Laugh* from her computer, as well as ditch the paper copy. She hated the idea of losing her hard work, but she had no choice.

She was greeted by her mother, who was cooking tea while listening to the radio and humming along with it. The comforting smell of roast chicken with sage and onion stuffing reminded Jaz that she hadn't eaten that day: she'd been too sick with nerves. Now, hunger and apprehension made her want to hurl herself across the kitchen and cling to her mother. 'I'm sorry,' she wanted to say. 'I'm sorry I've lied to you all. Please forgive me.' And maybe, if her brothers hadn't been standing behind her raiding the fridge for a drink, she would have done exactly that.

'Hello, Jaz,' her mother said, turning to see her. 'I see the boys found you. We wondered where you were. You didn't say you'd be late.'

'Sorry,' she murmured. 'It was a last-minute thing.' Conscious that she'd just lied again, she shook off her jacket and said, 'How're you feeling? Anything I can do to help?'

'I'm fine. Supper's nearly ready, so go and get yourself washed.'

She moved uncertainly towards the door. 'Where's Dad?'

'In his snug. Perhaps you could poke your head round the door and give him the five-minute warning that we'll be eating soon. Oh, now I come to think of it, he did say he wanted a word with you when you came home.'

Avoiding her brothers' eyes, she went to find her father.

'Ah, there you are, Jaz,' he said, as she stepped into the room he called his snug. It had its own bar in the corner, a couple of reclining leather armchairs, an enormous flat-screen telly – the largest in the house – and a display shelving unit that was home to rows of old car-racing magazines, as well as photographs of the various race horses he'd had a share in over the years. He had made it his private hide-away ever since Tamzin and Lulu had declared themselves too old for a playroom. 'Close the door after you,' her father added ominously.

He waved the remote control at the telly, then turned to give her a long, hard stare. 'Come and sit with me, Jaz.' He indicated the other chair.

She did as he said, sensing that his mood was different from the one he'd aired at breakfast that morning. There was something like kindness in his voice. Absurdly it made her want to cry. She loved her father and didn't want him to be angry with her. And she didn't want to go through another day like today. But she steeled her resolve, reminding herself that it could be a ruse to make her confess more than she wanted to.

'Jaz,' he began, 'out of all our children, your mother and I always had you down as the most sensible. The one with the brains we could trust. But now,' he shook his head, and she could see the disappointment in his eyes, 'well, now I'm not so sure. You've turned everything arse over tit. I don't know what to make of you. You've let me down. I think that's what hurts the most, finding out that you had it in you to deceive us all these months.'

He stood up, as if to give himself the advantage. It worked. Jaz felt small and unworthy as he towered over her. 'You probably know by now,' he carried on, standing in front of the television, his hands placed in the small of his back, 'that your brothers have spoken with your so-called friend, Jack Solomon, and if we're to believe him, and Phin and Jimmy reckoned he was kosher, apparently you've been sneaking off to some kind of group where you sit around writing.' He paused. 'Is that true?'

So, he and her brothers knew that much. 'You make it sound like a subversive activity, Dad.'

He widened his eyes. 'Well pardon me, Miss Hoity-Toity, but in my book, not telling us about it in the first place immediately makes it subversive. Why lie to us about it if it was so innocent? Unless, of course, it isn't. Well? I'm waiting.'

'Tamzin and Lulu are always lying,' she said, buying herself some time. 'You never go on at them like this.'

He dismissed her comment instantly. 'They tell childish fibs that are as transparent as water. Whereas you've wilfully misled us week after week. You looked us right in the eye and took pleasure in making fools of us.' His expression hardened. 'You should know by now, Jaz, that nobody makes a fool out of me and gets away with it. And what, I want to know, is the effect of this group on your college work?'

'I've always put college first, Dad.'

'And you'd better be telling the truth over that.' He let out his breath, and just as Jaz was beginning to think she might be off the hook, he said, 'But you still haven't explained why you acted the way you did.'

She swallowed. Her father wasn't going to let it drop. The truth, she decided, was the only way to satisfy him. 'Dad, I kept it from you and Mum because I couldn't face the backlash.'

'Backlash?' he repeated. 'What's that supposed to mean?'

'Phin and Jimmy would have gone on and on about me kidding myself I was a writer, and as for Tamzin and Lulu, they would have been forever nosing around in my room trying to find what I'd written. You know what they're like, always poking their noses into my stuff.'

He looked at her as if he hadn't understood.

'Dad, you don't get it, do you? I have no privacy in this family. None at all.' Her voice wavered: the strain of the day was catching up with her. 'Everything I do is made fun of. I can't even yawn without someone accusing me of yawning differently from everyone else. I don't fit in. I know I don't. Is it any wonder I keep things to myself?' She lurched to her feet, tears welling in her eyes. 'I'm sorry I lied to you, and that you're disappointed in me. But you'd better prepare yourself for more disappointment because I'll probably fail my exams next year and never be the brilliant success of the family you expect me to be. Why don't you save that honour for the next load of babies Mum's having?'

Shaking, she fled the room. She heard her father call after her, but she stumbled up the stairs to her room, threw herself on her bed and sobbed.

Chapter Thirty-Nine

*

Richard stalked back into the centre of the village, where he'd just been, knowing that his behaviour had been unforgivable. He should never have shouted at Angela like that. It wasn't her fault. It was his: the slightest thing set him off. 'Can't you do anything to keep them quiet?' he'd snapped at her yesterday, when Christopher's music had thumped overhead while he'd been trying to read a report. Just now, after he had collected the Sunday papers, he'd let rip at her over the state of the kitchen – piles of laundry waiting to be ironed, last night's grill pan in the sink, a row of bulging carrier-bags she kept meaning to take to the Oxfam shop, and the wreckage of breakfast still on the table. 'Look at this mess!' he'd shouted. 'It's nearly lunchtime and nothing's been done.' He'd thrown the newspapers on to a chair and started to roll up his sleeves.

'Good gracious, Richard, whatever is the matter?' she'd said, looking up from the button she was sewing on to one of the boys' shirts.

'How can you sit there and say that? Even by your standards the place is a tip. I've had enough of it, and if you won't put some order back into it, I will.'

Except he hadn't. He'd clenched his teeth, turned on his heel and stormed out of the kitchen.

Poor Angela. She really didn't deserve to be on the receiving end of his ill-humour.

Ill-humour! Could going half crazy really be described so simply?

It was three agonising days since Dulcie had ended their relationship. He couldn't sleep, couldn't eat, couldn't concentrate.

His mind was always on Dulcie. He'd nearly screwed up with a potential client on Friday. When a brash Yorkshireman, clearly used to getting his own way, had asked him a question too many, he'd said the first thing that had come into his head: 'Take it or leave it. Either way I don't give a damn. If you're looking for cheap, where safety is a secondary consideration, I suggest you go elsewhere. Find yourself a tin-pot outfit to match your own.' A shockwave of paper-shuffling and throat-clearing had gone round the table, and everyone had lowered their eyes, but not before Richard had read the look in them. Cavanagh's past it . . . Cavanagh's losing it . . . Cavanagh's on his way out.

But to their disbelief, and disappointment perhaps, the Yorkshireman had reached for the water jug and laughed, 'Now there's summat we don't often hear, a bit of plain speaking from a lawyer. Maybe we can do business, after all.'

He might have pulled off the deal by the skin of his teeth, but it meant nothing.

If he didn't see Dulcie again, he wasn't sure he could continue living. Every day was torture. The thought that she was able to carry on her life without him made the pain more excruciating.

How could she?

And how could she have destroyed what they had, when it had been so special and had meant the world to them?

He would give anything to turn back the clock, for Henry and Kate never to have met. He wouldn't have thought it possible that he could wish any of his children a moment's pain, but now he wanted Henry to know just a fraction of the misery he was experiencing.

He wasn't even ashamed of it. He didn't care that it was selfish of him to want something for himself at the expense of another. Dulcie had accused him of not loving Henry as much as she loved Kate – well, perhaps she was right. All he knew was that he loved Dulcie more than he'd loved anyone.

He passed the post office, then the newsagent, and continued through the village, towards the church and the footpath he had often used during his convalescence. He took the steep incline slowly, becoming aware of the warmth of the sun on his back. He glanced up, and saw that the sky was the clearest of blues, marred only by a scattering of billowing white clouds in the west towards Shropshire and the distant swell of the Welsh hills. He paused to catch his breath; anger alone wouldn't propel him up the slope – it might even kill him.

But who would miss him if he had another heart-attack and died?

Angela would miss him as a provider and the rock upon which she'd built her life, but not as a husband or a lover. As for the children, Nicholas and Christopher would mourn his passing, but the older ones were sufficiently established to get on perfectly well without him.

Despite the mildness of the day, he shuddered, chilled to think that he might die up here on this deserted hill and no one would truly grieve for him.

Not even Dulcie. She had cast him out of her life so easily, fobbed him off on the phone when he'd tried to speak to her, proving that she could not have felt the same for him as he did for her.

A frightening weight of depression cast its insidious black shadow over him and he flung back his head, wanting to berate whoever it was up there who was playing so cruelly with his life.

Then, filled with a desperate urge towards self-destruction he began to walk again, rage and despair quickening his step, his breath coming fast, his chest aching.

Chapter Forty

*

Beth was glad it was time to go home. It had been a long day and several of their more tiresome patients had appeared. Some people never grasped that the medical centre was where sick people came to get better, not an annexe of the Citizen's Advice Bureau, or an extension of the local pub where malicious gossip and bitchy complaints could be directed at the staff. She buttoned her coat, said goodbye to Wendy and braced herself for the cold walk home. When she let herself in Nathan was in his bedroom, head bent over several open books on his desk. 'Good day?' she asked, from the doorway of his room as she surveyed the mess. He'd always been untidy – clothes littered the floor, the back of his chair and the end of his bed, and a welter of papers, files and books filled the remaining spaces on the floor and the window-sill. For one as clear-sighted and analytical as he was, and so concerned about his appearance, it amazed Beth that he was content to live in such a muddle. She wondered what Jaz made of it.

He swivelled in his chair, the light from his Anglepoise lamp illuminating his handsome face, accentuating the strong line of his jaw and emphasising his dark eyes: how like his father he was. 'A *tour de force* of a day,' he said. 'Oh, before I forget, Barnaby called. He said he'd try again later.'

'Did he say what it was about?'

'Nope. But I should think it's to do with Grandma. Otherwise he'd have said something.'

'How astute of you, Nathan. Don't suppose your brilliance stretches to making a cup of tea for your old ma while she slips into something more comfortable, does it?'

While she exchanged her work clothes for a pair of jeans and a polo-neck sweater, Beth considered returning Barnaby's call. But what if Lois answered the phone? She really wasn't in the mood to speak to her mother-in-law. Better to leave it to Barnaby to ring when the coast was clear.

Beth was full of admiration for Barnaby. His plan to get Lois back on speaking terms with Beth and Nathan was to whisk away his wife on a luxury cruise. He hoped that after three weeks on the high seas she would feel like a new woman and would be receptive to an extended olive branch. While the two of them were exploring the Caribbean, Beth and Nathan would look after Marsh House. 'If we came home to find there'd been a cold snap and the pipes had burst, I'd be in no end of trouble. For the chop, good and proper.'

'Presumably you won't be telling Lois who'll be taking care of things?' Beth had asked, anxiously.

'Good Lord, no! I shall tell her I've got an agency involved and there's nothing for her to worry about. I've planned surprise weekends away before, and I'm confident I can pull this off too.'

'When do you plan to tell her the truth?'

'I don't. She'll be presented with a *fait accompli* on our return.'

It was a risky plan and Beth didn't think there were many husbands in the world who would go to such lengths. She gave Barnaby full credit for being so brave: railroading Lois was not for the faint-hearted.

After supper, leaving Nathan to continue with his homework, Beth went downstairs to see Adele. She was moving out the day after tomorrow – Jack was moving in on Friday – and Ben had promised to help with some of the more personal items of her packing.

Adele looked tired and flustered when she opened the door and, for the first time since the move had been planned, Beth wondered if the old lady was doing the right thing. Was it all proving too much of a strain for her? When she stepped into the hall, she soon realised the cause of Adele's discomfort. A balding man in a suit that didn't fit his squat chunky body and a thin woman in an unflattering short black leather skirt were unhooking a pretty Victorian watercolour from the wall above the radiator. Beth knew that it was a particular favourite of Adele's and she couldn't imagine her friend wanting to part with it. 'I'm sorry, Adele,' she said, 'I didn't know you had visitors. Shall I call back later?' She had no intention of leaving, but she had to make a show of courtesy.

'No, please, don't go.' A hand was placed insistently on her forearm. 'This is my nephew, Vernon, and his friend Sheila.'

'*Sylvia*.' The bald man corrected her. He held out his hand to Beth; there was a sheen of sweat on his top lip. 'And you might be?'

'Oh, Vernon, don't be so pompous. Beth is my neighbour from upstairs, and quite possibly the nicest person you'll have the pleasure of meeting. She's always looked after me so well.'

Beth smiled at Adele, but she saw Vernon's grey eyes grow sharper and the proffered hand fell to his side. She didn't much care for the look of him. Or his skinny friend. To her knowledge, this was the first time in ages he had called on his aunt, and he was manhandling one of Adele's favourite paintings. His showing up like this smacked of opportunism, and Beth was having none of it.

The telephone rang and while Adele went to answer it in the sitting room, Beth said, in her most commanding receptionist voice, 'I should be careful with that picture. It's extremely valuable.'

'Do you really think so?' Vernon took it from Sylvia, and held it up to the light for closer inspection.

'Yes,' said Beth. 'I'd go so far as to say it's practically priceless . . . to your aunt. So why don't I put it back where it belongs before it gets damaged?'

The grey eyes gleamed, and bored into her. But Beth held her ground and took the picture. 'Are you staying to help Adele pack, or do you have to rush away?'

Vernon looked as mad as a hornet. He opened his mouth to speak, but was cut short by Adele reappearing in the hall. 'That was Jack,' she said to Beth. 'Just wanting to reassure me that everything's going like clockwork. Oh, not stopping, Vernon?'

Still looking furious, Vernon had dug his car keys out of his jacket pocket and was jiggling them agitatedly. 'No,' he said briskly. 'We'd better be making tracks. You obviously have it all sorted here.' He threw Beth a hostile glance and jiddled the keys again. 'Well, good luck with the move. Call if you need anything.'

'Thank you, Vernon. It was nice of you to drop in.' Adele had relaxed and was acting the part of perfect hostess. 'You must come and see me in my new home. You too, Shirley.'

'It's *Sylvia*.'

'Of course it is, Vernon. Whatever was I thinking? It must be my age.'

They stood on the doorstep waving off the scavengers. Out of the corner of her mouth, Beth said, 'You wicked woman. You knew perfectly well what her name was, didn't you?'

One last wave and they closed the door.

'Beth, how could you think such a thing? Oh, but I'm so glad to see the back of them. For a moment I was quite unnerved. Now, where shall we start?'

Beth suggested the bedroom. 'If you're anything like me, that's where you keep your most personal possessions.'

Beth insisted that Adele direct operations from a chair, and took on the lion's share of the wrapping and packing. Before long they had cleared the contents of one chest of drawers and a bedside table and felt justified in awarding themselves a coffee break.

'What brought the dutiful nephew out of the woodwork?' Beth asked, handing Adele her cup. 'Apart from the opportunity to pick over the spoils.'

'Heavens, Beth, am I to take it that you didn't fall for my dear Vernon?'

'You assume correctly. And I didn't like his motives either. Sorry if that's too brutally honest.'

Adele smiled. 'I appreciate your honesty and your timely coming to my rescue. I've never seen myself as a dithery old lady before, but seeing Vernon sizing up my possessions so blatantly brought it home to me that I'm on borrowed time and the vultures are circling.'

'You're not dithery and you're certainly not on borrowed time, not by a good many years. Plenty of deviousness left in you yet.'

'I'd like to believe you, my dear, but sadly your kind words will not keep the bell from tolling for me.'

Later that night, Beth felt weary of spirit. Before the move business had taken root, Adele would never have spoken like that. It grieved her profoundly that her friend seemed to be giving in without a fight. And who would chivvy her along when she moved into the retirement home?

To cheer herself up, Beth switched on her computer. There were two emails. The first was from Simone, complaining about how hot it was and that if she wasn't careful she'd soon be able to get a job as a Mother Teresa lookalike.

The second was from Ewan.

She clicked on OPEN, her heart stepping up a gear or two, as it always did when she heard from him. It had taken a lot of courage on her part to agree to meet him. 'Let's not rush things,' she'd said, in response to his suggestion, 'but I'd like to meet you. Although you know what they say, curiosity killed the cat.'

Miaow! What are you saying, my feline friend? [he'd responded]. That you think I'm going to bump you off?!!!

No, but we might kill off our friendship with a dose of nasty reality.

Mmm . . . it's certainly a possibility, but sometimes you have to take a risk. I promise I won't press you. I'll leave you to decide when, how and if. If it makes you feel any better, my daughter thinks I'm off my head. She reckons I'm the one in danger, and that you could be a man – a crazed psychotic man – pretending to be a woman. You're not, are you?

She'd told him she was definitely a woman and that the only psychotic episodes she experienced were when she was suffering from PMT.

On the computer screen Ewan's latest email was before her.

BAD NEWS, I'VE BEEN REJECTED!

Tossed aside on the scrap-heap of failure. Not me personally (though it feels that way), my manuscript. The publisher, who seemed so keen, has now read the whole caboodle and thinks, and here I quote, 'Blah, blah, blah . . . not quite what we're looking for in the current climate . . . more blah, blah, and . . . therefore sadly not suitable for our list.'

Oh, to have one's fragile spirits soaring one minute only to have them dashed upon the rocks of one's shattered hopes and dreams! Don't worry, I'm not going purple-prosey on you. But I will admit to feeling a tad crushed. In fact, very crushed. Stupid, I know. But there we have it, a man felled by his own hurt pride.

Are you getting the hint that I'm feeling sorry for myself? No?

Well, believe me, there's plenty more self-pity at my disposal, but I shall manfully resist the urge to come across as a big-girl's blouse.

But something good did come my way today – the opportunity to attend a writers' conference. It's a week-long residential course near Harrogate where wannabe writers get the chance to meet agents and editors and attend talks and workshops.

The thought has occurred to me, that maybe – just possibly, at a pinch . . . erm . . . that you might like to . . . erm . . . attend said course as well.

A shocking suggestion, I know. But if you think about it, you'd be completely safe, surrounded, as it were, by so many other people. Granted I can't vouch for their sanity, and let's face it, writers are not the sanest lunatics in the asylum, but at least you'd have plenty of folk to protect you, should a full moon appear and I turn into a madman, or a howling wolf.

Hang on a tick, moonlight is streaming through the curtains and I can feel . . . oh, my saints, I can feel a tickling sensation working its way down my back and arms. Oh, no! Shaggy hairs are sprouting all over my . . . Ah-whoo-oo! Ah-whoo-oo!

Write back post haste and tell me something to cheer me up.

Ewan X

Beth smiled and began typing.

You're mad, Ewan Jones! Totally mad! As barking as the werewolf you pretend to be.

Glory be, one little rejection and you go to pieces. Get a grip, man! Pull yourself together.

Seriously, though, I'm sorry to hear you've had such a horrible knock-back. But you're a big boy and I'm sure you'll pick yourself up, dust yourself down, and try again. At least the publisher didn't tell you that you'd written a load of old rubbish – as I'm sure they'd tell me if ever I had the nerve to submit anything I'd written. As rejections go, that must rate as quite a nice one. Remind yourself that you haven't written a bad book, your only mistake was to send your manuscript to the wrong publisher.

Now then, and don't fall off your chair with shock, I think the writers' conference sounds a good idea. But you'll have to give

me more information before I commit myself . . .
  Forever cautious,
  Beth X

She still couldn't believe she was conducting such an enjoyable
relationship via the Internet. She was utterly charmed by Ewan's
ability to poke fun at himself, even when he must have been feeling
low. He was a refreshing change from all the men who took
themselves so seriously.

If meeting him was a risk, she was more than happy to take it.

Chapter Forty-One

*

With the three removal men now gone, Jack surveyed the mess they'd left behind them. Although he and they had worked hard at emptying boxes and placing furniture, there was still a lot to put straight. An hour ago his new home hadn't looked too bad, but now there didn't seem enough space for all his belongings.

First, before he unpacked anything else, he needed a drink. Luckily, he knew where to locate his limited drinks cupboard – it was in the dining room, lined up on the mantelpiece. He poured himself a large glass of single malt whisky, stood with his back to the door and faced the fireplace. When the original house had been divided into two flats, this room had suffered: space had been taken from it to provide a kitchen. As soon as he had the flat organised, but before he got too comfortable, he would get a builder in to open up the rooms. The work would cause massive disruption, but the end result would be worth it. He'd put a lot of thought into how he wanted the room to look. The old gas fire would be ripped out and the chimney opened up so that he could have a real fire, and in front of it a new sofa. There would be floor-to-ceiling shelves along the main wall, and he'd have two waist-high cupboards built either side of the fireplace and more shelves above for CDs and books. He'd have to do something about the lighting – spotlights and lamps, probably. The kitchen needed a complete revamp, new units and a new layout. He'd also buy a proper-sized table so that he and the girls could eat in comfort, instead of perching on stools at a breakfast bar as they had at his last house. He wanted to create a stylish room that would be the focus of the flat, somewhere Amber and Lucy would feel at home.

If they didn't go to America.

His throat clenched and he tightened his grip on the glass. Maddie's words from last Friday came back to taunt him. *It would be a fantastic opportunity for them.*

'And what about the fantastic opportunity of seeing their father?' he'd thrown at her, once he was able to speak without resorting to swearing.

'Keep your voice down, Jack,' Maddie had hissed. 'People are staring.'

'Let them!' He'd tossed his napkin on to his half-finished plate of pasta, his appetite gone. 'But it's good to see that you're more concerned about what people think of you in public than the welfare of our children. And talking of that, what the hell are you doing about Amber not eating?'

'It's just a phase,' she said dismissively. 'All girls go through it.'

'That's right, throw it into the okay bin along with everything else. Oh, it's okay that Amber's self-esteem is so low she's starving herself because every girl her age is doing it. Just as it's okay to cheat on your husband because everyone's doing that too!'

'Oh, for heaven's sake, stop it! Why do you always have to turn everything into a drama? You never used to be so bloody melodramatic.'

'You just don't get it, do you? You don't understand that there's nothing worse you could do to me. You sleep with my best friend, you leave me for him, and you limit the amount of time I can see our children. Then, and this is the best bit, you expect me to sit back and keep my voice down while you inform me that I'll be lucky to see them again. Well, pardon me if I don't play along with how you think I should behave.'

'I didn't say you couldn't see the girls again.'

'As good as,' he flung at her. 'So, come on, then, what's the big plan you and Tony have hatched? Do I get to see the girls every other summer holiday? Is that it?'

She picked up her handbag and plonked it on to her lap. 'If you're not going to talk reasonably, there's no point in continuing this conversation. There's nothing to be gained.' She retrieved her car keys from the bag and stood up. 'I feel sorry for you, Jack. You've allowed yourself to be blinded by your bitterness. Perhaps it would be better if Amber and Lucy did see less of you. I'd hate the girls to see you like this. It would harm them far more than anything Tony or I could do to them.'

Too angry and upset to follow her, he stayed where he was, weighed down with impotent fury. He was appalled by her vile accusation that he could ever hurt his children.

The unfamiliar ring of his doorbell interrupted his thoughts. He climbed over a coffee table and, sidestepping boxes, cushions and a stack of lampshades teetering on a pile of paperbacks, he made it to the front door, hoping that whoever it was wouldn't depress him even more. So long as he didn't think about Maddie and Tony, he was okay.

When he opened the door he was pleased to see that his first caller was Beth.

'Hi,' she said. 'I've just got in from work and wanted to make sure you hadn't forgotten you were having supper with us tonight.'

Smiling, he said, 'It's only been the thought of a decent meal to look forward to that's got me through the day.'

She peered round the door, to the war zone of the hall. 'Has it been awful?'

'Not really. If you're brave enough, come in and see for yourself.'

They stood in the middle of the hall, the perfect vantage-point from which to see into every room.

'Doesn't look too good, does it?' he said gloomily, overwhelmed by the enormity of the task ahead.

'It'll be fine,' she said. 'Every move is the same – you'll soon have it together. I could give you a hand tomorrow if you like. I'm not at the surgery in the morning. It's my weekend off.'

Touched, he said, 'That's really kind of you, but I'd hate to be accused of taking advantage.'

'Nonsense. Anyway, we're friends too. Comrades of the written word, as I think you once said. Now, I'd better get my skates on or there'll be no supper tonight. Eight o'clock suit you?'

As it turned out, Beth had time to set the table and grab a quick soak in the bath. Afterwards, while she was slipping a pair of pearl studs into her ear-lobes, she heard Nathan talking on the phone in the kitchen.

It was half-term, and to Beth's knowledge he hadn't spoken to Jaz all week. She had wanted to ask him if everything was all right between them but, respecting her son's privacy, she had held off probing. After all, she had her own need for concealment. She was beginning to feel guilty that she was behaving so furtively over Ewan. But her reluctance to tell anyone about him was based partly on embarrassment – how could she admit that she had grown fond of someone in such a way? – and partly on her enjoyment of the secrecy. It was fun to have a mystery man in her life. And exciting.

One day at work Wendy had commented that there was something different about her. 'I can't put my finger on it, but if I didn't know better, Beth King,' she'd said, 'I'd say you were indulging in more than a good night's sleep before coming into work. You're not seeing someone on the sly, are you?'

Smiling, Beth had said, 'Wendy, I can categorically tell you that I'm definitely not *seeing* someone on the sly. If I were, you'd be the first to know.'

Jack arrived promptly at eight o'clock, bottle of wine in hand. Beth thought he looked more cheerful than he had earlier, and was glad she'd invited him to dinner. During the meal she told him about Adele's ghastly nephew, Vernon, and he offered to accompany Beth when she visited the old lady in her new home next week. 'Why don't you bring Amber and Lucy as well,' Beth said, knowing how Adele had loved entertaining them some weeks ago.

'It wouldn't be too much for her?'

'I think she'd be tickled pink.'

They were clearing away the main-course plates when Jack asked Nathan, who was about to go out for the evening with Billy, if he'd ever met Jaz's brothers.

'No, but I get the feeling she isn't too keen on them. Why do you ask?'

'Oh, no reason.'

'Jack?'

He refilled his and Beth's glasses and looked at Beth, with a strange half-smile. 'Well, okay, I'll tell you, but I don't want this to get back to Jaz. She'd hit the roof if she knew what happened. Her brothers followed me last Friday and when they got the opportunity they bundled me into the back of their car and threatened me. They'd seen her in my car the night before and they thought I was carrying on with their little sister. Very laudable behaviour on their part, you could say.' He glanced at Nathan. 'And for the record, just in case you were preparing to swing a right hook in my direction, I'm *not* up to anything with Jaz.'

'That doesn't make sense,' said Nathan, with a frown. 'Her family know that Thursday night is her writers' group night. Why didn't they assume you were her legit ride home?'

'Ah, well, for reasons best known only to Jaz, it appears that she's kept her family in ignorance of that one important fact.'

Nathan looked thoughtful. 'Do you suppose that means she's been lying to them?'

'Almost certainly,' said Jack.

'Which would mean,' Nathan said slowly, 'that if she's been caught lying, she's probably been grounded.' Suddenly he smiled. 'Thanks, Jack, you've cleared up a mystery for me. Well, folks, I'm off out now. Don't wait up.' He left the flat whistling, the jaunty spring back in his step, which Beth now realised had been missing all week. She saw the puzzled expression on Jack's face, and said, 'I think you've just solved what's been bugging him. There hasn't been a peep from Jaz. No visits. No phone calls. Now he knows why. And it's nothing to do with him.'

'Well, if I were Nathan I'd be careful. If Jaz's brothers take a dislike to him, he'd better have some nifty self-defence manoeuvres up his sleeve. Do you think she's told her parents about him?'

Beth pondered this as she unwrapped the selection of cheeses she'd bought at lunchtime and arranged them on a plate. She decided Jaz hadn't. As far as she was aware Nathan had never been invited to the Raffertys' house. It was always the same arrangement: either Jaz came here or she met Nathan in town. She sat down. 'Dulcie told me yesterday that she'd given up trying to contact Jaz to tell her she was cancelling last night's meeting. She couldn't get a response from her mobile and the Raffertys' telephone number is ex-directory. At the time I'd thought that perhaps Jaz and her family had gone away for the week to their apartment in Tenerife. But if she's in trouble with her parents, perhaps they've punished her by taking away her phone.'

'How did she seem when you spoke to her?'

'Jaz?'

'No. Dulcie.'

'Oh. No better, really. Tired and subdued, feeling guilty too for letting the group down.'

'I would never have thought her capable of something like that.'

'Like what?'

'Deliberately moving in on a married man to break up his marriage.'

Beth knew how sensitive Jack was about the break-up of his own marriage, and chose her words with care. 'I don't think these things are ever deliberate. Besides, she hasn't broken the marriage up, has she?'

He helped himself to a cracker from the plate in the middle of the table and snapped it in two. 'She certainly wasn't strengthening it.'

A silence fell on them, until Beth said, 'You okay?'

'Since you ask, no.'

'Want to talk about it, or would you rather I minded my own business? By the way, do you want some cheese with those crumbs?'

He looked down at his plate ruefully. 'I'm turning into a wreck, Beth.' He sighed. 'Just as I think I'm getting my act together, another load of crap falls into my lap. The latest news from Maddie and Wonderboy Tony is that they want to go and live in California. It would mean I'd never see the girls. I'll – I'll lose them for sure.' His voice broke and he turned away, his jaw set hard.

For an awkward moment Beth didn't know what to do. Instinct told her that he needed physical reassurance, a gently placed hand, or a hug. But years of hiding her own emotions and keeping herself to herself held her back from showing physically how deeply she cared for his pain. She resorted to words. 'Oh, Jack, I'm so sorry. That's awful. Is there anything you can do to stop it?'

He swallowed, but kept his eyes from hers. She could see that he was close to the edge and her heart went out to him.

'I've spoken to my solicitor and he says all I can do is appeal to their mother's better nature.' His cynicism rang out in the quiet of the kitchen and he turned to face her. 'And I stand as much chance of doing that as I do of winning the Booker Prize.'

Beth gave him a small, tentative smile. 'Stranger things have happened,' she said softly. She poured the last of the wine into his glass. Why couldn't she just give him a hug? She hadn't always been like this. Before Adam had died she had never been afraid of physical contact with a man. It was as if the woman inside her had withered and died too. Inexplicably she felt like crying. But more inexplicable was the anger she suddenly felt towards Adam. How dare he still have the power to do this to her?

She got up abruptly to fetch another bottle of wine. While she

254

opened it, she asked Jack about the plans he had for Adele's flat – it would be some time yet before she saw it as his.

Plainly relieved to talk about something else, he apologised for the inconvenience he would soon be causing. 'I hope you won't be disturbed too much when the builders arrive,' he said.

'I'm sure it will be fine. And, anyway, I'll be out at work when they're here, unless you plan to have them hard at it during the night. Then I might have something to say.'

'Along with the rest of the neighbourhood, I shouldn't wonder.'

It wasn't long before Beth had drunk too much and she knew that she would pay for her recklessness in the morning with an almighty hangover. But she didn't care. And it didn't stop her switching from wine to spirits. Her anger had now given way to giggling mellowness. Jack, too, was laughing and smiling more than usual and together they sat on the sofa, finding whatever the other said absurdly witty and amusing. When she offered to make them some coffee, Jack pulled her back with a clumsy tug. 'Coffee's for wimps,' he said. 'How about another glass of that excellent single malt?'

'Sorry,' she said. 'Clean out now. I've got some inferior blended whisky if you like?'

He shook his head. 'I never touch the cheap stuff. It's guaranteed to bring on a hangover.'

'Adam used to like whisky,' she said, mournfully. 'He drank half a bottle of it the night he died. You mustn't tell anyone I said that.'

'Why?'

'Because it would be very, very, *very* disloyal to Adam.'

He leaned back on the sofa, put his arm around her. 'And you're a very loyal person, aren't you, Beth? Is that why you haven't remarried?'

'In part.'

'Which part in particular?'

She was enjoying the feel of his arm resting on her shoulder. 'The part other beers cannot reach.'

He joined in with her laughter. 'Oh, Beth, what a pair we make. But have you really never been tempted to get married again? You must have had offers – you're a very attractive woman.'

'Nobody's asked me.'

'Is that because you've had the drawbridge up?'

'It's not a crime to be discerning,' she said, with a hint of defensiveness.

'It *would* be a crime if you ended up depriving yourself of a happier life. But, then, who am I to talk? Look at the mess I made of things when I rushed into the arms of the first woman I came across.'

Hearing a maudlin tone creep into his voice again, Beth said, 'I have a secret. A whopping great secret no one knows anything about.'

His face broke into a wide smile. 'So what precisely are you hiding up your sleeve?'

'A man.'

'A man?' he repeated. 'Let me see.' He pulled her arm towards him and peered up her sleeve. 'I see no man.'

'That's because he's not there. He's—' She broke off and laughed. 'He's . . . he's a cyberman.'

He cocked an eyebrow at her. 'You sure about that? There's no chance you're muddling him up with the Dalek I saw in town the other week?'

Still laughing, she said, 'His name's Ewan Jones.'

'And?'

'And what?'

'Well, you'll have to fill me in on the details. All I've got so far is that he's a cyberman called Ewan Jones. Does that make him a Welsh enemy of the Time Lords?'

She shook her head, then waited for the room to stop spinning. 'He's a little older than me and has a great talent for making me laugh. He's also a fellow writer. Not published, but hopeful.'

'So where did you meet him? At a *Doctor Who* convention?'

She hesitated. 'Um . . . we haven't actually met.' She told him how they'd 'met' on-line and how their friendship had developed. 'I suppose it all sounds a bit silly to you, doesn't it?' she said, when she'd told Jack everything, even the possibility of meeting Ewan at the writers' conference.

He squeezed her close to him. 'I think it's bloody brilliant. How else should a writer meet his or her ideal partner but through the written word? Perhaps I should give it a go.'

'But what do you think about me meeting him in the way he's suggested? Tell me honestly.'

'Go for it, Beth. You know deep down you want to. So why not?'

'We might not like each other in the flesh. For instance, he might wear the most awful shoes – grey slip-ons – with white towelling socks.' She pulled a face. 'It might be disastrous. Stop laughing, Jack, these things matter. More seriously, he might turn out to be—'

'A roaring nutcase,' he interrupted her. 'In which case you need a chaperon.' He paused. 'Hey, and I know I'm almost as drunk as you, but I've just had the best idea of the night. Why don't we all go?'

'All who?'

'Hidden Talents – Dulcie, Jaz, Victor, you and me. We could go as a group. It'd be great. Just the thing to spur us on with our writing and at the same time we'd be checking out your bloke for you. What do you think?'

'I think, and I know I'm going to feel lousy in the morning, but we should both get drunk more often. You're a genius, Jack Solomon.'

'And to prove my brilliant idea isn't a one-off, here's another. Let's email your cyberspace boyfriend right now and give him the good news.'

'Now?'

'No time like the present. Then you won't back out. What's more, let's spice up the message and give him a taste of the real Beth King.'

She looked at him doubtfully, but he laughed and pulled her to her feet. 'Don't come over all wimpish on me, Beth. We're going to make him even keener to meet you in the flesh. You're always saying how good with words I am, well, tonight we'll put that to the test. I plan to have the man drooling at the thought of you.'

It was a mark of how drunk she was that she allowed Jack to drag her across the room to her computer. 'I hope you're not going to make me do something I'll regret,' she said.

Chapter Forty-Two

*

The following morning, in Suffolk, Ewan went for a brisk walk along the beach. A blustery wind blew off the North Sea, sending waves crashing in. It was an invigorating start to the day, and he felt better for it. One way or another, he'd had a lousy week. The rejection of *Emily and Albert* had hit him harder than he'd thought it would. He'd taken it personally. Put simply, the story mattered to him and he'd wanted to share it with others.

He bent down picked up a stone, hurled it far into the churning sea. 'I must be turning into a sentimental old fool,' he said aloud, his words catching on the wind. He threw another stone, then another. He never tired of the sea, could never imagine himself living anywhere else. At last, he turned his back on the shore, and tramped up the shingle incline towards the brightly coloured beach huts, one of which, so the local paper claimed last week, had been sold recently for a staggering ten thousand pounds. The world was a crazy place. The shelter of the dunes came as a welcome relief from the ravages of the shore, and he enjoyed the relative quiet and warmth before heading for the main street, where he stopped off at the handy open-all-hours shop for a newspaper and a packet of bacon.

While he was cooking his breakfast, cracking two eggs into the frying-pan alongside the bread and sizzling rashers, he thought of the dinner party he would be going to that evening. It was yet another attempt by some of his well-meaning friends to partner him off. That was the trouble with the happily married: they hated having a single person loitering untidily about the place. He hoped the woman he'd be seated next to tonight would have something interesting to say. The last woman at one of Phil and Susannah's dateline parties, had been an intensely bitter divorcee – an English lecturer and a foaming-at-the-mouth feminist to boot. She'd had only one topic of social chit-chat when she'd drunk too much wine: that all men were feeble and devious, and, come the revolution, deserved everything and more that they had coming to them. Hardly the type of engaging conversation to inspire any man to volunteer for active service. 'What in God's name did you think we'd have in common?' he'd asked Phil the next morning, when he'd called to thank his friends for their hospitality.

'Susannah thought you'd enjoy the intellectual challenge,' Phil had said. 'Not forgetting the literary connection.'

'Oh, yes. What was it she said about popular fiction? It should be strangled at birth. Phil, if she had her way, bookshops up and down the country would be cleansed of all gold-embossed jackets.'

He tipped his breakfast on to a plate and sat at the table, where he'd laid out the arts pages of the *Daily Telegraph*. After he'd read the book reviews he tidied the kitchen, and went through to his office, pretending, as he always did, that he wasn't eager to see if there was a message from Beth.

There was.

He read it twice, and hoped she wouldn't regret having sent it. It was a gem. Written, he presumed, while she was under the influence of something a little more intoxicating than a mug of bedtime Ovaltine.

Beth knew that something was terribly wrong even before she opened her eyes and found that the light penetrating the gap in the curtains was burning the back of her eyeballs. She turned on to her side and tried to sleep again. To pretend that her hangover was nothing more than a nasty dream.

But she knew it wasn't, and as she recalled the events of the night before, she drew her knees up to her chest, assuming the foetal position, as though it would protect her from the shame of her behaviour.

Drunk.

Oh, horribly drunk.

She remembered Jack kissing her goodbye and leaving, and Nathan arriving home to find her bent over the toilet. 'I don't think I'm very well,' she'd whimpered thinking of the countless lectures she had given him on the evils of alcohol. 'It must have been something I ate.'

'Yeah, that would be it, Mum,' he'd said, helping her into bed. She'd bet a pound to a penny he'd been laughing at her.

Then she remembered something even more shameful: the email she and Jack had sent Ewan.

She groaned, and sank further beneath the duvet.

'Oh, let the world end now,' she murmured.

Chapter Forty-Three

*

Dulcie had thought she was covering up remarkably well, but it was clear from Prue and Maureen's expressions that she had failed miserably. Under the full glare of her friends' gaze, the last of her defences crumbled.

'I'm not going to beat about the bush,' Prue said, with her customary directness, after their waitress had brought them their baked potatoes and salads, 'but what on earth is the matter with you, Dulcie? Are you ill?'

It took all her strength to inject a light-hearted quip into her response. 'Of course I'm not ill. What's more, I'll see the pair of you out.'

'Nonsense!' declared Prue, grinding a shower of salt over her lunch. 'I've never seen you looking so down in the mouth.'

In a less acerbic tone, Maureen said, 'She's right, Dulcie. You don't look your normal self. It's not Andrew or Kate, is it?'

'No, they're both fine. But thanks for asking.' She forced a cube of cucumber into her mouth.

It had been a mistake to agree to meet up with her dear friends. Why hadn't she cried off, with some plausible excuse? How had she thought she could ever convince them that all was well when she knew she looked a mess and that her demeanour told the world that she had undergone a dramatic transformation for the worse? Everything was slipping away from her. She'd had to cancel the writers' group last week and didn't think she'd be able to cope with it tomorrow evening either. Writing was the last thing on her mind.

And all because of Richard. Of what she had denied herself. Oh, how she missed him! With each day that passed, the pain grew worse. He phoned her every morning on his mobile, trying to make her see sense. He'd broken down this morning and she'd heard him sobbing. 'Don't do this to me, Dulcie. I'd rather be dead than not see you again.' Hating herself, she'd gently replaced the receiver with a trembling hand. The pain of hearing his anguish, knowing that she was the cause of it, was too much.

She had loved Philip, and had gone on loving him long after he'd died, but losing him hadn't been as painful as this. She could only conclude that it was because she had played no part in causing her loss and the heartbreaking devastation that followed. There had been no guilt to deal with. Only the purity of grief.

She looked up suddenly and saw that both Prue and Maureen were hunting through their handbags. She wondered what they were looking for. When Maureen handed her a small packet of tissues, she understood that the game was up, that there was no hiding from them now. She wiped her eyes, blew her nose and said, 'Would you mind very much if we . . .' She blew her nose again and cleared her throat. 'I think I ought to go home.'

While Maureen sat with Dulcie on the sofa, Prue pushed down the plunger on the cafetière and poured three cups of coffee. When they were all seated, Dulcie told them the whole story. She started at the beginning, with the day she had met Richard – the day he had changed her life. She told them how easily she and Richard had fallen in love, and even, with a degree of pride, what a wonderful lover he was: tender, considerate and infinitely passionate. 'He really was the most perfect man,' she murmured, knowing that her revelations were being received with more than a little envy.

'Except for being married,' muttered Prue.

'Yes. Except for being married,' echoed Dulcie. Then she told her friends about Kate and Henry. Which shocked them. They hadn't seen it coming. Who would?

'Is that why you've ended it with him?' asked Maureen.

Dulcie nodded. 'You understand, don't you? I had no choice. If there's a chance of those two young people being happy, I couldn't stand in their way.'

Prue put down her coffee cup. 'All I can say is, I hope they bloody well appreciate what you've done for them.'

'That's just the point, Prue,' said Maureen. 'They mustn't ever know. If they did it would ruin everything. Then no one would be happy.'

Prue looked at Dulcie in admiration. 'If I were in your shoes, I'm not sure I could be so selfless.'

Dulcie drained her cup and placed it carefully on its saucer. 'Anyway, it's all over now. And it's time I pulled myself together. I need to remind myself that I had a perfectly good life before Richard popped into it.'

Her friends looked at her doubtfully. Prue said, 'Dulcie, you need a break. You should get right away from Maywood. Why don't you go to London and stay with Kate or Andrew? You could treat yourself to leisurely trips to the galleries, lunches in smart restaurants, and no end of shopping sprees.'

Maureen warmed to the idea. 'And the theatre. Don't forget all those plays and musicals you could take in. Concerts too. It would be perfect.'

'It would also be exhausting.'

'Yes, but you wouldn't have time to dwell on . . . well, you know what I mean.'

Dulcie smiled at Maureen, loving her for her sensitivity. 'It's all right, you can say his name. I shan't faint at the sound of it.'

That evening, while she was listening to *The Archers*, Dulcie's mind kept wandering. What her friends had suggested wasn't so silly. But London didn't appeal. If she went there, she would inevitably end up seeing Kate and, very likely, Henry.

No. London was out of the question.

But now that the idea had been planted in her mind, she couldn't let it go. Prue and Maureen were right: time away from Maywood would do her good. It would also mean that Richard wouldn't be able to ring her.

Leaving Ambridge to its own devices, she went upstairs to the cupboard on the landing where she kept a stock of holiday brochures. The one on the top of the pile caught her eye – *Italian Escapes*. She took it downstairs to the kitchen, put it on the table, and made herself a sandwich, most of which she knew she wouldn't eat. But she needed something to occupy her while she let the thought of going to Italy take root. What would best suit her current frame of mind? The dramatic scenery of the Amalfi coast? The lakes? Como? Garda? Maggiore? Or should she venture inland to the hills and valleys of Umbria? Tuscany was a possibility too, although she had been there before.

Her sandwich made, she poured herself a glass of wine – Italian, as it turned out. An omen? She sat at the table and opened the brochure. Already she had dismissed the lakes: she wanted to keep them for a summer trip, as she'd previously planned. She flicked through the glossy pages, seeing images of Byzantine and Renaissance art, of rustic hotels nestling in rural idylls and snow-capped mountains, of piazzas, palazzos and stunning waterfronts, of perfectly ripened tomatoes, basil and creamy white mozzarella sprinkled with black pepper and drenched in olive oil.

For the first time in days, Dulcie felt hungry and she bit into her sandwich – the bread was past its best, and the lettuce had lost its crispness. Delving further into the brochure, she stopped at the section for city breaks. A photograph of St Mark's Square and the majestic domes of the basilica stared back at her.

Venice?

Oh, surely not. Venice was for couples strolling romantically hand in hand through the maze of narrow streets, or taking magical moonlit gondola rides along the Grand Canal.

It was a terrible idea. How could she consider rubbing salt into such a raw wound?

But how long was she going to allow herself to wallow in self-pity? Life had to go on.

She read on, scanning the range of hotels, looking for one that appealed. The Hotel Isabella was described as a hidden jewel, an oasis of tranquillity and refined charm reminiscent of a bygone era. Five minutes' walk from St Mark's Square, it was ideally situated and wouldn't inflict too large a dent in the bank balance, the brochure claimed. It sounded perfect. She bent back the corner of the page to mark the place, then realised that she'd finished her sandwich. It was the first meal that she had managed to eat in days. She took it as a good sign. Her friends would be pleased. 'You must eat,' they'd told her. 'How can you expect to think straight if you're not taking care of your body's needs?' They had left her with hugs of sympathy and repeated instructions that if she needed them she must ring, no matter what time of day or night. 'We're here for you, Dulcie,' Prue had said. 'I just wish you'd told us before.'

There had been no criticism of her affair with Richard, which was what she had feared. She had been convinced her behaviour would meet with their disapproval – people who were married, happily or otherwise, tended to take a dim view of others who appeared to ride roughshod over the sanctity of marriage.

How long, she wondered, before she would rid herself of the guilt? Not just for being party to Richard's betrayal of his marriage vows but for the pain she was now causing him.

Eventually she dragged her weary body upstairs to bed, telling herself that Richard was as culpable as she was, and that he had to take his share of the responsibility for what they had done. But men were different. Guilt slid off their consciences so easily.

She slipped her nightdress over her head, and tried to remember something Jaz had once said. Something clever about men and women and their response to guilt. It came to her while she was brushing her teeth. 'Show me a woman who feels no guilt and I'll show you a man.' Jack had taken issue with this, but Dulcie and Beth had laughed heartily.

How extraordinarily mature and perceptive Jaz was, despite her age.

Chapter Forty-Four

*

With a terrible feeling of *déjà vu*, Jaz listened intently to what her mother was saying.

'Now, Jaz, there's plenty of food in the freezer so you won't need to worry too much, not for a couple of days anyway. But if you could keep an eye on the girls, make sure they do their homework, it would be a great weight off my mind. I expect I'll be home by the weekend, so everything will be back to normal then.'

It was Thursday, almost two weeks since her father had found out about Hidden Talents. With no lesson after last break, Jaz had come home early from college to find her mother upstairs packing an overnight bag. 'What's going on, Mum?' she'd asked.

'Oh, nothing to worry about. My blood pressure's sky high so the doctor's ordered me to have a few days' bed-rest in hospital.'

Jaz's heart had plummeted. 'If there's nothing to worry about, why do you have to go into hospital?'

'Oh, I suppose they want some of those young trainee doctors to have a geriatric mother to practise on. Who am I to argue? Cheer up, Jaz, it'll be fine.'

But Jaz didn't think so. She watched her mother close her overnight bag. 'Where's Dad?' she asked.

'He's on his way with Phin and Jimmy. They'll be here any minute and then your father will take me to the hospital.'

'But if there's nothing wrong, Mum,' Jaz persisted, 'why the rush?'

She didn't get an answer because just then they heard the back door nearly crashing off its hinges, followed by the noisy entrance of Tamzin and Lulu, bags thrown on the floor, fridge door pulled

266

open and war breaking out over who was entitled to the last of the Sunny Delight.

'You will be patient with them, won't you?' her mother said.

Jaz took the bag from her, and walked with her to the bedroom door. 'I'll try, Mum, but they act up even more when you're not around.'

Her mother stroked her hair. 'We have to make allowances for them,' she said good-humouredly. 'They're throwbacks to the Rafferty side of the family, unlike you. You take after mine.' Out on the landing, she paused, and with one of the soft smiles that reminded Jaz of how much she loved her mother, said, 'I'm sorry how things seem to fall your way, Jaz. That's the trouble with large families. There's always one who attracts more than their fair share of responsibility.' Her expression turned serious. 'Now, I don't know what's going on between you and your father because he won't tell me. All he says is that he's got it in hand and that there's nothing for me to lose any sleep over, but if there is anything I should know about, you would—'

A loud crash from the kitchen made them both start. Jaz didn't want her mother to pursue this line of conversation any further so she said, 'Dad's right, Mum, there's nothing for you to worry about.'

Her mother smiled again and laid a gentle hand on Jaz's shoulder. 'He can be bombastic and sometimes irritatingly stubborn, but underneath it all he means well. I just want you to know that if you need anyone to talk to, please don't think I haven't got time for you.'

How tempted Jaz was to spill it all out there and then in the hope that her mother would take her side.

Her father's punishment hadn't been as bad as she'd thought it would be. She was allowed out now, but he'd banned her from Hidden Talents. It was this that hurt most. 'It's for your own good, Jaz,' he'd said. 'You've got a lot on your plate at college and the last thing you need is a distraction. Besides, you should be mixing with people your own age, not hanging around a bunch of arty navel-gazers.' She could have argued with him, defended the group – her friends – but she hadn't. Keeping quiet, she had learned, was the best way to handle her father. If she could win him round by doing as he said, that's what she would do.

It had been great when half-term had ended and she'd been able to see Nathan at college again. Explaining what had happened and admitting that she was being treated like a child had been mortifying, but Nathan was fantastic about it. 'And there was me thinking you'd got bored of my amusing company,' he'd said, during lunch in the cafeteria.

She was so grateful to him for his understanding and for not laughing at her. He said it was because he knew better than most that families could be weird. She'd even confessed to him that she'd switched off her mobile so that he couldn't get in touch with her. 'I was feeling so sorry for myself, I knew if I spoke to you I'd burst into tears.'

Vicki and Billy had said she should stand up to her father.

'You're seventeen, you don't need to take this crap,' Billy had said. 'Stopping you going to a writers' group must be against some kind of human-rights law. Hey, you sure your father isn't a member of the Taliban? Any sign of him growing a beard and wearing a tea-towel on his head?'

'Shut up, Billy!' warned Nathan. 'Haven't you sussed yet that not everything in life is a big joke?'

'Why not talk to your mum?' Vicki had asked. 'Mine's great for getting round my dad and making him do what we want.'

But Jaz knew, as she stood on the landing, looking at her mother's tired face, that she couldn't confide in her. Not with her going into hospital. 'I'm okay, Mum, really. You mustn't worry about me.' She peered over the banister towards the front door. 'Sounds like Dad's back.'

She was right. Her father burst through the front door like a member of the SAS. He flung down his jacket and called, 'Moll, where are you?'

'Up here, Popeye.'

For such a large, heavy-set man, he flew up the stairs, taking them two at a time. 'You okay, Moll?' he said breathlessly; he folded her into his enormous arms. 'Holy Mother of God, I've probably been caught on camera that many bloody times I'll be facing a lifelong ban. Are you sure you're okay?'

At their mother's insistence, no one but their father was to go with her to the hospital, and waving them off, with Phin, Jimmy, Tamzin and Lulu, Jaz realised that her father loved her mother very much and would do anything to keep her safe. How many husbands, after so many years of marriage, felt so strongly for their wives?

But that evening as she cooked supper, at the same time reading through some history-of-art notes she'd made for an essay, a worrying thought occurred to her. What would dad do, if the unthinkable happened and something happened to mum? How would he cope without his beloved Moll?

She buried the thought deep. Nothing was going to happen to her mother. She was pregnant, not ill. She wasn't suffering from an incurable disease. Just as soon as the doctors had her blood pressure back to normal, her mother would be home.

Chapter Forty-Five

*

Never in the history of Most Embarrassing Moments had Beth experienced such head-hanging shame. What had she been thinking when she'd sent Ewan that email? And what must he have thought of her when he'd read it?

Oh, he'd been pleasant enough about it in his response, had only teased her mildly, but deep down, he must have been quietly reviewing his opinion of her. What else could he have done in view of what she'd suggested she might like to do with him and a bar of chocolate?

Top tip, Beth [he'd emailed back]. Be sure to melt the chocolate first. But for the sake of clarity, would that be Galaxy or Cadbury's? I'm rather partial to a bar of Fruit and Nut, if my personal preferences ever need to be taken into account.

It was now March, and nearly two and half weeks since the night she and Jack had got so thoroughly plastered. The embarrassment should have passed by now, but it hadn't.

The next day Jack had apologised to her when she'd summoned the energy to go downstairs and help him with his unpacking.

'I'm struggling to piece together the exact details of last night,' he'd said, 'but I'm pretty sure I didn't behave too well. I can't remember the last time I woke up feeling so ropy. I didn't let the side down too much, did I?'

'I don't think so,' she'd murmured, 'but if you could lower your voice, I'd be eternally grateful.'

Smiling – obviously not feeling quite so ill as she was – he'd offered her a cup of coffee.

'When I'm convinced I'll be able to keep it down, that would be great.'

They didn't get much done in the first hour, but after Jack had forced her to drink several glasses of water, building up slowly to her eating a whole Rich Tea biscuit, they made some headway on the boxes in the kitchen. 'For a single man, you have a surprising amount of stuff,' she'd said, when the last of the boxes was empty.

'That's because Maddie didn't want any of it. I think she fancied the idea of taking Tony by the scruff of the neck and starting from scratch with him. Women like to do that, don't they?'

'I wouldn't know.'

He closed the door on the cupboard they'd just filled with a set of glass fruit dishes and a cut-glass punch bowl complete with cups – classic wedding-gift stuff that rarely, she guessed, saw the light of day. 'Okay, point made,' he said, 'I'm guilty of condemning the whole of womankind based on the actions of one particular woman. I retract the statement.'

And that's what Beth wished she could do with Ewan – retract that drunken email. Despite his reply, she hadn't had the nerve to correspond with him again, and wondered if she ever would. During the week, when Jack had given her a lift into work – this was now a regular occurrence – he'd asked her about Ewan and how things were going.

'Things aren't going anywhere. I blew it with that email we sent.'

He'd frowned. 'I can remember us writing it, Beth, but I can't recall precisely what we said. Remind me.'

Shame and disappointment – disappointment that she'd ruined things between her and Ewan – made her turn on Jack. 'But it was all your idea! You dictated it to me.'

'Did I?'

'Well, not all of it.' She had to accept her part in the sorry tale. She told him what they'd written.

He looked appalled. 'Oh, Beth, I'm really sorry. Did he take offence?'

'It's hard to tell, but perhaps not.'

'So what's the problem?'

'*I'm* the problem. I can't shake off the embarrassment of what we – I – said.'

When he dropped her off in the health-centre car park, Jack had said, 'If he's half the man you think he is, he'll treat the whole thing as a joke. Especially if you explain to him that you were drunk and aided and abetted by your new neighbour, who was in a far worse state than you.'

Since Jack's BMW had become a regular feature in the car park the tongues had been wagging furiously at work, and Wendy was in danger of wearing herself out with all the nudging and winking she was doing. 'I knew all along that you were seeing someone on the sly,' she declared triumphantly, the first morning she caught sight of Jack. 'He's a looker too. How much younger than you is he?'

'Wendy, how many times do I have to tell you? He's just a friend from the writers' group.'

'Who just so happens to have moved into the flat below yours. The man's got it bad for you, if he's gone to all that trouble.'

It didn't matter how often or how vehemently she denied the charges, Wendy would have none of it. But it made Beth register a happy truth: Jack was a friend, a good *platonic* friend with whom she felt quite at home. Maybe because she knew he felt the same about her. The age difference between them wasn't that great, but it provided a natural barrier over which neither of them had any intention of climbing.

But now there was this barrier between her and Ewan, which she didn't want. Yet how was she to dismantle it? What could she say to convince Ewan that she wasn't the wanton woman she'd made herself appear?

After work that evening, Beth drove to Marsh House to help Barnaby pack. Lois was at her South Cheshire Women's Group, listening to a guest speaker talking about her midwifery work in Calcutta. Barnaby had told Beth on the telephone that if there was any sign of Lois's car she was to drive on and come back later.

But the coast was clear, and Beth rang the doorbell to join in Barnaby's act of skulduggery. First thing tomorrow morning Lois, unknown to her, was being whisked off to Manchester airport to fly to Miami where she and Barnaby would embark upon their cruise.

Upstairs on their double bed was a large open suitcase: every wardrobe door and drawer was open. 'I've put a list together of the type of clothes I think Lois will need,' Barnaby said, 'but I want you to choose shoes and jewellery, and . . .' he lowered his eyes '. . . those all-important undergarments. You being a woman, I thought you'd know how these things work better than me. I'll be downstairs making us a drink if you need anything.'

It was a strange experience to sort through Lois's clothes, especially when it came to selecting her underwear. It was doing this that caused Beth to see her prim mother-in-law in a different light. Here was a woman who indulged herself in exquisite lingerie – M&S didn't get a look-in. La Perla – she'd heard Simone talk about it in tones of hushed reverence – featured heavily, as did another make she'd never heard of, and Beth was astonished by the amount of silk and delicate lace that took up three entire drawers. Every item was carefully folded and laid out like a shop display; she hesitated to disrupt its pretty order. In comparison, her limited range of worn-out chain-store bras and knickers would never pass muster. I've lived on my own too long, she thought. I've let things slide.

She looked at her reflection in Lois's dressing-table mirror. Her hair needed cutting, but otherwise she didn't think she was beyond redemption. There were a few too many lines around her eyes, a shadow or two, but with a lick of paint here and there, she'd almost get away with it. Whatever *it* was. Thank goodness she'd never been able to afford expensive holidays in the sun so hadn't ruined her skin. Her figure wasn't too awful either: she was still a size twelve and could wear the same clothes from years back. It was a boast she shouldn't be proud of, she realised. Those old clothes should have been thrown away a long time ago.

She held one of Lois's black lacy suspender-belts against her – she'd never worn stockings – and decided that one day she would like to spoil herself with something as frivolous and pretty.

'Here we are then, coffee. Oh . . .'

She whipped round from the mirror to see Barnaby looking almost as embarrassed as she was. She added the suspender-belt to the case on the bed and took the proffered mug. She smiled awkwardly. 'I – I was just thinking how lovely all these things are. Lois has exceptionally good taste. I'm ten shades of green with envy.'

For a moment Barnaby looked as if he didn't know what to say. Then he chuckled. 'Between ourselves, it's a little weakness of hers, and one I'm rather fond of.'

'You sweet man.'

They stood in silence, staring at the open suitcase. Then: 'I've never said this before, Beth, but you're a very attractive woman, who . . . who ought to have remarried by now.'

She blew on her coffee. 'To be honest, Barnaby, it's not as if I've had much choice in the matter.'

'But it's not right. I don't like the way things have worked out for you. You deserve better. A nice man, to make you feel . . .'

'To make me feel what?' she prompted.

'Complete.'

She laughed. 'There are women beyond these four walls who'd pluck out your nose-hairs for saying that.'

He squared his shoulders. 'Yes, and they doubtless live alone and will never know the joy another person can bring into their lives. I know Lois and I don't always give the impression of being in accord, but for the most part we've been happy. I suspect you and Adam would have been the same.'

'Maybe,' she demurred. 'Who knows?'

He looked at her. 'You *were* happy, weren't you?'

Smiling, she said, 'Oh, yes, extremely so. If we hadn't been, then perhaps I *would* have met someone else.

Another silence grew between them.

'You won't leave it too late, Beth, will you? Even I know it gets harder for women to find a partner as they grow older. Stupidly, men think a woman half their age is the answer.'

'Gracious, Barnaby, I didn't know you were so clued-up on these things.'

'I take in more than most people give me credit for. I also understand the pressure you've been under from Lois. She's never fully recovered from Adam's death, and I doubt she ever will, but one day I pray that she'll accept you have every right to move on and fall in love again.' With his free hand, he put his arm around her. 'You've always been more than just a daughter-in-law to me, Beth. You're the daughter I never had. And I'll move heaven and earth to see you happy. Hence the drastic measures.' He indicated the bed with its half-packed suitcase.

Unable to express her gratitude in words alone, she leaned into him and buried her face in the warm softness of his woollen sweater so that he couldn't see her tears.

*

274

It was almost nine o'clock when Jack came off the telephone. He'd just been talking to Dulcie, who, after much apologising for letting down the group again, had told him she was going away for a brief holiday. 'I feel awful for bailing out like this, but I need a break,' she said. 'I'm hoping the change of scenery will do me good. You've seen for yourself what a state I'm in, so I've decided to do something positive, to shake me out of the doldrums.'

'Good for you,' he'd told her, marvelling at the human capacity for understatement. Dulcie had given up the man she loved, was clearly suffering for it, yet was prepared to make light of her pain. Although he hadn't changed his stance on what she'd done – adultery would always be unacceptable to him, and he didn't give a damn how judgemental or holier-than-thou it sounded – he liked Dulcie and didn't want her to be unhappy. 'Going anywhere nice?' he'd asked. 'Somewhere hot and exotic?'

'Somewhere pleasantly warm and extraordinarily beautiful. Venice. I've never been before.'

'That sounds great. Anything you need doing in your absence?'

'Yes. That's why I'm calling. Jack, I know this is a terrible imposition, given that you've just moved house and must be very busy, but I'd feel inordinately better if you could keep the group going while I'm away. I've failed you all, these last couple of weeks, and I want to make amends somehow.'

'Is it worth it, with so few of us able to attend?' he asked. 'Jaz still can't join us and Victor doesn't seem keen.'

'Even if it's just you and Beth who get together, I'd feel better about it.'

'Okay, then,' he conceded. 'But how long are you going to be away?'

'I'm keeping my plans flexible. A week, maybe two. Perhaps longer. I'll see how the mood takes me. And how well the money lasts. Now, tell me about your new flat. How's it going?'

'I'm gradually getting it sorted. Which is stupid because I'm going to mess it all up next week – I've got the builders coming in on Monday. They're knocking through from the kitchen to the dining room.'

'Oh, I wish you luck in that enterprise. The dust will be horrendous.'

He was just about to ask her what type of exercises she wanted the group to do while she was away when she said, 'If it all gets too bad for you, Jack, you're more than welcome to stay here. In fact, you'd be doing me yet another favour, house-sitting for me. Shall I let you have a set of keys, just in case?'

While he heated up a microwave meal for one, Jack wondered why Dulcie had asked him to lead the group. Why not Beth? She was just as capable as he was. It might have something to do with Victor, he concluded. Perhaps Dulcie had thought Beth would find it difficult to stop Victor dominating what was left of the group. He was a real oddity, that man, the sort who'd never fitted in anywhere.

But Jack was more concerned about Jaz than he was about Victor. It wasn't his place to interfere in the affairs of another family, but he felt that Jaz's father had overreacted. Dulcie had thought the same. 'Do you think it would help if I spoke to her parents?' she'd asked, on the phone. 'I could explain to them that we're a perfectly respectable group of people, not a cabal of local nutters.'

'I don't think our sanity or standing in the community is at the root of the problem,' he'd said. 'It's that she lied to her parents to hide what she was up to.'

'What a silly girl. And what a waste of all that talent. I do hope her father relents and lets her join us again. She's a bright girl and he should be proud of her. He ought to take a long, hard look at the situation and understand why she felt compelled to lie.'

Dulcie had hit the nail on the head, he thought, as he ate his supper in the sitting room and channel-hopped through a selection of make-over programmes and medical dramas. There was nothing worthwhile to watch so he admitted defeat and switched it off. Anyway he didn't have time to waste: there was plenty to do before the night was through. He wanted to do some writing as well as get the girls' bedroom ready. He was picking them up tomorrow morning and he wanted the flat to look its best for their first proper stay. They'd only seen it when it had belonged to Adele Waterman and secretly he wanted them to be impressed at the transformation. And that was before the builders moved in.

There had been no more talk from Maddie about California, but he didn't think that was because the threat had gone away. His fear was so great that the girls might go away that he didn't trust himself to raise the subject with Maddie or Tony. It was all he could do to contain his anger, some of which he used in his writing, venting it late at night in controlled bursts of passion. On a more practical level, he had instructed his solicitor to write to Maddie's, asking her to think what would be most beneficial to Amber and Lucy, stressing that they had to come first, and that an obvious basic need for them was to see their father regularly. He'd insisted on seeing a copy of the letter before it was sent – he didn't want it to inflame an already volatile situation – and he could only hope Maddie would take it in the spirit it was meant and respond accordingly. But the bottom line was, if he had to go to court to settle the matter, he would.

On the other side of town, Victor tried to ignore the person who was knocking on his front door. Why couldn't people leave him alone? He could keep himself to himself so why couldn't they?

Bent over his typewriter, his skull throbbing with the headache he'd had since he woke that morning, he closed his eyes and covered his ears with his hands. Go away, he willed whoever it was. Leave me be.

At last the knocking stopped. But the intrusion wasn't over. He heard the sound of metal on metal: the letterbox was being opened.

He pushed himself to his feet unsteadily, feeling lightheaded. He took the stairs slowly, wondering why he couldn't move faster.

There was no one at the door when he reached it, but on the floor was a single white envelope. With shaking hands he ripped it open. It was a handwritten note from Dulcie Ballantyne. What did she want *now*?

He read the few lines she'd written, then tore it up in disgust, letting the shreds of paper fall at his feet. She was going away: in her absence that jumped-up estate agent would be in charge of Hidden Talents and they'd be meeting at his new flat in Maywood Park Road.

What did Jack Solomon have that Victor Blackmore didn't? Why hadn't she thought to ask him if he'd lead the group? He was more experienced than any of them. He was the one with the most complete manuscript.

He dragged himself back upstairs, the thumping inside his head almost unbearable, as if all his blood had surged to his brain and was threatening to burst out through his eye-sockets. He yanked the page he'd been writing from his typewriter, laid it on the desk and inserted a fresh piece. Then he hunted for the notes he'd made earlier, remembering, ten minutes later, that he'd written them on the wall behind him. This was a new technique he'd adopted, using the walls as four large noticeboards: it was a foolproof method to keep his notes safe. He was rather proud of himself for coming up with such a simple, clever idea.

Shivering, he rewound the scarf around his neck and rubbed his hands. He went over to the Calor Gas burner to make himself a drink. But when he tried to light the gas, it spluttered, hissed, and the flame slowly died: the cylinder was empty.

Silently, and not knowing why, he crouched on the bare floorboards, covered his unshaven face with his hands and wept.

Chapter Forty-Six

*

Dulcie was glad she had taken Prue and Maureen's advice: without question, Venice was a wonderful distraction, the perfect tonic.

From the moment the water taxi had dropped her off in the Castello district, and despite being tired from a day's travelling, she had felt at peace. Walking the short distance to her hotel, she had become absorbed in her surroundings and had marvelled at the early-evening sky, a glorious infusion of fading blue and subtle shades of pearly pink: it was simply the most beautiful sight she had seen and for a minute it had held her motionless. Tourists had buzzed around her, probably annoyed with the obstruction she was causing, but she had ignored them, continuing to drink in the still, magical atmosphere of the lagoon as day surrendered itself to the dusky mist of twilight.

Enchanted, she had reluctantly torn herself away and, armed with her map, had wheeled her suitcase in the direction of the family-run three-star Hotel Isabella. It had taken her ten minutes to locate it and, within the blink of an eye, she had fallen in love with its unmistakable Venetian charm and hospitality. The sixteenth-century building didn't offer a view of the lagoon or any of the waterways but, at the end of a narrow alleyway, it lived up to the brochure's claim that it was an oasis of tranquillity. She had at once felt perfectly at home.

This had been two days ago, and her love of the city was growing with each hour. 'Today,' she told herself, 'I will not walk too far.' She made the promise as she helped herself to a sweet pastry and a bowl of fresh fruit from the breakfast buffet in the small hotel dining room. She exchanged a smile and a 'good morning' or a '*buon giorno*' with her fellow guests – they were mostly American with one or two Italians – then sat down, knowing that her promise would be almost impossible to keep. Such was the temptation to explore every square inch of Venice, lest she miss some unrivalled gem of architecture, yet another Tintoretto or a spectacular reflection of light on water, that she was in danger of wearing herself out.

She laid her napkin on her lap and smiled at the young waiter who appeared silently at her elbow to pour her tea. '*Grazie*,' she said, loving the special treatment she was receiving. One of the joys of travelling alone as a single woman, even an ageing one, was the preferential treatment she received. She was all too aware that she was an object of curiosity to the staff at the hotel, as well as to the other guests, but she didn't mind: it worked to her advantage. Alberto, the impeccably well-mannered concierge, about the same age as Andrew, fussed over her at every opportunity: 'Signora Ballantyne, you know where you are going? You have a map?' The waiters saw to it that each morning at breakfast she had a table looking out on to the pretty courtyard where shade-loving shrubs grew in terracotta pots and the walls were covered in creepers so rampant there was hardly any discernible brickwork.

Wearing her most comfortable shoes, she set out for another day of adventure. She left the narrow alleyway, Calle Lorenzo, behind her when she turned into Calle della Pietà and stopped in front of the church of Santa Maria della Pietà. There was a board outside the *chiesa* advertising a concert for that evening. Alberto had told her that there were many concerts to enjoy in Venice and, making a snap decision, she climbed the steps and went inside. There was a small ticket booth at the entrance and, the transaction quickly made, she left the church to walk the length of the Riva degli Schiavoni looking forward to an evening of Vivaldi.

It was a beautifully warm March day and, arms swinging, she walked through the crowds of tourists, past the world-renowned Hotel Danieli, which, according to her guidebook, had once been a haunt for nineteenth-century writers and artists; Ruskin, Balzac and Dickens, to name but a few. Perhaps one day she would write a bestseller and be able to afford to stay there herself. The thought made her smile.

Until now she hadn't thought of her writing, but Venice was a place of unique inspiration and she knew it wouldn't be long before she would be itching to get back to it. Maybe she could buy herself a notebook and write here in Venice. She could find an open-air café and sit in the warm sun to let her convalescing mind take on the challenge of a blank page. Excited by the prospect, she knew she was recovering. 'I'm on the mend,' she said aloud, causing the striking young woman walking alongside her – so obviously Italian in her stylish black trouser suit and chic sunglasses – to glance at her and hurry on ahead.

She passed the colourful souvenir stalls on her left, which lined the busy waterfront, and came to the Ponte della Paglia, more commonly known as the Bridge of Sighs. Hordes of tourists were congregated here to photograph each other in front of the bridge but, considering herself practically a local now, Dulcie barely slowed her step to admire the view – she had snapped a selection of pictures yesterday.

The Doges' palace was the next point of interest, followed by the two soaring columns of San Marco and San Teodoro. For several centuries the granite pillars, one topped with a marble statue of St Theodore and the other a bronze of the Lion of St Mark, had framed a place of execution; now they were the focal point for the flocks of pigeons and tourists alike. From what Dulcie had read in her trusty guidebook during dinner last night, even in these enlightened times superstitious Venetians eschewed walking between the two columns for fear of bringing bad luck on themselves.

Leaving behind her the hubbub of the *piazzetta*, she headed for the *vaporetto* stop for the water-bus that would take her to the Dorsoduro district and the Guggenheim. Yesterday she had covered the major sites, such as the basilica, the campanile, and The Doges' palace; now she was giving her attention to what she called her B list. Peggy Guggenheim, an accomplished art collector and a woman who had certainly lived life to the full – if a little recklessly – struck Dulcie as an interesting role model. Just recently there had been an article in *The Times* about the fabulous collection of modern art housed in Venice and Dulcie was keen to see it.

The *vaporetto* was packed and, not for the first time, Dulcie wondered how the rickety diesel-run motorboat kept afloat with so many crammed on to it. Ahead of her, at the entrance to the Grand Canal and bathed in brilliant sunlight from a sky of powder blue, was the magnificent Baroque church of Santa Maria della Salute. It was true, Dulcie thought, as a man beside her pointed his video camera at the church, that every way you turned in Venice there was a view of breathtaking beauty. Who needed physical love, when the senses could be touched so satisfyingly with this heaven-like perfection?

The same thought struck her again that evening. She had had dinner in a nearby trattoria – her appetite had fully returned – and she was now being seduced by a string quartet. It was irrelevant that the Four Seasons had become such a cliché: to hear it played in a church where the great composer himself had written and directed performances of his own work was a joyful experience, which she hoped she would never forget. The music sounded so fresh, so vital, that it was as if she was hearing it for the first time.

During the interval, when there wasn't anything to do but go outside for some fresh air or wander around the church, she stayed where she was, avoiding the crush of a large audience on the move. When the initial rush had passed, she looked across the nave and recognised an American couple from the hotel. The woman, a tiny slim thing in her mid-forties, stylishly dressed, with large brown eyes, waved at her. Dulcie returned the greeting and wasn't surprised when they came over and introduced themselves. They were an engaging couple, who were quite at ease talking to strangers. Dulcie took an instant liking to them. Their names were Cathe, pronounced Cathy, and Randy Morris. 'Oh, I know what you're thinking.' The woman laughed. 'My husband's name is such a joke where you come from.'

'Well, only—'

'No, it's okay, we can laugh as well as the next person. Isn't that right, Randy?'

He nodded and smiled. 'How're you enjoying the concert? The acoustics are great, aren't they?'

'I'm loving it. It's the perfect end to a perfect day. Have you visited Venice before?'

'We sure have. We came here for our honeymoon. We're doing a kind of re-enactment twenty-two years on, you could say.' The man put his arm around his tiny wife's shoulder and looked deep into her eyes, which Dulcie could see now were skilfully enhanced by carefully applied makeup. But the man's gesture was so loving, that Dulcie was reminded of Richard. She caught her breath.

'Are you okay?'

Dulcie dropped her programme to give herself time to restore her equilibrium, and made a great play of fumbling for it at her feet. 'Goodness, what a butterfingers I am,' she said, when the fear of crying had passed and she was able once more to meet their gaze.

Other members of the audience were making their way back to their seats and she was relieved when her new friends said they ought to return to their own chairs, but not before they had invited her to join them for a drink afterwards.

She spent the rest of the concert trying not to allow memories of Richard to intrude, forcing herself to focus on Venice and how much better she was feeling and what she had planned for tomorrow. But, remembering that today was Thursday, her thoughts strayed homeward. Would Mr and Mrs Rafferty have forgiven their daughter for deceiving them? Would Jack have been successful in getting the group together? She wasn't a fanciful woman, but Dulcie had a gut feeling about Jack. She was convinced that he would become a published author. There was an incisive honesty about his writing that she was sure would have huge appeal. That was why she had asked him to keep the group going while she was away: she had wanted to be sure that he would keep his own novel flowing.

Jaz perched on the edge of her mother's bed. For once she was glad that her father believed in throwing his money around: Mum had a private room and could have visitors more or less whenever she liked.

'So how's everything at home?' her mother asked. 'The girls behaving themselves?'

'Oh, I've got them well under my thumb,' Jaz said breezily. It was a lie, but she felt justified in telling it. She didn't want her mother to worry. She'd been in hospital for a week now, and her blood pressure was still too high for her to come home. Her ankles had ballooned and Jaz doubted they would ever go back to how they'd been before. There were other complications with her pregnancy too, something to do with too much amniotic fluid. There was even the threat that the babies might be born too soon. So, no, she could not tell her mother that Tamzin and Lulu were as out of control as they had ever been. More so, perhaps. They played up at the slightest provocation because they knew they could get away with it. Dad was so preoccupied with work and worrying about Mum that he didn't seem to notice what was going on right under his nose. Phin and Jimmy were doing their usual double-act of Dumb and Dumber, so no change there.

But the good news was that, at Mum's insistence, Dad had got in touch with an agency and now Mrs Warner came in every day to cook, clean and do the ironing. She was a godsend and Dad was thinking of keeping her on when the babies arrived. 'But, Popeye, I've always done my own housework in the past,' her mother had complained.

'And you never had twins to deal with in the past,' he'd argued back. 'A bit of help round the house will give you a much-needed break.'

They had visited Mum every day, and Dad usually came twice, but this evening he, Phin and Jimmy were out on the town in Liverpool: it was St Patrick's Day and they probably wouldn't be home until the early hours. Dad had made a few unconvincing noises last night about not bothering this year – 'Oh, Moll, it wouldn't be worth it. How could I go, knowing you were stuck here in this blasted hospital?' – but he hadn't needed much encouragement from Mum to go off and enjoy himself.

'Popeye, there's no point in both of us being miserable. Go and have some fun. But to make me feel better, fix up a babysitter for Tamzin and Lulu so that Jaz can come and visit me on her own. These days, we never have a chance to natter, just the two of us.'

As it turned out, they didn't need to arrange for anyone to keep an eye on Tamzin and Lulu: friends, whose parents presumably hadn't met them, had invited them both for a sleep-over. Her father had given Jaz the money for a taxi to and from the hospital so, for one fantastic night, it was just her and Mum.

'Is anything bothering you, Jaz?'

Her mother's question made Jaz look up from the pattern on the blanket, which she had been tracing with a finger. 'No. Why would you think that?'

'It must be the serious expression I keep seeing on your face. How's college? You hardly mention it these days.'

'It's great.

'Really?'

'Really.'

'So what *is* troubling you? Come on, Jaz, talk to me. Why do you think I made the trade-off with your father? He gets to go to

Liverpool to be with his old friends, and I get the chance to talk to you alone.'

'I didn't know you were so sneaky, Mum.'

She smiled. 'I play by my own rules. Now, then, spill it all out. I want to know what's been going on behind my back.'

Jaz was dying to share everything and knew she would feel better for it, but she couldn't forget why her mother was stuck here in bed. She held her tongue.

As though reading her thoughts, her mother said, 'If you're worrying about upsetting me and sending my blood pressure off the chart, don't. Think about it – there's no better place I could be for receiving bad news.'

Worn down by her mother's gentle insistence, and the need to talk to her, Jaz said, 'You won't like it, Mum.'

'I'll be the judge of that. Now, come on, do us both a favour. Let's get this over and done with and I guarantee you'll feel better for it.'

Jaz told her everything. About Hidden Talents, and how she'd been going to the group most Thursday evenings while pretending she was at Vicki's. She explained her reasons for her secrecy. Also about Dad's ban on her attending the group for the foreseeable future. 'They're a really nice bunch of people, Mum. There's nothing weird about them, like Dad seems to think there is. Dulcie lives in a lovely house in Bloom Street where we meet, and she's the one who's in charge, though she tries to make out that she isn't and—'

'A bit like me, then,' her mother interrupted, with a twinkling smile.

Jaz smiled back at her, gaining confidence now in the telling of the story. 'And then there's Beth . . .' She hesitated, thinking of Nathan. 'Um . . . I'll tell you about her in a minute. Jack's great, he's an estate agent in town and a really cool writer. Only trouble is, Phin and Jimmy jumped to the conclusion that something was going on between us.'

Her mother's eyes widened.

'There isn't, Mum, honestly. It was because Jack always gave me a lift home and they saw me in his car. How're you doing? Blood pressure okay?'

'Go on. I'm fine. Tell me more about the group.'

'Well, the only other person is Victor, and he's seriously cranky.'

'I thought you said there weren't any weirdoes?'

'He's the exception. Delusional too. He reckons he's writing the book of the century. God, Mum, he couldn't write a shopping list, never mind a novel.'

Her mother laughed, reached out to Jaz and hugged her.

'What's that for?' Jaz asked, when her mother released her.

'For making me laugh. For taking my mind off being pregnant. I'm sick of mother-and-baby talk.'

'You're not angry, then?'

'I'm cross with your father for overreacting. So typical of him. In his daft way, he thinks he's protecting you. He hasn't learned to trust you yet. Trouble is, he judges others by his own standards and mistakes: he was a terrible tearaway before he met me. You've only got to look at Phin and Jimmy to get a glimpse of what he was like in his old wildcat days.' She leaned back against the pillows and sighed. 'But if that's the height of it, I'm sure I can sort it with your father. Leave it to me.'

But Jaz wanted to have everything out in the open: no more secrets or lies. 'Um . . . actually, Mum, there is something else. Something I haven't told Dad.'

'Oh?'

'I've been seeing this really nice guy from the upper sixth. His name's Nathan King and his mother is the woman I mentioned earlier, Beth.'

'So what's wrong with him? Why keep him hidden from us? Is he covered from head to foot in tattoos and body piercings?'

'No! Nothing like that. He's great. But . . . but I didn't want anyone to know about him. I thought Phin and Jimmy would scare him off.'

Her mother gave her one of her soft, knowing looks. 'He wouldn't be much of a boyfriend if he was that easily put off. It's you he's interested in, not your brothers. And presumably he's intelligent enough to reason that you're as sane as you're pretty. A bit silly at times, but nothing that a dose of self-belief and common sense wouldn't cure.'

Jaz took a moment to consider what her mother had said. She was right. Jaz had told countless lies because she had been convinced that the slightest thing would frighten Nathan away. But it wasn't just her insecurity that was to blame: pride had clouded her vision and caused just about the entire mess she now found herself in. She felt a hand on hers.

'Did you hear what I said, Jaz?'

'I'm sorry, Mum. I was thinking. But, yes, you're right.'

'Good. Now, when do I get to meet Nathan? Don't look so horrified. If we're to get round your father, I ought to meet the young man so I can put Popeye's mind at rest. Perhaps we could pretend that you've only just got to know him. That way we can avoid a lot of unnecessary trouble.'

Jaz flung her arms round her mother. 'Oh, Mum, you're the best.'

'A pity you didn't think that some months back and confide in me. Think of the hassle-free life you could have been enjoying.'

Jaz rode home in the back of the taxi happier than she'd been in a long time. Mum had been brilliant. And, even better, she was interested in her writing. She'd asked to see some of it. 'I could do with something good to read,' she'd said.

Jaz hadn't had the heart to tell her she'd wiped her novel off her computer and thrown away the only paper copy.

At home, she paid the taxi driver, let herself into the house, and stood in the hall in the darkness.

Instinctively she knew something was wrong. The burglar alarm wasn't on: the little red light above the window wasn't winking as it should have been. Her mouth went dry and her heartbeat quickened. She walked nervously towards the sitting room, her footsteps slow, her knees trembling. Holding her breath, she pushed open the door and switched on the light.

It was difficult to be certain, but it looked as if anything that had been worth taking was gone: hi-fi, telly, video-player, silver ornaments, pictures. Worse, the place was trashed: sofas turned over, cushions ripped open, curtains pulled down, lamps and the glass-topped table smashed, walls and carpets smeared with God knew what.

Chapter Forty-Seven

✳

'Don't worry, I'll be there in seconds. Just hang on.'

Nathan switched off his mobile and looked at Jack and his mother's concerned face. 'Sorry to break into your two-man writing group, but it's Jaz. She's just got back from visiting her mum and found they've been burgled. I'm going round to make sure she's okay.'

'Is she on her own?'

He was already out in the hall pulling on his coat. 'Yes.'

'In that case,' his mother glanced briefly at Jack, who nodded, 'we're coming with you. She's called the police, I take it?'

'I didn't ask, but I expect so.'

Jack drove, and when they got there they found a police car on the drive and lights blazing from every window of the house. Nathan was glad the police had arrived so quickly. He hadn't said anything to Jaz on the phone, but his primary concern had been the possibility that the burglar – or burglars – was still in the house.

A WPC opened the door to them, and after they'd explained who they were, they were shown through to the kitchen, where Jaz was pacing the floor wringing her hands. Nathan went straight to her. 'Dad'll kill me when he finds out,' she cried, holding him tight. 'He'll say I didn't put the alarm on. But I did.' She stifled a sob. 'He'll blame me, I know he will. Oh, *why* did this have to happen?'

'Of course your dad won't blame you,' he reassured her.

'Your friend's right.' Another police officer joined them in the kitchen. He held a pair of wire cutters. 'The alarm's been tampered with. They knew what they were doing and broke in through the french windows in the dining room. Same as the house broken into last night. Place trashed, no room untouched. Looks like we're in for a run of it. Little sods.'

It wasn't until the two police officers had gone, just after midnight, that Jaz managed to get an answer from her father on his mobile. Nathan could tell when she held the phone away from her ear what his reaction was.

'It's okay Dad,' she said, when he allowed her to speak. 'I'm fine. I've got some friends here with me. Dad, you'll have to speak up, I can hardly hear you ... Well, tell them all to shut up! Look, the place has been trashed. It's awful ... every room ... Oh, Dad, they've written on the walls ... ruined the carpets ... There's ...' She gulped. 'Mum must never know. We'll have to get it sorted before she comes home from hospital. She'll be devastated.' When Jaz started to cry, Beth stepped in and took over the conversation.

'Hello, Mr Rafferty. You don't know me, but I'm a friend of your daughter's from the writers' group ... Yes, that's right, Hidden Talents. I'm here with my son and Jack, who's also from the group ... Oh, ... Thank you, but there's no need. We came as soon as Jaz called. She's shaken but, on the whole, I'd say she's doing pretty well ... No, there's nothing more to be done. The police have been and gone and Jack's boarded up the broken pane of glass in the dining room where they got in. What I was going to suggest was, rather than you come rushing home, Jaz could stay the night with Nathan and me ... Okay, I'll hand you over to Jaz and she'll give you our address.'

'Thanks, Mum,' Nathan said, when they were back at the flat. Jack had gone downstairs and Jaz was in the bathroom, getting ready for bed.

'What for?'

'Being so nice.'

'Nice doesn't come into it. I wouldn't have dreamed of leaving the poor girl on her own. And if you'd spoken to her father, you would have known there was no way he could drive home. He and everyone he was with sounded as drunk as skunks. A shame we had to spoil the party for him. I hope he remembers our address in the morning.'

He helped his mother to make up a bed on the sofa for Jaz, and just as they were hunting for a spare pillow, Jaz appeared self-consciously in a pair of oversized Winnie the Pooh pyjamas. 'Don't you dare laugh,' she warned him.

'It never crossed my mind.'

'And if it does, you have my full permission to pinch him hard,' his mother said. 'Anyone for a drink before we turn in for the night? No? In that case, I'll wish you both sweet dreams.'

'I'm sorry I was a bit of a headcase earlier,' Jaz said, when they were alone and she was curled up beneath the duvet on the sofa.

'When was that? I must have missed it.'

She nudged him with her foot. 'Don't patronise me.'

'I wasn't.' He stroked her face, then tugged one of her plaits. 'Anyway, how could I do that to someone wearing such a colossally cute pair of pyjamas.'

Her face reddened. 'My mum bought them for me years ago, thinking I'd grow into them. I never did.'

'I'm glad you didn't – otherwise you'd be huge.'

She laughed, and he moved in to kiss her. But she frowned and pushed him away. 'It's okay,' he said, 'I'm not going to do anything silly.' He smiled. 'Certainly not with my mother in the next room.' The frown vanished and she put her arms round him.

He lay down next to her and closed his eyes. Before long they were both asleep.

In the morning, Beth found them lying on the sofa, her son fully dressed and wrapped in Jaz's arms. Who was protecting whom?

For a man who had to be nursing a monumental hangover, Jaz's father was hiding it well. As were her brothers, Beth suspected.

The flat didn't seem large enough to accommodate these three large, imposing men and, given what she knew of Mr Rafferty and his sons, Beth was relieved that they'd arrived long after Jaz and Nathan had woken. Any evidence that the two had slept together, albeit quite innocently, had been tidied away, and Beth was now handing round cups of coffee as if she was perfectly used to entertaining at this time of day: it was five to eight with college and work to get to. 'You must have been up early,' she said to Mr Rafferty. 'Sugar?'

He helped himself to three spoonfuls. 'I couldn't sleep for worrying. The boys and I hit the road at seven.'

'Have you been to the house yet, Dad?'

The big man turned to his daughter. 'No. I wanted to make sure you were okay first.'

'I'm fine.'

Her voice sounded tight and edgy and Beth could see that Jaz's main concern this morning had nothing to do with the burglary, but everything to do with Nathan being in the same room as her father and brothers. She hadn't so much as glanced at Nathan since her father's arrival when he'd swamped her in a massive hug.

Stirring his sugar-laden coffee, Mr Rafferty returned his attention to Beth. 'Look, Mrs King—'

'Please, it's Beth.'

'Well, Beth, I just want to say how grateful I am for what you and your son did last night, leaping into the thick of it and taking care of my Jasmine at such short notice.'

Jaz cringed. 'No one calls me that, Dad.'

He pointed at her with his spoon. 'They do if they really care about you, sweetheart. And this Jack bloke, I need to thank him as well. Holy Mother of God, what the sweet Fanny Adams is that?'

From beneath them came the noise that Beth and Nathan had grown used to. It was Jack's builders starting work. From what he had said, they were a shambles. They arrived inconveniently early and left shortly after lunch – Jack knew this because he'd seen their van driving past his office on Tuesday. When he had confronted them, they had admitted they were double-booked and had another job on the go.

Beth explained about Jack living downstairs and the work he was having done.

'Who's he got in to do it?' Mr Rafferty shouted, above the racket. 'Someone reputable, I hope.'

'I'm sorry,' she yelled back, just as the noise stopped, 'I don't know their name. They're a small outfit, I think.' She told him how unreliable they were.

All three Rafferty men rolled their eyes. 'Bloody cowboys. Here today, gone tomorrow. If he needs someone decent, tell him to get in touch. I owe him.' Mr Rafferty drained his cup, put it down carefully on the table and pulled out his wallet. He handed Beth a business card. 'Right, then, are we set?' This was to Jaz.

She reached for the bag she'd brought with her last night. 'It's okay, Dad, I've got all my stuff for college. I'll walk with Nathan.'

'Don't be an eejit, Nathan can have a lift too. There's plenty of room in the Jag. That okay with you, lad?'

Nathan nodded. 'Thank you. I'll just get my things.'

While he was gone and Beth was clearing away the cups and saucers, she heard Jaz's father whisper, 'Nice boy that, Jaz. You could do a lot worse.'

Turning on the tap and filling the sink, Beth smiled to herself. Funny how things worked out.

Chapter Forty-Eight

*

With his impressive track record for cocking things up, Jack should have known better than to court disaster by getting any building work done. Given the opportunity, he would have sacked the builders: they'd been as good as useless. As it was, they'd done a runner, leaving the job half done and his flat practically uninhabitable, brick dust and rubble everywhere – they hadn't bothered to organise a skip – and bare wires dangling. Was he depressed? Was he downhearted? Yes. Yes. And bloody *yes*!

But it wasn't all bad, as Beth had been quick to point out. She'd handed him a business card and told him to get in touch with Jaz's father. 'I got the feeling he'd do it for a good price as a favour to you. He was very grateful to us for helping Jaz on the night of the burglary. I received a gorgeous bouquet of flowers from him and, from what Nathan says, he's had a change of heart regarding Jaz and Hidden Talents. Having met me, and seen for himself how normal I am, he's decided she can come back.'

That had been yesterday morning, Saturday, and since then things had moved apace. Jack had spoken to Mr Rafferty, feeling slightly guilty for bothering him at the weekend, especially as he had his own problems to deal with, and had arranged for one of his men to visit on Monday – tomorrow. Then he'd moved out of the flat to take up Dulcie's offer. 'She wouldn't have suggested it if she hadn't been serious,' Beth assured him. 'Dulcie's not that kind of a woman.'

So that was where he was now. He'd moved in this morning, having rung Dulcie in Venice to check that it really was okay for him to set up temporary camp. 'Of course it's all right, Jack.

293

Though I'm sorry to hear the reason why you've resorted to making use of my house. Still, at least my mind is at rest to know you're there.' Stupidly he'd told her about the Raffertys' burglary, although not the possibility that Maywood was in for a spate of them. He hoped the news wouldn't spoil her holiday. She'd asked if he'd managed to get the group together on Thursday evening, but he'd had to admit that only he and Beth had met, and that was before they'd had to abort and go to Jaz's aid. 'It was a very informal evening,' he'd confessed, 'but it was quite useful in as much as I bored Beth to tears with a chapter I'd just finished writing.'

'I doubt that you bored her,' Dulcie had admonished him. 'You're an extremely able writer, Jack, and I have high hopes for you. You have a real talent for telling a good story. Now, what about Victor? What's the latest on him?'

'I tried ringing him as you asked, but the number doesn't work. If I have time during the week, I'll call on him one evening.'

He'd also told her that Jaz might be allowed to join the group again.

'Goodness, Jack, I turn my back for a few minutes and everything happens. Perhaps I should leave you in charge more often.'

'And that's not all.' He told Dulcie about the writers' conference. He omitted to say how Beth had come to hear of it, or that there was now a chance that she might not want to go. 'What do you think, Dulcie? Should we go as a group?'

'I think it's an excellent idea. These conferences can be so encouraging. Where's it being held?'

'Somewhere near Harrogate, so not too far away.' He'd then gone through a few domestic details with her about the central-heating system and which bedroom he should use. Finally he said goodbye, conscious that she had a holiday to get on with.

He'd brought a selection of work suits with him, some shirts, two pairs of jeans and a sweater, plus basic provisions, some ready-made meals for one and, most importantly, his laptop and printer. He wanted to make the most of any spare time he had. There hadn't been much so far: today he'd taken the girls swimming, then on to McDonald's and the cinema before driving them back to Prestbury. The original plan had been for Amber and Lucy to stay the weekend with him but, given the chaos of the flat, it had seemed sensible to cut short their visit. He had hated doing this and Amber had taken him to task. 'It's not fair, Daddy.' She'd pouted. 'I wanted to see you for the whole weekend. It doesn't matter to me how messy the flat is.'

'It would matter to me if bricks started falling on top of you,' he'd said.

'I bet you're exaggerating. It can't be that bad.'

'Believe me, Amber, it is.'

It was now eight o'clock and an age away from the Double Mac and fries he'd had for lunch. He opened a bottle of Budweiser and started to fix himself some supper with the intention of getting down to Chapter Thirty-five afterwards. He reckoned he only had another five to do before *Friends and Family* – his first book – was finished. He liked the sound of that: *his first book*. It implied there would be more. He had a feeling that, now he had started, nothing would stop him. Writing was addictive.

He grilled some sausages and buttered some slices of soft white bread, adding a squirt of ketchup – which he had been surprised to find in Dulcie's kitchen – then sat down to eat his culinary masterpiece. In front of him was his laptop plugged in and ready to go. But a ring at the bell stopped him mid-bite. With a mouthful of sausage, he answered the door. He stared at the grey-haired man on the step, not recognising him – it was hardly likely that he would: this was Dulcie's house, after all. Sensing that it would be imprudent to admit to this stranger that the owner was away, he waited for the man to speak first.

'Is . . . is Dulcie in?' the man asked awkwardly.

Jack hedged: 'Um . . . not just at the moment.'

Suspicion passed across the man's face. 'Can you tell me when she'll be back?' His voice was scarcely polite now.

Finishing what was in his mouth, Jack said, 'Sorry but I can't.' His words came out more belligerently than he'd intended.

They pushed the man over the edge of politeness and into hostility. 'Look, I don't know who you are but, please, go and find Dulcie and say that Richard wants to speak to her. Please, do that much for me.'

Jack hadn't considered that while he was in Bloom Street the man from whom Dulcie had run away might turn up. There was something so desperate about him as he stood on the step pleading to see Dulcie that Jack stood back from the door and said, 'I think you'd better come in.'

Richard's hopes soared.

At long last he was going to talk to Dulcie face to face. Suddenly he no longer cared who the unknown man was who had deigned to allow him across the threshold, and who was now walking through Dulcie's house as if he owned it.

He had tried so hard to get her out of his mind, but he couldn't. She had torn his life apart. Finally, he had the chance to repair it. But when the stranger led him into the kitchen and he saw no sign of Dulcie, hope drained out of him. He took in the sandwich on the table, the laptop, the open bottle of beer. 'What's going on?' he demanded. 'Where's Dulcie? And who are you?'

'I'm a friend of hers,' the man said calmly. He held out his hand. 'Jack Solomon, a member of the writers' group.'

'And Dulcie?' Richard prompted, ignoring Jack's hand. 'Where is she?'

'She's away, and I'm house-sitting for her.'

'Away? Where? With Kate and Andrew?'

'Why don't you sit down? Beer?'

Richard shook his head, irritated that someone other than him was acting host in Dulcie's house. He repeated his question: 'Where exactly is Dulcie?'

'On holiday.'

Exasperated, Richard began to pace the floor. 'Look,' he exclaimed, 'I'm getting the feeling that you're playing games with me. Do you know who I am?'

'I know exactly who you are. You're Richard Cavanagh, Dulcie's ex-lover. Now, before you get any more uptight, why don't you just accept that until Dulcie returns from her holiday you won't be able to speak to her? Perhaps you should go home to your wife and children.'

The directness of the man's words brought Richard up short. 'How dare you?'

'A bit of straight talking too much for you?'

'Who the hell are you to judge me?'

Jack reached for the bottle of beer on the table. 'I'm a man who knows what it feels like to wake up one morning and find that his wife has been sleeping with someone else.' He drank deeply from the bottle, eyeing Richard as he did so.

Richard winced. He passed a hand across his face. Oh, hell. What could he say? 'I don't suppose that offer of a beer is still on, is it?'

They sat at the table, the laptop shut down, and a barely touched sausage sandwich between them. 'Don't let me stop you eating,' Richard said.

'Would you like half?'

'No, thank you . . . Oh, go on, then. I'll get another plate.'

They ate and drank in an awkward silence.

'This feels very peculiar,' Richard admitted.

'I know what you mean. And I'm sorry for coming on so strong. It's really none of my business what you and Dulcie have been up to.'

'Neither of us planned it.'

'Maybe not, but the result's the same. People get hurt.'

'I'm not making excuses, but I've never loved anyone the way I love Dulcie. I don't expect someone as young as you to appreciate that love is just as exhilarating and wonderful at my age as it is at yours.' He paused. This was the first time he had spoken to another person about his relationship with Dulcie. It felt strange, but it was also a welcome relief to speak openly about her. 'Dulcie means everything to me,' he said simply.

'Still? Even though she's finished with you?'

'I'll go on loving her for ever. It's the rightness of our love I can't turn away from. Where's she staying, Jack? Is she in London visiting her children?'

'No. And I'm not sure she wants you to know where she is. That's the whole point of her going away. She needed to put some distance between the two of you.'

'Do you have any idea how long she'll be away?'

'A week. Perhaps two. She was very unhappy before she went.'

Richard nodded. 'I understand. But she's got it wrong if she thinks a holiday will solve anything. I'll still be here when she comes home.'

'And your wife and family? Where will they be?'

He felt the stab of Jack's question, pushed away his plate and leaned back in his chair. 'I've told Dulcie that if she wants to make a go of it, I'm prepared to make my choice . . . and bear the full brunt of the consequences.'

Jack fixed him with a disdainful stare. 'I have two young daughters who are currently bearing the full brunt of their mother's choice, so I know what I'm talking about when I say it's never the straightforward business you think it will be. Being a part-time father is an emotional minefield. You want to do your best, because you feel so damned guilty, so you pack too much into too small a chunk of time. And every little disagreement you have with your children gets magnified by your guilt, reminds you, yet again, that you've failed. You even begin to wonder if you should cut your losses because maybe, just maybe, they might be better off forgetting all about you. How old are your children?'

Richard swallowed. This wasn't what he'd come here for. This critical directness was too much. 'Please, if you don't mind, I'd rather not discuss my children.'

'No, I guess not. Another beer?'

'No, thanks.' Richard watched Jack help himself from Dulcie's fridge. He caught a glimpse of the kind of stuff he'd never seen in Dulcie's kitchen before: processed meals for one – a curry, a cottage pie, and a packet of haddock in cheese and broccoli sauce. Bachelor food. Or, more accurately, separated-man food.

He was about to try once more to get out of Jack where Dulcie was when the phone rang. It was the faint tone of a mobile. 'Excuse me a minute,' Jack said. 'Hi, Des, how's it going?' He wandered out of the kitchen, into the hall.

Left on his own, Richard relaxed. Dulcie's house-sitter was a nice enough man, but there was something disturbingly judgemental about him. He saw things only in black and white. Life wasn't like that. He got to his feet, and put the empty plates into the sink, then went back to the table for his beer bottle and glanced at Dulcie's noticeboard. Pinned to it were the familiar photographs of Kate and Andrew, plus one of Dulcie wearing a large straw hat. It was a particular favourite of his: he'd taken it in the garden last summer. It was a picture he would dearly love to have on his desk at work or in his wallet so that he always felt she was close to him. He was tempted to slip it into his pocket, but his attention was diverted by a piece of paper. On it, in Dulcie's expressive handwriting, was the name and address of a hotel in Venice. He looked out to the hall and, seeing that Jack was still deep in conversation, he grabbed a pen and a square of paper from the pad Dulcie kept by the phone. He scribbled down the details and, just in time, pocketed the scrap of paper as Jack came back into the kitchen.

'Sorry about that,' he said.

Richard waved aside his apology with a smile. 'No, it's me who should apologise. I shouldn't have come here and ruined your evening, not to mention scrounge half your supper. Which was great, by the way. It's a long time since I've had a sausage sandwich. Anyway, I'll leave you in peace now.' He held out his hand. 'No hard feelings, then?'

Chapter Forty-Nine

*

Jaz and Nathan both had a free period so they were able to leave college early that Tuesday afternoon to drive to the hospital.

When Jaz had asked Nathan if he'd like to meet her mother – 'the sanest and nicest member of my family' – he'd agreed and said he'd see if he could borrow his mum's car.

To Jaz's horror, her father was now encouraging her to go out with Nathan. 'He looks a regular decent boy to me,' he'd said, at breakfast only that morning. 'Smart, too.' As he tucked into his plate of bacon, black pudding and scrambled eggs, he'd added, 'I could do with a tame lawyer in the family. Think of the fees I'd save.'

'Dad!' she'd remonstrated. 'I'm only seventeen. I'm not thinking of marrying anyone, let alone Nathan King.'

'Aw, get away with you, girl. I'm looking to the future.'

Blushing to the ends of her toenails, and seeing her brothers sauntering into the hotel restaurant for their breakfast with her sisters tumbling in behind, she'd finished her toast and made a hasty exit. It was difficult to decide which was worse: her father taking a hard line with her or being too interested in fixing her up with Nathan. But as he'd given her the go-ahead to rejoin Hidden Talents, she was happy to let him think whatever he wanted.

It had been Beth and Jack's kindness after the break-in that had won him round. 'Anyone who takes that kind of care of a child of mine is okay in my book. That Beth struck me as a sensible woman. Nice with it.'

Jaz was so happy she'd given him a huge hug. 'Thanks, Dad.'

Trying to look stern, he'd said, 'Just you see it doesn't get in the way of your studies. And no more lying to your mum and me.'

She'd told her mother that there was no need for her to have a word with Dad, that it had all been sorted. Of course, she couldn't tell her why he'd had this change of heart – 'He must be in a particularly good mood,' was all she could come up with. 'Maybe the thought of being a father all over again is mellowing him.'

'Well, to make sure there's no misunderstanding, I'm going to tell him that I know all about Hidden Talents,' her mother had said. 'It's best that we're straight with him, Jaz.'

But her father had much more to think about than Hidden Talents.

On seeing the house, he had taken one look at the mess and moved them lock, stock and barrel into the Maywood Grange Hotel. 'If I ever get my hands on those bastards, I'll bloody staple them by their friggin' ears to the walls of their own homes and leave them there to rot!' He was incandescent with rage that this had happened to him of all people.

Jaz had never seen her father so angry, or so upset. Unable to take out his anger on the burglars – who had struck again he had learned from the police – he had vented some of it on the police officers in charge, accusing them of incompetence and wasting tax-payers' money. Apart from Mum's jewellery, he wasn't bothered about the stuff that had been taken: 'That can all be replaced,' he'd said matter-of-factly. 'That's what insurance is for.' It was the damage that had been done to the house that incensed him. 'I built that house for your mother,' he'd said. 'It was her dream home. Now it's a friggin' nightmare.' High on impotent fury, he'd threatened to wash his hands of it and put it on the market. Jaz was surprised by how sad this had made her. It made her realise how attached to her home she really was. Her own bedroom had been trashed, like all the others: clothes pulled off hangers and randomly ripped, her mattress hacked to pieces, files and important college work thrown around the room. Her CD player and all her CDs had been taken, as had her computer. She was glad now that she'd wiped her novel. For a stranger to have had access to something so personal would have left her feeling even more violated.

It had been a crazy few weeks, what with worrying about her mother being in hospital and the burglary, but the experience had forced her to get things into perspective. As a result, she had come to see that *Having the Last Laugh* had been a cruel parody of her family. It had had its funny moments but, over all, it had been childishly spiteful. Where had been the depth and integrity she so admired in other writers?

Once her father had overcome his anger, he had decided not to sell the house. 'I'll not let the buggers get the better of me,' he'd cursed. And so, after Phin and Jimmy had arranged to have everything removed that had been ruined, he had pulled out all the stops to get the house put right. An army of professional cleaners had worked round the clock, and now the decorators were doing their bit. When they had finished, every carpet was to be replaced and Jaz couldn't begin to calculate how much money her father was throwing at the problem to resolve it. And all so that Mum would never know the worst of it. 'This is the last thing she needs to worry about,' he'd said to her, her brothers and sisters. 'You're all sworn to secrecy,' he'd added, looking pointedly at Tamzin and Lulu, who hadn't been allowed to see the state of the house – another instance of his desire to protect his family. 'If you breathe a single word of this to your mother, you'll regret it. Got it?' For the first time in their lives her sisters seemed to understand that a serious response was expected of them. Coincidentally, from that moment on, their behaviour in the hotel improved: they stopped mucking about in the lifts, raiding the ice machine or ringing Room Service for a midnight feast.

Breaking into her thoughts, and, as if reading them, Nathan said, 'Jaz, how does your father expect to pull off such an elaborate stunt? I mean, your mother will know that something's gone on. The smell of fresh paint, new wallpaper, new carpets, new everything – it'll be a dead giveaway, won't it?'

'Of course he plans to tell her, but he wants everything to be as normal as he can make it before she comes home. He wants to lessen the shock.'

'He must really care about her.'

Jaz noted the thoughtful expression on his face. 'He does. Funny thing is, I'm only just seeing how much. I always knew he was mad about Mum, but I'd put it down to exactly that – madness. You don't think about your parents actually being in love with each other, do you?' She immediately regretted what she'd said. 'Sorry, that was insensitive of me.'

'It's okay. But I know what you mean. I think my parents probably loved each other a lot too.'

In the quiet that followed, Jaz's thoughts turned to her father again. As a small child she had grown up listening to people telling her what a great man Popeye Rafferty was. If a friend or relative of the family was in need, he was always the first to offer help. She could remember being so proud of him. When had she become so critical?

At the hospital, Jaz reminded Nathan not to say a word about the burglary to her mother.

He took her hand. 'This might come as something of a shock to you, Jaz, but there's nothing wrong with my attention span. I'm fully on board with the scam. And do you really think I want to incur the mighty wrath of your father, and just as he's taken such a shine to me?'

'Don't push it. One word from me and you'll be history!'

They were both smiling when Jaz poked her head round her mother's door. She was relieved to see that her mother was looking better than she had in days. She was sitting up in bed, wearing her best nightdress. She had applied some makeup and her lovely auburn hair had been washed and nicely blow-dried. Jaz ushered Nathan inside and said, 'Hello, Mum, how are you?'

'All the better for seeing you.' She put down the magazine she'd been reading. 'Ah, now you must be Nathan. Close the door and come on in.'

They drew up two chairs and Nathan handed over a prettily wrapped box of chocolates. 'I thought you might like these,' he said. 'That's if they're allowed.' He glanced at the large basket of fruit on the other side of the bed.

'They'll make a welcome change from the healthy stuff I'm being forced to eat. Last night I dreamed I was cooking Jaz's father's favourite meal, a large suet-crust steak and kidney pudding. I woke up starving.' She took the box from Nathan and thanked him. 'We'll have one right now, shall we?'

Jaz was touched that Nathan had gone to so much trouble for her mother, but she was equally pleased to see how well received the gift had been. Mum was good like that. Jaz supposed it was one of the reasons why Dad showered her with so many: he received much more in return, in terms of love and affection. A distant memory surfaced, something she once heard her mother say to her father: that it was easy to love the lovable, the child who always smiled and raised its arms for a cuddle, but it meant so much more to get a hug from the quiet, withdrawn one. Only now did she understood that her mother had been talking about her.

Jack could think of any number of ways he would rather spend his evening, but he'd promised Dulcie he would call on Victor. After locking up the office, he drove out of the car park and turned on to Bridge Street where he joined the queue of busy rush-hour traffic waiting to negotiate the town's main roundabout. He inched his way forward, and finally reached the head of the queue then turned towards Station Road. He passed the large pay-and-display car park on his left, then Maywood College, and watched the house numbers on his right. He knew Station Road well – Norris & Rowan currently had three properties for sale along this stretch of terraced houses; they had always changed hands regularly.

He parked between a shiny Astra and a less than well-maintained Peugeot, which he recognised as Victor's. He knocked at the door.

Knocked again.

And knocked again.

Nothing. From what Dulcie had told him on the phone, it had been the same when she'd tried to call on Victor. 'But I felt sure he was in,' she'd said. 'Don't ask me how, I just felt it.'

Jack felt it too. Standing back from the house, he looked up at the windows, which were thick with grime. Was it his imagination or was there a flicker of light coming from one of the upstairs windows? It was so faint he thought it might be a reflection from the street-lamp behind him, which had just come on with a pale orange glow. But no: the more he looked up at the window, the more convinced he became that a light was on inside. He decided to walk to the end of the row of houses and see if he could get round to the back.

He walked along the cinder path to the rear of the properties until he drew level with Victor's. It was then, when he looked up at the back of the house, that he realised that what he'd thought to be a softly glowing light was a fire. Victor's house was on fire.

Quick as a flash he phoned for the emergency services on his mobile, then tried the gate. It was locked. He threw his weight against the rotting timber, burst through it and stumbled into the small backyard. The door into the house was locked, but he seized a wooden broom that was propped against the wall and swung it at the kitchen window.

Once inside, he called to Victor as he peered into the dining room, then the sitting room. He got no response so he went back to the kitchen, grabbed a tea-towel and shoved it under the cold tap. When it was soaking, he took a deep breath and made for the stairs. On the smoke-filled landing, with the wet cloth pressed to his face, he braved the room where the source of the fire was. Thick smoke stung his eyes and made them water. He forced them to stay open, and saw a body on the floor: flames were licking over and around it. He pushed himself forward, grasped Victor under his armpits, and dragged him from the room. Out on the landing, he took off his jacket, wrapped it around Victor's apparently lifeless body to snuff out his smouldering clothes. Then he heaved him down the stairs, to the hall, where he laid Victor on the floor, and allowed himself to catch his breath. Just as the shock hit him of what he'd done, and what might happen if he didn't get out of the house fast, he heard the high-pitched wail of a siren. Jack fumbled with the front-door lock and carried Victor to safety. Within seconds a team of firemen was on the scene, a crowd of onlookers too: neighbours who claimed to have smelt smoke but had put it down to a bonfire.

Jack rode in the ambulance with Victor to the hospital. His own injuries were superficial – a raw soreness in his throat and chest, some cuts from when he'd climbed through the window and a few burns – nothing that wouldn't heal within a week or two. But Victor looked like he'd be damned lucky to live.

Chapter Fifty

*

With the curtains drawn back, Dulcie lay in bed looking at the surrounding jumble of rooftops and chimneys. She was listening to the church bells clanging softly and thinking what a perfect way it was to start the day.

She had been in Venice for over a week now, and she had never felt so settled in a foreign place as she did here. Perhaps it was the compact size of the city that made it feel so homely. And so safe. In all the times she had wandered the maze of narrow streets, night or day, she had never felt she was in any danger. Recently, though, her solitary nocturnal strolls had dwindled. Her American friends, Cathe and Randy, had seen to that by discreetly taking her under their wing. 'We can't have you on your own too much,' her petite protector had declared, and once or twice Dulcie had allowed them to have their way. It would have been churlish to do otherwise. Besides, she enjoyed their company – they were refreshingly honest and direct: qualities Dulcie admired.

The past two evenings they had enjoyed an exorbitantly priced nightcap at Florian's in the Piazza San Marco. The atmosphere was enchanting, and listening to the small orchestra as it attempted to outplay the competition from the bar across the square was an added delight. Last night, when they had finished their drinks, they had browsed the display of pictures on sale around the square, the artists vying enthusiastically for their attention. Dulcie had fallen in love with a beautiful etching of the island of San Giorgio Maggiore – it was the view she saw every morning when she left the hotel and stood for a moment on the Riva degli Schiavoni to admire the lagoon and all its activity. She had purchased it from a young girl with jet black hair, and looked forward to taking it home and having it professionally framed. She knew exactly where she would hang it: in her study above her desk so that she could lose herself in it when her writing wasn't going well.

But for now, and since she had bought herself a notebook, her writing was flowing effortlessly. She had written two short stories so far, and was eager to start another. The muse was definitely performing for her and its reappearance was a sign that she was almost back to normal. It meant that she could think of the future and getting on with her life without Richard.

She had thought hard about the writers' conference Jack had mentioned on the phone, and had concluded that the group should go. Having attended similar courses in the past, she knew it would be a marvellous opportunity for them all. If it was well run there would be interesting guest speakers to learn from, tutors on hand to give advice, and possibly one or two agents and editors to talk to. She hadn't said anything to Jack, but she harboured a real hope that he might be 'discovered'. It was a long shot, but these things happened. He wrote so compellingly that she was convinced *Friends and Family* was publishable, that a professional eye would see it as a potential hit. What she liked most about Jack was that he had no inkling of the extent of his talent. Too often would-be writers had an overly inflated view of themselves and their work.

Would-be writers such as poor old Victor.

Any dislike or critical views she had once held for Victor had now been subdued by her concern that something was terribly wrong with the man. She sensed that the group had only half a picture of him, as if he were a character in a book who had been badly sketched in. She hoped that Jack had found the time to call on him. 'I know it's asking a lot,' she'd said to Jack, on the phone, 'but I'm worried about Victor. Didn't you think he'd lost an awful lot of weight when we last saw him?' She trusted Jack to do the right thing: he was a good man.

A glance at her travel clock on the bedside table told her it was time to get up. She was having breakfast with Cathe then going on a trip to the islands in the northern lagoon. Randy had opted to forgo the excursion, saying he had some important phone calls to make.

As they set off for the waterfront, where Alberto had told them to pick up the boat, Cathe linked arms with Dulcie and said,

'Randy is the sweetest man alive. His phone calls aren't that important, he just thought we'd prefer to have a girls' day out.'

Dulcie smiled understandingly. 'I can't think of many men who would want to spend a day looking at glass or lace.'

They paid for their tickets and joined the chattering group of tourists who had already climbed aboard the vessel and taken their seats. Last to get on was their guide for the day, a tanned Italian man of about the same age as Dulcie. With his distinctive Roman nose, his swept-back grey hair and lightweight cotton sweater draped around his shoulders, she thought him exceedingly handsome. As the boat pulled away from the jetty, he smiled at her and slipped on a pair of fashionable wraparound sunglasses. After he'd turned away, Cathe nudged Dulcie. 'Cute, wouldn't you say?'

'And some,' Dulcie whispered back. 'But he knows it.'

Murano was their first stop, and after the group had disembarked, their guide, Antonio, filled them in with some background information about the island. His English, though heavily accented, was excellent and he explained how Murano had been the centre of the glassmaking industry since the thirteenth century. 'Here, on this little cluster of islands that make up Murano,' he told them, 'mirrors were made a long time before anyone else thought of it.'

'Trust the vain Italians to be the first to spot that niche market,' murmured Cathe.

'And spectacles too,' Antonio continued. 'It is thought that they were also invented here. It was truly a marvellous and creative place. During the sixteenth century, Murano glass became the must-have accessory all over Europe. Every palazzo had to have its share of exquisite crystal, and today you, too, can be a part of the rich history left to us by those early-glass artisans. Come, I take you now to see some glass-blowers at work. And then I invite you to join me in the showroom to see the many splendours on offer for you to purchase and take home.'

Following Antonio, as he strode ahead of the group, Cathe said, 'Don't you just love the understated way they try to relieve us of our dollars?'

Dulcie laughed. 'Shame on you for being such a cynic.'

Most of what was for sale – stunning handmade chandeliers and exquisite sets of wine glasses – was wildly expensive and would require shipping home, but both Dulcie and Cathe settled for some modestly priced scent bottles. Next the tour moved on to the island of Burano. 'This is the prettiest of the islands in the lagoon,' boasted Antonio, handing out roughly drawn maps. 'Nowhere else will you find such a collection of colourful houses, a rainbow of colour that will delight your senses. *Sì, sì,* it is the truth I tell you, no exaggeration. And wait till you see the lace. Ah, the lace, you will fall over yourselves for this. Here you will see local Buranese women hard at work with the stitching. But before all that excitement, we stop for lunch.' He smiled broadly. 'Where I promise you will taste the best fish in the best trattoria Burano has to offer.'

Everyone laughed, by now used to Antonio's effusive gilding of the lily.

'*Sì,*' he exclaimed, 'I know this restaurant to be the best because it is my youngest son Giorgio who runs it. It is the one marked on the map I have just given you. If you follow the directions, I will meet you there in . . .' he looked at his watch '. . . in precisely thirty minutes. Do not worry about getting lost, it is impossible. Burano is a very easy place to be.'

'And is Giorgio as handsome as his father?' asked Cathe, as Antonio helped her out of the boat and on to the jetty.

'Oh, he is even better-looking. He is the image of your Tom Cruise.'

He offered his hand to Dulcie, who was last to get off, and said, 'You permit me to invite you to join me for a drink before lunch perhaps?'

Dulcie was so taken aback that she nearly lost her footing. He held her firmly. 'Was that such a dreadful shock to you?'

'Yes,' she said, flustered. She straightened her sun hat, which had become dislodged.

He smiled. 'In that case I will have to make amends by insisting you accept my invitation. It is a deal? *Sì?*'

Not one to be bamboozled, even by a man as attractive as Antonio, Dulcie said, 'I'm afraid it isn't possible. I'm here with a friend and it would be rude of me to abandon her.'

But when she looked for Cathe to corroborate this, there was no sign of her on the jetty: she'd gone on ahead with the rest of the group and was waving at Dulcie, a sly grin on her small elegant face.

'It looks to me as if you are the one who has been abandoned,' he observed, with a smile.

He took her to a bar in a small, shady square where he was greeted by a number of elderly men who obviously knew him well. She wondered how many times a week they witnessed this very scene – Antonio with yet another woman from one of his tour groups. He removed his sunglasses, placed them carefully in the breast pocket of his shirt, and, without asking her what she would like to drink, called through to a man behind the bar and ordered two Bellini cocktails.

'You look surprised,' he commented, when the waiter brought them their drinks.

'Frankly I am,' she said. 'It doesn't look the kind of place that would serve a cocktail. Or do they keep a bottle of Prosecco here specially for you?'

He laughed and raised his glass. 'Here is to many more surprises for you during your stay in Venice.' He took a slow sip, then lowered his glass. 'How long are you here for? But wait, before you answer that tell me your name. After all, you have the advantage, you know mine.'

She swallowed a refreshing mouthful of sparkling wine and fresh white peach juice. 'It's Dulcie,' she said, 'and I've been here for just over a week.'

'And you leave when?'

'I haven't decided.'

'Oh. So you are a flexible lady?'

She laughed. 'Perhaps not in the way you might be thinking.'

He slapped his forehead and laughed too. 'Oh, my English, it is not always so good. Please, forgive me.'

A wiry dog came over to their table and sniffed at their legs. Finding nothing of any interest it soon wandered off.

'Dulcie, that is an unusual name, is it not?'

'I suppose it is. It comes from the Latin *dulcis*, meaning—'

'Meaning sweet,' he finished for her. 'Yes, I am a man of education too. The name suits you. And is there a husband for the sweet-natured English lady?'

'No.'

'Divorced?'

'Widowed.'

'Ah. I am sorry. Did your husband die recently?'

'No.'

He drained his glass. 'One-word answers, they tell me to mind my own business. You are here on holiday to enjoy yourself, not to be interrogated by an Italian man with too much curiosity. Come, it is time for us to join the rest of the group and your American friend, who will want to know exactly what you have been up to. The friend who thinks that we Venetians are only after one thing . . . your bucks and pounds.'

Disappointed to be leaving so soon, Dulcie hurriedly finished her Bellini and gathered up her bag. 'Thank you for the drink,' she said. 'I enjoyed it.'

'*Prego*. I almost believe you.' He slipped his sunglasses back on, making her feel as if he'd pulled down the shutters on their conversation.

'Look,' she said, feeling as if she owed him an explanation, 'it isn't anything personal, I'm just quite a private person.'

He put a hand under her elbow and led her across the square. 'And do such private people ever risk having dinner with men they hardly know?'

Again taken aback, she thought of Richard and how easily she had accepted his invitation to have dinner with him that first day they met. 'They do if the situation feels right.'

'It's only dinner,' Dulcie had to keep reminding herself later that evening when she was relaxing in a hot bath at the hotel.

Then why did she feel so guilty, and that she was being disloyal to Richard?

Oh, it was ridiculous. Richard was a married man whom she'd sensibly shooed off back to his wife, where he belonged. Now she could do as she pleased. She was a free agent.

So long as she didn't hurt anyone, a faint voice whispered to her.

She chased it away. 'The only person likely to get hurt is me,' she said aloud, while reaching for a towel and stepping over the edge of the bath.

She chose her clothes with care – nothing too dressy, she didn't want Antonio imagining that she'd gone to extra trouble for his benefit, and equally nothing too casual – she suspected that Antonio, like most Italian men, would be smartly turned out. She opted for a pair of loose-fitting black silk trousers and a cream overshirt. Then she applied some strategic touches of makeup and appraised her reflection in the dressing-table mirror. She was particularly pleased with her eyes. They were a toned-down version of Cathe's and she was impressed with the subtle transformation. Not too old to learn a few tricks, then. She picked up her hotel pass key, hooked her bag over her shoulder, and went downstairs to wait for Antonio in the hotel foyer, as arranged.

From behind his desk, where he was on the telephone, Alberto greeted her with a smile and a wave. She didn't have to wait long: Antonio appeared through the revolving door almost at once. She'd guessed correctly: he was wearing a jacket and tie and the confident air of a man who knew he could still turn the head of a woman half his age. Once again, and after he'd politely told her how nice she looked, he placed a hand under her elbow and steered her out of the hotel, much to the amusement of Alberto – who, Dulcie knew, had been watching them keenly.

'Would you like to walk or take the *vaporetto*?' he asked, when they were facing the waterfront.

'It depends where we're going,' she answered.

'I have booked a table at my favourite restaurant near the Rialto Bridge. It is not far.'

She smiled. 'But a *vaporetto* ride is so pretty at night.'

He smiled too. 'In that case I would be a heartless man to deny you such a pleasure.'

Dulcie soon discovered that Antonio was known to nearly every local they came across – the woman from whom they purchased their tickets addressed him by name, the man who drove the boat waved to him, and the waiters at the restaurant all smiled and joked with him, one even slapping him on the back. 'I have lived in Venice all my life,' he explained, when they were sitting down with a ringside view of the brightly illuminated Grand Canal with all its passing traffic, 'apart from a brief time in London when I was a student.'

'What were you doing there?'

'Studying, of course.'

She caught the playfulness in his voice. 'I meant, what were you studying?'

He straightened the cuffs on his shirt, lining them up an inch beyond the cuffs of his jacket, then said, 'I was a medical student, training to be a doctor.'

'Really?'

'Aha, once again I have surprised you! Yes, the simple guide turns out to be more than you thought.'

'That's not fair,' she said defensively. 'My husband was a doctor. And so is my son. I was merely thinking of the coincidence.' She took the menu their waiter handed to her wondering why on earth she was here being goaded by this monstrously egotistical Italian.

'I'm sorry,' he said, when he had taken it upon himself to order aperitifs without asking her what she would like, 'I have upset you with my twisted sense of humour. To make amends I shall bore you with my life story. But, fear not, it is not long. You won't be in need of resuscitation at the end of it, though to give you the kiss of life might be rather pleasant. Aha, that is better, now you are smiling again. Well, as I said earlier, I have always lived in Venice. My wife, too, was a local girl and we had five children.' He laughed. 'They say that doctors always have large families, and I am proud to say that I did my part in upholding this belief.'

'So what kind of doctor were you?'

'An excellent one!'

'You're impossible.'

Their drinks arrived, and after she'd taken a cautious sip and found it to her liking, he said, 'I was an eye surgeon at the local hospital here in Venice, but I retired two years ago, not long after my wife passed away. It was time for me to lay down the tools of my trade, my hammer and chisel, and try something new.'

She winced at his joke and said, 'So you became a tourist guide?'

He shook his head vehemently. 'No, no. I became an *excellent* tourist guide. I do everything with great skill.'

He was incorrigible, had no understanding of the concept of modesty. But he was amusing company, she decided, and felt herself relax into the evening. They ordered their meal along with a bottle of wine, and the spotlight was turned away from Antonio and on to her. He wanted to know where she was from in England and why she was travelling alone. In the end she told him much more than she had intended, probably because of the quantity of wine she was drinking.

'So this Richard from whom you are running, you still love him?'

'Yes.' The admission was out before she could stop it.

He topped up her glass. 'I do not understand this need you have to punish your heart so cruelly.'

'It's for the best. For Kate and Henry, for Richard's wife and his young sons.'

'But not the best for Dulcie. Or Richard, I would dare to suggest.

To have pestered you so intensely before you came away shows the strength of his love for you.' Suddenly he leaned forward in his seat, his face barely inches from hers – it made her wonder how many of his patients had been dazzled by him when he'd been examining their eyes. 'Dulcie,' he said, 'permit me to be straight with you. I believe you have made a terrible mistake. To be blunt, at our age we have to grab the chances that come our way. No, no, do not argue with me. A stranger sees these things more clearly. Let the young people, Kate and Henry, sort themselves out. If they truly love each other they will find a way to continue their relationship.' He held up a hand to stop her interrupting him. 'Please, I know what you are going to say, but you are wasting your time protecting Richard's wife. Do her the kindness of letting her live a happier and more fulfilling life. Oh, yes, it will be difficult in the beginning, I do not dispute that, but by being honest about your love for Richard, you will give his wife the opportunity to find her own happiness and she will stop clinging desperately to a man who loves another. There, I have finished. It is now your turn to speak.'

But Dulcie couldn't. She was literally struck dumb by the man's audacity . . . and maybe by the sense of what he'd said.

Chapter Fifty-One

*

Dear Beth,

I have the distinct impression that you are hiding from me. Is it
something I said? Did I push you too hard over the writers'
conference? Just because I'm a writer, (a recently rejected
writer at that!), it doesn't mean I'm any good at subplots and
subtexts. I'm just an idiot who blurts out the first thing that
comes into his head. Some of which – most of which – he
instantly regrets. (There are those who hold the view that my
ramblings should come with a government health warning.) If
I've done anything to offend you, please don't hesitate to show
me the error of my ways.
  Yours, confused-and-disappointed-of-Suffolk,
  Ewan

PS I can take constructive advice and criticism as well as the
next thick-skinned man, though I do tend to bottle out sometimes
and wear a hard hat when the brick-bats really start to fly. I can
even take rejection, as recently demonstrated. But what I'm not
so hot on is seeing a blank screen every night when I log on to
see if there's a message from my favourite correspondent from
Maywood . . .

PPS For all I know you might have been away for the last few
weeks, or have had such a busy time of it you haven't had a
spare minute to keep in touch. If so, disregard all of the above
and accept the apologies of a pathetic man whose only excuse is

that he's turning into the whingeing sad old fool he promised his daughter he'd never become.

Beth finished reading Ewan's email, then scrolled back up to the beginning, and read it through once more. Without giving herself a chance to change her mind, she clicked on REPLY and started typing fast.

Dear Ewan,
Please, please, PLEASE don't berate yourself. My silence had nothing to do with you, but everything to do with me. Or, rather, everything to do with being so embarrassed. I'm ashamed to say that when I last emailed you I was disgustingly drunk. I half hoped you'd realise this and therefore make an enormous allowance for me, but I didn't want you thinking that I made it a regular feature of my evenings to get off my head – as Nathan would probably describe the state I was in. Truly, I am the most temperate of souls. And please believe me when I say I wouldn't dream of sending such an outrageous message in a more sober state. I've been hanging my head in shame ever since, wanting very much to put the episode behind me.
    And to change the subject completely (I'm reddening like the proverbial beetroot as I sit here making my excuses and apologies), I'll fill you in on what's been going on. You won't believe the half of it!

She told him about the Raffertys' house being broken into and of Jack staying at Dulcie's while she was away in Venice recovering from the end of her affair with Richard.

But more dramatic than any of this is [she wrote], was that Jack called round to see Victor (he was the peculiar man from the group who wouldn't take any advice), at Dulcie's request, only to find his house on fire. Jack had to smash a window to get in and rescue Victor, who is now in hospital recovering from the most awful burns. It looks as if the fire was started by a candle falling on to a pile of papers. According to the hospital, Victor must have collapsed before the fire got going. He was incredibly lucky to survive. Lucky, too, that Jack called on him when he did. I feel really sorry for Victor, especially as he's lost what was most precious to him. When Jack and I visited him, we had to break the news to him that his manuscript had perished in the fire – it was probably what fuelled the flames in the first place. And because he wrote it on a typewriter, he doesn't have a copy of it. It was heartbreaking to see him cry, Ewan. Poor man, he was utterly devastated. He doesn't seem to have any friends or family, and from what the nurses tell us, we're his only visitors, so Jack and I are trying to see him as often as we can – Jaz has also said she'll call in on him tomorrow after she's been to see her mother.

Well, that's about the height of it this end. Oh, only to add that my in-laws are away on their cruise and Barnaby emailed me from the ship (such technology!) to say that all was going very well. To his great relief (and mine) Lois was thrilled with the surprise he'd pulled on her. She didn't even mind him packing her clothes behind her back – she doesn't know yet that he asked me to do it for him. Barnaby is hoping that, on their return, Lois will be more receptive to the idea of calling a truce to our big bust-up over Christmas. Fingers crossed!

I've also been to see my old neighbour, Adele, (who used to live in the downstairs flat). I'm so relieved that she's enjoying the retirement home she's moved into. She's made lots of friends and joins in with the occasional outing to a National Trust property or the theatre. It's the future, Ewan. It's what awaits us all . . . if we're fortunate enough.

That really is all the news from Maywood. Nathan is at the cinema with Jaz, which leaves me with a nice quiet evening and a chance to do some writing, which has taken a bit of a back seat this last week, what with the many hospital visits to see Victor.

Best wishes,
Beth

PS I've decided to take the plunge and go to the Writers' Conference. Jack's coming too, to act as my chaperon . . .

PPS I don't think there's anything remotely whingeing or sad about you. The old is yet to be verified!

Conscious that her message was overly factual and not in the least witty like Ewan's, she clicked on SEND, then logged off. There, she'd done it. She'd put the humiliating incident behind her and committed herself to meeting Ewan. Anticipation outweighed any last remnants of her embarrassment, and happiness swelled inside her.

It was a long time since she had experienced the butterfly sensation in her stomach at the prospect of meeting a man, but there was no denying that she felt it now as she left her computer to make herself a cup of tea. The conference wasn't until next month, which meant she either had plenty of time to change her mind, or weeks of distracted thoughts to endure.

At work today Wendy had caught her tapping a pencil absently against her teeth while staring into mid-air and daydreaming about Ewan. 'Thinking of that gorgeous man again, are you?' her friend had teased.

Flustered that Wendy had read her thoughts so clearly, she dropped the pencil. Then came to her senses and realised that Wendy was referring to Jack. 'Oh, don't be so ridiculous,' she'd responded – the jokes about him were wearing thin. 'Jack is the last person I'd be daydreaming about. I've told you before that I don't go for younger men.'

But it would have to stop. Daydreaming was for the young. A grown woman of forty-three ought to know better. Yet more and more she was finding that being a sensible adult was such a chore. Why shouldn't she indulge herself in a little harmless frivolity?

Having decided to go to Harrogate, her next hurdle was telling Nathan about Ewan. She didn't have to, but she felt she should. Trouble was, she knew what his reaction would be: 'Let me get this straight, Mum. After all those lectures you gave me about not talking to strange men in public loos, you've struck up an email relationship with an unknown man?'

It was gone eleven when she finished writing and, knowing that Nathan would be back soon, she logged on to see if, on the off-chance, Ewan had responded to her email.

There was a message awaiting her: she clicked on READ.

Do my eyes deceive me? Or is this really an email I see before me from my sweet maiden in Maywood?

Gadzooks, it is!

And what an extraordinary time you've been having. I'm surprised CNN isn't covering the events going on in your little town and beaming them around the world. Just think of the book it would make!

Seriously, though, that poor guy Victor has my full sympathy. Was his house badly damaged in the fire? And, if so, where will he go when he's well enough to be discharged from hospital? As for losing his precious manuscript, there are worse things that could happen, but not many for a writer. On the other hand, perhaps this will give him the chance to start afresh. After such a harrowing ordeal, he's bound to want to explore a whole new area in his writing. Or does that sound too glib? For what it's worth, I think that's the approach I would take. Would have to take.

But to move on to less grim matters. I'm polishing my shoes in readiness for meeting you at the conference. I know all too well that women judge men by their shoes, and I'll have you know you won't find me wanting in that oh-so-crucial department. Hands and nails are important too, so nearer the time I shall be booking myself into the nearest beauty parlour and arranging a full-buff manicure. From there the hair will have to be groomed to within an inch of its life and the best suit dry-cleaned. As you can tell, I aim to make an excellent impression. If I have a nervous breakdown in the interim period, then so be it: the cause will have been a good and noble one.

Now to a slightly tricky problem. Since your last email, I've been stockpiling bars of chocolate, but now it appears I won't have a use for them. Any ideas what I should do with two dozen catering packs of Fruit and Nut?

Time to dash for the bunker. I feel a Scud missile heading this way from Maywood.

Yours, so-very-glad-to-hear-from-you,

Ewan X

PS Please don't waste any more vital energy worrying about THAT email. It will be wiped from the memory banks, as of now.

PPS Hey, what's with all the Jack references? Do I have a rival for your affections? If so, you'd better warn him that it will be quills at dawn the first day of the conference.

Hearing Nathan's key in the lock, Beth logged off hurriedly and decided that now was the time to tell him about Ewan.

Chapter Fifty-Two

*

The pleasing rhythm of Dulcie's stay in Venice had changed subtly.

Cathe and Randy had left for Paris first thing in the morning – before Dulcie had made it downstairs – and already she felt their absence. She had become accustomed to starting the day by seeing the couple at breakfast, then catching up with them in the evening in the hotel bar before they went their separate ways for dinner, maybe getting together later for a nightcap. They had been easy to grow fond of, had never overstepped the mark or imposed themselves on her, just offered simple friendship, expecting nothing in return. Last night they had exchanged addresses and Cathe had impressed upon Dulcie that she was welcome to stay with them any time she wanted. They lived in Maine, and the thought of visiting them during the autumn – the fall – was tempting. Likewise, Dulcie had said her home was always open to them.

And home was somewhere she would have to return soon. Perhaps prompted by Cathe and Randy's departure, her thoughts were increasingly of Maywood and everything she'd left behind. Antonio's words during dinner, two nights ago, had also had an effect on her. Was there a chance he had been right? If so, could she really put her own happiness above anyone else's?

'Trust me, these things resolve themselves, Dulcie,' Antonio had said, as he walked her back to her hotel that night. 'If only we let them.' He had kissed her lightly on the cheek and wished her luck. 'It is time to stop being a coward, Dulcie. Go home to the man you love. *Arrivederci.*'

Now it was just gone two o'clock and she had been wandering the labyrinth of alleyways in the San Marco district, after a visit across the Grand Canal to the Accademia. Finding herself in the Campo San Stefano, she decided to stop for a late lunch. Her legs were tired after several hours of walking and she was thirsty. In honour of Antonio she ordered a glass of Prosecco and selected a sandwich from the *tramezzini* menu. While she ate, she took out her notepad and pen and continued with the short story she had started yesterday – appropriately it was set in Venice. Before she knew it, and after she'd ordered a second glass of Prosecco, two hours had sped by and the sun had moved round the square. Feeling it on the back of her neck, she paid her bill and set off for the hotel. She had another concert planned for the evening, and if she was going to avoid falling asleep during it, a siesta was in order. Drinking at lunchtime was invariably a mistake and, holding tight to the rail on the *vaporetto* as it bumped against the San Marco Giardinetti stop, she yawned hugely. People clambered off, their places on the boat immediately filled by more passengers. Then they were chugging away, the smell of diesel filling the air.

As they drew level with the stately granite columns that marked the entrance to the *piazzetta*, Dulcie shaded her eyes from the glare of the afternoon sun. For the craziest moment, she thought she saw Richard among the blur of tourists. She strained her eyes, telling herself it couldn't be him, that she was imagining things – the result of too much sparkling wine. But, yes, unbelievably it *was* him.

Her heart thumped wildly and she was seized with the urge to wave madly and call his name, as she willed the boat on to the next landing-stage. It seemed to take for ever, but at last she was off and pushing through the queue of people waiting to board. On the waterfront, she almost broke into a run, rushing passed the Hotel Danielli, over the Ponte della Paglia and on alongside the Doges' palace. She was out of breath when she reached the *piazzetta*: the stitch in her side was so painful she had to stop to recover. She feared now she would lose track of Richard, that he would be lost in the crowds, or vanish into one of the many alleyways. But, amazingly, she caught sight of him again. He was side on to her, his gaze fixed rigidly on the rows of gondolas gleaming in the sunshine, water lapping at their sides. He didn't hear her approach or know that she was now standing next to him until she said, 'It's a stunning view, isn't it?'

He turned, did a double-take, then flung his arms around her. The strength of his embrace was so great it nearly knocked her off her feet. They were both in tears when they released each other. Around them, people were giving them odd looks, and a wide berth.

'Oh, Dulcie, don't be cross with me,' he said, clasping her hands in his. 'Don't be angry that I followed you here. Just let me talk to you. Hear what I've got to say, then I'll go . . . if you want me to.'

She took him back to the Hotel Isabella. Smiling broadly, Alberto handed over her key. 'And, Signor Cavanagh, *your key*?'

Dulcie glanced at Richard as he took it. He looked shamefaced. In the small mirrored lift, and in answer to her unasked question, he said, 'It's a long story, and I'm all too aware of how devious I must seem. Forgive me, please?'

'Nothing to forgive,' she said, still dazed with shock that he was here. She let them into her room. The chambermaid had been: the bed was made, and sunlight streamed across it. She stood for a moment at the foot of the bed, acknowledging that words could wait: now she wanted to feel Richard close to her. She wanted to lie beside him and feel the tender warmth of his hands on her body. But if she allowed that to happen, as she knew she would, she would never let him go. She couldn't live as she had in the past. Selfishly, she wanted him for herself. All of him. There would be no more half-measures. She wanted to live her life to the full. The hiding had to stop.

Behind her, she heard him moving. She closed her eyes, anticipating what he would do next. She felt his breath on her neck as he gently pressed his lips to her skin: oh, he'd always known the effect it had on her. He turned her round and kissed her. They made love in silence, with an intensity that left them both exhausted.

They fell asleep, Richard's arm wrapped protectively around Dulcie's shoulders. His last words, before he drifted away from her were 'I love you, Dulcie. Be with me . . . always.'

Dulcie hadn't been asleep for long when a flash of memory jolted her awake. She recalled the moment, on the *vaporetto*, when she'd seen Richard in the *piazzetta*. Something was wrong. Something jarred. But what?

She was almost asleep again when the answer came to her. Richard had been standing between the two granite columns where . . . where superstitious Venetians never set foot.

It was irrational, but in her drowsy state she lifted her head from the pillow to check that Richard was all right. His breathing was steady, and when she laid a hand on his chest she felt the reassuring rhythmic beat of his heart.

She closed her eyes and chided herself for her stupidity.

All thoughts of a concert that evening were abandoned, and as Dulcie and Richard lay in bed, he explained how he'd found her. 'You mustn't blame Jack. He played no part in this.'

'Jack? You've spoken to him?'

'Yes. I went to see you, to throw myself on your mercy one more time, and found myself confronted with a strange man who was giving nothing away. I have to confess that initially I was far from polite to him. To give him his due, he was the model of guardianship, and refused point-blank to tell me where you were staying. He made it clear he didn't approve of me.'

She told Richard about the break-up of Jack's marriage, that it was still painfully raw for him. 'So how did you find out where I was?'

'It was on your noticeboard in the kitchen. You're too organised for your own good, Dulcie, not that I'm complaining. I wanted to book the first flight available, but I had to wait for things to calm down at work. I couldn't believe it. We've had a relatively quiet spell for some weeks, then suddenly a large contract I thought we'd sewn up started to unravel. I was convinced, the way my luck was going, that I'd arrive too late, that you'd already have flown home.'

'And Angela? Where does she think you are?'

The mention of his wife's name was the first hint of reality to cloud their happiness, to remind them that, beyond the walls of the Hotel Isabella, the real world awaited them.

He rolled on to his back and stared up at the ceiling. 'In Bristol, at a corporate ra-ra. You know, the usual kind of thing, wall-to-wall team building and effective management training. Dawn-till-dusk bonding.'

His words hung heavily in the silence between them. She ran her fingers over his chest and said, 'What happens when we go home, Richard?'

He took her hand and raised it to his lips. 'I do what I should have done a long time ago. I tell Angela the truth. I've been a coward and I'm not prepared to go on hurting either of you the way I have till now.'

Over dinner that evening, in a trattoria only a short walk from their hotel, where Dulcie had eaten on several occasions, he asked her what had changed her mind. She told him about Antonio. 'I know it sounds far-fetched, but he made it seem, oh, I don't know, reasonable somehow. I've come to the conclusion that Kate and Henry will have to decide for themselves what to do. And Angela, well, I feel this terrible weight of guilt every time I think about her, but maybe she really will be better off without you. Who knows? Learning to stand on her own two feet might be the making of her.' She reached across the table and placed her hand over his. 'Are you sure you want to do this, Richard? The ramifications will go on for the rest of our lives.'

'I know, but believe me, I've never been surer about anything. I love you, Dulcie, and while I won't be able to offer you all that I'd like to in the way of financial security—'

She removed her hand from his, stopping him short. 'Richard, I don't care what money you may or may not have. It's you I love, not your bank balance.'

'Which will be seriously depleted by the time I've squared things with—'

She stopped him again. 'Put your wretched male pride back into its box, and listen to me. It's *you* I want in my life. I'm not in the least interested in your worldly goods and chattels. All I expect you to bring to our relationship is commitment and honesty.'

He looked serious. 'Some might say, in view of how I've treated Angela, that I'm incapable of either of those things.'

After dinner, arm in arm – something they had never been able to do back in England – they went for a stroll: it was a perfect night wrapped in moonlight and gently lapping water. Richard hadn't been to Venice before, and Dulcie found herself wanting to share her love of this romantic place with him. To her delight he was equally taken with Venice's unique charm and beauty. I shall always remember this night, she thought, as beneath a starry sky they lingered on a tiny bridge overlooking a narrow waterway of shimmering inky blue. It was a peaceful backwater of neglected buildings and crumbling brickwork; humble, magical and stunningly beautiful. How could a city of such faded grandeur touch

324

the hearts of so many? But answering that was like trying to dissect the very essence of love – like trying to catch hold of quicksilver.

Standing behind her, his arms around her, chin resting on the top of her head, Richard said, 'One day, when we're married, we'll come back here and stand on this same spot and I shall tell you that you've made me the happiest man alive.'

'Not before then?'

'No.' He turned her round to face him. 'I want us to be married as soon as we can. I wish it could be tomorrow, but I'm afraid we'll have to be patient.'

She shushed him with a kiss. 'One step at a time.'

They took the *vaporetto* back to the hotel, and went straight to bed. But they couldn't sleep. There was too much to think about. The days ahead, when they returned to Maywood, were going to be fraught with pain, particularly for Richard and Angela. Dulcie hoped they were all strong enough to survive the ordeal.

Victor was sick of people telling him how lucky he was to have survived the fire. Would any of those infuriating nurses feel lucky if they were going through this pain? It was worse during the night when he was alone and all he had to think about was the agony he was in. The painkillers and sleeping-pills never seemed strong enough, and by four in the morning he was wide awake and wishing he'd never been rescued.

He didn't remember a thing about the fire. His last memory was of sitting in front of his typewriter, feeling dizzy. Jack had explained that he'd found him on the floor and had carried him downstairs. He'd also told him that there was no sign of his manuscript in the room where the fire had started. To his everlasting shame he had cried when he'd heard this. That Beth woman had looked near to tears too. He'd asked them to leave him alone. They'd gone, but had returned the following day. And the day after that. He'd lost track of how long he'd been stuck here in the burns unit – it felt like for ever. No one would give him a straight answer when he asked when he'd be able to go home. The worst of his burns were around his neck, chest, right shoulder, arm and hand, and the doctors spoke of the risk of infection, that there would have to be skin grafts. He was hooked up to an intravenous drip, which fed in antibiotics and God knew what else. His throat and lungs were still suffering from the effect of smoke inhalation, and he could only speak in a hoarse whisper.

If he was honest, he didn't want to go home. Both Jack and the policeman who had come to talk to him about the fire had said the damage to his house was confined to just two rooms. Again, he had been lucky. But were they telling him the truth or merely sparing his feelings? What they didn't know was that the insurance company wouldn't pay up. Because of his redundancy, he'd let the monthly payments slip. If his throat hadn't hurt so much, he would have cried out his frustration. But all he could do was lie in this wretched bed as helpless as a baby. Sometimes just opening his eyes was all he could manage.

The next morning brought a troupe of trainee doctors to gawp at him. Lunchtime came and went, followed by a bossy nurse who spent an age fiddling with his dressings and made him cry with the pain. When at last she left him alone, he lay back exhausted, pitying the man in the bed alongside him who was in for the same treatment.

Hours later he woke up from a deep sleep to find a girl staring down at him. Through the crack in his eyelids she looked vaguely familiar, but indistinguishable from the hundreds of young nurses he saw every day.

'Hello, Victor, how's it going?'

He closed his eyes. 'Go away,' he croaked.

'Charmed, I'm sure.'

Still with his eyes shut, he said, 'I'm tired. I just want to sleep.'

'That's okay. I'll sit here and eat my way through this bunch of grapes I've brought for you.'

He forced his eyes open and focused on the girl sitting beside the bed. 'It's you,' he said, in disbelief. 'You're that lippy girl from the writing group.'

She grinned. 'Nice one, Victor. You sound like my father. How are you?'

'How do you think I am?'

'Well, for a man who's gone through what you've been through, I reckon you don't look so bad. The husky voice is an improvement. Almost sexy.'

'If you've come here to mock me, have your fun, then go.'

'Now why do you think I'd do a thing like that?'

'Why else would you be here?'

326

'To see how you are. Jack and Beth told me you didn't have any visitors other than them, so I thought you'd appreciate a friendly face. Oh, and I brought you these.' She delved into a small black-leather rucksack, pulled out a newspaper and a box of chocolates and put them on his bedside locker. 'They're contraband,' she said, her voice lowered. 'Liqueurs. I thought you might be in need of the alcohol.'

'And the paper?'

'There's an article in it about you.'

'Me?'

'You and Jack. Because of you, he's a hero.'

'I thought you said something about grapes.'

'I was kidding. Of course, if you'd rather have the vitamin C, I could take the choccies away and bring you something healthy instead.'

'No,' he said. 'I'll make do with those.'

She laughed. 'Good to see you've not lost your touch, Victor. You're still a miserable old goat.'

He stared at her, incensed. 'How dare you talk to me like that?'

'I dare because you're stuck there in bed unable to do anything about it. Now, when are you going to start writing again?'

'That's none of your business.'

'Yes, it is. We're members of a writers' group. We're supposed to support and encourage each other.'

He sighed. His voice was growing weaker and the pain in his throat was getting worse. 'I doubt I'll be able to hold a pen for months.'

She looked at him solemnly, her gaze taking in the wreck of his body. 'Is it very bad?'

He swallowed, and to his horror tears filled his eyes. With an effort that sent waves of unbearable pain shooting through him, he turned his head. 'I'd like you to go now.'

To his immense relief, he heard her get to her feet. But the relief was short-lived. 'I'll see you tomorrow, Victor. Take care, won't you?'

Chapter Fifty-Three

*

Jack had said he would visit Victor during the afternoon, between clients, and with Beth working late, Jaz had said she would do the evening slot. It fitted in well with seeing her mother first, who was still under orders to stay in bed – her blood pressure was showing no sign of coming down.

Jaz had been warned by Beth that Victor looked awful, but on her first visit nothing had prepared her for the sight of him. He was straight out of a horror movie. She'd done her best yesterday to hide her shock and had chatted to him as though nothing was wrong, even being rude to convince him she wasn't there out of pity. When he'd started to cry, she hadn't known what to do or say – other than to go, as he'd requested.

But she was back to see him today, as she'd said she would be. She'd asked Mum how she ought to handle things, and had been advised to be herself. 'If you do anything else, he'll know you're uncomfortable with the situation, which in turn will make him feel worse. Just be your usual self, Jaz. And if he starts to cry again, don't be embarrassed, find him a tissue.'

It was great being able to talk so openly with her mother. It was like it used to be between them.

The house was looking better now, too: the decorators had almost finished and the carpets were being fitted next week. But they'd nearly been found out. Tamzin and Lulu had been arguing at the end of Mum's bed and Dad had told them to keep the noise down. When Lulu had pushed Tamzin off the bed, Dad had roared, 'Just you wait till I get you monkeys home! I'll knock your stupid heads together!'

'Don't you mean when you get us back to the hotel?' Tamzin had said.

Jaz had thought her father would explode and throttle her sister on the spot, so she stepped in and said, 'Will you listen to the girl? She treats the house like a hotel and now even *calls* it a hotel.' With much tutting and rolling of eyes, she'd dragged her sisters out of the room, saying their sugar levels were probably at an all-time low and she'd get them a can of Coke. Later that night her father had thanked her for her fast thinking. He'd even apologised for having punished her so harshly over Hidden Talents. 'Your mother's taken me to task,' he admitted. 'She says I've got to treat you more like the adult you are. Thing is, Jaz, I still want to keep you in my pocket where I'll know you'll be safe.'

'Oh, Dad, less of the cheesy routine.'

'It's true. You're the special one in our family and I don't want you to come to harm. Tamzin and Lulu are natural-born fighters, like the boys, but you're so small. Nothing but a waif of a girl who needs someone to look out for her.'

'Dad, I'm more than capable of taking care of myself. I've been doing it for years. You've taught me all you know.'

He'd laughed and left her to get on with her homework while he went to check on Tamzin and Lulu in the room next door.

Now Jaz stepped out of the lift on the third floor of the hospital and followed the signs for the burns unit. Victor was lying in exactly the same position as he'd been in yesterday, flat on his back, staring up at the ceiling.

'Hi, Victor,' she said. 'I threatened you with another visit, and here I am. Don't ever accuse me of short-changing you. So, what's new? I'm afraid I've come empty-handed this time.' She noticed that the box of chocolates she'd given him yesterday was open on his bedside locker and that three barrel-shaped chocolates were missing.

'Nothing's new,' he whispered morosely.

She repositioned the chair next to his bed and sat down. 'I've just been to see my mother – did I tell you she was here? No? Well, she's been stuck in bed for much longer than you. She's expecting twins, and she's been told that if she doesn't do as the doctors say she might lose the babies. Pretty serious, eh? Hey, you know what we ought to do? Fix the pair of you up with walkie-talkies and you can moan to each other about how awful it is in here.'

She rambled on, chattering nineteen to the dozen, only occasionally eliciting a response from Victor – a roll of his eyes or a
disapproving croak. She told him about the burglary and the house
being wrecked. 'They messed up all my college work, but I've
managed to sort it out.'

A flicker of something, possibly understanding, passed across his
face and he said, 'What about your writing?'

'Ah. Long story. I had to ditch it. It was rubbish, anyway. I'm
waiting for inspiration to hit me so I can start something new.
What will you do next?' Jaz saw his lips move, but she didn't catch
what he said. She leaned towards him. 'Sorry, Victor, I didn't hear
you. What did you say?'

'I said, I'll give up.'

She was shocked, and poignantly nostalgic for the old Victor: the
pompous, ego-inflated Victor. 'You'll do no such thing,' she said.
'If I can start again, so can you.'

'I think we can safely say our circumstances are very different.'

'And that's where you're wrong. We have one very important
quality in common with each other: we're writers. And once a
writer, always a writer. You just need to get going again. It would
be great therapy for you. Once you start using your brain again,
you'll soon be feeling less sorry for yourself.'

'Sorry for myself?' he echoed, in a hoarse whisper. 'Next you'll
be telling me to pull myself together.'

She smiled. 'I hadn't thought of that. It's not a bad idea, is it?'
She waited for his response, to see if she'd gone too far. For what it
was worth she thought she had. But something about his beaten
manner made her want to shake him up, to make him believe in
himself again. She didn't have to be a brain surgeon to know that if
he didn't believe his body would heal he'd never get better inside.
What spurred her to carry on talking to him in this no-nonsense
way was the hope that, while she had his attention, he wasn't
thinking about his appalling injuries. At least there was no sign of
him crying as he'd done yesterday.

He'd made no response to her comment, so she said, 'Did you
know that the writers' group hasn't met for a while?'

'No, I didn't,' he murmured. 'I've had more important things to
occupy me.'

'That's right, so you have. Anyway, Jack and Beth thought that

330

while Dulcie was still away on holiday, and you were stuck here, there wouldn't be any meetings.'

'I'm overwhelmed by the group's consideration, as I'm sure Dulcie will be.'

'Okay, that's me done here. I've got a stack of homework to get through this evening.' She stood up. 'Shall I come again tomorrow?'

She had to hide a smile of satisfaction when, in a tired, strained voice, he said, 'If it isn't too much trouble, perhaps you could bring me a book to read.'

'Consider it done.'

As she waited for the lift to take her down to her mother's ward, where her father would be waiting to give her a lift back to the hotel, she had the weirdest thought: *Consider it done.* It might have been Popeye Rafferty speaking.

Now, there was a scary thought. Was it possible she was more of a chip off the old block than she'd ever given herself credit for?

Despite knowing what he would have to face when he and Dulcie returned home, Richard had never enjoyed a day more. Or maybe it was because he knew they had to make the most of it that it had passed so happily. For a brief period he and Dulcie had been an ordinary couple. There had been no hiding, no fear of a chance encounter with someone who knew either of them. And this was how the rest of their lives would be, once the initial horror of telling Angela that he wanted a divorce had passed. They were returning home tomorrow. Returning, paradoxically, to the future. *Their* future.

While Dulcie was in the bath, he checked his mobile to see if there were any messages for him – he'd deliberately left it in the hotel room, not wanting a second of their day to be ruined. There was only one message, from Juliette at the office. The first time he listened to it, he frowned at its cryptic content. When he pressed the button to play it again, the frown deepened and he sat down on the edge of the bed.

'Sorry to do this, Richard, but I needed to get hold of you. I thought you ought to know that I've just spoken to your wife and, well, I must have got my wires in a tangle because I had no idea you were on a course in Bristol. I thought you were on holiday. Lucky you'd briefed your wife so thoroughly on that point or I would have looked very silly. Anyway, sorry again, hope I haven't caused any problems. Oh, and we've got a bit of a crisis here, but that can go on hold until you're back. We'll muddle through without you. Speak to you soon. 'Bye.'

Oh, hell. It had started.

Chapter Fifty-Four

*

It was raining when they landed at Manchester airport. The dirty grey sky and the strong gusting wind that met them were a far cry from the beautiful weather they'd enjoyed in Venice. For most of the flight, they had sat in silence, nervous of what lay ahead.

As she held Richard's hand, Dulcie's heart went out to him. Shortly after he'd listened to Juliette's message, Angela had phoned: most of the conversation was audible in the small hotel room. 'Exactly where are you?' she'd asked. 'Because I know you're not in Bristol. I've phoned round, and no one knows anything about the course you told me about.'

'Angela, please, I'll be home tomorrow. We can discuss it then.'

'I want to discuss it *now*. You're . . . you're having an affair, aren't you?'

'Angela—'

'Please tell me it isn't true,' she had cried. 'Tell me I've got it wrong.'

'I'm sorry, but it is true.'

'Are you . . . are you with her now?'

'Yes.'

She had ended the call. Ten minutes later Richard had tried ringing her back, but the line was engaged: either she was speaking to someone else or she had taken the phone off the hook.

Dulcie hadn't wasted her breath on reassuring Richard that it didn't matter how Angela had found out, that he had been going to tell her the truth anyway. She knew it made all the difference to him. He had wanted to spare his wife's feelings as far as he could, to break it to her gently and help her over the worst of the shock.

To let her know that he would stand by her and the children, and do everything in his power to make the situation more bearable.

Richard had left his car at the airport and he drove them to Maywood. Dulcie had telephoned Jack late last night to warn him that she would be arriving home today, and when they let themselves into her house, she saw that he had been as good as his word: everything was just as she'd left it, with the bonus of a well-stocked fridge and the mail left in an orderly pile on the kitchen table. There was also a vase of daffodils with a note attached: 'Thanks for letting me stay. See you soon. Jack. P.S. Hope Venice did the trick.'

Richard didn't want to stay long. He prowled anxiously around the kitchen, refused the offer of lunch, drank half a cup of coffee and said, 'I ought to go. The sooner I get this over with the better – and before the boys come home from school.'

She stood on the doorstep and reluctantly let him leave, then rushed after him to give him one last hug, no longer concerned if any of her neighbours saw them. 'I wish I could be there with you,' she said, 'to give you moral support.'

He held her tightly. 'This is definitely something I have to do alone, Dulcie.'

'I know.' She stepped back from him. 'I love you, Richard. Remember that, won't you? Call me when you can. It doesn't matter how late. Or how early. I'll be here.'

It was raining hard as Richard drove out of Maywood. With the wipers swishing back and forth, he was on auto-pilot, passing familiar buildings, road signs, hedges and swathes of open farmland but not seeing any of it. He was thinking of the day he'd first met Dulcie. It had been the most extraordinary and glorious moment of his life. Until then he had never believed in anything as rhapsodic as love at first sight. But it had happened. And to a middle-aged sceptic such as he.

He had been sitting in the lounge of Maywood Grange Hotel when he had heard someone say his name. The voice was distinctively low and, to his ears, incredibly seductive. He'd looked up from the crossword he'd been doing in *The Times*, and had literally felt his heart jolt. He could still remember her exact words: 'Sorry, I didn't mean to make you jump.' If he had started, it was not because she had taken him unawares, it was because she had rocked his world.

They had slipped into an easy rapport and he had spent the rest of the day in bewildered astonishment, trying to conceal his attraction to her as she showed him round the selection of houses she had arranged for him to view. But that evening he had lowered his guard and invited her to join him for dinner. It was then that he had sensed the attraction was mutual.

And what of his wife and family while all this was going on?

Out of sight, out of mind.

He wasn't proud of it, but that was the truth. In the course of that one day the rest of his life had been changed. He hadn't intended it to happen, he had always dismissed men who embarked upon affairs, but he'd been unable to withstand the force of his attraction to this unusual woman. With her sense of fun and independence, her uncomplicated love of life, she made the world seem a better place. She was strong and refreshingly direct.

It was unfair to compare her with Angela, but she was everything his wife wasn't. She was both restful and exciting to be with, and if he had to sum up the effect she had on him in a single phrase, it was that she allowed him to be himself. Once, when he had felt lousy and knew that he looked far from his best, he'd apologised to Dulcie for it. She had given him one of her level stares and said, 'It's okay, Richard, off-days are permissible. You're not on parade with me.'

Oh, if only they had met in their twenties. What a rich and fulfilling life they would have had together.

He swung through the gates and came to a stop in front of the garage, next to Angela's mud-splattered Range Rover. He switched off the engine, looked up at the house through the pouring rain – the house Dulcie had found for him and his family. Could he really put the boys through such an ordeal? Would they ever forgive him? And how would he feel if they refused to see him again? It happened. Children caught in the crossfire of divorcing parents often saw things in black and white and clung protectively to the parent they considered to be in the right. Henry and Victoria would probably do that, initially. Although Henry might have reason never to speak to him again.

He groaned and lowered his head to the steering-wheel.

335

He roused himself and went inside. The house was eerily quiet. He put down his case at the foot of the stairs and called to Angela.

No reply.

Without removing his raincoat, he went through to the kitchen. No sign of her there either. But, on stopping to look out of the window, he saw her sheltering beneath an umbrella at the bottom of the garden. His heart thudded.

It must have rained solidly for some time, for when he walked over the lawn his shoes sank into the sodden grass. He didn't want to startle her, so he called softly, 'Angela, what are you doing out here?'

She turned, slowly, as if she had been waiting for him. He could see that she'd been crying. Inside his chest, his heart thudded again, painfully.

'Oh, Richard . . . why? Why have you done this to us?'

'I'm sorry,' he said, 'more sorry than I'll ever be able to say.'

'I don't understand. I thought we were happy. I know I'm not the easiest of wives, that I irritate you with my silly—'

He stopped her. 'It's not you, Angela. You must never think that. It's me. I . . . I changed. I became someone different. I didn't mean to.'

The rain was coming down harder now and he was drenched, but he made no move to seek refuge beneath her umbrella. She didn't offer it. Tears flowed down her cheeks. She said, 'I suppose it's some young girl from the office. A pretty bit of ego-boosting fluff half my age.'

'Don't do this, Angela.'

She sniffed defiantly. 'Why not? Why shouldn't I be allowed to know who you've been with? Is she very pretty? Is she—' Her voice faltered and she began to cry in earnest, her sobs loud and choking. 'Oh, God. Why, Richard? Why did you have to do this?'

He stepped forward, took the handle of the umbrella and walked her back to the house. He sat her in the kitchen and knelt on the floor at her side. And still she cried. He hated himself for doing this to her. She didn't deserve such pain. 'I'm sorry,' he said. 'I never meant to hurt you.'

She lifted her tear-soaked face to his. 'Tell me about – about this other woman. Don't shake your head as if I'm a child to be protected. I want to know. I *need* to know.'

336

He stood up and went to the window. 'It's not what you think. It isn't someone from the office.'

'Do I know her? Is it someone from the village?'

'No. It's Dulcie. Dulcie Ballantyne.' He heard her sudden intake of breath. And then, unbelievably, he heard her laugh.

'But she's *old*!'

He swung round. 'No, she isn't.'

'But she's old,' Angela repeated. She threw back her head and laughed. It was a cruel, mocking laugh, which he'd never heard from her before. But as suddenly as it had started, it stopped. 'She's not even remotely beautiful,' Angela said. 'And she's certainly not slim. Dumpy isn't far off the mark, I'd say. My God, Richard, is that the best you can do? What on earth is the attraction?'

He clenched his teeth. He understood that Angela needed to vent her fury, but he wouldn't countenance a disparaging word about Dulcie. 'You don't have to resort to being spiteful,' he said.

'Oh, that's wonderful. That woman can wreck my marriage but I'm not allowed to say a word about her age or her crabby old looks. Now I've heard everything.'

Richard kept his face impassive. 'I know you're upset and angry, Angela, but if we're going to sort this mess out, we need to remain calm and level-headed.'

She cleared her throat. 'You're right,' she said. 'I'm being my usual stupid self. I need to—'

'You're not being stupid,' he interrupted impatiently. Then, in a more placatory tone, 'Please don't keep saying that. Shall I make us some tea?'

They sat at either end of the table, divided by a pile of laundry that was waiting to be ironed and several days' worth of newspapers destined for the recycling collection point in the village.

'Right,' Angela said, after a sip of tea, 'what happens now? Do I make you promise never to see her again and we carry on as if nothing has happened?'

His heart slammed against his ribs. Angela had no idea of what was coming next. She thought he had stepped out of line and assumed that, because he'd been caught, he would get back where he belonged, his 'misdemeanour' discreetly tucked away.

'Or do I,' she continued, 'for the sake of the boys, have to accept that there'll always be this . . . this third person in our marriage?'

He closed his eyes briefly. When he opened them, he said, 'I'm afraid neither of those options will work, Angela.' He swallowed. 'I want a divorce. But I want you to know that nothing here,' he glanced around the kitchen, 'will change. This will always be your home, yours and the children's. You won't have to worry about money. I'll see to all that. I promise I'll take care of everything.' But as he tried to fill the yawning gap between them with words, wanting to reassure her, he knew she wasn't listening.

'A divorce? You can't be serious.'

'I'm sorry, but I am. I – I want to marry Dulcie.'

She shook her head. 'No. No you don't. You're having a silly mid-life crisis.' Her voice had reached a high hysterical pitch. 'Oh, why couldn't you have just made do with growing your hair and buying a motorbike?'

'I think you'd agree that I'm too old for either of those choices,' he replied.

'Well, you're too old to have an affair,' she retorted. Then, more calmly, she said, 'It's because you had a heart-attack, isn't it? It's made you realise you're getting older. That time is running out. But it'll pass. You'll soon be your old self.' She was pleading with him.

He said nothing.

'So, when did the affair start? After our Boxing Day party?'

He knew the truth would hurt, but there had been enough deceit. If he lied to her now, they would get nowhere: she would carry on believing that it was just a phase he was going through. She had to know he was serious about Dulcie. 'Since I first met her, when we were house-hunting to move up here.'

Angela's mouth dropped open, a small cry escaped her, and then she fled from the room, crashing the door after her.

With his elbows on the table, he leaned forward and hung his head. The worst, or so he hoped, was over.

Chapter Fifty-Five

*

The flat was looking less like a bombsite now and more like the airy, comfortable home Jack had envisaged. He had Rafferty & Sons to thank for that. Because of his connection with Jaz, he knew he'd been treated as a priority. However, it had occurred to him that maybe the real reason he was getting such gold-star treatment was because of what her brothers had done to him, that this was the Rafferty way of settling the account. But he'd soon dismissed the idea: he couldn't imagine Patrick Rafferty conducting business that way. He didn't strike Jack as a man who would condone what his hot-headed sons had done. Odds on, they had acted without his approval. And hadn't they told him to keep schtum? Especially where Jaz was concerned.

The men Patrick Rafferty had organised to do the job had been one hundred per cent reliable. Most days, and during his lunch break, Jack had called in to see how they were getting on, but his supervision wasn't required. They knew what they were doing and planned to finish the job next week, when they would return to see to the odds and ends. One had a mate who was a joiner and specialised in fitting kitchens. 'I could give you his number, if you like, so you can get him round here to give you a quote. I'm not saying he's cheap, but he'll do you a quality job for a reasonable price. He did the boss's kitchen, so that tells you all you need to know. Assuming, that is, you're planning on losing those old units. A right seventies nightmare, aren't they? Floor's not much cop either. You wanna rip up them old lino tiles and get some laminated wood down.'

Jack had formed no lasting relationship with the antiquated

kitchen – fake teak-fronted units with the obligatory aluminium edging – and was only too pleased to be given the name and phone number of someone who came so highly recommended. He lost no time in ringing the joiner and arranging for him to come and see what the job would entail.

Now, as Jack stood in the soon-to-be demolished kitchen beneath the harsh glare of a fluorescent strip-light, he went through his mail. The only envelope of any interest had been addressed by hand: it was from the organisers of the writers' conference in Harrogate. In reply to his phone call they had sent him several copies of the programme with some application forms. He slipped the pieces of paper back into the envelope and took it upstairs with him.

Yet again Beth was bestowing more neighbourly generosity on him: he was looking forward to the day when he would be able to return her kindness by inviting her and Nathan to eat *chez* Solomon.

Nathan opened the door. 'Hi, Jack. Mum's just getting changed, she won't be long. Jaz and I have nearly got supper ready. Don't look so worried, we washed our hands before we started.'

'That's not worry on my face, Nathan, it's awe. Hello, Jaz. What's cooking?'

'Chilli con carne.'

'And pudding?'

'Banoffee pie.'

'Now I *am* impressed. Anything I can do to help?'

'Absolutely not,' said Nathan. 'We promised Mum a night off, and we're not going to be accused of being incapable because we've taken on extra help.'

Beth joined them in the sitting room. 'Aren't they sweet, Jack? I'm racking my brains as to what they're after. More use of the car, perhaps? Or more money?'

During the meal they caught up with each other's news. Anyone observing them, thought Jack, as they laughed and joked, would think they were a regular family going about its evening business. The thought made him sad: he wished Amber and Lucy were there too. He still didn't know if Maddie and Tony were going to up sticks and move to the States. His solicitor's letter had prompted a guarded reply, informing Jack that no decision had been made as yet, but that his concerns regarding the children had been duly noted. Meanwhile, all he could do was hope and pray that the move wouldn't come off. He didn't know how he would handle being so permanently apart from the girls. He saw them little enough now, but just once or twice a year would be intolerable.

'More chilli, Jack?'

Shaking off his morose thoughts, he helped himself from the dish Jaz was offering him, and said, 'How was Victor when you saw him yesterday?'

Nathan laughed. 'Ah, yes, the other man in Jaz's life.'

Jaz elbowed him. 'You leave poor Victor alone. Actually, Jack, he's being almost polite to me.'

'And she's being too modest to sing her own praises,' said Beth. 'Against all the odds, Jaz has done the impossible. She's got Victor writing again.'

'No? How?'

'She was downright rude to him, from what I can gather,' said Nathan. 'Shook him by his singed shoulders and told him to stop whingeing.'

'I did no such thing!'

'So what words of encouragement did you offer him?'

'I merely suggested that having something else to think about would give him less time to feel sorry for himself.'

Jack smiled. 'That's my girl.'

'She's thinking of joining the UN next,' teased Nathan. 'I can't think how they've managed till now without her obvious skills in diplomacy.'

'You're all making too big an issue of it,' said Jaz. 'He asked me to take in a book for him, so I gave him a notepad and pen as well, just in case anything came to him in the middle of the night.'

Beth passed her the basket of garlic bread. 'I think you've been brilliant. You've done more for Victor than the rest of us ever could. You even got him to admit that he'd been made redundant.'

'I just gave him the opportunity to talk. It must have been hard on him, losing his job like that, after so many years.' She bit into a piece of garlic bread. 'Do you want to know what my latest plan for Victor is?'

'Go on,' urged Jack. 'Let's have it.'

'Now that Dulcie's back, I think we ought to start up the group again and hold our meetings at the hospital so that he can join in.'

Jack looked at Beth. 'Can we do that? Will the hospital allow so many of us to visit at the same time?'

'I don't see why not. I've seen quite large families gathered round patients' beds. So long as we don't make too much noise and only stay for the specified time, what harm would we do?'

'And who'd have thought we cared enough about him?'

Beth glanced at the burns that had almost healed on his hands. 'And there speaks the hero who risked his own life to rescue Victor.'

'But it's true, isn't it?' persisted Jaz. 'He's the biggest pain going, but you can't help feeling sorry for him.'

Nathan put his arm around her shoulders. 'I had no idea you were such a sentimental softie.'

'I'm not,' she warned. 'Tough as old boots, me, so watch your step.'

The banoffee pie was a triumph and, after accepting their praise, Jaz confessed that the chef at the Maywood Grange Hotel had made it for her. 'It turns out that he and Dad know one another from way back and now we're getting whatever Dad fancies to eat,' she explained. 'It's so embarrassing – the other guests must hate us.'

'Oh, let them,' said Jack. 'Your father's a top man. The flat's coming on a treat.'

'I'm surprised you've come back to this lowly neighbourhood,' said Beth, handing him a bottle of wine. 'After whooping it up in Bloom Street, Maywood Park Road must be something of a drop in standards for you.'

'Oh, I'm making do,' he said, with an exaggerated shrug. 'I'm sure I'll get used to being back in such a rough area.'

'And talking of Dulcie, how do you think she's faring? I did ask her to join us tonight, but she said she wasn't in the mood for company.'

It was four days since Dulcie had returned from Venice and, from the limited conversations he and Beth had had with her, they'd learned that her affair with Richard was now back on and out in the open. As for what would happen next, Dulcie had refused to comment. Perhaps she didn't know.

'I haven't a clue,' Jack said, in answer to Beth's question. 'She doesn't give much away, but when I called round last night to thank her properly for letting me use her house, she seemed

342

okay-ish. I think she's dreading Richard's wife turning up on her doorstep wanting an all-out confrontation.'

'I still can't believe that Dulcie's been having an affair,' said Jaz, scraping up the last of her dessert. 'She just doesn't seem the sort.'

'Why's that?' asked Beth, with a wry smile. 'You wouldn't be casting aspersions on her age, would you?'

Jaz missed the implied criticism. 'There is that. But, well, she seems so nice and normal, not the man-eater type. The opposite, in fact.'

'I didn't know adulterers had a certain look. What would it be? A lascivious leer?'

Jaz rolled her eyes. 'Don't be obtuse, Nathan. All I meant was, she doesn't fit the profile.'

'And which profile would that be?'

While Beth made the coffee, Jack pondered this thought. Had he demonised Maddie and Tony because of their actions? Weren't they really just two people who had fallen in love? And if Maddie had been any other woman, wouldn't he have wished his old friend all the luck in the world?

From across the kitchen, while she waited for the kettle to boil, Beth watched Jack's face growing ever more solemn. She could guess what he was thinking of. How long, she wondered, would it be before he could think of Maddie and Tony without it hurting? A year? Two? A decade? Maybe never. Perhaps something like that stayed with you for a lifetime.

To lighten the mood for his benefit, she said, 'You wouldn't believe what I've had to put up with these last few days, Jack. I told Nathan about Ewan and it's been non-stop innuendoes, warnings and advice. It's got to the stage where I'm thinking of running away from home. Only I know he'd come looking for me, wagging his finger.'

'Too right. Honestly, I teach her how to use the Internet and the next thing I know she's cosying up with some bloke. Irresponsible or what?'

'Oh, give your mother a break, Nathan. I think it's cool what she's done. And, ooh, *so* romantic.'

Beth blushed. 'It's not like that, Jaz. We're just friends. How could it be anything else when we haven't met?'

'But that's about to change,' said Jack. He got up, went over to the sofa where he'd been sitting earlier and came back with a thick envelope. '*Voilà*! Application forms for the writers' conference. What's more, Beth, you and I are going to sit here this evening and fill them in, ready for posting tomorrow morning. And, Nathan, I promise I'll give this Ewan chap a thorough vetting when I meet him. Your mother will be in safe hands.'

Late that night, after Nathan had driven Jaz back to the Maywood Grange Hotel and Jack had left, Beth switched on her computer hoping there would be a message from Ewan. There was.

Dear Madly Teased of Maywood,

Oh, how I feel for you! There's nothing like the brutal teasing of one's offspring to make one squirm. I'm convinced Alice has switched courses and has abandoned her degree in politics for one in how-to-humiliate-one's-ageing-father. At the rate she's going she'll get a first, no problem!

Why do children turn themselves into boringly mature adults? Or, in our case, fussy carers? Lord help us when we're so infirm we genuinely need their assistance. I hope I die before Alice shows an unhealthy interest in stair-lifts and incontinence pads.

I wish I could reassure your son that my intentions are perfectly honourable, that he shouldn't lose any sleep worrying that your reputation might be sullied by meeting me. But I fear I'll be whistling in the wind. If he's anything like Alice he'll have made up his mind that you're incapable of making a reasoned decision for yourself. It's called love, Bethany. Don't be too hard on him. Because of your circumstances, he's had to grow up very quickly (as Alice did) and has assumed responsibility for you.

And don't worry that you suspect his comments contain a more serious undertone beneath the surface of the lighthearted joshing. They probably do. It's his way of protecting you. He needs to put thoughts into your head that he thinks you're too naïve to come up with on your own – as if! Alice's comments vary from making you out to be a man who gets off on pretending to be a woman or a potential Fatal Attraction bunny-boiler. Her favourite put-down is, 'Oh, *ple-ease*, you're not still corresponding with Ms Loony-Tune are you?' (Sorry if any of this causes offence, but by giving you the picture of what I'm up against, I hope you'll understand that you're not the only one being put through the mill!)

Anyway, I must away now and do some writing. I haven't been able to do much recently owing to a hundred and one other commitments. If you don't hear from me over the next couple of days, worry not, it'll be a hectic schedule that's kept me from getting in touch, not a moody turn.

All the best,

Ewan X

PS How very rude of me, I haven't enquired how your writing is progressing. Do you ever hit a wall when a blank screen cruelly mocks you? It happens to me now and then. I find the only solution is to brew up some hot Ribena and switch on the telly for some daytime revelry. There's nothing like a shout at Trisha or Kilroy to stir up the juices first thing in the morning. Though my preferred choice, later in the day, is a languish on the sofa with Watercolour Challenge.

But what am I saying? This giving away of my innermost secrets has to stop. I dread to think what kind of an impression you are forming of me. Be assured I am ALL man, there's not a wimpish bone in my body. Well, none that I'm prepared to own up to.

(Oh, hell, now I come to think of it, on top of the appointments I've made for the beauty parlour and hair salon, I will now have to firm up my wilting pex at the gym before we meet! I said PEX, Beth!)

As ever, Ewan's self-effacing humour made Beth laugh. Behind her, Nathan said, 'I do hope he's keeping it clean, Mum. We don't want the Vice Squad hammering on the door in the middle of the night with allegations of improper use of the Net.'

Beth turned round. 'You'll be relieved to know that every word he writes is squeaky clean.'

Nathan came and stood next to her. She sensed he wanted to say something important.

'Mum?'

'Yes?'

'You will be careful, won't you?'

'I know what you're saying, but do you have any idea how

careful I've been all these years? I'm tired of being so circumspect. Everyone else is allowed to have some fun and take the occasional risk. Why can't I?' She switched off the computer and sighed. 'The truth is, Nathan, I don't want to end up boring myself to death.'

He smiled. 'You'll never do that, Mum.'

'Can we call a truce, then? No more lectures?'

'Maybe just the odd one. To counter the hundreds of warnings you give me every time I go out in the car.'

She reached up and, just as he often did to her, ruffled his immaculate hair. '*Touché.*'

Chapter Fifty-Six

*

Fourteen days after they'd flown home from Venice, Richard moved in with Dulcie. He brought with him clothes, a selection of his favourite books, a small album of photographs, some files, and a heavy heart. Seeing him so downcast, so worn down and wretched, Dulcie had doubts about what they had done. 'You don't have to do this,' she told him, as she watched him hang his clothes in the wardrobe she'd cleared for him. 'It's not too late to change your mind.'

He stopped what he was doing. 'Is that what you think is going through my head?'

'You wouldn't be the man I love if you weren't wondering whether you were doing the right thing.'

He tossed the remaining clothes on to the bed and came to stand with her in front of the window. He stroked her cheek. 'Thank you,' he said.

'For what?'

'For always allowing me to be me. For giving me the space to doubt and yet not be doubted.'

She turned her face into his hand and kissed it.

Leaving him to finish his unpacking, she went downstairs. For once the house was quiet. Was it too much to hope that a restful calm had been reinstated?

In the days immediately after Richard had told Angela the truth, the phone seemed never to stop ringing. She had been tempted to wrench the wires out of the wall sockets, but the thought of Richard being unable to talk to her prevented her succumbing to such an action. The first person to ring her had been Richard,

347

to say that Angela now knew everything: with whom he'd been having an affair and his intentions.

'How is she?' Dulcie had asked, wishing that he wasn't speaking to her on his hands-free mobile as he drove to his sons' school to bring them home: the reception was so poor she had to strain to hear his voice.

'Devastated. As I expected. The worst part was she thought that we'd put it behind us and carry on as normal.'

'That was brave of her. It's not every woman who would be prepared to forgive so easily. And how are you?'

'I think my feelings are irrelevant.'

For a moment the line fizzed and crackled and she missed what he said.

'I said it's going to take a while, Dulcie. She's going to need a lot of help to recover from the shock. I can't just walk away immediately.'

'I understand. Believe me, I do. However long it takes, Richard.'

The connection had broken then, and she'd spent the next few minutes standing by the phone willing it to ring again. But it didn't.

Not until the following morning when Kate phoned her. It was the call Dulcie had dreaded most, knowing that it would only be a matter of time before either Angela, with a need to turn to her elder children, or Richard, wanting to explain it all to them, made Henry aware of the difficult situation he was now in regarding his relationship with Kate.

Disbelief, anger and horror were at the top of Kate's agenda and Dulcie could say nothing to appease her daughter.

'Oh, Mum, you of all people! How could you?'

'I don't see what makes me any different from anyone else,' Dulcie had countered.

'But with a married man! And young children are involved.' Kate's voice was shrill with condemnation and righteous disgust.

'I'm well aware of the situation, Kate. Are you sure your view of me isn't coloured by the delicate position in which you now find yourself?' Dulcie enquired, with an edge to her voice.

It was then that she felt the full force of Kate's wrath. 'I'm in no such position, Mum. For your information, and because of your sordid goings-on, Henry's dumped me. I'm back in my flat now. How does that make you feel?'

'How very short-sighted of him,' Dulcie said drily, recalling

Antonio's advice in Venice: if Kate and Henry loved each other they would find a way round the problem.

A four-letter expletive she'd never heard Kate use hurtled down the line followed by, 'How can you be so bloody insensitive?'

Dulcie tried to interject, but the question had been rhetorical: Kate was in full flow. 'You've wrecked two relationships in one go, quite a feat, wouldn't you say? I don't know how you can justify what you've done. It's the most appallingly selfish thing I've ever heard of. And I can't believe you've been seeing Henry's father for so long. Why didn't you say anything? No, don't answer that. Deep down you were ashamed of what you were doing. Well, I sincerely hope you feel even more ashamed now.' She drew breath, but not for long enough to give Dulcie time to speak. 'And what was going through your mind when Henry and I started seeing each other? Why didn't you stop me? You could have saved me all this – all this pain.' She started to cry, and at once Dulcie's animosity towards her daughter vanished: she longed to take Kate in her arms and make everything right for her.

'I'm sorry, Kate,' she said, 'but there's nothing I can say or do to make amends, I know that. I just hope that one day you'll forgive me.'

The phone went dead and Dulcie replaced the receiver.

An hour later Andrew phoned. Without preamble, he said, 'I've just had Kate ranting and raving on the phone, Mum. How're you doing?'

'Coping. Just.'

'Anything I can do?'

'Yes. Make it all go away.'

'It'll sort itself out in the end,' he said pragmatically.

He sounded so like his father, so optimistic – even when he was dying Philip had remained upbeat – that Dulcie had to swallow against the tightness in her throat. She said, 'I wish I had half your certainty.'

'She'll be okay, Mum. Trust me. I might be the gay one in the family, but we both know that Kate's the real drama queen.' He paused. 'That was an attempt at a joke, by the way. You were supposed to laugh and feel better for it.'

'Oh, Andrew, what would I do without you?'

'Shall I see if I can get some time off and come up?'

'That's sweet of you, but there's no need. I'm just reeling from the shock of Kate's anger.'

'Look, I can't speak for long now. Shall I call again this evening?'

'That would be nice.'

And so the days had progressed, with Kate phoning regularly to take out her anger on Dulcie and Andrew to pick up the pieces. Poor Andrew, he was also on the receiving end of his sister's fury because he had known since Christmas about the affair and not told her.

Then one day, around lunchtime, Angela phoned. There was reproach in her voice, but skittish desperation too. 'Why can't you leave him alone?' she cried. 'He's my husband, the father of our children.'

'I don't think this conversation is a good idea,' Dulcie had said. 'I can't say anything that will help – other than that I'm sorry.'

Her apology had been flung back at her. 'Don't patronise me with your smug sympathy. I don't need it. Perhaps it will be you who'll need the words of pity when you find that Richard won't leave us. He loves his children and would never do anything to hurt them.'

Dulcie went out into the garden, thinking of Richard and what he was doing upstairs – transferring his life from one home to another – and felt an even bigger weight of guilt and sorrow towards Richard's wife. If Angela had thought their two young sons would be her trump card in keeping her husband, she was now facing the agonising truth that it had failed her.

Richard was sitting on the edge of Dulcie's bed – *their bed* – talking to his eldest son. Henry had phoned because he'd just heard from Angela that his father had moved in with Dulcie.

'Henry, there's no point in going over the same ground again and again. At some stage you have to accept that this is the decision I've made and I'm sticking with it. And, no, it isn't a spur-of-the-moment thing. It has nothing to do with having a heart-attack and wondering what the hell I've done with my life.'

'But, Dad, it's so not you.'

'What? Being happy?'

'No. Being such a bastard to Mum.'

Richard flinched. 'That's exactly what I'm trying to avoid, Henry.'

'Yeah, it really looks like it. Next you'll be spouting crap like you have to break eggs to make an omelette. Do you have any idea what you've done? Mum says Christopher and Nicholas won't stop fighting, they're turning into a pair of hooligans. And all because of you.'

'Credit me with sufficient—'

Henry cut him dead. 'Right now, Dad, I can't credit you with anything but gross stupidity. For God's sake, all marriages go through a rocky period, but most couples pull through and get on with it. Especially couples who've been married as long as you and Mum. Security is more important than a momentary fling of passion that stands bugger-all chance of lasting.'

Losing patience, Richard said, 'And what would you know about marriage? You, whose idea of commitment is to remember a girl's name after you've bedded her!' He heard his son gasp. 'I'm sorry,' he said hastily. 'That was out of order. I shouldn't have said it.'

'Why not, if that's how you feel about me? It's good to get these things into the open and know where we stand with each other. But I'd like you to know that Kate – yeah, how about that? I can remember her name! – well, Kate and I thought we had a future. But you've put paid to that.'

'It needn't be so.'

'Get real, Dad. How can I possibly go on living with her when you, to use your own choice expression, are *bedding* her mother? You might not have any principles, but I do. I wouldn't hurt Mum in so vile a manner.'

Richard sagged beneath the vicious onslaught. 'We're not getting anywhere, Henry, so I suggest we say goodbye.'

'Suits me. I only called to let you know that Victoria and I will be up at the weekend to stay with Mum. I thought it might matter to you.'

No, thought Richard, when he'd rung off. You called, Henry, because you still can't accept that your boring old father has dared to do this dreadful thing. He's chosen love over staid security. One day you'll understand that you only get one chance. And, yes, there was some truth in what his family was throwing at him: his heart-attack had had an effect on him. It had opened his eyes to what was important to him.

He got up and went to the window. Dulcie was in the garden,

sitting on the wooden bench in her favourite spot, surrounded by clumps of daffodils. With her face tilted towards the pale spring sun, she looked so content. He felt a rush of love and knew that, between them, they would get through this mess. The strength of their love would ease his conscience and eventually he wouldn't feel as bad as he did now. Already he missed Christopher and Nicholas and he was scared of the terrible division that would come between him and them. Victoria had spoken to him only twice, and although she hadn't been as forthright as Henry, her disdain had been evident.

Initially Angela had insisted that they keep the younger children in ignorance of his affair with Dulcie: he would soon come to his senses and they should avoid putting the boys through any unnecessary upset. But he had been insistent. 'Angela, please don't make this worse by pretending it's not happening.' In the end, he had to move out to make her understand that he was serious. It was brutal, but she had left him with no choice.

By far the hardest part had been telling Christopher and Nicholas. Christopher had stared at him, sullen and tight-lipped, while Nicholas had kicked the wall and said, 'That makes five of us.'

'Five what?' Richard had asked.

His youngest son had given the wall another kick, denting the plaster. 'Five of us in my class at school whose parents have split up.'

Still staring out of the window at Dulcie he made a promise to work hard to repair the damage he'd inflicted on his family. With Dulcie's support, he would do it.

'Family,' announced Popeye, beaming round at his, 'that's what it's all about. You can't beat it.' His eyes moist, he bent down and kissed his wife, then the tiny bundles in her arms. Even Jaz was moved by his speech, and by the sight of the wizened little faces blinking in the light.

Five hours ago her mother had unexpectedly gone into labour and given birth to two healthy babies, a girl and a boy, as yet unnamed. Although premature they were a good weight, according to the midwife, and Jaz was relieved that her mother's difficult pregnancy was over.

'Shall I take some photographs now?' she asked.

'Yes,' her father answered. 'Come on, Tamzin and Lulu, get yourselves lined up here, you too, Phin and Jimmy. Right, then, everyone smile.'

'Hang on,' said her mother, 'that's not right. Jaz has to be in the picture as well. Someone go and fetch a nurse to take it.'

Phin obliged and returned with the prettiest he could find. As they all posed for the camera, Jaz allowed her eldest brother to put his arm around her, which she had never done before. If he or anyone else noticed, they didn't comment on it.

When they were driving back to the hotel, leaving her mother to rest, Jaz reflected on how weird it was that they had all started to get on better with each other since mum had gone into hospital. In a funny kind of way the break-in had also brought them together.

The latest news about the house was good. The decorators had finished and so had the carpet-fitters. Dad was planning for them to move back in tomorrow. Which was perfect timing because if Mum and the babies were okay they would be allowed home at the weekend. Between now and then he was going to come clean with Mum. Jaz had the feeling that her mother would be so preoccupied with feeds and nappies she wouldn't have time to worry about how bad the damage had been to their home.

As Dad had said, it was family that counted. And as none of them had come to any harm, what did they have to complain about? When she thought about Victor, alone and in pain, the Rafferty troubles paled into insignificance. In fact, as her father was in such a good mood she was going to ask him an important favour: she wanted to see if he'd help sort out Victor's house. 'It's only small,' she intended saying to him, 'so it wouldn't take long.' She just hoped she was right – because if they didn't help Victor, she didn't know how he'd get things put straight. When he'd told her he'd lost his job, he'd admitted that he hadn't kept up his insurance. 'I was looking for ways to save money,' he'd said.

'You idiot, Victor. Even I know that's a short-cut not worth taking.'

She was also going to ask her father if she could go up to Harrogate with Dulcie, Jack and Beth for the writers' conference during the Easter holidays. She had exams to do after the break, which her father would probably use as a reason for her not to go, but now that she had her mother's support, she was quietly confident that any objections he made would be overruled.

Chapter Fifty-Seven

✳

It was the weekend and Richard was driving home. Or, as he corrected himself, to his former home.

Last night he had decided to accept Angela's invitation to join them all for Sunday lunch – Henry and Victoria were up from London, and for once the boys didn't have a sporting fixture to fulfil. His reluctance to give an unequivocal yes straight away, when Angela had called him at work, had prompted her to say, 'We need to put on a united front for the sake of the children. But, of course, if you can't tear yourself away from *that woman* for a couple of hours, I'm sure Christopher and Nicholas will understand.'

'Angela, please don't use the boys to manipulate me.'

'I'm not! I'm merely stating the obvious. Your sons would be disappointed to know that *she* comes before them. But I suppose you've proved that to them already.'

'She's understandably upset and needs you to know it,' Dulcie had said, when he told her of the conversation.

'But does she have to be so bitter?'

'Wouldn't you be?'

That was the thing about Dulcie: she could be uncomfortably honest, unfailingly fair-handed, and was disposed to see a situation from every viewpoint.

Instead of parking in his usual space, next to Angela's Range Rover in front of the double garage, he came to a stop beneath the dining-room window. It was a symbolic gesture he needed to make: there was no point in thinking, or letting others think, that nothing had changed. Respecting his new status, that of a guest, he rang the bell.

Victoria opened the door. She looked at him for a moment or two, as if sizing him up as friend or foe.

'Okay if I come in?' he asked.

She stepped back. 'Don't be stupid, Dad. You don't have to ask permission to come into your own house. Why didn't you use your key?'

'It didn't seem appropriate.'

She brought her eyebrows together in a frown of intense disapproval – she had done it so often as a young child, usually when confronting food that was green and described as good for growing children. The memory made him put out his arms. 'How about a hug?'

The frown vanished and she slipped into his embrace, burying herself inside his coat. 'Oh, Dad, why have you left us?'

He held her tight. Finding it difficult to speak, he breathed in the sweet smell of her freshly washed hair. 'I haven't left you,' he murmured. 'I'll always be there for you, you know that.'

'Ah, so it was you I heard.'

It was Angela, and to Richard's consternation, Victoria almost leaped out of his arms: she stood with her hands behind her back against the radiator. To hide his awkwardness, he took off his coat and hung it in the cupboard under the stairs. 'What can I do to help?' he asked Angela.

'Oh, nothing,' she said airily. 'It's all done. Henry's opened the wine and, with Victoria's help, the boys have set the table.'

Disappointed that he had nothing with which to occupy himself, and getting the message that Angela was making a point, he said, 'I'll go and have a word with the boys, then.'

He found them upstairs in Christopher's bedroom. Their eyes fixed on the small television on the desk, they were playing a rowdy shoot-'em-up game, blasts of gunfire preceding animal-like cries of death and destruction. He placed himself in their line of vision. 'Hi, boys, how's it going?'

They switched off the game and the room was instantly quiet: neither seemed to know how to answer him. And how could he ask them so glibly how it was going when very likely all they wanted to do was hit him? Angela was right: as far as they were concerned, he had given them an uncompromisingly clear message. But he had to convince his young sons that, when it came to his love for them, nothing had changed: they still meant the world to him.

He heard Angela calling. 'Sounds like lunch is ready. We'd better go.'

Downstairs in the dining room they threw themselves on to their seats, one either side of Richard at the head of the table. 'I've sharpened the knife for you,' Angela said. He felt her watch him as he made a start on carving the pork. In silent concentration, he sliced it with slow, deftly precise movements, each piece the same thickness as the last. He wondered how he could appear so calm before his family after all that he'd done to them. At the other end of the table Angela blew her nose, then excused herself.

Victoria asked Christopher to pass the plates round, and by the time Angela reappeared, with a jug of apple sauce, a stilted conversation had sprung up. 'One of these fine days,' she interrupted them, 'I'll produce a meal and won't leave half of it in the kitchen.' The conversation ground to a halt.

Lunch with his family was proving as great a strain as Richard had feared it would. Henry looked as if he wanted to kill him, Victoria was quiet, and the boys were more interested in a noisy contest over whose jaws could accommodate the largest roast potato than in answering any of his enquiries about school or their friends. Their fidgety kindergarten antics annoyed him, but he felt in no position to reprimand them – he was learning fast what it was to be an errant father. Opposite him, Angela was firing off random statements that bore no relation to the reality of the situation. Twice now she had referred to the change in the weather and how unseasonably warm it was. 'More like June than the beginning of April,' she had enthused.

His being here was a mistake. It was too soon. He should have said no, waited until they were all feeling calmer about his leaving.

'So, Dad, when are you going to stop this nonsense and come home?'

Everyone stopped eating and turned to look at him. He put down his knife and fork and steadied his nerve with a sip of wine. 'Henry, I don't think this is the time or place to—'

'I would have thought it was exactly the time and place.'

'Henry—'

'No, Mum, this has to be said. One of us has to drill some common sense into Dad's befuddled head. He's made his point, and now he has to grasp that enough is enough. What he's doing to you, to *us*, is wrong, and it has to stop.'

'It's not a matter of making a point,' Richard said calmly, conscious that Christopher, was banging a foot against the table leg and Nicholas was biting his nails, which he'd never done before. 'And I really don't want to discuss it now.'

'More apple sauce, Victoria?' asked Angela.

'When, then?' Henry's voice was querulous and demanding.

'No thanks, Mum.'

'I said, when, Dad?'

'I heard you, Henry, and I'm not prepared to answer you when you're behaving with scant regard for anyone's feelings but your own.'

'Nicholas? Any more to eat? Another potato?'

'I've had enough, thanks.' Nicholas dropped his cutlery on to his plate with a deafening crash.

'Me behaving with scant regard for other people's feelings? Oh, that's good. And where does that leave you, I wonder?'

'Please, Henry, don't spoil what's been a perfectly pleasant lunch. Simmer down and pass me the gravy.'

Henry switched his gaze from Richard to his mother. 'Are you completely mad, Mum? No one in their right mind would describe the last hour as having been pleasant. Wake up and smell the divorce papers!'

'Don't you dare speak to your mother like that.'

'It's all right, Richard, Henry doesn't mean it. Do you, darling? He's just upset. Nicholas, stop biting your nails and, Christopher, please don't keep kicking the leg of the table. How would you like it if—'

'I don't give a shit about the table.' Christopher lashed out with a vicious, well-aimed kick. 'And if you'd cared more about Dad, he wouldn't have needed to go off with some other woman. It's all your fault.'

Angela's face turned white. 'Christopher!'

'Oh, shut up, all of you!' cried Victoria. 'Can't you see that none of this is helping? The simple truth is that Dad no longer loves Mum, and no matter how much she or we pretend otherwise, he's not coming back. He loves someone else and all we can do is accept that and get on with it.' Her voice wavered, and she added, 'Painful as it may be.'

'Nice one, Victoria, that really hit the spot,' muttered Henry when Angela had slowly risen from her chair and walked out of the room. 'I suppose, and as I'm the only one here with a sensible and sympathetic thought in his head, I'd better go and make sure Mum's all right.'

'Stay where you are,' instructed Richard, scarcely able to keep his fists from pounding the table. '*I* will go and see how your mother is, but not before I've said this.' He folded his napkin, placed it neatly on his side-plate. 'While I have to take full responsibility for what I've done to your mother, I will not,' he looked around the table, 'I repeat, I *will not* tolerate any one of you speaking to her like that. None of this is her fault. Do you understand that? Christopher?'

Christopher chewed on his lip and nodded.

'What's more,' Richard continued, his voice still low and severe, 'Victoria was correct when she described the situation I've created as being painful. It is, and will remain so for some time yet. We need to help each other, not argue and dish out blame that isn't deserved.' He rose to his feet. 'Now, while I go to your mother, I suggest you do your part by clearing away the lunch things.'

He found Angela upstairs in what had been their bedroom. She was on the bed, sobbing, her face turned into the pillow, her knees drawn up to her chest. 'Leave me alone,' she said. 'Go back to the woman who means so much to you.'

He bent down and offered her a tissue from the box on the bedside table. She ignored it, kept her face turned away from him.

'Shall I bring you up a cup of tea?'

'No.'

'What can I do to help?'

'Please, just leave me alone.'

'There must be something I can do.'

She turned over and looked at him through swollen, tear-filled eyes. 'There's nothing. Can't you see you're doing more harm than good by being here? Haven't you humiliated me enough? Go, Richard. *Go!*'

He was so upset that he had to stop the car on the way back to Dulcie's. He sat motionless for a full ten minutes, overwhelmed by the icy chill of being cut off from his children.

Chapter Fifty-Eight

*

While Nathan checked Ceefax to see if Lois and Barnaby's flight was still on time, Beth fiddled with the vase of tulips she'd spent the last ten minutes arranging. She was convinced that their presence at Marsh House when Lois and Barnaby arrived home would not be met with the forgiving acceptance Barnaby was hoping for. She hated the thought that Lois might turn on him after all he'd done: 'How could you be so devious? I told you I never wanted to speak to them again.'

Originally Barnaby had wanted Beth and Nathan to meet them at the airport but – imagining the drive home with a poker-faced Lois sitting in the back of the car – Beth had suggested that it might be better for them to come home in a taxi and be greeted with a warm house, a cup of tea and a piece of cake. 'Just as you think best,' Barnaby had conceded. 'I'll trust your judgement in the matter. Women usually know what's what.'

Smiling at this typically old-fashioned remark of Barnaby's, Beth thought that if she really knew what was best, she would have taken hold of Lois a long time ago and shaken her out of her refusal to leave them all, Adam included, in peace.

When they heard the sound of a car at the front of the house, Beth gripped Nathan's hand. 'Now, remember, we're doing this for Barnaby.'

'No, Mum, we're doing this for *all* of us.'

They stood in the hall, listened to car doors being opened and shut and luggage hauled out of the boot. Only when they heard the taxi driving away did Beth steel herself to open the door. Smile fixed firmly in place, she said, 'Hello there, you two, welcome home.'

359

To her relief there was no hostility in Lois's face, just confusion, followed swiftly by alarm. 'Beth, what are you doing here? And you too, Nathan? There's nothing wrong with the house, is there? Oh, please don't say we've been broken into.'

Barnaby cleared his throat. 'Beth and Nathan have been keeping an eye on things, Lois, while we've been away. At my instruction, I might add.'

Frightened of what Lois's next words might be, Beth reached for one of her bags, and handed it to Nathan. 'Everything's absolutely fine with the house. The kettle's on and I've taken the liberty of turning up the heating for you. After the lovely hot weather you've been enjoying, I thought you'd need to acclimatise slowly. The weather has been quite warm just recently, but the evenings are still on the chilly side.' Beth could hear herself talking too much and too fast but, unable to stop the nervous flow, she carried on while she ushered Lois and Barnaby inside, telling them where she'd put the enormous pile of mail, that the milkman was due to come first thing in the morning and that they'd missed nothing on television. 'Only repeats,' she informed them, 'and an excess of cookery and gardening programmes.' On catching a bemused look from Nathan that told her to calm down, she finally drew breath. 'Tell you what, I'll stop fussing, make the tea and let you settle in.'

She beetled off to the kitchen. She was just pouring boiling water into the teapot when she heard footsteps behind her.

Lois.

She put the lid on the pot and turned round. 'You look fantastic, Lois,' she said, speaking the truth. 'I've never seen you so tanned. And you've had your hair done. Did you have it cut on the ship? It looks great. Very elegant.' When Lois still didn't say anything, Beth gave in, her heart sinking fast. 'Please don't be cross with Barnaby. He thought he was doing the right thing, that this would help. If you'd rather we left, just say the word.' Beyond the kitchen, and out in the hall, Beth could hear Nathan offering to carry the heavy luggage upstairs. Oh, how she wished she could change places with her son, and not be here, face to face with Lois, who, as she stood with her hands clasped in front of her, was giving no indication as to how she was going to retaliate to the supreme act of meddling that had gone on behind her back.

Beth was just about to apologise again, when Lois raised a hand. 'It's all right, Beth. It's me who should be making the apologies. I'm sorry, so very sorry. I don't deserve your forgiveness, not when I've behaved so badly, but please, if you could find it in your heart to . . .' She trailed off.

'Oh, Lois, there's nothing to forgive. Really there isn't.'

But Lois disagreed and, with great stoicism, she met Beth's eye. 'I've given the matter a lot of thought these last few weeks and I'm left with the conclusion that I could have treated you and Nathan a lot better. And I'm not just talking about my refusal to see or speak to you since Christmas. It . . . it goes a long way back.'

Beth knew that this conversation was costing Lois dear and, acting on impulse, she put her arms round her. It was only a brief embrace for Lois was not a demonstrative woman – she considered hugs an emotional extravagance. She patted Beth's shoulder. 'Perhaps we could have a proper talk some time.'

The next day Lois came to the flat. It was Saturday: Nathan was out with Jaz, Billy and Vicki, and Beth had a good feeling about the outcome of her mother-in-law's visit.

They sat at the kitchen table, sunshine streaming in through the windows, catching on the jug of daffodils on the sill and lighting the room with a golden warmth. The preliminaries had been dealt with – a pot of tea stood between them, as well as a plate of expensive all-butter cookies that Lois had brought with her: she never had been able to turn up empty-handed, it simply wasn't in her nature.

'Beth,' she began, 'you've been a part of my life for more than twenty years, and yet, in all that time, I've seldom been truly honest with you.'

This didn't come as a shock to Beth: she knew that when Adam had first introduced her to his parents, Lois had not been overwhelmed by her son's choice of girlfriend. Beth had always suspected that she had wanted someone a little more top-drawer as a daughter-in-law; a younger version of Lois, perhaps. In those far-off days, Beth had been a carefree and independent young woman who regularly threw caution to the wind, who had lived her life as she wanted to. As students, she and Simone had thought nothing of throwing a handful of clothes into their backpacks to go island-hopping round Greece for an entire summer.

'You see, Beth,' Lois pressed on, a finger playing with the biscuit crumbs in front of her, 'I'm not one of those people who would survive on their own. You might find this hard to believe, but I've always admired you. You coped so well with Adam's death. Alone, and with a young son to bring up, you stood there as solid as a rock. While I floundered hopelessly. I almost hated you for that. I even tried to convince myself that you couldn't have loved Adam, or how else could you have managed without him?'

'It always felt the other way around to me,' murmured Beth. 'You seemed so strong. So in charge.'

'I shut down, Beth. I closed off my emotions. Whereas you, you didn't hide your grief. To me, that showed real strength. And I'm sorry to say I despised you for it.'

'But I only kept the show going because of Nathan. And because of your and Barnaby's help. I felt I owed it to the three of you. And, of course, there was Adam. It was as if I had to keep going for his sake.'

Lois looked up. 'Yes, there was always Adam, wasn't there?'

'That's been the problem, Lois. He's haunted us all these years. For too long. We can't go on living in the past. It's not fair to any of us. Especially not Nathan.'

'I know, and I'm truly sorry that poor Nathan has suffered as he has. I had no idea of the harm I was doing to him. But, please, let me finish saying why I admired you so much for coping on your own. You see, I'm frightened of being alone, of losing those I care for most. If anything happened to Barnaby, or if he left me, I don't know what I'd do. And I know what you're thinking: why do I give him such a hard time if that's the case? It's my way of trying to prove to myself that I don't need him as much as I do.'

'So when you lost Adam . . . when he killed himself,' Beth said gently, 'you were confronted with one of your worst fears?'

'Yes. I couldn't accept the way he'd died. How could he have taken his own life when he was surrounded by people who loved him? How could he possibly want to leave you and Nathan? And his own mother. I don't think I'll ever understand why he did that.'

'For what it's worth, I don't think I will either. I've made myself accept that he simply wasn't the Adam we all knew and loved on the night he died. Perhaps the plain truth is that we never truly know another person. He hid his unhappiness well . . . just as we all do,' she added.

'But, Beth, it was only money he'd lost. A stupid investment that had gone wrong.'

'It was pride he lost too. He'd borrowed extensively to make that investment and he couldn't face the fallout.'

Lois's shoulders sagged. 'He could have come to us. We would have helped. He only had to say. We would have done what we could.'

'He chose not to.'

Lois frowned. 'Doesn't that ever make you angry? That he deliberately made the wrong choice?'

'It used to. Now I'm more concerned with making the right choices for myself. And for Nathan. Of course, these days, he's making his own.'

They both fell silent, until Lois said, 'Aren't you frightened of being alone when Nathan leaves home?'

'I was. But now I'm just beginning to discover the wonderful opportunities that await me. What's more, I've come to the conclusion that I deserve a little fun.'

'Lois sighed. I wish I had half your pluck.'

'But you do, Lois. You just haven't got round to using it.'

'Maybe you're right. All I'm sure of now is that I've lived in a state of fear for too long. When Adam died I was terrified I'd lose you and Nathan as well. That's why I tried to keep things as they were, making sure you stayed close to me. I did everything I could to make you believe you didn't need anyone else.'

'Oh, Lois, a caged bird thinks of nothing but flying away.'

Lois nodded. 'I dreaded the day you'd fall in love with another man and not need Barnaby and me any more. I was terrified of losing our only grandson. Watching Nathan grow up was almost like having Adam all over again. The most precious gift I had been given.' She wiped away a tear and Beth reached out a hand to her.

After a minute's silence, Lois said, 'Goodness, you must be wondering what's brought this on.'

As she topped up their cups, Beth said, 'I'm assuming it has something to do with Barnaby.'

For the first time since she had arrived, Lois's expression relaxed. 'When he wants to be, Barnaby can be quite an adversary. Beneath that gentlemanly exterior he can be as cunning as a wily old fox.' For a moment, staring down at her wedding ring, she was lost in her thoughts. Then: 'One night when we were away, we were sitting on the veranda of our cabin watching the sun go down and I suddenly realised I was happy. And happier than I could remember being in a long time.' She smiled unexpectedly, the tightness gone from her face. She looked almost young. 'And that was when Barnaby took advantage of me.' She laughed. 'As a result of too much of the high-life in its liquid form, I might add. He told me in no uncertain terms that if I didn't apologise to you and Nathan when we arrived home, I would lose you both for ever. He also said he would never forgive me if that were to happen. He didn't say as much but it was implicit in his tone, that if I didn't do as he wanted, I might lose him too.'

Beth was shocked. Who would have thought he had the nerve? Three cheers for good old Barnaby.

That evening, when Nathan came home, Beth told him about her conversation with Lois. 'I don't think we should hold out for a miraculous change in your grandmother,' she concluded, 'not right away, but let's do all we can to help this dramatic change of heart. By the way, I've invited them to spend Easter Sunday with us. Is that okay with you?'

'Fine. But won't you be busy preparing yourself to meet the Chosen One?'

She blushed – and it wasn't a faint glow in her cheeks, but a full unexpurgated redness that covered her, or so it felt, from head to toe.

He laughed. 'It's okay, Ma, you're allowed to slap me for my impudence, but only if you can catch me.' Grinning, he dodged out of her reach and went chortling off to his bedroom, leaving her to squirm alone.

The Chosen One, indeed!

That was how Nathan now referred to Ewan, and as the day of the writers' conference drew near, her son had upped the pace of his teasing. 'How long till D-Day?' he'd joked at breakfast that morning. D-Day, to give it its full title, as dubbed by Nathan, was Dénouement Day – the final outcome – the day on which she would meet Ewan.

'I think you might be getting carried away, Nathan,' she'd responded mildly, hiding her face behind the packet of Special K. 'Perhaps your own budding romance with Jaz is getting the better of you.'

Never missing a beat, he'd pulled aside the cereal packet and said, 'In your dreams, Ma.'

The writers' conference was the day after Easter Monday, hence Nathan's comment about her being too busy to cook for Lois and Barnaby. Apart from Victor, who was still in hospital but making a surprisingly good recovery, everyone in the group was going, although only for the first three days of the week-long course – Jaz couldn't spare any more time away from home as she had exams to face at the start of the summer term, and Jack hadn't wanted to use up too much of his valuable holiday entitlement. He'd kindly offered to drive, which had come as a relief to Beth – her car had been playing up recently and she hadn't relished the idea of it breaking down. The only aspect of going away that she didn't like was that Nathan would be on his own. It was silly, but she hadn't left him alone for any length of time before, and while she trusted him she felt guilty leaving him on his own to revise for his exams. 'It's fine, Mum,' he'd said, when she'd started backing out of the trip, 'I'll get far more done without you here.' He'd also accused her of trying to find an escape route. 'It's too late now to use guilt as a means to avoid the Chosen One.'

He was right, of course. She *was* suffering momentary attacks of cold feet. What if she didn't like Ewan? What if he had bad breath? What if he smoked – a habit she abhorred? She had confessed to Dulcie about him – after last week's group meeting, which they'd held at Victor's bedside. Dulcie had said, 'If you don't like him, that's an end to it. But if there's more chance of the opposite happening, then it would be a lost opportunity, wouldn't it? You'd always wonder how things might have turned out if you'd only had the courage to meet him.'

Now that Richard had moved in with Dulcie, Beth was inclined to think that her advice came straight from the heart.

Victor was looking forward to something, which he couldn't remember having done in a long, long time. The last time it had happened was when he'd sent some chapters of *Star City* to a publisher in London. He had walked home from the post office as if on air. It had been one of the most exciting moments of his life, knowing that soon his dream would come true: he would be a published author.

But once more his moment of acceptance had been denied him.

He'd waited days, then weeks without hearing anything, until finally he couldn't stand another day of not knowing. During his lunch break at work he had telephoned the publisher, only to be told that his manuscript had not yet been read. Another month came and went, and finally a letter arrived telling him that the editor wished him luck elsewhere with his manuscript. Luck! It wasn't luck he required, it was recognition, acknowledgement of his talent. But it was perhaps what he should have expected. Life had never played fair with him.

However, that was behind him now. As were the days of mourning his manuscript. Now he was really on to something. That extraordinary girl, Jaz, had set him on this track. 'I've brought you something else to read,' she'd said. 'I thought it would cheer you up.'

He'd taken the book from her reluctantly and read its title. 'But it's for children,' he'd said.

'Get real, Victor. Harry Potter's for everyone – he cuts across all boundaries. That's half his charm. I bet you a shiny pound that when I see you next you'll have finished the book, and if you're really nice to me, I'll bring in the next in the series.'

To his astonishment she'd been right. He'd read *Harry Potter and the Philosopher's Stone* in a day, finding it both gripping and strangely comforting. He'd scrounged a pound from one of the nurses and put it on his bedside locker next to the book ready for when she next visited.

Smiling, she'd handed over the next instalment.

'Of course, it's nothing but money for old rope,' he'd said. 'Simple enough idea that anyone could have dreamed up.'

She'd nodded and agreed. 'It's always the simplest ideas that are the best. Now, I can't stop long today, I promised Mum I'd take care of the twins so that she can run Tamzin and Lulu to their gymnastics class.'

'Oh,' he'd said, trying not to show his disappointment. He never told her as much but he looked forward to her visits and her bulletins on the world outside the walls of the hospital. 'How is your mother?'

'Pretty good, considering she's recently given birth and then discovered Dad tried to cover up the burglary and that everything worth stealing had gone. But she's forgiven him, and that's cool.'

The day after that he'd had the surprise of being visited by Hidden Talents *en masse*. 'We thought we'd hold the meeting here with you tonight,' Jaz had told him.

'Is that allowed?' he'd asked doubtfully, casting his eyes in the direction of a nearby nurse – she was the bossy one and he was sure she took pleasure in making him cry out when she changed his dressings.

'We checked with the top brass,' said Jack, 'and were told that, so long as we keep the noise down, nobody will mind.'

'A pity you didn't think to check with me first,' he'd said peevishly. He didn't like it when people got above themselves and started organising him.

'Quit whingeing, Victor,' snapped Jaz, 'or I'll cut off your Harry Potter supply, and where will you be then? Trawling the streets for a new dealer.'

As it turned out, he'd enjoyed the group being with him. Not that he'd said anything, of course. Give that Dulcie woman too much praise and it would go straight to her head. The only downside to their visit was that they told him about the writers' conference they were all attending. He'd felt left out.

Jaz had promised to bring in the third Potter book for him, and he'd decided to tell her this evening when she visited that his next novel was going to be something along similar lines. Obviously his would be better, and with less emphasis on the gimmickry and clever names, but it would appeal to children and adults. To get started, he needed Jaz to buy him a new A4 pad and a proper fountain pen. He was able now to sit up for longer periods and writing would kill the hours of boredom he had to endure.

But as the clock in the ward ticked away that evening's visiting session and there was no sign of Jaz, all the anticipatory excitement he'd been experiencing slowly drained away. She wasn't coming. She'd let him down. Looking about the ward, he saw that everyone else had a visitor. He was the only one with an empty chair beside his bed. Feeling depressed and very alone, he closed his eyes, pretending to anyone who might glance his way that he was asleep and in no need of a visitor.

Minutes passed.

'Sleeping on the job again, Victor?'

He recognised the voice instantly. He opened his eyes. 'You're late.'

'And you're a miserable old devil, but I try not to let that get in the way of our special time together.'

He smiled. 'Have you brought me the next book?'

'Would I ever let you down, Victor?'

'Everyone else has. Why should you be any different?'

'First, I *am* different. That's why I go to all the trouble to visit you and deny myself an evening with my gorgeous boyfriend. And second, you can switch off the self-pity tap. Any more of that and I'll spill the beans about what happens in *The Prisoner of Azkaban* and spoil the ending for you. Deal?'

Later, when she was leaving, he asked her why she kept coming to see him.

She slung her small leather knapsack over her shoulder. 'Didn't I tell you? It's my care-in-the-community work. I'll get a nice gold badge to wear when I've got you back on your feet. See you.'

He watched her go. What *was* in it for her? Certainly not a gold badge.

Chapter Fifty-Nine

*

The Rafferty builders had finished work on Jack's flat, and now that it was just how he'd wanted it, he felt a growing desire to tidy up the loose ends of his life. This Easter Sunday was destined to be a turning point, and if Christ's Resurrection was to be taken as a symbol of new life, then it was apposite that today he should do his damnedest to put the past behind him.

An excited cry from Lucy, who had her nose pressed to the window, made him look up from the garlic he was crushing. 'Dad, they're here!'

He washed his hands quickly and called through to Amber, who was in the bedroom listening to a CD by a bunch of teenage boys he'd never heard of – that was before she had first started playing it at eight o'clock last night. Sixteen hours on he was practically word perfect on the title track, which had been given full-volume treatment every time it came round. Upstairs, Beth and Nathan, who had their own guests coming for Sunday lunch, were probably singing along too.

First to arrive was Julie with Desmond Junior who, on seeing Jack, grinned from his car seat, reached for a foot and proudly pulled off his sock. He stuffed it into his gummy mouth and gurgled, as if to say, '*Ta-daa!* And my next trick will be to swallow my Osh Kosh dungarees.'

Des brought up the rear with what looked like enough survival gear to aid a party of ten to the top of Mount Kilimanjaro. 'It's his travel cot and duvet, and a small collection of toys,' Des explained, when the door had been closed. 'Oh, yes, and his high chair.'

'Don't say you've forgotten his changing mat and bag,' complained Julie.

Des checked out the contents of his arms, his back and his shoulders. 'No, my sweet, I think that's here somewhere. Hello, girls, long time no see.'

In the crowded hall, Amber and Lucy stepped forward, their interest not in Des and Julie but in the smiling Desmond Junior, whom they'd not met before. 'Look, Dad.' Lucy had been waiting particularly anxiously for his arrival and was itching to play with a real baby. 'He's eating his sock.'

Julie clicked her tongue. 'Anyone would think we didn't feed him, the way he carries on. Do you want to help me take him through to the sitting room, Lucy?'

'Hey,' said Des, standing in the middle of the large room and giving it a professional once-over, 'this is great. Must make the hassle with those cowboy builders seem almost worth it.'

'Oh, don't remind me. Bodge It and Run will be marked on my psyche for the rest of my life.' He helped relieve Des of his load. 'Now who's for a drink?'

'I drew the short straw today, so I'll have some orange juice, please.'

'Des?'

'Any beer on offer?'

'Need you ask?'

Leaving Amber and Lucy to watch over Desmond Junior, Des and Julie followed Jack to the far end of the L-shaped room and into the kitchen. 'Now, this I do approve of,' observed Julie. She ran her hand over the polished granite work surface, then opened one of the cream-painted cupboards to inspect the racks and shelves. 'I hope you're taking note, Des, because when we get round to gutting our pathetic excuse for a kitchen, this is just the kind of design I'd like.'

'Damn you, Jack,' Des smiled, 'why do you have to have such good taste? More to the point, how in hell did you manage to get it done so quickly? I thought these jobs dragged on for months.'

'You know the old maxim,' Jack said, as he poured their drinks, 'it's not what you know, it's *who* you know. Rafferty and Sons were excellent, and the kitchen fitter they recommended rated this as a piddling little job, compared to the large-scale kitchens he usually works on. I guess I was lucky.' He almost added, 'For once,' but didn't. During the last week, he'd come to the conclusion that he was luckier than he'd ever realised. He had two beautiful daughters, a relatively secure job, a great roof over his head, and a circle of friends that now included those who shared his passion for writing. The members of Hidden Talents were of varied ages and backgrounds, with little else apparently in common, but the bond that held them together was strong, and one way or another they had all been looking out for each other this last month or so. He handed round the drinks. 'If it doesn't sound too corny or pretentious,' he said, 'I'd like to propose a toast.'

Des raised his eyebrows. 'Oh, yes? That sounds ominous.'

'I finished *Friends and Family* last night.'

'Come again?'

He smiled, enjoying the look on his friends' faces. No one outside Hidden Talents knew about his writing. 'I've written a book.'

Des looked incredulous. '*A book?*'

'Yes, one of those strange objects with rows of letters covering the pages. I know you're not the most literate of men, Des, but you must have come across one at some time.'

'Ha, ha, *ha*. How long has this being going on?'

'Since last October.'

'But you never said anything.'

'Sorry, Julie. Don't be offended, it wasn't personal.' He frowned. 'Or maybe that's the point. I've found the whole exercise extremely personal, and I couldn't bring myself to tell anyone who might think I was crazy for doing it. I mean, whoever heard of an estate agent having the wit to write a book?'

Julie laughed. 'Certainly I couldn't imagine the one I'm married to having the wit.'

'Hey, what is this? Gang Up On Poor Old Des Day?'

'Ah, is diddums feeling got at?' She pressed a kiss on his cheek, and got one in return.

'No more than usual.' Then Des turned back to Jack and, with an arm round his wife, he said, 'So, what's the book about? Is it a saucy exposé of the world of estate agents? Any car chases in it?'

'Ignore him, Jack, he's a Philistine. Who's it aimed at? You must have an audience in mind.'

He thought about this. At length he said, 'People like us,' then added, 'With the exception of Des, perhaps,' and grinned.

'On what ground am I being excluded?'

Both Jack and Julie laughed. 'Being a nincompoop,' said Julie.

He tipped his nose in the air. 'In that case I'm taking my beer and going to mix with more congenial company.'

They watched him join the children, getting down on the floor and letting his small son out of his seat. A moment passed and Jack said, 'Thanks for burying the hatchet, Julie. I really appreciate it.'

She gave him a hard stare. 'There wasn't ever a hatchet. It would never have come to anything half so drastic.'

'But I upset you over Clare, and I'm sorry for that.'

'That's water under the bridge now. Clare is only too happy with the way things are currently shaping up.'

'Yes, I'm intrigued to meet the new man in her life.'

Less than five minutes later, his curiosity was satisfied when the sound of the doorbell heralded the arrival of Clare and Colin. Inviting Clare for lunch had been, he liked to think, the first step on the road to his very own *glasnost*. He had expected her to turn down his offer, and he would never know if she had accepted just so that she could flaunt Colin – *See, now I'm with a man who really cares about me*. But whatever her motive for coming, he knew that he had done the right thing in contacting her. 'Of course you can bring him,' he'd said, when she'd mentioned a new boyfriend. 'The more the merrier.'

Colin, an accountant, had a good sense of humour, and before long they were having a classic battle of estate agents' versus accountants' jokes. 'Right, then,' said Des, rolling up his sleeves and getting into the swing of it. 'Why were estate agents invented?'

'Don't know. Why?'

'To give accountants someone to look up to!'

They all laughed, except Lucy, who said, 'I don't understand any of your jokes. I think Desmond is much funnier than any of you.'

'Would that be Desmond Junior or his brilliant father?' asked Des.

'Don't ask the question if you don't want the honest answer,' warned Jack. 'Now, who's for dessert? We have a choice of M and S's finest crème brûlée or their equally fine lemon tart.' He started to gather the plates and dishes from his end of the table, noting that Amber had eaten more than she had of late. He took it as an encouraging sign.

Clare passed him her plate. 'Need a hand?'

He sensed that she wanted to be alone with him and, knowing that this would be their only opportunity, he said yes. Between them they cleared the table and took everything through to the kitchen. 'I love the flat, Jack,' she said. 'You've put a lot of thought into it.'

He stopped what he was doing. 'Perhaps if I'd put as much thought into what I was doing with you, I wouldn't have hurt you so badly.'

'It works both ways. If I hadn't been in such a hurry I wouldn't have scared you off so effectively. I think we can safely say it was too much too soon for both of us.'

'Does that make us friends now?'

'I'd like to think so.'

'That's good. I'm pleased.' He carried on stacking the dishwasher. 'Colin seems a really nice bloke. If it's what you want, I hope it lasts between the two of you.'

From where she was standing, by the fridge, she looked towards the table, to where Colin was chatting to Amber and making a rabbit out of a paper napkin for her. 'He is. He's a lovely man. More importantly, he's not divorced.'

'So, no baggage?'

'Travelling light, you could say.'

'Even better.' He wanted to offer her a word of caution – 'Don't rush him, Clare, let things take their natural course' – but he knew it wasn't his place. Only a very close friend like Julie could offer such advice.

That evening, a few hours after the lunch party eventually broke up, Jack drove the girls home to Prestbury. 'That was nice today, Daddy,' Lucy said, from the back of the car. 'Can we see Des and Julie again?'

'I don't see why not.'

'When I was a baby, did I dribble like Desmond and blow bubbles with it?'

'Oh, all the time.'

Sitting in the front seat, Amber wrinkled her nose. 'That's disgusting.'

'But it's nothing compared to what you did as a baby.'

She shuddered. 'I don't want to know.'

373

'Oh, go on Daddy, tell us. How horrible was Amber when she was little?'

Jack laughed. 'I didn't say your sister was horrible.'

'I bet she was.'

'Bet I wasn't.'

'You were both as cute as buttons, and that's an end to it.'

They drove on, Lucy humming to herself and Amber perfectly still, her eyes closed.

'Have you really written a book, Dad?'

He looked at Lucy in the rear-view mirror. 'Yes, Luce, I have.'

'Is it for children?'

'No. Grown-ups.'

'Is it good?'

He smiled. 'I don't know. I'm not really the right person to ask.'

'Yes, you are, you wrote it.' This was from Amber: her eyes were open now.

'It doesn't work like that, sweetheart.'

She didn't look as if she agreed with him. 'What's it about?'

'A family,' he said, hoping to leave it at that. He didn't feel entirely comfortable about telling the girls any more. But children have an in-built knack for knowing when a parent is hedging.

'And?' prompted Amber.

Keeping his eyes on the road, he said, 'It's about a family who, one minute, is happy, but then everything starts to go wrong and . . . and the parents split up because—'

'Is it about us?' interrupted Lucy.

'In some ways, yes, but in other ways, no.'

'What happens in the end?' Amber's voice was cool. 'Do the parents get back together?'

'No. But they promise each other never to do anything that would hurt their children.'

'And do they keep their promises?'

'In the end, yes.'

374

Chapter Sixty

*

'There's no need for you all to see me off,' Jaz said, coming down the stairs with a heavy bag.

When she reached the bottom step her father took it from her and plonked it by the front door. 'I agree,' he said, 'absolutely no need to do anything half so daft, but we'll do it all the same, if that's okay with you, you silly eejit.'

She smiled, first at him, then at her mother, who asked, 'You've got everything you need, haven't you? Did you find your favourite black jeans? I put them on your bed.'

'Yes, Mum. Thanks.'

'And you have enough money?'

'Plenty. Dad's seen to that. Now, will you all stop fussing? I'm only away for a few days.'

Phin gave her a punch on the shoulder. 'Yeah, but who will we spat with while you're gone?'

She gave him a playful kick in return. 'You won't have time for that, now that you're occupied with the lovely Nurse Della. How long have you been going out with her? If it's more than a week, it must be a record. In fact, if you're still seeing her when I come home, I'll know that it's serious and I'll have to help Mum find a mother-of-the-groom outfit.'

Phin rolled his eyes at her and was about to offer a suitable riposte when they heard a car pull into the drive.

'Okay, stand aside, everyone, that's my ride out of here.'

If she had thought she would be able to sneak off without any further embarrassment, she had miscalculated the new mood of family-togetherness her father had been so keen to foster since the arrival of the twins – they had been named Declan (Tamzin and Lulu were delighted with that as they were mad about Ant and Dec) and Amelia Jane. 'How come the boys get the Irish names and we girls don't?' Jaz had asked her father.

'Because that's the way the cookie has crumbled,' he'd replied. 'Any complaints?'

'None at all,' she'd said. 'I'm just relieved I didn't end up as Bernadette or with something I couldn't pronounce or spell.'

Jack, Beth and Dulcie were coming towards the house when Jaz broke free of her father's hug and escaped outside. While she added her bag to the luggage already in the boot of Jack's car, a round of hand-shaking ensued.

'Don't worry, Mr and Mrs Rafferty,' Beth was saying, 'we'll take good care of your daughter.' Jaz noticed that her brothers were talking to Jack, a little apart from the rest of the group. She wouldn't put it past them to bribe him to keep an eye on her. She crept up behind them, pretending to listen to Dulcie as she congratulated her mother on the twins' birth, and tuned into what her brothers were saying. None of it made any sense: Jack was laughing and saying something about treating the whole thing as a joke, that maybe one day he would immortalise the incident in a book. 'All the same,' muttered Phin, his face oddly serious, 'fair play to you for taking it so well. The flat okay?'

'It's great. I wish I'd come to Rafferty's in the first place.'

'You'll know another time. And if we hadn't been tied up with a job in Crewe, we'd have done the work ourselves. Anything else you need doing, just give us a bell. It's the least we could do.'

. . . *the least we could do*. Jaz took this as positive proof that something was going on. And what on earth had Jack taken so well? Over the coming days in Harrogate she planned to get to the bottom of it.

The mood in the car as they headed towards Harrogate reminded Dulcie of long-ago school trips. The excitement and anticipation were the same, and as she twisted round to offer a bag of Murraymints to Beth and Jaz in the back, she felt that all that was missing from their excursion was a hearty rendition of 'One Man Went to Mow'.

The traffic on the M62 was light, and Jack was an able driver who drove smoothly and confidently; he wasn't one of those aggressive types who swoop in close to the car in front and jab at the brakes every twenty seconds. Feeling relaxed, and enjoying the music that was playing on the radio, she closed her eyes and gave in to her tiredness.

Richard had been tense all last night, and at half past three they had given up trying to sleep and had gone downstairs for some tea. With his head in his hands, he had sat at the kitchen table and groaned. 'My children hate me,' he said, despairingly, 'and I can't see them ever changing their minds.'

'Give it time,' she had said soothingly, hating to see him so wretched. 'It's too soon to make judgements like that. You mustn't be so hard on yourself. Be patient with them. Let them be angry for a while, and eventually it'll pass. They'll come round when they're ready. They just need time to adjust.'

And wasn't that exactly what she was doing with her own daughter? The angry telephone calls had stopped, and instead there was now a stony silence: Kate was refusing to speak to her, and it hurt. Andrew had tried talking to Kate, but she was almost as angry with him as she was with Dulcie.

Half an hour before Jack had come for her that morning, Richard had left for work, his face ashen from lack of sleep and worry. 'Why don't you take the day off?' she'd said, concerned how drained he looked.

'I can't,' he said. 'I have two important meetings to chair.'

She had kissed him goodbye and warned him not to overdo it while she was away.

'Early to bed every night,' he'd said, with an attempt at a smile. 'You will ring me this evening, won't you?'

'Of course.'

'And you have the mobile I gave you?'

'Yes. I might even remember how to work it.'

She had watched his car move slowly down the road, already missing him. But she cheered herself with the thought that when she came home she would be greeted not by an empty house, as she was used to, but by the man she loved.

Unlike Dulcie, who was now asleep, Beth was wide awake and fidgety, her mind racing. She couldn't settle with the book she'd brought for the journey and she certainly couldn't sleep. The prospect of meeting Ewan was tipping her over the edge of reason.

She had fully intended to go to bed early last night but she'd been up until nearly two, dithering over what clothes to pack. Nathan, usually so helpful, had made things worse by appearing in her bedroom with a silly smirk on his face as she refolded – for the umpteenth time – her smartest pair of jeans. 'Make one single remark about the Chosen One and D-Day,' she'd warned him, 'and I'll never let you use the car again.'

'Cool it, Ma. I only came to see if there was anything I could do to help. Do you think that top's a good idea?'

She looked at the top she'd been about to add to the bag. It was one of her favourites: a rare item in her wardrobe that she thought flattered her figure – it was a hug-tight fit. 'What's wrong with it?' she asked, holding it up for closer inspection.

He sucked in his breath. 'You don't think it's a touch risqué for a first date? You don't want to give the wrong signals by wearing something too revealing.'

'*Out!*' she cried. He was having her on. 'Go to bed, you tiresome boy.'

When she had called a halt to the dithering and the last item of clothing was neatly folded inside the bag, she sneaked back to the kitchen – she didn't want Nathan to know what she was doing – and quietly switched on her computer. Ewan had promised to send her one last message before they met in Yorkshire. She had checked earlier, before the ten o'clock news, but there hadn't been a word from him.

Now there was.

Hi Beth,

No time to chat for long – so much to do, so little time, blah-de-blah.

Glad to hear things have been resolved between you and the in-laws. Barnaby sounds like a veritable saint on wheels. Thank goodness he's so fond of you and Nathan. And you mustn't worry about leaving Nathan on his own to do his revision – from what you've told me of him, he sounds motivated enough to get the work done.

And here's me telling you not to worry, when I'm down to the very beds of my nails at the thought of meeting you.

What if she doesn't like the colour of the anorak I've bought specially for the occasion?

What if she susses I'm wearing a syrup fig?

And, oh, I hardly dare write this for fear of instant rejection, but what if she doesn't go for a man who likes to keep his small change in a handy little purse?

These questions, and many more, have kept me awake at night over Easter. All I ask of you, Bethany, is to be gentle with me. I'm a sensitive soul who cries every time the Andrex puppy on the telly is replaced with a new one. Where do all those cute superfluous puppies end up? Are they flushed away with all that loo paper? Ah, 'tis a cruel world out there.

But I digress. Tomorrow dawns. I aim to arrive at Norton Hall around supper-time – save me a scrap or two of stale bread and gruel, won't you?

Looking forward (it goes without saying, but feel it would be an appalling omission if I didn't) to meeting you. Travel safely.

All best,

Ewan X

PS You'll recognise me by the aforementioned anorak.

PPS On the other hand, it might be better if I look out for you – an attractive blonde woman trying to avoid the furtive gaze of a man playing nervously with the snap-fastener on his faux leather purse . . .

Apart from a brief hitch near Cambridge, where a lorry had jack-knifed, Ewan had had a good run across the A14 to join the M1, and so far the traffic had moved at a steady pace. He was now skirting Leeds and reckoned he'd arrive at Norton Hall earlier than he'd anticipated.

According to the programme of events, Norton Hall had once been a private residence, but since the mid-seventies it had been extended and converted into a conference centre. He'd stayed in many such places over the years, but this one was new to him. He hoped there would be a few basic necessities, such as a decent supply of hot water, edible meals and an electrical system that didn't fail. During the last conference he'd attended there had been a complete power failure and at bedtime everyone had been guided to their rooms by torchlight. Just before they'd been despatched to their rooms, he'd needed to visit the loo. Fumbling in the dark to find the urinal was not an experience he was in a hurry to repeat.

The organisers of the Harrogate conference boasted that Norton Hall had a swimming-pool, a croquet lawn and two tennis courts as well as a large canteen, a bar, a central conference hall that seated four hundred, a library, and a small computer room. There were half a dozen rooms for discussion groups and workshops, two lounge areas, and even the ruins of a small chapel in the grounds, which, so the author of the programme declared, were 'of an extensive nature and worthy of a constitutional stroll'. The accommodation was situated in a modern two-storey block adjacent to the original house, and, while basic (in the author's opinion), was warm and clean, and came with tea- and coffee-making facilities.

What more could anyone want?

An *en suite* bathroom would be nice, thought Ewan, as he overtook a people-carrier. A power shower and a mini-bar bursting with salted cashew nuts wouldn't go amiss either.

He cruised along at a blistering speed for the next mile or two, then eased off the accelerator when he spotted a police car in the inside lane further up the motorway. All around him the traffic slowed as they played Grandma's Footsteps, trying to slip past the police car without being seen.

The games we play, he thought.

And the game he was playing with Beth, he reminded himself, had every chance of backfiring on him. While he hadn't actually lied to Beth, he had been less than straight with her. He hadn't meant to mislead her for as long as he had, but before he knew it, he had been caught up in a mire of his own making and unable to admit the truth. It seemed easier to wait until they met and she could take the facts at first hand, then decide for herself what she thought of him. And his reasons for his deviousness.

Alice had expressed her opinion in her customary blunt fashion: 'I can't believe you're going through with this crackpot idea,' she'd exploded, when he'd got round to confessing. He'd had her on the phone for nearly an hour last night, listening to her last-ditch attempt to make him see sense.

'Look, Alice,' he'd said, as patiently as he could when she finally allowed him to speak, 'I'm not the innocent schmuck you think I am.'

'Then which schmuck are you?'

'Ho, ho! Now, stop being so bossy and cut your decrepit father a bit of slack.'

'But, Dad, if I don't look out for you, who will?'

He sighed, exasperated. 'Where did I go wrong with you? Did I love you too much when you were growing up? Is that it?'

'Don't try to sidetrack me by getting mushy or I'll think you've really lost it. Now, promise you'll ring me, and if she starts wanting to check your credit rating, get the hell out of there.'

'Yes, Alice. No, Alice. Anything else, Alice?'

'That's it for now, but if something else occurs to me I'll give you a ring.'

'Oh, no, you won't. I'm switching off my mobile, as of now. Goodbye, Alice.'

'But, Dad, that's not fair!'

'Yes, it is. 'Byee.'

He almost missed the sign for Millingthwaite, the village where Norton Hall was, and he had to brake sharply to make the turning. He slowed his speed as he took the narrow lane – it was so tight the hedges almost brushed the sides of his car. He silently chastised the author of the programme of events for not warning conference delegates of this potential hazard.

But a scratched car would probably be the least of his concerns after Beth knew how he'd deceived her.

Chapter Sixty-One

✤

With conference participants having to share bathroom facilities, the accommodation was appropriately segregated: girls at one end of the block, and boys at the other. Wedged between them were two dozen rooms for couples and committee members, along with visiting guest speakers and anyone deemed important enough to warrant their own bathroom. Unless you were a VIP, there was an extra charge for this luxury, as the conference administrator had informed Jack when they arrived to register at the designated meeting point. They were given name badges – 'It's for security,' they were advised. 'We've had problems in the past with strangers wandering in and helping themselves. Make sure you lock your rooms.' It wasn't the most auspicious start, but perhaps a sensible one, and as Jack unpacked his bag, putting the few clothes he'd brought with him into the rickety old wardrobe, which smelt faintly of vanilla, he looked out on to the grounds of Norton Hall.

Some early arrivals were already sitting on the benches dotted around the croquet lawn, others were sprawled on the grass enjoying the afternoon sunshine, and in the shade of a large oak tree, a woman dressed in what looked like a kaftan was sitting cross-legged with her palms extended, as if checking for rain. Dulcie had warned them during the journey that writing courses had a tendency to attract a rich and varied mix. It looked as if she was right.

A knock at the door made him start. He opened it and was confronted with yet more proof of Dulcie's theory. A gangly man in sagging jogging trousers and a T-shirt stood before him. His hair was very grey and tied back into a bushy ponytail. He wore copper bangles on both wrists and around his neck hung a golf-ball-sized crystal on a leather thong. The crowning glory of his attire was a pair of scruffy green slippers; through a hole at the front of one poked a yellowing big-toe nail.

'Hi,' he said. 'Just thought I'd make myself known to you.' He pointed to his name badge, which Jack hadn't noticed until now – it was lost in the Celtic knot design of his T-shirt. 'Zed Wane. I'm in the room next door. This your first time?'

Jack nodded.

'Aha, a Norton Hall virgin. I thought I didn't recognise you. I came last year, and the year before that, so I'm what you might call an old hand. I could show you round, if you like. They'll be serving afternoon tea any minute. But a word to the wise, get there quick or there'll be nothing left. You could come with me now, if you want.'

'Er . . . I'll be along shortly,' Jack said, judging it prudent not to become Zed's best new buddy too soon. 'I want to finish unpacking first. I'll catch up with you later.'

'I'll keep an eye out for you.' His neighbour shuffled away, shoulders hunched, slippers slapping at his heels.

Jack closed the door and wondered if he was going to regret coming.

At three o'clock, as arranged, he knocked on Beth's door. Dulcie and Jaz had got there ahead of him, and after they'd swapped notes on the quality of their accommodation – Dulcie's window wouldn't open and Jaz's bed creaked – they set off for a cup of tea and a slice of cake. It was being served in one of the lounge areas in the main part of the house, and this was reached by a covered walkway that joined the two buildings. They tagged on to the end of a small queue and Jack noticed that Zed was at the front of it: he was loading slabs of fruit cake on to his plate. 'Someone to watch out for,' Jack told the others, in a low voice. He explained about his friendly neighbour.

Beth laughed, but Jaz said, 'You're sure he said his name was Zed? It wasn't Ewan, by any chance, was it?'

'Hey, now you come to mention it, he did say something about a pseudonym.'

'Jack,' warned Dulcie, with a smile, 'Beth's going through enough turmoil as it is. Behave yourself. You too, Jaz.'

A hubbub of voices filled the high-ceilinged room, and it was obvious that many of the delegates knew each other from previous conferences. But unlike Zed, if their dress sense was anything to go by, they gave the impression of being relatively normal. There was a wide range of ages, but Jack reckoned Jaz would win the prize for the youngest participant.

Zed wasn't alone in his eccentricity: grouped around a sofa in the far corner of the room was a noisy crowd of men and women sporting identical black T-shirts with the name Jared Winter emblazoned across them. Jack knew him to be a well-known science-fiction writer. Or was he a fantasy writer? The distinction had always been lost on Jack. He'd never been interested in either genre, especially fantasy – those wacky book covers showing women with unfeasibly large breasts and powerful thighs put him off. Jared Winter was one of the guest speakers at the conference, and Jack decided, from the look of his devotees, that the man was in for some serious hero-worshipping.

He turned to Beth. 'I think I've found Ewan for you.'

'Oh, Lord, have you? Where?'

He inclined his head towards the far corner of the room. 'See the big fella with the mane of black hair and purple-tinted sunglasses? It has to be him.'

Beth dug at him with one of her elbows. 'Not funny, Jack. That's a woman.'

'Good God! Is it?'

At four o'clock they made their way to the main conference hall and listened to the formal introductions made by several committee members. Beth craned her neck to see if she could spot a half-decent-looking man with the name Ewan Jones pinned to his chest. In the end she gave up and concentrated on what she'd come to Norton Hall for. Once the introductions were over, they were given the dos and don'ts of the conference: smoking was allowed out of doors, voices were to be kept down after midnight, high jinks kept to a courteous minimum, and no pestering of guest speakers, editors and agents would be tolerated. Then they were dismissed and the conference got under way.

With her file, borrowed from Nathan, clutched to her chest, Beth set off with the others for a workshop on characterisation. They took their seats – in the back row, as dictated by Jaz – and Beth saw that the session was to be led by a formidable woman with a face plastered in makeup; chunky rings adorned all but one of her fingers. Her name was Dorothy Kendall and she reminded Beth of Fanny Craddock. She was about to whisper this to Jaz, when she realised that the observation would be wasted on someone so young.

The first half of the session flew by, and Nathan's file of A4 paper now contained several pages of useful notes. 'Just goes to show,' she said to Dulcie, when they were given a five-minute break, 'never judge a book by its cover.'

'I know what you mean,' Dulcie said. 'She gave the impression she might horsewhip us if we didn't pay sufficient attention.'

In the second half of the workshop they were paired off and after a ten-minute conversation they had to write a hundred-word description of the other person. 'And don't any of you insult me by going for the obvious,' Dorothy Kendall barked at them, 'such as the colour of hair and eyes. I want you to look out for interesting mannerisms, turns of phrase, and use them to give a fresh, cliché-free character sketch. The writer who comes up with the worst offering has to buy me a drink in the bar tonight.'

Beth concentrated hard, as if her life depended on it: she didn't fancy spending any time alone with the awesome Dorothy Kendall. Later, and relieved to survive the workshop without being humiliated as the class dunce, she slipped out of the room before their teacher changed her mind and hauled her back in for an extra session. 'I had no idea it would be as scary as this,' she said to Jack – Dulcie and Jaz had gone on ahead of them. 'I hope the rest of the course tutors aren't like her.'

'But she got us working, didn't she?'

'But at what cost? I'm exhausted. Thank goodness we're only here for three days.'

'Come on, I'll see if I can rustle up a strengthening cup of hot sweet tea for you.'

'Bugger that! I need something stronger. Lead me to the bar!'

He laughed. 'Beth King, hush your mouth! Whatever would Nathan say? Less than twelve hours away from home and you've turned into a fishwife.'

The bar area was packed. Jack left his file and pen with Beth, and joined the crush of thirsty writers. He eventually surfaced and gave her a tall glass clinking with ice. 'Vodka and tonic,' he said, 'as the lady requested. Any sign of Jaz and Dulcie?'

'No, we seem to have lost them.'

'And there's still no sign of the elusive Ewan Jones?'

'I told you before, he said he wouldn't be here until supper-time.'

Jack glanced at his watch. 'Which is served in just over an hour and a half.'

'Stop it, you're making me nervous.'

The bar was even busier now, and as they were unable to hear each other, Beth suggested they find somewhere quieter. They squeezed through the throng, heading in the direction of the glass-roofed extension and some comfortable chairs. When they were almost there, Jack said, 'You go ahead, I need to make a trip to the little boys' room.' She tucked their files under her arm, took his drink from him and made a beeline for the last unoccupied squashy sofa. She settled into the cushions and waited for Jack. It was a full ten minutes before he returned, and when he did, he was grinning from ear to ear. 'I hardly dare ask what you've been up to in the gents' loo to make you smile like that,' she said.

He sat down next to her, still grinning. 'I've just had the pleasure, as it were, of standing side by side with Felix McCallum.'

'Who?'

'You know – the editor I have an appointment to see tomorrow.'

'The one who's giving you a critique on the chapters of *Friends and Family*?'

'The very man.'

'And?'

'He saw my badge and asked if I was the one who'd sent him the stuff last week about a bloke whose marriage goes belly up.'

'Good with words, is he?'

'Don't nitpick. It's what he said next that's important. He said he hoped I'd brought the rest of the manuscript with me because he was very keen to read it.'

'Jack, that's brilliant. Well done, you!'

Jaz was starving so she was stuffing herself with one of the Mars bars her mother had given her – typical Mum, she'd packed her a supply of goodies just in case the food wasn't up to much. Home seemed a long way away, and it was just as well it was. Jaz was furious with Phin and Jimmy. During the car journey up here, she had asked Jack what he and her brothers had been discussing before they'd set off for Yorkshire. He'd refused to tell her at first, but had then relented, concluding that it didn't matter now.

But it did! She felt so ashamed. How could her brothers have done that to him? She was so furious that she had nearly phoned home from the car, but Jack, Dulcie and Beth had persuaded her not to. 'They were only looking out for you,' Jack had said. 'Leave it be. Besides, you don't want to let anything spoil the next few days.'

She threw the empty Mars bar wrapper into the bin, licked her lips and smiled: her dim-wit brothers had inadvertently given her the means to get Victor's house sorted for him. When she got home she would blackmail them into doing the job; they wouldn't have any choice in the matter. As they had tried to hush up the incident, she knew they didn't want Mum and Dad to find out what they'd done. And rightly so. Dad would be livid that his name had been associated with such low-life behaviour, and Mum, well, if anyone upset her they would have Popeye Rafferty to answer to. Thank you, boys!

She locked her door and went to meet the others in Jack's room. Amazingly, and after a chance meeting in the men's loos, Jack had handed over the manuscript of *Friends and Family* to an editor called Felix McCallum, and they were having a glass of fizzy wine (the best Norton Hall could come up with) before dinner to celebrate.

When they joined the queue for dinner, and were scanning the conference noticeboard for information about tomorrow's activities, Jaz found she had something of her own celebrate. As a result of Dulcie's encouragement to take advantage of whatever competitions were on offer, she had submitted a short story. To her delight, it had been shortlisted for a prize and the winner was to be announced later in the week – when, unfortunately, they wouldn't be around.

Dinner was surprisingly good – pork in green peppercorn sauce with glazed carrots and creamed potatoes, then lemon cheesecake. When coffee had been served they were told that there would be a fifteen-minute break before the guest speaker took the floor in the main conference hall. The title of Jared Winter's talk, they were told by the committee chairman, was '*The Perception of Honesty in Novel Writing – What You Can and Cannot Get Away With*'.

From across the dining hall a loud cheer went up from his fans and, as one, they scraped back their chairs and made a noisy exit. 'Wow,' said Jaz, 'they're eager to get front-row seats, aren't they?'

The rest of the audience trickled into the hall more sedately, and once again Jaz insisted they sit in the back row. 'Last thing we want is to be associated with a bunch of crazies. Polo mint, anyone?' She passed the tube to Jack, who passed it to Beth – but just as Beth moved to take it from him, the lights went out, a hush fell on the audience, and the tube dropped to the floor. Beth leaned forward to retrieve it, but the mints had rolled under the seat in front of her. When she had rescued them and had straightened up, everyone was clapping the guest speaker who was making his entrance into the hall. 'Sorry about that,' Beth said to Jack, whose leg she had knocked several times during her scrabbling. She was just about to join in with the applause when she froze. Up on the podium, taking his seat beside the conference chairman, she could see a man wearing a navy blue anorak holding, of all things . . . a small purse.

Ewan?

Chapter Sixty-Two

*

'You lied.'

'I'm sorry.'

'But you *lied*. And you did it all the time. Every exchange we had was a sham. You conned me.'

'Are you going to let me try to explain?'

'Why? So you can fool me with yet more lies?'

'Please, Beth. I owe you an explanation and I want you to try to understand why I lied. Which, if I wanted to be pedantic, I'm not guilty of doing, not in the true sense. What I *am* guilty of is keeping things from you, but not of lying to you. If you don't believe me, it's all there in the emails I wrote.'

Enraged, she said, 'So now you're saying I should have been more clued-up and read between the lines?'

He shook his head. 'No.' A group of delegates was approaching, including the conference chairman. 'Look,' he said, 'I can't talk now. I've got to sign some books. Will you meet me later? In the bar?'

'I don't know.'

'Please, Beth. It's important.'

She gave in with bad grace. 'Oh, all right. But don't expect me to be falling over you like all those adoring fans of yours.'

For the first time in their conversation, he smiled. 'That's exactly the point, Beth.'

She joined the others – when Ewan (Jared?) and she had left the hall, they had followed then withdrawn to a discreet distance.

'You look like you could do with an extremely large drink,' Jack said.

'Make it several,' she answered grimly.

The bar wasn't as busy as they'd expected, and the lad who served them said it was always the same when a popular author was signing copies of his latest book. 'I'm hoping to nip along in a minute myself.'

'So just how popular is he?' asked Jaz.

The lad gave her a pitying look. 'Don't tell me you've not heard of him.'

'I'm not into science fiction.'

'Strictly speaking, he's fantasy.'

Beth snorted. 'I'll say he is.'

They took their drinks to a nearby table and sat down. Beth still couldn't get over how shocked she had been when she'd recognised Ewan. Amid the applause, he'd stared out at the audience, his eyes sweeping the rows of faces. Frightened he'd spot her, she'd sunk down in her chair. Jack had asked her if she was okay. 'It's him,' she'd hissed. 'It's Ewan.' Jack had glanced at the people around them.

'No, up there. Jared Winter is Ewan.' She'd only ever seen the one photograph of him, but she knew she wasn't mistaken – the hair was the same, and the smile.

'You're kidding?' exclaimed Jaz, who'd overheard.

'I wish I were.'

Jaz had passed the news to Dulcie, on the other side of her, but there was no time to say any more: the chairman of the organising committee was on his feet introducing the speaker and telling them how honoured and fortunate they were to have Jared Winter with them. 'These days, he rarely has time to make such a commitment, but what some of you may not know is that Jared got his lucky break on a writers' conference just like this one, and he feels it's important to put something back into the system. Ladies and gentlemen, I give you Jared Winter.'

More applause followed and Jared – Ewan – rose to his feet and adjusted the microphone. 'You might be wondering why I'm dressed like this,' he began, as he put the purse into his anorak pocket, 'and the answer is twofold. The theme of my talk this evening is honesty, or its perception as carefully orchestrated by the author. The way I'm dressed is to prove how easy it is to manipulate and mislead the reader into believing what you, as the writer, want them to believe. Put a character into an anorak and show him sorting through his loose change in a purse, and you've created a shy mummy's boy. More sinisterly, he might be a shy mummy's boy by day, but a potential serial killer by night. According to convention, what he isn't – based on those two simple details – is a red-blooded Adonis with a taste for fast cars and even faster women. Or is he?' He waited for the laughter to die down. Then, scanning the rows of faces, he said, 'And the other reason for my turning up like this is that I'm sharing a private joke with a friend in the audience.'

At this, Beth had sunk even lower into her chair. How could he have said that?

'But if no one objects, I think I'll dispense with the theatrics.' He unzipped the anorak, creating a stir among the women in the front two rows – several wolf-whistled – and tossed it onto the chair behind him. His talk was self-effacing, entertaining and informative, and had it been delivered by anyone else Beth would have enjoyed it, but she sat motionless for the next forty-five minutes, stunned by the depth of his deviousness.

'Well?' said Dulcie, as they sipped their drinks, while around them the number swelled at the bar: it was impossible not to notice that a good many paperbacks bearing Jared Winter's name were now in circulation. 'I think it's obvious why he lied to you, Beth.'

'Yes,' agreed Jack. 'He was seeking anonymity.'

'It doesn't help,' Beth said. 'I feel as if he's made a fool of me. If I'd known who he was I'd never have kept up the correspondence.'

'And he probably knew that,' said Jaz.

Three pairs of unblinking eyes stared at Beth.

It was another hour before Ewan reappeared. Beth saw him searching the bar for her. 'He's here,' she said to the others.

'In that case, we should go,' said Dulcie.

'No,' said Beth anxiously. 'Please stay.'

'Absolutely not. If there are apologies to be made, he deserves the right to make them in private. Goodnight, Beth. Breakfast is at eight, I'll knock on your door at ten to. Come on, Jaz. You too, Jack.'

Ewan looked tired as he came over to Beth. 'Have I scared your friends away?'

'No. They're being diplomatic and giving you the benefit of the doubt.'

'Am I allowed to sit down?'

She nodded.

'And how about you? Are you prepared to give me the benefit of the doubt?'

'That depends on how convincing you are.'

He leaned forward, but just as he was about to speak, a woman in tight black leather trousers tapped his shoulder. Beth couldn't catch what she said, but the gist was plain: she wanted him to sign a book. He obliged politely, but Beth could see that he was frowning as he reached for a pen from the inside pocket of his jacket. No sooner had she thanked him and turned to go than another appeared wearing a pair of dangly earrings made of pink feathers.

'Could we go somewhere else?' Ewan asked, when they were alone again. 'Somewhere quieter?'

They ventured outside. He said, 'Did you know the grounds were extensive—'

'And worthy of a constitutional stroll,' she finished for him.

'You've read the programme, then.'

'From cover to cover.'

In the darkness, he pointed to a bench across the lawn and led the way. The wooden seat was conveniently private, shielded from view by a rhododendron bush. 'Are you warm enough?' he asked.

She nodded.

'Sitting comfortably?'

Another nod.

'Okay, then, time to start the grovelling. But you must have sussed now why I did what I did.'

She nodded again.

'In which case, you must have also sussed that I'm the most extraordinarily attractive man you've ever set eyes on.'

She turned and looked at him incredulously.

'Aha! At least that elicited more than a passing nod.'

'Don't play games with me. You've done enough of that already.'

'Okay, I admit I kept things from you because I'm sick of meeting people, women in particular, who think of me as Jared Winter.' He inclined his head towards the house. 'Believe it or not, that bunch in there is pretty typical.'

'And how many other women have you conned in this way?'

'None. I swear it. You're the first.' He groaned. 'That didn't come out right. What I meant was, I've never chatted with anyone on the Internet before. The night I met you was the first time I'd tried it. And, you have to admit, we hit it off. If we hadn't, we wouldn't be sitting here now.'

'But I feel as if I wasn't chatting to the man I thought I was. Who are you, really? Jared Winter or Ewan Jones?'

'I'm Ewan Jones. JW, as I think of him, is a pseudonym. He's not even an *alter ego*.'

'Why didn't you tell me before now? All right, not at the start, I can see that. But why not tell me the truth once we'd got to know each other? Why wait to spring the surprise on me here?'

'I had to be sure.'

'Of what?'

'That it was me, boring old Ewan Jones, you wanted to get to know better, not JW, the zany fantasy writer. You should see some of the mail I get from my female readers.'

'Fond of you, are they?'

'I don't think fondness comes into it. Some of the things they say they'd like to do to me . . . Well, let's just say it's reading those letters that's turned my hair grey.'

She laughed, but stopped short when she remembered her drunken email and what she'd suggested she might do with several bars of chocolate.

'It's not funny,' he said.

'I'm sorry. But just for a minute, you sounded like the Ewan I know.'

He leaned back on the seat. 'Thank goodness for that. Here, you're shivering, have my jacket.'

'You should have hung on to that ghastly anorak.'

'I suppose that joke fell flat, didn't it?'

'As a pancake.'

'When I first saw you in the audience, I thought perhaps you'd lied about your height.'

She looked at him, puzzled.

'But then I realised you were trying to hide from me and weren't vertically challenged after all.'

She blushed. 'You spoke very well. You had the audience hanging on your every word.'

'But not you, I suspect.'

'I was in shock.'

'And now?'

'Mm . . . coming round, slowly.'

'Excellent. So tell me what you've done today. Which workshop did you attend?'

'"Characterisation" with Dorothy Kendall.'

He whistled. 'And you survived? You're made of stronger stuff than I thought. Did she threaten the group with having to buy her a drink if you didn't perform well enough?'

'Yes, and it put the fear of God into me. Is she always so fierce?'

'Legendary for it.' He lowered his voice, although there was no one within eavesdropping distance. 'I met her years ago at a similar writers' conference and I was so struck by her I used her in my next novel. Trouble was, the readers loved her as she strutted about in her red leather basque and shiny thigh-high boots. She had to become a regular turn in all the subsequent books.' He smiled. 'I owe it all to that woman.'

'I'm afraid I haven't read any of your books,' Beth admitted.

'I was hoping that might be the case.'

She turned to him, remembering something important. 'You *did* lie to me. You said your book was rejected.'

He shook his head. 'Sorry, but that was true.'

'But how? If you're so successful, why—'

'I wanted to write a novel that was totally different.'

'Wouldn't the Jared Winter name sell it anyway?'

'I wanted it to be accepted in its own right, so I submitted it under another name.' He smiled ruefully. 'And I experienced a healthy dose of rejection, just as I did before I started writing as JW.'

'I'm sorry. That must be hard for an established writer to come to terms with.'

'In some ways, yes, but occasionally it's good to be reminded of one's strengths and weaknesses.' He paused. 'Any chance that I've been forgiven yet?'

'I'll let you know in the morning.' She slipped off his jacket and handed it to him. 'I ought to be turning in.'

'Am I allowed to show how gallant I am by walking you to your room?'

She got to her feet. 'I doubt you'll make it past the security guards. But thanks for the offer.'

'Of course – I was forgetting the single-sex accommodation. I'll walk with you as far as the cross-border checkpoint, then.'

Ewan's room was on the first floor, overlooking the croquet lawn. Unusually, given the rattles, creaks and clunks that a strange room invariably yielded, he'd slept well. At the last conference he'd attended, the one when there had been a power failure, the room had been unbearably hot. The central-heating pipes had run along the length of his bed and he'd ended up throwing open the window, only to wake at three and find that a downpour of rain had soaked the notes for his talk, which he'd left on the desk under the window. Immediately after breakfast he'd had to address a three-hundred-strong audience feeling as if he'd passed the night shovelling coal into the furnaces of hell.

But this morning, drawing back the curtains and seeing that the warm spring weather was holding, he felt refreshed. He was looking forward to the workshop he was leading.

And to seeing Beth again.

He'd known all too well the risk he'd taken with her, and had anticipated her reaction right to the last accusation. All he could hope for was that she had calmed down since last night and was prepared to carry on as before. The plus side of it was that while he had been explaining himself and apologising, they had been spared the awkwardness of sizing each other up. But, then, that was only his take on the events of last night. For all he knew, Beth might have been disappointed with him in the flesh – hair too grey, waistline too full, wrinkles too many. And that was on top of discovering that he was your bog-standard, no-good devious man with a score of ulterior motives.

But there hadn't been any disappointment on his part: Beth was just as attractive as her photograph had led him to believe. He'd had no trouble spotting her in the audience – the look of horror had helped. When he'd left her last night, he'd apologised again for misleading her. She hadn't said he was off the hook, but he was hopeful that, after a good night's sleep and maybe a chat with her friends, she would have forgiven him.

Washed, shaved and dressed, he locked his room and took the staircase down to the ground floor. With luck an enthusiastic fan wouldn't waylay him, or an overly efficient conference organiser insist that he had breakfast with the committee members.

He entered the dining hall. Many of the tables were already occupied by conference participants tucking into plates of eggs and bacon, and taking care to avoid eye-contact with anyone, he sought out Beth and her friends. Eventually he located them and went over to their table.

In for a penny, in for a pound. If she'd decided he was *persona non grata*, he was about to find out.

The afternoon was going slowly for Jack. The workshop he'd signed up to do on the importance of dialogue was interesting, but his mind kept straying to his manuscript, which had been with Felix McCallum since yesterday evening. How much of *Friends and Family* had he managed to read? And had he liked it? Jack knew he would have to wait until after dinner, when he had an appointment with Felix, to find out.

At last the workshop was over. He had arranged to meet up with the others in the garden before they went back to their rooms to change for dinner, so he headed in that direction. Dulcie, Beth and Jaz had all opted for a talk entitled 'Women on Top'. It was led by an author called Jessica Lloyd, a romantic novelist from their own neck of the woods in Cheshire. Amusingly, they had gone to great lengths to assure him that it wasn't a gender-bashing session, but an in-depth study of the changing image of romantic fiction.

Jack saw that all the benches had been taken, so he tested the grass. On finding it quite dry, he sat down. Too late, he saw Zed approaching. From the look of him, he hadn't changed since yesterday: same baggy jogging trousers, same T-shirt, same slippers. He sat heavily on the grass next to Jack, his knees drawn up to his chin. 'I'm glad I found you, I wanted to ask you something.'

Warily, Jack said, 'Oh, yes?'

'Yeah, I'd really appreciate you having a squint at my novel. I've almost finished it and I'm getting a good vibe off it. I think you might too.'

Jack was reminded of Victor. Perhaps he was getting soft in his old age, but he felt sorry for Zed, so he said, 'I'm no expert, but I'll have a look at it if you like.' That opened the floodgates and for the next ten minutes he was subjected to a detailed account of a book that sounded as quirky as its creator. He had never felt so relieved as he did when he spotted Dulcie, Beth and Jaz coming across the lawn towards him. Give me women on top any day, he thought, as they apologised to Zed for dragging him away.

*

'Can you believe we're nearly half-way through our time here?' said Jaz, during dinner.

'I know what you mean,' replied Dulcie. 'The time is flying by. Are you glad you came?'

'Oh, yes. I'm having a fantastic time. I thought Jessica Lloyd was brilliant and incredibly encouraging. I'm going to read all her books when I get home. How about you, Beth?'

Caught with her thoughts elsewhere, Beth said, 'Mm . . . sorry? What did you say?'

It was Jack who was brave enough to ask, 'So, how're you getting on with Ewan? Have you forgiven him for wanting you to like him for *who* he is not *what* he is?'

She had been thinking of the conversation she'd had with Ewan after lunch, when once again her friends had left them discreetly alone. 'I think we've reached an understanding.'

'And?'

'And nothing, Jack.'

As the conversation returned to the afternoon's talks and workshops, and then more importantly to what Felix McCallum would make of Jack's novel, Beth's thoughts wandered again. Ewan had invited her to go for a drive tomorrow. 'I don't know this area of the country,' he'd said, 'and I'd like to explore. I wondered if you'd consider taking some time out of the conference to come with me.'

'Only if you promise not to wear that appalling anorak or bring your purse with you.'

'I think I could agree to those terms.'

They had both seemed relieved by the ease with which the deal had been struck, and had chatted happily while they finished their coffee. When they left the dining hall together, Beth had the feeling they were being watched. She had assumed Ewan was the focus of attention, but she was almost through the doorway when she saw two of Jared Winter's groupies looking daggers at her.

She held her head high. 'Look all you like, girls,' she felt like saying. 'The name's Beth King, and I'm licensed to make you green with envy.'

Chapter Sixty-Three

*

Dulcie was bursting with pride and happiness: Felix McCallum had read Jack's novel, liked it, and wanted to make an offer for it.

Late last night, while they'd been celebrating in the bar, Ewan had advised Jack to find himself an agent. 'You shouldn't agree to anything until you have someone to act on your behalf, someone who understands how the business works.' Ewan had offered to ring his own agent in London and put him in touch with Jack.

'I'm so proud of you,' she'd said to Jack, when they'd finally called it a night. 'But didn't I say all along that you had that magic touch publishers are on the lookout for?'

'Search me if I know what it is,' he'd said.

'It's called talent,' Beth and Jaz had said together.

In an uncharacteristic display of emotion, he'd thrown his arms around all three of them, and said, 'But I couldn't have done it without you. If you hadn't been so encouraging and supportive I might never have finished writing the book.'

'And just you remember that when you're filthy rich and famous,' Jaz said.

Dulcie had wanted to share the good news with Richard, but decided not to bother him so late. Now, with a few spare minutes before breakfast, she tapped in his number on the tiny phone he'd given her. He answered straight away and she could tell from the background noise that he was in his car using his hands-free mobile. He sounded pleased to hear from her, which gave her a lovely warm feeling inside and reminded her how much she missed him.

'Sorry I didn't call you last night,' she said, 'but it was very late when I got back to my room.'

'Ah, so you were out partying all hours, were you?'

'And with good reason. Jack has a publisher interested in his novel.'

'That's marvellous! He must be cock-a-hoop. Give him my best wishes.'

'I will, darling. And how are you?'

'Oh, okay. Missing you.'

'I miss you too. But I'll be home tomorrow and we'll be able to make up for lost time.'

She heard him laugh. 'Is that a promise?'

'A dead cert.'

The line crackled noisily. 'Are you still there, Dulcie?'

'Yes. The line's awful. Where are you?'

'On the M6 heading for Worcester. The traffic's horrendous.'

'Well, just you make sure you drive carefully. I'd better go now, the others will be waiting for me. Take care.'

'You too. And remember to pass on my congratulations to the star of your writers' group.'

She rang off, inordinately happy. Happy for Jack, and for herself, for the deep sense of commitment that existed now between her and Richard.

Although Beth had been hopping mad that Ewan had hidden his true identity from her, she could now see the situation from his point of view. Much to her surprise, the conversations she'd had with her son had also helped her to accept that Ewan wasn't the monstrous liar she had at first thought him to be. 'Nathan, I feel so stupid,' she told him, when she called to make sure he was all right.

'Why, because for a moment you thought you might have to admit your cocky son was right? Now you see what I was trying to protect you from? People who use the Net aren't always what they make themselves out to be.'

'I know. Please don't make me feel any worse than I already do.'

'But look on the bright side. This guy, Ewan, Jared, whatever his name is, felt he had more to lose than you. So I guess that makes him okay.'

'Really?'

'Yeah, he has a profile he needs to protect. He must have decided you were worth the risk. Any chance you can get me a signed copy of one of his books?'

'Is that approval I hear in your voice? Are you giving me the go ahead?'

'Do you need it?'

Beth was glad she had agreed to take time out from the conference to see some of the local countryside. The first surprise of her expedition was Ewan's car: a slinky black Porsche.

'I make no apology for being a big kid who likes a flashy motor,' he said, opening the door for her.

She slid into the low slung seat and thought of Nathan and what a kick he would get from driving such a beauty. 'You're not going to terrify me by showing what this is capable of, are you?'

'Certainly not. But if it reassures you, the button for the ejector seat is right here.' He pointed to a small red button on the dash. 'Or maybe that's the cigarette lighter, I forget. You any good with a map?'

'Since you ask, yes; I have a PhD in navigation.'

'Good, you can do the honours, then.' He passed her an OS map, already folded to the appropriate section.

'Where are we heading first?'

'I fancied going up to Brimham Rocks.' He leaned in towards her, and pointed to what had been marked on the map as a place of interest. 'It's only a short drive, so we should be there in no time at all. Depending, of course, on your skill as a navigator.' This was said with a smile and, being so close to her, when he looked up she noticed the colour of his eyes for the first time. Blue.

She lowered her gaze back to the map. 'I think you'll find my map reading ability will more than make up for any inadequacy on the driver's part.'

Laughing, he started the engine and carefully reversed out of the space. He proved to be a man of his word and didn't frighten her once. The rock formation was enormous, much larger than either of them had expected. Leaving the car, they set out on foot to explore. The view was spectacular and, beneath a cloudless blue sky, they could see for miles.

'It's beautiful,' she said. 'Stunning.' When he didn't respond, she turned and was surprised to find that he wasn't looking at the view. 'Ewan?'

'Sorry, I allowed myself to be distracted by a far more interesting sight.' He groaned and covered his face with his hands. 'Tell me I didn't say that! Tell me I didn't say something so clichéd. Dorothy Kendall would flay me alive!'

She laughed. 'You did, and you should be ashamed of yourself.'

'Oh, I am. Believe me, I am.'

When he suggested they walk on, it seemed perfectly natural that he should take her hand. Quite at ease in his company, Beth said how much she was enjoying herself.

'Good,' he said, 'because I am too. Thank you for coming.'

'Thank you for the invitation.'

'And thank *you* for being so polite.'

'Are you making fun of me?'

'Just a little.'

'Well, don't.'

'Not ever?'

'Only if you don't object to me getting my own back.'

'How will you do that?'

'I shall tell on you to La Kendall. About the basque-wearing character in your books and the gratuitous clichés.'

He burst out laughing. 'Ooh, go straight to my Achilles heel, why don't you?'

From Brimham Rocks they followed the road back towards Norton Hall, then took the route to Harrogate.

'We can't possibly come to this part of the world and not experience afternoon tea at Betty's,' he told her. 'I hope you're a cream tea person, Beth, or there'll be no hope for us.'

'I'll have you know I can eat my own weight in scones and clotted cream.'

They had only a ten minute wait before a waitress in traditional black skirt, white blouse and pinny showed them to a table. They ordered a selection of sandwiches, cakes and scones, and sat back to observe their surroundings and the other customers. When their food arrived, Beth looked at Ewan in horror. 'Did we really order so much?'

He shrugged. 'That's just yours, mine will be along in a minute.'

They tucked in.   'I hate to be so picky,' Beth said, 'but I've just thought of a whopping great lie you told me in one of your emails. You said you ran your own public relations business.'

'And you think I don't?'

She frowned. 'But you're a writer.'

'Correct. And to be a writer who sells well these days, you have to get out there on the road and do your share of PR work. I've been doing it for years, showing my face at writers' conferences, signings, interviews, meeting booksellers. You name it, I've done it.'

'That's cheating.'

He smiled. 'I also recall telling you that my job is to make people suspend their disbelief, that it's all in the spin.'

'You mean, it's the way you tell 'em?'

'Exactly.'

She poured out more tea, passed him his cup and said, 'Tell me about the book you had rejected. The other night you said it was very different to a Jared Winter novel. In what way?'

He finished the sandwich he'd been eating, wiped his mouth with his napkin. 'Confession time. You see before you a man who is trapped by his own success. I've written twelve fantasy books now and I've reached the point when I'd like nothing better than to switch horses mid race.'

'You mean try a different genre?'

'Yes. I wrote a love story; about my parents. Back in the righteous fifties, they caused a heck of a rumpus when they scandalously fell in love. Dad was already married but they persevered and despite the stigma of living in sin, which really meant something then, especially as they had a child, me, they were immensely happy. Until sadly my father died.'

'What an interesting story. Will you try again with it?'

He smiled. 'Eventually, when my bruised ego has recovered. You can't keep a good man down. It's what I tell every rejected would-be writer I meet at these conferences. Get back into the saddle and give it another go.'

'So what's wrong with the books you're so successful with?'

'I'm bored with them. I need to do something different. If it doesn't sound too pretentious, I feel confined. I want to spread my creative wings. But all is not lost. I have a plan. I write phenomenally fast and currently I can produce two books a year. I'm hoping to stockpile a few then take a break from JW and write something else.' He helped himself to another egg and cress sandwich. 'Well, does that satisfy you? Are you convinced now that I haven't lied to you?'

Respecting him for his honesty, she said, 'You did lie to me, about something else.'

'Go on?'

'You played down how nice you are.'

She could see from his expression that for a split second she'd wrongfooted him. But then a slow smile worked itself across his face. 'Got you on a technicality again. That wasn't an untruth, that was an omission. The same one you made.'

All in all it had been a good day. The meeting Richard had driven to Worcester for had gone well, and the mood of everyone around the table had turned from weary pessimism to optimistic determination to wrap the job up. The turning point came when the lawyers of the customer they were dealing with, a large retail organisation, finally accepted the newly offered terms: this was after weeks of frustration, when draft after draft of the logistics contract had been written and summarily rejected. Motivating a large team during such delicate negotiations took time and effort, but when the result was good, it made the job all the more worthwhile.

He'd left his jubilant team in the Worcester office to celebrate and driven home. He was now on the M6, not far from Maywood, but the traffic was heavy and slow. Knowing that he was bone tired, and probably not concentrating as he ought, he wound down the window and decided to stop at the next service station for some strong black coffee.

He pulled into the car park, found himself a space, and switched off the engine, tempted to take a short nap. As he turned the key, a pain shot through his left arm. He let out a cry, drew his fist to his chest and clutched his shoulder, waiting for the pain to subside. But it didn't. Light-headed, suddenly covered in sweat and feeling as if he were being crushed, he fought for breath. He tried to keep calm, knowing that he was having another heart-attack, that possibly a worse agony was inevitable. He fumbled for his mobile – just inches away – but another spasm of pain shot through him and he jerked his head back against the head-rest.

'Oh, God,' he gasped, 'this is it . . .'

His last conscious thought was of Dulcie. Of never seeing her again.

Chapter Sixty-Four

*

Dulcie was worried. It was unlike Richard not to answer the messages she'd left on both his mobile and the telephone at home in Bloom Street – her own voice informed her each time she tried that she was unable to come to the phone. During breakfast, while Beth and Jaz had been chatting with Ewan, Dulcie had shared her concern with Jack. His advice was to call Richard at work. It was the obvious solution, but it had been one of her many golden rules throughout their relationship that she never rang him at his office. But, as Jack rightly pointed out, the nature of their relationship had changed; he was openly living with her.

She put off phoning until lunchtime, two hours before they would be leaving Norton Hall. The weather was so warm and bright that she went outside to make the call. She wandered in the grounds until she came to the chapel ruins. No one was about so she sat on a bench and tapped in Richard's work number. The telephone in Cheshire was answered by a young girl with a sing-song voice, whose tone changed immediately when Dulcie asked to speak to Mr Richard Cavanagh.

'Oh – I'll – I'll just put you through to someone who can help you. What did you say your name was?'

'I didn't. It's Mrs Ballantyne.'

Dulcie had expected to be put through to Richard's secretary, and was taken aback when she heard the resonant timbre of a man's voice. For no real reason, anxiety twisted into the piercing stab of certainty. Something *was* wrong. 'Is Richard there, please?' she asked.

'I'm afraid not,' the man said. 'May I ask who's calling?'

She noted his cautious tone. 'My name is Dulcie Ballantyne and I'm – I'm a close friend of his. I've tried ringing him on his mobile but I can't get an answer.'

'I see.' He cleared his throat. 'I'm sorry to be the one to tell you but Richard died yesterday.'

Her hand flew to her mouth, held back a cry of disbelief. *No! Oh, no! Not dead. Not Richard. He can't be.*

'Hello? Are you still there?'

She uncovered her mouth and tried to speak. But she couldn't. As her eyes filled with tears, she swallowed hard and forced the words out. 'Yes, I'm still here. When did Richard . . .' Her voice broke. She tried again. 'How did . . .?' But it was no good: her throat was clenched and nothing would come out.

The man came to her rescue. 'At the moment the only information we have is that it was another heart-attack. He was on his own, driving back from Worcester yesterday afternoon and—'

This time she couldn't stop the cry escaping. 'No! Not on his own!' She ended the call and held the phone to her chest. She sobbed aloud, her whole body shuddering with the shock. Above her, a cloud passed over the sun and she felt as if the whole world had just gone dark.

While Jaz and Jack finished their packing before lunch, Beth volunteered to look for Dulcie. There was no sign of her anywhere and, on the verge of giving up, thinking Dulcie might have gone ahead to the dining hall, Beth decided to widen her search to the chapel ruins. It was there that she found Dulcie. Her head was bowed and she was weeping silently. She didn't notice Beth until she had joined her on the bench and put her arms around her. Instinctively, Beth knew what had happened. She let Dulcie cry some more, and then almost in a whisper, she said, 'Is it Richard? Has something happened to him?'

It seemed an age before Dulcie raised her head from Beth's shoulder. 'He's dead, Beth. Another heart-attack. I – I should have been with him.'

Beth held her tightly again. 'Oh, Dulcie, I'm so sorry. So very sorry.'

Shivering, Dulcie pulled away from her. She stared up at the sky, her mouth and chin trembling. 'I can't believe I'll never see him again. And just as we'd begun to plan a real future for ourselves. It was really going to happen.'

Reminded of her own grief when she had been told Adam was dead, Beth blinked away the tears that were pricking the backs of her eyes. She held Dulcie's hand: it was icy cold. 'Come on, Dulcie, let's get you back to your room. I'll ask Jack to rustle up something for you to eat.'

'No. I want to go home. I want to be nearer Richard.'

Dulcie could remember little of the journey home. She must have dozed at some time because when she next opened her eyes they were back in Maywood and turning into Bloom Street. Beth helped her out of the car and Jack carried her bag. Seeing the look of concern on Jaz's face, Dulcie felt a wave of pity for her – death wasn't for the young, they weren't equipped to cope with it. As if she had been thinking the same, Beth suggested that Jack took Jaz home. While he was gone, Dulcie watched Beth move about the kitchen as she made them some coffee. There was no milk, but Dulcie didn't care. She wasn't going to drink it. Instead she warmed her hands on the mug.

When Jack reappeared the three sat at the table, which reminded Dulcie of the night she had first told them about Richard and how she had just ended their relationship. She thought how cruel she had been and how desperate she had made him. The memory was too much and she buried her face in her hands and wept for the man she had lost, for what she had done to him and the effect it must have had on him. 'This is all my fault. I made this happen. If only I hadn't fallen in love with Richard he would still be alive, his heart wouldn't have—'

'You're not to think like that,' Beth said firmly. She placed a hand on her arm. 'The weakness must always have been there – it had nothing to do with you.'

'But if it wasn't for me causing the stress in his life, the weakness might never have shown itself.'

'You can't know that. And that way madness lies so clear it from your mind. Now.'

She had never heard Jack speak so severely and it helped. She stopped crying.

They sat with her for the rest of the afternoon and late into the evening. Beth had suggested she stayed the night to keep her company, but Dulcie wanted to be alone.

Except she wasn't alone. In the silence of the night as she lay in bed, she felt Richard's presence. The smell of him was still on the pillow and sheets and the book he'd been reading was at his side of the bed. Next to it stood a silver-framed photograph of the two of them in Venice – it had been taken by a tourist, a man who had slipped briefly into and out of their lives and unwittingly provided Dulcie with a keepsake she would always treasure.

She fell asleep lying on her side, her hand resting on the space where Richard had once been.

Chapter Sixty-Five

*

Since they had returned from Yorkshire, Beth and Ewan's email correspondence had tailed off. It was more common now for them to phone each other: they had swapped telephone numbers and addresses during Beth's last night at the conference.

'I don't suppose there's any chance that I've convinced you I'm not a serial killer with a penchant for bumping off fellow writers, is there?' he had asked, as they took a late-night stroll through the grounds of Norton Hall.

'You might have. Why?'

'Oh, no reason.'

When she didn't push it, he said, 'You're not playing the game properly. You should have pressed for the reason.'

'Is that so?'

'Yes. So go on. Press away.'

'Do I have to? I'm quite happy walking along in the dark minding my own business.'

'You're making this very difficult for me, Bethany King.'

She tried not to smile. It was ages since she'd played the flirting game: she was rather enjoying it. 'If I knew what I was making so difficult for you, I might do something about it.'

Coming to a stop, he said, 'Okay. I'd like to ask you two questions. The first is this. Can we stay in touch, and not just by email but by that antiquated device known as the telephone?'

She had no hesitation in agreeing. 'Yes. I'd like that very much. And your second question?'

'Crikey, not so fast, Beth, it took all my courage to get that one out. I need to psych myself up for question number two.'

'Is it that bad?'

'You might think so.'

'Oh, well, when you're ready.'

He started walking again, but this time with his arm around her shoulders. He wasn't wearing his jacket tonight and she could feel the warmth of his skin through the soft cotton of his shirt. She could smell his aftershave, a fresh citrus fragrance that she knew would always remind her of this moment. And how attracted she felt to him. She had hoped he might want to kiss her, and had to acknowledge that if he didn't she would go home disappointed.

Plenty of other people were taking advantage of the mild night, and after several women – diehard Jared Winter fans – had stared openly at Beth, she had suggested he might like to remove his arm. 'Your book sales are going to plummet if you don't,' she added.

He surprised her by leading her towards the middle of the floodlit croquet lawn. And there, for all to see, he said, 'This is my last night with you, and even if I have to spend the rest of my life dodging looks that could kill, it's a price I'm prepared to pay.' He took both of her hands in his. 'Prepare yourself, Bethany King, here comes question number two.' He coughed. 'Would it be too much of a liberty to ask if a lowly wretch such as I, a simple soul who is scarcely worthy of your attention—' He took a breath. 'Well, would he be allowed one small kiss? And to hell with the book sales!'

She had laughed. 'For that, I'll grant you a colossal kiss.'

And she had. A kiss that was so perfect that even now when she recalled it – thought of his arms around her and his lips moving slowly against hers – her legs went weak. Suddenly a loud cheer had gone up behind them. They hadn't noticed the crowd of onlookers who had spilled out of the bar.

'Okay,' he called. 'Show's over. Nothing more to see. Go about your business.'

Then, laughing, Beth and Ewan had slipped away to a less visible spot in the garden, and after he'd apologised for sullying her good name, he held her close and kissed her again, tenderly, lovingly. 'Thank goodness our children aren't here to witness such appalling behaviour,' he joked, as he stroked her cheek, his eyes never leaving hers. 'I'd be grounded for at least a month if Alice knew what I was up to.'

That was what she liked so much about Ewan: his sense of

humour. He could make her laugh and was sexy too – it was a winning combination in her book!

But it didn't feel right to be so happy when she knew how sad Dulcie was. Poor Dulcie was torn apart with grief. It was heartbreaking to see. Especially as Beth knew just how it felt and that the painful memory would never leave her entirely. As she'd told Ewan on the phone, to experience that depth of loss once is bad enough, but twice, as in Dulcie's case, with her husband and now Richard, was unthinkable.

She had been touched that Ewan had sent Dulcie a card of sympathy: he was as sincere as he was generous. He'd kept his word about speaking to his agent on Jack's behalf, and as a result Jack had sent a copy of *Friends and Family* to London and was now waiting to hear what kind of offer Felix McCallum would make. It was all very exciting. She was glad that Jack had been the one from Hidden Talents to find success with his writing; he richly deserved it. She had no illusions about her own scribblings – in comparison with what Jack could do, she was still in kindergarten. But getting published had not been her *raison d'être* for joining Hidden Talents.

Back in October, when she had plucked up the courage to respond to the card in the window of Novel Ways, she had hoped it would provide her with an opportunity to meet new people and explore a shared interest. To her delight, it had given her a whole new lease of life far beyond anything she could have imagined: with a new circle of friends and revitalised self-confidence, Nathan's leaving home in the autumn didn't look half so daunting now.

On top of that, and to her amazement, there was also the potential for romance. She and Ewan had arranged to meet again in a couple of weeks' time. She was going to stay with him in Suffolk and secretly, like a child waiting for Christmas, she was ticking off the days on the calendar.

The other day Simone had phoned, and howled with laughter when Beth had told her what she'd been up to all these months. Her reaction was partly based on the coincidence that Ben had recently discovered Jared Winter's books and had taken to reading them in bed at night. 'And you know what an infuriating laugh Ben has – he's like a pressure cooker about to explode. Tell your new friend to stop writing such off-the-wall books or I'll be citing him in my divorce petition. By the way, is he as quirky as Ben says the books are?'

Since coming home Beth had read several of Ewan's novels, so she could answer her friend's question from an informed standpoint. 'Not really. He's funny, but never at the expense of anyone else.'

'Does he remind you of Adam?'

'No.'

'Good. Adam took life too seriously. That was why he killed himself. Now, go and have some fun, Beth. Don't, whatever you do, talk yourself out of this one – it sounds as if the two of you have really hit it off. Maybe it's because you've taken the time and effort to get to know one another as friends.'

As a consequence of her improved relationship with Lois, and wanting to continue the new sense of understanding between them, Beth had decided to tell her and Barnaby about Ewan. She chose to confess when she and Nathan were at Marsh House, having been invited to look through the holiday snaps and watch an hour-long video recording of cruise highlights. While Nathan was out of the room answering a call on his mobile, she made her announcement. 'I thought you ought to know, not that there's much to tell, that I've met a man I'm quite fond of. He lives in Suffolk, so there's no danger of . . .' she lost her nerve.

'No danger of what?' prompted Lois, a hand playing with a tiny pearl button on the cuff of her blouse, her faded blue eyes blinking behind her reading glasses.

She summoned her courage by reminding herself how Ewan had made her feel when he'd kissed her so publicly; she quickly found the right words. 'Of making a fool of myself or getting too involved too soon.'

Barnaby picked up the remote control for the video-player and said, 'I would have thought it was high time you threw caution to the wind and got involved with a man, Beth. Wouldn't you agree, Lois?'

'Does he make you happy when you're with him?'

The question was so unlike any other Lois had asked her that Beth responded with equal candour. 'We haven't had the opportunity to spend much time together yet, but yes, he does.'

'Well, then, what else is there to say? Does he have a name?'

'Ewan Jones.'

'And what does he do?'

'He's a writer.'

For a moment Beth waited to hear Lois exclaim, 'I knew all along that you had an ulterior motive for joining that writing group!' But she didn't. She smiled stiffly and said, 'That's nice. At least you have something in common. Something on which to build.'

'He also has a twenty-year-old daughter who he's brought up on his own, so he understands how important Nathan is to me and the special relationship we have.'

At that point Nathan had come back into the room and, hearing his name, had said, 'Talking about me behind my back, Ma?' But before Beth could reply, his grandmother had tactfully changed the subject. Certain things would never change: Lois would always be a firm believer in the not-in-front-of-the-children school of thought.

Jaz stood back to admire their handiwork. Not bad.

For the last week she and her brothers, with help from Nathan, and even, occasionally, from Billy and Vicki, had been secretly working on Victor's house. Her brothers had seen fire-damaged houses before and said that Victor's was only singed in comparison. As it was, the work was restricted to the bedroom in which the fire had started and the room immediately below, because the ceiling had given way under the deluge of water the firemen had used to put out the flames.

She had seen the house for the first time when Victor had asked her to have a look at it, then report back to him. 'Why me?' she'd said. 'Why not Beth?'

'Because I know you won't lie to me. I want to know just how bad it is.'

So, using the key he had entrusted to her, of which she had a copy made, she had let herself in. She had been relieved to see that things weren't as bad as she'd thought they would be. It was the smell that really got to her: the acrid stench of smoke filled the small house. What also came home to her, as she stood at the top of the stairs, was that if Jack hadn't been the kind of man he was, Victor would be dead. And as far as she knew, only she, Jack, Beth and Dulcie would have been upset by his death. She thought of Dulcie and the state she'd been in since they got back from

Harrogate, and hurriedly pushed away the thought of death. Victor was very much alive and would soon be home.

What she hadn't anticipated when she'd enlisted her brothers' help was that Dad would be so impressed by their apparent enthusiasm to help a man they'd never met – and in their free time – that he wanted to pitch in too by supplying the materials and tools. 'Don't think I'm going soft, though,' he'd said, when Jaz thanked him. 'I'm after the publicity. When your friend comes out of hospital, we'll get the local rag round to do a feature.' Jaz wasn't fooled: she knew her father couldn't resist a good cause.

And now, a week on, with only the replastered walls in the bedroom to be painted when they'd dried out, the small terraced house was habitable again. She couldn't wait to see Victor's face.

It would be almost as interesting as her brothers' faces had been when she'd impressed upon them the reasons why they had to help her. 'Boys,' she'd said, not long after her return from Norton Hall, 'I have a job for you.'

'Oh, yeah, little sis,' said Phin. 'What's that? You need a hand counting your winnings?'

Everyone at home at been amazed when she'd received the letter from the organising committee of the writers' conference telling her she'd come second in the short-story competition and had won fifty pounds. Tamzin and Lulu were now scribbling stories of their own in the hope that they, too, would earn money so easily. Dad had been particularly chuffed and had slipped another twenty pounds into her hand, saying, 'Well done, Jazzy, I'm dead proud of you.'

'No, I don't need any help with that, Phin,' she'd said, 'but I'd like your assistance with something I know you can do.' She'd explained about Victor's house and they'd laughed at her. Until, that was, she'd said, 'Do you think Mum and Dad will laugh when they hear what you did to Jack?'

They'd looked at each other in silence, then back at her. 'What're you saying?'

'Oh, Jimmy, did I not make it simple enough for you? Well, here's the thing. You help me put Victor's house in order and I shan't spill the beans about what second-rate villains you are. You know how Mum thinks the sun shines out of your bums, it would be a shame for her to discover that her boys used undue force to push a respectable pillar of the community into the back of their car and threaten him.'

413

'She wouldn't believe you.'

'Prepared to take that chance, are you? And think how mad Dad would be if he found out what you did. *And* that you'd upset Mum.'

They gave in. The only irritation was that now Dad was holding up her brothers as paragons of charitable good will. 'If only everyone had a social conscience like Phin and Jimmy,' he kept saying. It was all Jaz could do to hold her tongue. Reluctantly, she came to the conclusion that her brothers would always come up smelling of roses.

Standing alongside Phin and Nathan in Victor's hall, she clapped her hands. 'We've done it, boys. Well done.'

Already stripping off his overalls, Phin said, 'And now we're quits, right?'

'Absolutely. No question.'

Jimmy came out of the dining room, a pair of stepladders over his shoulder. 'We'll leave you two to lock up, then.'

When they were alone, Nathan said, 'Happy now?'

'I will be when Victor comes out of hospital next week and sees what we've done.'

'You're sure he'll approve? You don't think he'll accuse you of interfering?'

'Nah. He'll be beside himself with joy.'

'You reckon?'

'No. He'll be as ungracious as he always is, but inside he'll be okay about it. He just won't know how to express his gratitude. I get the feeling he hasn't had much experience in that area. Anyway, what's the worst he can do? Shout at me for poking my nose in?'

Wiping his hands on an old cloth, Nathan smiled. 'And I can tell him right now he'd be wasting his time.'

'You guess right. I switch off when Victor starts moaning, and he knows it.'

'I almost feel sorry for the man.'

Nathan took Jaz home, then drove to the health centre to pick up his mother. It was Adele Waterman's birthday today and they were treating her to dinner. It seemed ages now since she had moved out and Jack had arrived, but that was the funny thing about change, he supposed; once it had happened, the new became the old. The same would be true once he left home for college – before long both he and his mother would have adjusted to the changes in their lives. Last year he'd been worried how she would cope on her own, but not now. With Jack living in the flat downstairs, he knew help would be on hand, should his mother need it, and with Ewan on the scene, he was sure she would soon start to live her life quite differently from the way she had since his father had died.

Thinking of his father, he was glad that things had been resolved with his grandparents, and happier still to know that he no longer had to compete with the distorted memory of a man he could scarcely remember.

Change, he'd come to realise, happened all the time. Whether they wanted it or not.

Chapter Sixty-Six

*

Once again Victor was being told how lucky he was, and he was almost tempted to believe it. He was being allowed home next week and, compared to the man who had come in yesterday afternoon with burns far worse than Victor's had ever been, he had a lot to be grateful for.

It was the endlessly chatty WRVS woman who brought round the trolley of papers and magazines every day who was currently telling him how fortunate he was. She had only started the job last week and he'd noticed that since Monday she'd developed the habit of hovering around his bed as if she had nothing better to do. 'We'll miss you when you've gone, Mr Blackmore,' she was saying, 'but all good things must come to an end. You're a lucky man to have recovered so quickly. It must be the combination of the excellent nursing care here and your devoted little girlfriend who visits you so regularly.'

He looked up from his A4 pad, horrified. 'My devoted what?'

She smiled. 'The pretty redhead.'

'For your information Jaz doesn't have red hair, she has *auburn* hair.' For a split second he wondered why he'd said this. Then he remembered Jaz telling him that she hated anyone describing her hair as red.

The woman's smile broadened. 'The two of you are the talk of the ward – you're the envy of every man here.'

'But I'm old enough to be her father – her grandfather!'

'For most of them here,' she threw a glance at the rest of the patients, 'that's what's driving them mad. They want to know what your secret is and if they can adopt her as their special visitor when you've gone.'

'That's disgusting! There's absolutely nothing between Jaz and me. We're . . .' he sought to find the right word. Acquaintances? No. They were more than that. Writing associates? Again, it didn't sound adequate. 'Friends,' he said, surprising himself with the admission. 'And I take great exception that you should think otherwise. You can tell this perverted lot that—'

'Calm down, Mr Blackmore, I'm only teasing you.' The woman, who was about the same age as Victor, clicked her tongue. Then, just as he thought she was moving away she said, 'Oh, I hope you don't mind me saying, but I really like what you're writing.'

He eyed her suspiciously. 'And what would you know about that?'

'I've read it. It's very good.'

'When have you read a single word of what I've written?' he demanded, outraged.

'Ssh – don't get so worked up.' She gave a faintly embarrassed shrug. 'Perhaps I shouldn't have done it, but, well, there we are, I did.'

'But *when*?'

'Oh, here and there. When you were paying a call of nature, or were busy with—'

'You went behind my back? Is that what you're saying?'

'You left your notebook on your bed. I thought you wouldn't mind. I mean, why would you? If you're hoping to get published one day you've got to get used to people reading what you've written.'

'But it's private! It's at a raw, unstructured stage. It's not fit to be read, least of all by a woman I hardly know. It's an invasion of my privacy, that's what it is, and I'm going to report you.'

She looked alarmed. 'Oh, please, Mr Blackmore, don't do that. I didn't mean any harm. I was curious. And the trouble was, once I'd read the first couple of pages I couldn't stop. I wanted to know what would happen next. I felt so sorry for the poor little boy, I just had to know if he'd get his own back on those rotten bullies.'

The heat of his anger began to cool. 'You wanted to know what would happen next?' he asked. 'Really?'

'Oh, yes. I was hooked.' She lowered her gaze, shamefaced. 'I don't suppose you'd let me read the rest when you've finished it, would you?'

Victor's annoyance disappeared. 'I'll think about it,' he said. He watched her trundle her trolley along the row of beds and returned her wave as she left the ward. He made a note to find out her name. An objective opinion from someone with such a refreshing view of his writing might prove invaluable. The thought occurred to him that she might also help him after he had been discharged next week. He would need the odd errand running for him, and she seemed pleasant enough.

All the members of Hidden Talents had said they'd lend a hand when he went home, but it was Jaz's offers of help that had surprised him most. She had always been rude to him, but he liked her because she was so remorselessly plainspoken with him. That was why he'd trusted her to look at his house. Anyone else would have tried to put a gloss on the state of it to spare his feelings. Jaz hadn't done that. 'Well, Victor,' she'd said, after she'd taken a look at it, 'it's not as bad as you'd think it would be. Sure, there's a mess, but I reckon you've been lucky. Tell you what, why don't you leave it to me to get it sorted for you?'

'But it must be worse than that? It has to be.'

'Victor, would I lie to you?'

'Mm . . . maybe not. How will you get it sorted, though? You can't do it alone. And I told you about the insurance—'

She'd interrupted him again and tapped her nose with a finger. 'I have contacts. Don't forget, I come from a family of builders. If you want, you can settle the money side of things when you're back on your feet. Meanwhile, stop twittering and give a girl a break. I'm trying to do something nice for you and you're being boringly negative. Just give thanks that luck, at long last, is shining on you.'

Victor closed his eyes and thought over the last six months of his life. The shame of being made redundant seemed lost in the mists of time, as did those depressing days and nights of sitting, cold and alone, in the spare room writing *Star City*. He knew now that he'd made himself ill doing that, had very nearly lost his life. But how could he ever have believed he would produce his best work by writing in that stifling vacuum? Nowadays, and because he was used to having company twenty-four hours a day, he felt a hundred times more creative. As soon as he was well enough, he would start looking for a new job and attend Hidden Talents more regularly. And he'd go on a course like the one everyone else from the group had gone on.

Jack was finding it difficult to concentrate at work. His mind was constantly elsewhere, his fingers metaphorically crossed every second of the day as he waited to hear the latest news from London.

Other than Des, who had been sworn to secrecy, no one at work knew that Jack had been spending his spare time writing a novel, and while he had wanted to share what had happened at Norton Hall with Des and Julie, he was keeping quiet until he had something concrete to tell them. He'd last heard from Nick Ellis – Ewan's agent in London who had read *Friends and Family* – two days ago. 'Leave it with me, Jack,' he'd said, on the phone, 'but I think we can safely say you should get in a bottle of your favourite drink. You're going to need it. I don't suppose you've started on the next book, have you?'

'Are you joking?'

'Get to it, Jack. Publishers like to know there's more of the same in the offing. I'll tell Felix you're well on your way with book number two.'

Jack had the feeling that literary agents could knock spots off estate agents when it came to wholesale flannel and brass-necked cheek.

At five thirty, he left his staff to lock up the office and drove to Prestbury to fetch the girls, his thoughts switching from the outcome of Nick Ellis's negotiations with Felix McCallum to the rehearsing of the script he'd put together for tonight. If only he knew that the others concerned would stick to the lines he'd written for them, he'd feel a whole lot happier. As it was, he knew only one thing: he was about to leap into the unknown and he wasn't sure he had it in him to be as magnanimous as he needed to be.

He'd mentioned to the girls on the phone last night that he wanted to talk to Mummy and Tony when he came to pick them up. 'Do you think you could be really good and stay upstairs while we have our chat?'

'You're not going to argue again, are you?' Amber had asked.

'No,' he'd said, ashamed that she'd witnessed such scenes before.

Maddie answered the door. She looked anxious, probably wondering what it was he wanted to discuss.

'Is it okay if we talk in the kitchen?' she said. 'Tony's in the middle of cooking supper.'

'That's fine by me,' Jack said, amused by such a notion. But, sure enough, there was Tony, the one-time dedicated bachelor who had sworn never to learn to cook, standing at the Aga stirring a large pan. 'I'm experimenting with vegetarian cuisine,' Tony said. 'Lentils. It's a Jamie Oliver recipe that he claims is foolproof. Glass of wine?' He replaced the lid on the pan and reached for an opened bottle of Merlot that was warming at the back of the Aga.

'Just a small one,' Jack said.

The wine was poured and glasses were handed round. They each took several sips before anyone spoke.

'Look,' said Jack, needing to clear the air, and put them at their ease, 'I haven't come here to fight or make a point. I just want to talk to you.' He took a sip of his wine. And another. 'The thing is, I doubt I'll ever feel totally happy seeing the pair of you together but, for Amber and Lucy's sake, I have to learn to appear that way. To achieve that, you two have to help me.'

'How? Every time I try to discuss anything with you, you fire off at me,' Maddie said defensively.

'I know. But sometimes . . . sometimes it's as if you deliberately fail to see things from where I'm standing.'

'That's what you always say. What you don't realise is—'

'No, Maddie,' Tony intervened gently. 'There have been occasions when Jack's been right and we've been wrong.' She looked at him as though he'd slapped her. He touched her arm lightly. 'We're only human,' he said, 'it's inevitable that we'd make mistakes.' He turned to Jack again. 'What do you want us to do?'

Jack put his glass on the table in front of him, pushed his hands into his trouser pockets. 'I don't know.'

'Would saying sorry help?'

The unexpectedness of Tony's suggestion, its sheer simplicity, brought Jack up short. He crossed the kitchen to look out of the window, giving himself time and space to think.

'Jack?'

He turned his head, and saw before him . . . not the man he'd come to hate, whom he'd vilified for everything wrong in his life, but his exuberant boyhood friend. Memories of their glory days flashed before him. Until this moment he had thought that writing *Friends and Family* would be the last word in catharsis, but now he knew differently. He had to hear that Maddie and Tony were genuinely sorry for what they'd done.

'Would it help, Jack?' his old friend pressed.

'Yes, Tony,' he murmured, his voice shaky. 'I can't explain why, but I think it would.'

Tony put down his nearly empty wine glass and passed a hand through his hair. He glanced briefly at Maddie. 'I've known you nearly all my life, Jack. I've loved you as a brother. To all intents and purposes, you *were* my brother and what I did to you was wrong. I was a shit for falling in love with Maddie, but I did and I can't change that. All I can say, and I'll say it for the rest of my life if it helps, is that I'm sorry. I'm sorry for wrecking everything between us, and to prove it there'll be no more talk of California. I just couldn't do that to you and the girls.' He glanced again at Maddie, who was standing next to him now. 'Sorry if you're disappointed.'

She shook her head. 'Far from it.'

'But I thought you wanted to go?'

'I only went along with it because I thought you wanted it so badly.'

Tony groaned. 'Oh, the great unsaid. It must be responsible for nearly all the world's troubles.' He put his arms around Maddie and held her.

Jack stiffened, then forced himself to relax. Maddie caught his eye and slipped self-consciously out of Tony's embrace. 'I suppose it's my turn to apologise now,' she said. She moved towards Jack and, in an elegant gesture that reminded him of when they used to dance together, she held out her hands and waited for him to take them. When he did, she said, with tears welling in her eyes, 'I'm sorry, Jack. Truly I am. Please don't hate me for what I did. I couldn't bear it.'

'I don't hate you,' he murmured. 'I never have. And never will.' Then, unbelievably, he took her in his arms, something he hadn't thought he'd ever do again.

The phone was ringing when he let Amber and Lucy into the flat and the answerphone kicked in before he could get to it. He let the caller leave her message – he would deal with it later after the girls had gone to bed. He played back the only other message that had been left for him. It was from Nick Ellis. 'Give me a call, Jack, I've got great news for you. I'm in the office till late, so you'll catch me here until about eight thirty.'

While the girls helped themselves to a drink, Jack dialled Nick's number in London. The phone was answered instantly.

'Oh, hi, Jack. How are you?'

'Fine. Actually, better than fine. I'm over the moon. I've just had some excellent news.'

'It must be your lucky day. How does a two-book contract for a six-figure sum sound to you?'

His heart racing, Jack gestured to Amber and Lucy not to switch on the television. 'Depends what the six figures are. What have you in mind?'

'I was thinking of a cool one hundred and fifty thousand pounds.'

Jack swallowed. 'Did I hear right?'

'You did. Felix loved the book, he said it was amusing and poignant and straight from the hip. Or did he mean heart? Whatever. I've told him I had to okay the offer with you, but if I were you I'd take it, Jack. It's a good one.'

Laughing, Jack said, 'You don't have a clue how good.'

'I do, actually. It's my business to sift the wheat from the chaff, and this is definitely a wheat situation. Shall I say yes to Felix?'

'Affirmative. You might like to add on a thank-you from me.'

'Steady on! Let's not give him ideas above his station. And don't be surprised if he wants you to change the odd thing here and there. From what you've told me, you wrote the book at lightning speed, so there's bound to be some rewrites on the cards. But it'll be a breeze. Now, go and do the sensible thing and celebrate.'

'Do you fancy going out for supper?' Jack asked the girls, when he came off the phone.

'McDonald's?'

'I was thinking of something a little more up-market, Luce. How about Chinese?'

'Spare-ribs and lemon chicken?'

'The whole shebang! Whatever you want. Our objective tonight is to celebrate a double-whammy.'

'A double-what?' asked Amber.

He hugged them both. 'We're celebrating two mega-fantastic events in my life. One, you're not moving to America, which is pretty fantastic, and two, against all the odds, I'm suddenly the happiest man in Cheshire. Hey, scrub that. I'm the happiest man in the whole wide world!'

Amber squirmed in his arms. 'You okay, Dad?'
'You know what? I think I am.'

Dulcie was driving to Maywood station to meet Andrew and Miles. They had insisted they would grab a taxi from the rank outside the station, but she'd told Andrew, 'I might have lost the man I love, but as yet I've not lost the ability to drive a car.' They had wanted to come up sooner so that they could make a fuss of her, as Miles had put it so sweetly, but work commitments had dictated otherwise and this was the earliest they had been able to get away. She was looking forward to their company – not that she'd spent much time on her own. Prue and Maureen, Beth, and Jack had seen to that. With their kindness, which was sometimes gentle, sometimes firm, depending on her state of mind, they had ensured she wasn't left to her own devices for long.

It was a fortnight since Richard had died, and initially she had thought that keeping her mind on anything other than him would be the answer, that blocking him out would get her through the lonely days and nights. It had been a vain hope. Nothing could keep her thoughts from him. She had wanted to spend her every waking moment recalling their happy times together. And there were so many of them. Their time in Venice would always be special to her. She would never forget the beauty of the moment when they had stood on the small bridge in the twinkling darkness of the night and he'd said that one day they would return as man and wife, that he would be the happiest man alive.

Occasionally she tortured herself by questioning whether she had made Richard happy. If they'd never met he would not have had to endure the pain of choosing between his wife and her. She still couldn't rid herself of the thought that it was her fault he'd died.

She wasn't alone in thinking that: Angela had written to her, a letter of vengeful cruelty blaming Dulcie for Richard's death. 'You caused the stress that ultimately tore his heart apart,' Angela had written. 'I just hope you never know a moment's peace for what you did.'

Jack and Beth had been firm with Dulcie when she'd shown them the letter. 'You're not to believe a single word of what she's written,' Beth had said.

Jack had been more forthright. He'd taken the letter from Dulcie and ripped it up. 'We all understand why she felt the need to write it, but it helps no one. Least of all her.'

Even now the letter, though it was long gone, still hurt Dulcie. But it didn't hurt as much as not being able to attend Richard's funeral. She had accepted that she had no right to be there and had only found out when and where the funeral would take place the day before it happened. Juliette Simpson had phoned to explain that she still felt badly about what she'd done. 'Richard never held you responsible,' Dulcie said. 'He was on the verge of telling his wife anyway, so please don't feel guilty. It's quite unnecessary.'

'I know, he told me about ... about the two of you when you came back from Venice.'

Dulcie was surprised by this admission. 'Richard confided in you?'

'Yes. He wanted me to have your telephone number in case I ever needed to contact him out of work hours and I couldn't reach him on his mobile. He said he was going to tell more people in the office when you returned from Harrogate. He wanted to be honest with everyone. I don't suppose you'll be at the funeral tomorrow, will you? Everyone from his department will be going. Richard was very popular. He was a good man to work for. One of the best.'

'No, I shan't be there,' Dulcie had said, 'but perhaps you should tell his wife what you've just told me, that he was so well liked.'

Another woman might have sent an anonymous wreath to the funeral, but Dulcie planted a climbing rose against the back of the house where she and Richard had often sat. Patting down the soil, she spoke aloud as if Richard was there with her: 'I once promised you I would never play the part of a possessive lover, my darling, and now I'll make you another promise. I will do my best to grieve for you quietly and lovingly. I will think only of the good times we shared. Just as you'd want me to.'

The following day she had a surprise visitor.

Richard's daughter, Victoria.

'I haven't come here to make a scene,' she said. 'I just want to talk to you. But I'll go away if you'd rather.'

'No. Come in. Please.'

She took her through to the sitting room, then regretted it. The kitchen would have been better: it would have been less formal and helped them to relax. She waited for Victoria to sit down. 'I

424

suppose you've come for his things,' Dulcie said, sitting opposite from her.

Victoria frowned. 'What things?'

'All the things he brought with him.' She was thinking of his clothes and books upstairs, and more importantly, his papers and documents. 'I was going to post some of it, but . . . but somehow I haven't got round to it.'

The frown was still on Victoria's face – reminding Dulcie of Richard – and she said, 'That's not why I've come.'

'Why, then?'

'I need to understand why you meant so much to him. It was so out of character what he did. I still can't accept how he could do it.'

'You probably won't believe me, but we felt the same ourselves. Neither of us felt proud to be deceiving so many.'

'But you still went on doing it?'

Dulcie nodded. 'Yes. I don't expect you to condone what we did, but we loved each other. I didn't throw myself at him, didn't trick him into an affair. It was love. I'm sorry if that hurts, but it's the truth.'

Dulcie watched Victoria chew her lower lip, and then, to her horror, the poor girl started to cry. Dulcie went to her. 'I'm sorry,' she said, 'perhaps I shouldn't have said that.'

'No, it's okay. In a way it's what I came to hear. I wanted to know that Dad was happy before he died. The last time I saw him he looked so sad. I hated seeing him like that. Henry was bullying him into coming home, back to Mum. He caused an awful scene. I knew then that Dad would never come back. I felt as if we'd lost him. As if *we* were lost to him.'

'Oh, no. That wasn't the case. He loved you. You four children meant the world to him. He was terrified you'd stop loving him. It was why he stayed as long as he did. He was a good man, Victoria. A devoted father. You must never doubt that.'

She left an hour later, after Dulcie had given her the documents she felt belonged to his family rather than to her. 'What will you do with his clothes?' Victoria had asked when she was at the door, ready to go.

'Give them to charity when I can bear to part with them,' she said. 'The books I shall keep. Unless you want them?'

'No. You have them.'

They had parted with a handshake, which was more than Dulcie felt she deserved. But, that night, she had slept peacefully for the first time in days. She had woken in the morning, with a sense of calm. She might have found herself thrust into yet another new role – that of a grieving mistress – but she knew she would cope. Her love for Richard would see to that.

She had been waiting for no more than five minutes when a stream of people emerging from the station caught her attention. She twisted her head round to look out for Andrew and Miles. But when they appeared, she saw they weren't alone.

Kate was with them, a tentative smile on her lips. Dulcie's heart soared. To be reconciled with Kate so soon was more than she could have hoped for.

Dear Beth,

I've just heard the news from my agent about Jack's book offer. Please pass on my best wishes. I know exactly how he'll be feeling, as if he's won the Lottery ten times over.

Now, while I have your attention, and knowing what a worrier you are, I'd like to put your mind at rest. I want you to know that when you come to stay here next weekend, there won't be a trace of the bars of chocolate I'd stockpiled in the garage apropos an earlier suggestion on your part. I'd hate to think of you having sleepless nights fretting over this and just wanted to reassure you that I will be the epitome of the perfect gentleman during your visit. Only trouble is, I've eaten the aforementioned chocolate and have ballooned into the size of a humpback whale. Hope this won't put you off coming to stay.

  Lots of love,
  Ewan X

PS Alice will be putting in a brief appearance while you're here, so be warned, Attila the Hun will be on the prowl to give you the once-over!

PPS How about I nip out and buy us the one bar of Fruit and Nut? Just in case . . .

Dear Ewan,
I have a sweet tooth, better make it two . . .
  Love Beth